MW00873284

The Greenlanders
A Tale of Sea and Steel

Hannah Ross

© Copyright 2017 by Hannah Ross
All rights reserved

Prologue

Thorvard strained against the ropes that bound him to the mast. His fury could not find release even in a shout, for his mouth was gagged. All he could do was stare helplessly at how his few loyal men were bound as well and dragged aside, while the rest scurried like rats to do Freydis's bidding. *Weak treacherous cowards. They will regret this.*

He made sure to remember each one – how they moved, spoke, looked. He would deal with them as soon as opportunity presented itself, and he would not be forgiving.

Freydis came over with a confident step, her head held up high. *She knows no shame, this one. I should never have trusted her. I should never have married her.*

"I'm sorry, Thorvard," she said, but her expression was quite the reverse from an apology – it exuded arrogance, defiance and triumph. "Once we do what must be done, I'll release you. You'll see that I was right. Raise the sail, men. We take course southwest."

Nobody asked where they were headed. Thorvard knew it as well. *Vinland.*

It was sheer madness. It would be the death of them all. The Skraelings would finish them off with a flick of a finger, given how few capable men were on the ship. *But with me out of the way, who is left to beat some reason into Freydis?*

Thorvard remained bound to the mast like a misbehaved dog for many hours. Bitterness, pain and fury left no room for hunger, but his throat was parched and his tiredness soon began to kick in. His legs trembled as he leaned against the mast for support. The ropes were too tight to allow him room to sit, and he wondered how much longer he would be able to hold on before he slumped unconscious with exhaustion.

"Nod your head if you promise to be quiet, and I'll take this gag out of your mouth and give you a glug of beer," Erlend, a weasel-like balding thin man, said with a nasty leer. Thorvard never trusted the bastard, and glared at him with a murderous expression, not moving his head an inch. "Suit yourself," Erlend shrugged and moved away. Freydis didn't return to look at her vanquished husband again. She was up front, giving directions to the men.

She wants to go back to Vinland to avenge Helgi, Tur and Gudrid, but she is deluded. We are too few. Will Valhalla admit those who seek death in so foolish a way?

A futile effort to find a more comfortable position offered Thorvard an unexpected sliver of hope. There was a splinter on the other side of the mast, just where his bound hands were pressed. The ropes snagged on it. Thorvard attempted to rub the ropes against it, straining them at the same time. He had nothing to lose. His movements were small enough to go unnoticed. A half-hour of such strained, painful chafing rewarded him with a slight loosening of the rope. Thorvard kept working away, every muscle in his body quivering with weakness and pain and tension. A stubborn strength came from somewhere and didn't let go. He kept straining. A gale rocked the ship, splashing him in the face with salty water, but though it drenched him and stung his eyes, Thorvard didn't care. *Odin, Father, let me get out of these bounds before it's too late.*

A few strands in the rope split with a taut noise that went unheard over the sound of rushing waves. Taking heart, Thorvard kept chafing and straining. The bulging muscles of his arms were hard as steel; his wrists bled, but he didn't heed that. With a last mighty effort the rope gave away, and he was free. He pulled the gag out of his mouth and roared with fury, drawing fearful glances. They had taken his hand-axe and skinning knife, but in his frenzy he was scarcely less dangerous even unarmed. His mighty fists felled men left, right and center, and when he reached Erlend he grabbed him by the scruff of the neck.

"Goodbye," Thorvard said, hurtling the accomplice overboard, arms flailing. Nobody made a move to pull him back up, and the waves and flapping sail and creaking mast soon drowned the man's weak desperate pleas for mercy. The storm raged on, and so did Thorvard.

When he reached Freydis, she cowered, all her former self-assurance gone. He was sorely tempted to place both hands on her neck and squeeze with all his might, but he restrained

3

himself and only grabbed both her wrists, holding them in a vice-like grip. His face was distorted with hatred.

"I've grown to expect all sorts of things from you," he growled, "but not this."

"Thorvard, listen," she mumbled, satisfyingly contrite all of a sudden. "You have to understand, the Skraelings must pay – "

"You would have us all killed for naught," Thorvard went on, giving her a rough shake. "You don't even know how to navigate. You betrayed me and humiliated me in front of my men. I'm through with you."

He flung her away, still seething. Freydis crouched down with a low hiss, nursing a bleeding lip. She lost, and she knew it.

"Take course to Brattahlid," commanded Thorvard, "unless you want to go the same way as Erlend. And get this scheming bitch out of my sight. I never want to see her again."

Part 1

Chapter 1

Leif's sharp eyes sought the shore and found it a while ago, but despite the relief he felt – the relief of every sailor upon seeing the longed-for firm land on the horizon - he did not know how the country would welcome him. He had never seen it, had never stepped upon it, and his father was banished from it for life by a despicable, shameful decree. But lo and behold, here he is, returning to Norway by explicit invitation from the king.

He knew the journey would soon be over, and so he became more aware of the sights, sounds and smells that always accompany a sea voyage – the movement of the deck beneath his feet, the creaking of wood, the sounds the oars made as they hit water, the misty drizzle that sprayed his skin and left a salty taste upon his tongue when he licked his lips. All of this would be over soon, for months, until his spring journey home.

At the same time he thought of the letter he had directed to the king, a letter in which he let His Majesty know that unexpected currents had carried him into lands far to the south of his intended route - and that he foresees, therefore, to arrive rather later than he expected. He hoped the message reached its destination – and he hardly knew why, but he well remembered the scribe he had hired to perform this task. He didn't bother to learn his letters himself, and never needed it. In the scribe's modest little home, they had sat talking for a long time.

Looking back, he was even glad of the unexpected detour. This was the first time he chanced to journey so far south, and the lands he reached fascinated him, even though he had never thought much about the south – he was far more interested in the north and west and the unknown lands which captured his heart and soul and usurped his dreams.

About a thousand years passed since the birth of the man Christians proclaimed to be god, and Christianity ruled throughout the entire south and middle of Europe. There, he and his people were received with obvious mistrust, suspicion and fear, although he had made it clear from the beginning that they did not come as raiders. Now the church had turned its steps north, and he knew that in the royal court of Norway, too, he will find the same images and statues of the Crucified Man, the same glum temples and the same conversations about saving one's soul by accepting the new Faith.

He expected that a considerable part of his men will be affected by this new influence, and will probably carry the Faith with them onward, to the remote settlements where his father had been pioneer. His father would not like that, he knew. As for his people, he couldn't do much more than wonder whether this will affect their spirit for better or for worse, or not at all.

Still, he knew that in the north, the Old Gods will not resign their place so easily, and the people will stick to their faith despite the king's intentions to create alliances with the other rulers of Europe. His father, for example – he was certain – would never convert.

The man he had paid to write the letter was short and rather dark, thin-faced and stoop-shouldered, and a black, soft leather cap covered his dark curls. His name was Nathan Ben Yossef, and in his home he did not see the image of the Crucified Man.

"The locals fear you," he told Leif, "you, the Vikings who came to raid, to rape and burn and leave desolation after them."

"I am no Viking," protested Leif. "I am only a sailor."

"It matters not. Just as much as they fear you, we, the Jews, fear the locals amongst whom we live. Sooner or later their viciousness will be turned against us, and the daily humiliations will escalate to threats, and those to robbery and violence, rape and murder. And once again, we will have to travel far from the places we have grown used to, just as our forefathers had."

These words created an echo in Leif's heart. His father was banished from Norway, the country he loved, for crimes of blood and crimes of gold and crimes of love, and perhaps those last ones were what played the most crucial part in his verdict.

...His sister appeared behind his shoulder, walking like a quiet, dangerous wild animal, and shook her red hair off her face. Leif repressed a sigh. *Women at sea...* among things he considered a nuisance, the presence of women on board of a ship was a prominent one, but for his mother this was a chance to see Norway again, for the first and perhaps only time in many years – and this chance she was unwilling to forgo. His mother was also the one who insisted on taking Freydis with them.

"I know your father will feel lonely without Freydis and me," she said, "but a young woman needs to be under the watchful eye of her mother. I wouldn't trust anyone else to look after Freydis."

Leif was highly skeptical regarding how much influence the watchful eye of a mother will hold in the case of Freydis, but did not object. He could say in his sister's favor that she did all she could to stay out of his way during the journey. She was unusually, almost suspiciously quiet. And now, coming towards him, she looked amused - as if she succeeded in tricking them all. Leif looked directly in her eyes. Both brother and sister had regular, handsome features, but while one of Freydis's eyes was icy-blue, like Leif's, her other eye was a dark chasm, almost

7

black, with flecks of copper around the iris. This gave her an appearance which many found unnerving.

"We are very close to land, Freydis," he told her, "and I must warn you, Norway is not Greenland or Iceland, where you might feel free to do whatever comes into your head. We will arrive straight at court, and I expect you to be obedient and quiet, and never leave Mother's side for as long as we stay there."

It didn't escape his eye that the left side of her mouth, the sensual mouth with the full red lips, moved in a brief, sarcastic twist which plainly stated how she felt about whatever he had to say on the matter. But when she spoke, her voice was placid enough.

"I do not mean to bring you trouble, Leif," she said. "I know how important it is to you to be accepted at court."

It was so. This was his chance to turn from a lifelong exile into a respectable, influential man. If all goes well, he might even get ships, goods, people – everything that is needed to enlarge the distant settlements of Greenland and to sail west again, following the coast that had captured his heart. He did not want Freydis to know how much he fears she might damage his chances of success, though.

"This is not about me," he told her. "I say this mainly for Mother, and for your sake as well. If you don't behave too foolishly we might even find you a husband."

The derisive twist of the mouth became more prominent. "I have no need of a husband," said Freydis. "I was already married once, remember?"

"And I am sorry to tell you this, sister," said Leif with quiet confidence, "there will probably be men around – many men, even – but not anyone who can compare to Thorvard."

"I care nothing for Thorvard," said Freydis. Her voice was calm, but her eyes burned, and Leif saw the pain behind the anger. He and Thorvard had always been like brothers, and though he knew it would probably do no good, he warned his friend when he noticed the growing attachment between Thorvard and his sister. But all was in vain. Thorvard would not give her up – not until he paid the full price and found himself betrayed, humiliated and nearly killed. He was forced to leave Greenland and Leif didn't blame him. He would have done the same.

A jolt of mute anger towards his parents flickered in his heart every time he thought of Freydis. It was only natural that the first and only daughter born into the family after three boys would grow up spoiled, but one could still expect his parents to be a little firmer concerning her upbringing. For instance, whatever reason could there be to allow and even encourage a girl to learn her letters? Leif himself was certain that a man has no need of reading or writing if for most of his life his hands hold an axe, an oar or a bow. A woman had even less business with literacy.

If Freydis had not been allowed to start with the stupid reading in the first place, she would never have discovered the accursed scrolls that planted such destructive ideas in her head; her studies brought her, eventually, to excessive self-confidence, dealings with dark magic, a dangerously rebellious attitude, and the ruin of her marriage. And it did not come as a surprise, either – as her older brother, one who had known Freydis all her life, protected her and teased her alternately, he knew it was only to be expected. He loved Freydis, but had no illusions as far as her character was concerned.

He looked at his sister's receding back, at her thin and upright figure, and the head full of red hair. He was so deeply immersed in thought that he did not notice his mother coming near him until she stood quite close.

Even after many years of life in wild, mostly unsettled Greenland, Leif's mother had managed to preserve her smooth, calm countenance and her slim womanly figure. Her dark hair, though it was liberally streaked with grey, was thick and collected in a shiny sleek knot at the back of her head. When Leif looked at her, he could easily imagine how captivating she had once been to his father, Erik, whom everyone called Erik the Red – how she made him struggle against the boundaries of his social standing and do all in his power to induce a daughter of a rich and influential man to marry him in secret. This caused fury among his mother's relations, and certainly played a part in the king's decision to banish Erik from Norway for as long as he lived.

"I did not think I would ever see these shores again," his mother said, and her joy mingled with melancholy.

"Sometimes I wonder," said Leif, "how it would have been if I were born and raised here. We could all have lived a different life."

"I am not sorry for what had come to pass," his mother said with determination, "but your father and I had been treated unfairly. Our only crime was that we loved each other and got married."

Leif smiled at her affectionately. The love and devotion of his parents to each other never failed to touch his heart.

"It might have been *your* only crime, Mother. My father, I fear, had a few other deeds that spoke against him."

"Norway is not what it had been thirty years ago," said his mother, ignoring his last words although she knew, of course, that her husband was renowned for the mischief of his youth. "You, my son, have an opportunity to make your home in Norway again... if you wish it, and after you complete another journey into the West. The king was highly impressed by what you managed to achieve, and he knows it is in his interest to bring you closer to him. His invitation did not surprise me at all."

"I do not know if I want to make my home in a land that slammed its doors in my father's face," said Leif. "Besides, in Greenland we have a name, an established consequence, a home my father had built... here, we have nothing. We'd be about as valuable as the dirt under one's feet."

But his mother went on as though she didn't hear him. "I want you to know, son, that I mean accept the new Faith. It will be to the benefit of us all. I advise you to do the same."

He shrugged his shoulders. "I don't know what to say. You, of course, may do what you think is right, Mother. But you must understand my father will not see it in a favorable light."

A slight crease appeared on her brow but was gone almost as soon as he perceived it. "I know your father is very much devoted to the old gods," she said, "I do not expect to convert him at once, but I know he will allow me to arrange such matters for myself in the manner I see fit. And maybe I will be able to convince Freydis as well."

"Freydis will accept any god, if she thinks she might gain from it," said Leif, "but you and I both know what her declarations of faith are worth."

"The most important thing is that she is done with her folly. She must not go back to it. She had already caused enough damage, to herself more so than to anyone else."

"With this," said Leif, "I most definitely agree."

Chapter 2

As the ship got closer to the coast, Freydis grew more excited. After the isolated settlement in Greenland and the remote farms in Iceland, and an unbearably long journey in the affectionate but exasperating company of her mother and brother, the arrival at Trondheim was a blessed release to her. In Norway she would regain her freedom, in Norway she would be able to detach herself from the overbearing protection of her family, and no one will prevent her from spreading her wings. She was too clever to declare this openly, but she had not the least intention of accepting any authority – not of her father, not of her brother, not of a husband and not of the Church.

Freedom. The freedom to do whatever she wants – it is worth, all that had happened, is it not? So she told herself, repressing the heavy, leaden feeling that nestled in the pit of her stomach when she thought of the price she had paid for studying the lore of magic and connecting with certain people; the price she paid for her aspiration to leadership.

As a rule, girls were not supposed to be brought up free and independent. They were supposed to turn dull and obedient and be interested in nothing more than keeping house and finding a husband, and once they found him, pleasing him and popping out a brood of children.

Was I really so much to blame? Freydis only wanted her life to be a little more than that – not just for her own sake, but for that of her family. Power, respect, consequence. They deserved it, all of them - Red Erik and her brother Leif, and she, Freydis, with her intelligence and talent. However, in this world one cannot sit back and expect to receive all one deserves on a silver platter.

One must fight for it. One must reach out with a strong, grasping hand, and take it. And that was what she had tried to do – and be damned the bastards that stood across her path. *It was their fault, not mine*, Freydis told herself again, clenching her fists. She couldn't leave it be, and so a new ambition joined the old ones – revenge. Thorvard did not understand it. No one could understand it.

Once again she was trapped in her contradictory feelings regarding this invitation Leif received to the Norwegian court. On the one hand, the invitation was a rare opportunity for their family after so many years of exile. It was a chance for Leif, and therefore for his siblings as well, to climb another rung of the ladder. *If Leif acts wisely, of course.* On the other hand, it was very clear the timing of the invitation was not decided by chance. Undoubtedly, rumors of Leif's achievements reached the king's ears, and he sensed an opportunity to gain even more power and influence for the throne. *The king, the earls that acted for the banishment Erik the Red like a mad dog – they will take advantage of what he and his son had done.* The idea grated on Freydis's pride. What her family deserves, she thought savagely, is not royal pardon – it's an apology and the elevation of their father to the position he might have had if he had not been sent into exile.

It was not very difficult to guess what the king wanted. They – Erik the Red, his family and his people – were the founders of the Greenland settlement. That land, frozen and unwelcoming as it might be, belonged to them now. And despite the difficulties of life in those parts, the land held treasures – skins of white bears and seals, whale ivory and walrus tusks, and inside the country perhaps layers of silver and copper, as her brother Thorvald suspected and hoped. He had taken great pains to travel up and across the country. The people were few, lonely in the icy land that was called Greenland not without a fair bit of irony, but at least no one bothered them. In Greenland, among his loyal men, Red Erik was as good as a king.

Her brother Leif sailed even further to the west, in that journey she insisted to partake of, the journey she would never, ever forget. She shuddered. The tortured faces of Helgi, Tur and Gudrid still stood against her closed eyes, as if burned on the inside of her eyelids. She didn't mean for it to happen. She loved Tur and Gudrid, two innocent youths who had just been wed, and even silly Helgi, who was devoted as a puppy to her, even though he knew full well she was a married woman and faithful to her husband. *Yes, I had been faithful,* Freydis insisted stubbornly. But during that trip, Thorvard was left behind and Helgi took advantage of that and trailed her every step, which eventually led him to his death.

Thorvard didn't want her to go. He pleaded, reasoned, begged and threatened. After he despaired of influencing her directly, he spoke with Leif. Still, Freydis would go to that beautiful, new, enticing land. And the face of the sorcerer, terrifyingly calm, stood before her eyes as he spoke and said – though she could not tell how she understood his words -

"You we shall not harm. It brings on the wrath of the spirits, to harm a woman who carries a child."

A great terror went through her, for though then she did not know with absolute certainty she is pregnant, she sensed it was true. And indeed, it turned out that Thorvard's seed had been planted in her womb, that last night they spent together before the journey – the last night when she had lain in her husband's arms.

Revenge, she told Leif that morning when she pretended she had only just gotten up, and the lifeless bodies of Helgi, Tur and Gudrid were found by their camp. Revenge at once. But Leif said again and again that they are too few, that it would be too dangerous, that they came only to explore, not to conquer, and that he did not plan to go into any confrontation with the natives. They must turn back, her brother had decided, go back home and return later on with more people - and soon after, they raised sail.

"I cannot risk the lives of the other men," Leif had said quietly, watching how her furious tears fell as they threw a last look upon the receding coast of Vinland. "And something else, Freydis – as insufferable as it may seem now, it might be that someday we will have to negotiate with these locals. The bodies of our poor friends give hint of being sacrificed in some religious rite, and I have no doubt that the natives offered them to their gods as a gift. They returned the bodies, and did not attack our camp, although they could have done so easily. This can be seen as a warning. Maybe they are too few to try and fight us all, or maybe they aren't interested in an open battle with us. I intend to go back there with more people and better weapons, ready to fight if need be. Still, I do not exclude a possibility of reaching some sort of agreement with the locals."

Agreement! Freydis had gone white with fury every time she remembered that conversation. No, no agreement can exist after what had come to pass. Only revenge.

Of course, later on some meddlesome fool asked why Helgi, Tur and Gurdid walked out of the camp in the middle of the night in

16

the first place, and how come the watchmen who were on duty at the time did not notice them. Someone threw this query into the air in the presence of Leif, and Leif directed that same question to their father, and Erik wondered aloud in front of Thorvard – and he, who had had his suspicions already, drove Freydis into a corner and demanded answers. The revelation of her lie caused the situation to deteriorate pretty quickly.

It was not my fault, Freydis told herself time and time again. *It was not my fault.*

And still... a new land, fertile and forested, with clear fresh water and abundant game. And a promise of even fairer places beyond it. It is no wonder the rumor had traveled and reached the king. If he succeeds to wheedle an oath of complete fealty out of Leif, Greenland and Vinland will fall into his lap like ripe fruit.

But to her brother's credit, Freydis could not imagine him being so servile.

Chapter 3

Leif's heart missed a beat as he beheld the fjords his father had described in such detail. This was home, even though he had never been here before. Though it was impossible, it seemed to him he recognized every outcropping of rock, every curve of the shore. He shadowed his eyes with his wind-beaten hand and watched the wooded green mountains and their sharp fall into the steely blue of the sea. The buildings of Trondheim and the harbor presented themselves before his eyes. By his side, his mother grabbed his arm in excitement - while Freydis raised her head, prepared to step upon the land of Norway not as an exile come to knock humbly on doors, but as an earl's daughter making her return to the rightful land of her forefathers.

"Look, there is the king himself!" Leif heard his sister's quick, urgent whisper in his ear when the ship came into harbor and they began disembarking.

"Nonsense," he dismissed. "Why would the *king* come out to meet the likes of us?"

But a few minutes later he had to acknowledge that Freydis was right. It truly was King Olaf himself, and all his retinue with him, and Leif could only wonder to what he owes this impressive welcome. He did not prepare for this. After such a long journey at sea his clothes were, of course, tattered and covered with salt stains, and he was far from being clean himself. His hair and beard were tangled and he was very much in need of a wash.

The king was a short, rather stout man near the middle of his life, with an almost bald head, a protruding belly, grey hair and very light eyes. Overall, he was not very impressive. His sons, who stood by his side, were much more prominent in their stature, their dress and their air. The group that surrounded the king and the princes moved forward once the king made a few steps in the direction of those who had just landed.

Leif was by far the tallest among all the men. He could not dislike this, and he suppressed a smile as he inclined his head in a proper welcome. Quite apart from his tall stature, he also radiated a powerful energy – the same unmistakable, unconquerable energy that was a gift bestowed by the gods upon Erik the Red, who made people leave everything behind and join him on his quest after an unknown land. Leif, his son, had inherited this quality.

King Olaf might not have had an awe-inspiring record of bravery or heroic deeds or anything very distinguishing, but he was a shrewd man. He understood in that very moment that the man standing in front of him is a natural leader, a man of vision, and capable of making people follow. He was more than just a sailor and the king was glad he heeded his instincts and came out to meet the party from Greenland himself. This man, Erikson – one had better see through him as soon as possible. He can be highly useful – and also highly dangerous.

His Highness received the newcomers in a cordial, though reserved way.

"Welcome home, Leif Erikson," he said. "Not every day do we see a ship that has made a journey such as yours. We are all eager to hear of the lands you have seen."

"Of course, Your Grace," Leif said politely, but without servility. "If I am permitted, I shall be glad to describe all that might interest you of our journeys and discoveries."

"I appreciate your readiness," the king nodded, "but of course, first of all you will be taken to your quarters, as I expect you will want to refresh yourselves."

Leif gave his polite thanks, and felt dirtier than ever among the king's men in all their finery. He was eagerly anticipating a bath, a trimming of hair and beard, and a change of clothes.

He was about to open his mouth and say some other phrase of insignificant politeness, but at that moment he chanced to look at a young woman who stood quite close to the king, a little behind him. Her slim, willowy, very graceful figure would have made her stand out even if it weren't for the dress she wore – a dress in deep red, made of sleek, shiny and obviously costly fabric. Her hair, lush and thick, the color of dark copper, was put up in a braid that coiled around her head and caught the rays of the autumn sun. Her skin was white as milk and, by the look of it, as soft as a ripe peach. The features of her face were exquisite, as if created with more special care than those of an ordinary human being. The emeralds in her ears and about her neck matched her eyes, which were adorned by long, dark eyelashes.

For a split second her eyes met Leif's, and she inclined her head slightly. He was rendered mute.

He searched for something else to say, but the king already turned around and began distancing himself from them and, following his cue, the two princes and the woman in the red dress walked away as well. The retinue continued after the king and those closest to him, except a few servants who stayed behind to show Leif and his men the way to their intended quarters.

"Have you seen Princess Thorgunna?" Leif heard his sister's voice again. "The one who stood on the king's left. It must be her. She is even more beautiful than people say."

"Princess?" Leif finally began to recover. "She is the king's daughter?"

"No, she is his niece, the daughter of his late brother," said Freydis. "The king fostered her from a young age. I heard he loves her as a daughter and intends to marry her to his son and heir soon, even though the prince had received more ambitious offers. So it appears Princess Thorgunna is going to be the queen of Norway," she added with a hint of envy.

The emeralds still sparkled and shifted before Leif's eyes, striking in their green like the forests that kissed the sea.

...He had almost forgotten what it feels like to immerse his body in hot water, Leif privately acknowledged when he entered the bathhouse which was prepared and heated for them by the servants. One of them came in to help him trim his hair and beard, but Leif sent him away. He was used to doing that himself.

When he was done, the powerfully chiseled features of his face appeared to better advantage. His face was handsome in a rather rough, weather-beaten way. The clothes that were prepared for him were simple, as befits a man of his rank, but properly sewn and clean.

He vigorously scrubbed his body with a stiff brush, and layers of dirt began to dissolve in the water. Soon, the bath water turned black. It took three changes of steaming hot water, a feat which demanded a considerable portion of firewood, until his body was satisfyingly clean.

When Freydis entered his room, shortly before nightfall, he was already dressed, bathed and as groomed as he was like to get. His sister, too, looked much better after a refreshing rest and bath. She was wearing a dark embroidered dress, one he had never seen before, which looked very well on her. Her red hair was brushed but not braided, and fell on her shoulders and back in a mass of red waves. A simple white ribbon prevented it from falling across her face, which was smooth and calm, and no innocent onlooker could have guessed that this young woman witnessed the terrible murder of her friends.

"Well, well," said Freydis, "I came to find out whether you had seen Mother, but was left speechless as I beheld you, Leif. You really are very handsome when you bother to bathe and comb your hair."

He ignored the sting, which was most unjust, of course, as until a few hours ago he and Freydis were each just as dirty as the other.

"Mother probably met some old acquaintance," he said with an artless smile, "and is now busy discussing marriage proposals for her headstrong daughter Freydis."

Freydis made a derisive snort, but by the look upon her face he could tell she did not take this threat all too lightly.

"You are the one who needs to marry again, Leif, not I," she said. "It has been five years since Maura. We all loved her, and I know it was a harsh blow for you. But it is time to move on, is it not?"

Leif's expression became inscrutable, as always when the issue came up.

"I have no intention of marrying again," he said succinctly.

"You have no sons," Freydis insisted – more to distract his attention from herself than for any other reason, he knew.

"Of this I cannot be certain," he said with a feeble attempt of a jest. It was in vain.

"You know very well what I mean. You have no son to continue your work after you, and you should know it grieves Father. You are thirty years old, Leif."

"My father has other sons. Thorvald will marry soon, the way things look, and Thorstein will probably follow suit. The family will continue through them."

"We all love Thorvald dearly, but he is not like you. He will always be a poet, full of dreams and tales, with his head up in the clouds. And Thorstein... he is so quick-tempered and reckless it is a wonder he hadn't been caught in some blood feud or other yet. *You* are Father's heir, Leif. You know it well."

"Thorvald will become more practical, and Thorstein will grow up," insisted Leif.

In his heart he could not deny that he had thought of a second marriage in the past years. There were offers enough, despite the limited size of the Greenland settlement and its distance from other lands. He could have taken an innocent virgin girl, or a widow with a steadier mind and more life experience. But he did not hurry to promote a match, and actually, saw no reason to.

There was, of course, the wish and desire of every man to have a son he would raise and bring up, but this need was not very urgent in Leif's eyes. His brothers and friends would continue where he left off. Besides, he did not like to think of death and what comes beyond it. He was a man of strong body and mind, active and energetic in thought and deed, and he had certain needs which, of course, had to find some outlet – and they did, it must be said. He did not live the life of a hermit and knew how to take advantage of the opportunities that had fallen to his lot.

But he was no longer the careless youth he had been before he met Maura.

Maura changed him, changed his entire life, and never again would he become what he had once been. In the months following her death he was alone most of the time, driving the pain deep within, and after a while he went on as usual, or so it seemed – but those close to him knew how much he had suffered. It was as if a part of him, the best and most vital part, died together with her.

Most of his relations and friends found it best not to speak of Maura, of his grief and the possibility of his marrying again, but Freydis sometimes pressed him to discuss the matter with a glaring inconsideration of how he felt. As usual when that happened, he shrugged her off.

"I suggest you go and look for Mother, Freydis," he said. "If she lost her way, she might be late for the feast."

Chapter 4

Thjodhild did not lose her way. In her wanderings she found the court church. It was Sunday, and the priest made a spirited, heart-warming sermon. Her eyes brightened as she sat listening to it. The message of compassion, humility, friendship, loyalty and peace touched her tender heart. She regretted that Erik was not with her, although she presumed that he, in his gruff manner, would have snorted in contempt as he listened to the spirit of gentleness in the priest's speech. If the message should eventually get through to him, it will call for a long period of cajoling from her side, she knew. After over thirty years of marriage, Thjodhild had no illusions.

Still, she was determined to bring this wonderful new faith to her home land. In the eyes of her mind she already saw a little chapel, much humbler than this one, serving as a spiritual gathering place for the people of their settlement, the distant country they managed to turn into a livable place by sheer work and the sweat of their brow, an achievement that was now almost entirely attributed to Erik the Red, the despised exile who could never step upon the land of his birth again.

All of a sudden she heard someone calling her name and turned around. She recognized the man not by his face, for it had become wrinkled, and not by his hair, which was once chestnut-colored and thick but had thinned and greyed over the years; nor by his firm and upright figure, for a great kettle-belly now adorned the front of his body – but by the deep, melodic voice which she often heard in her youth, singing songs and telling tales, a voice that did not change even after three decades.

His name was Bergsveinn Snorrason. His father was friendly with hers, and the two of them often visited. Her father once even talked of his plans concerning a match between Bergsveinn and herself – the two were more or less of an age – but Thjodhild exhibited a high degree of indifference to the scheme, and the boy as well, so the match did not take place. Even back then Thjodhild did not doubt that Bergsveinn would eventually find his way to a more prosperous, profitable marriage, and it did not surprise her in the least to meet him after all these years here, at court.

Bergsveinn looked at her and smiled a wide, uninhibited smile of an old childhood friend. His eyes went over her face, looking for traces made by time. No doubt he noticed the wrinkles on her brow and at the corners of her mouth and eyes and saw the grey that wove itself into her dark hair. But the blue eyes that looked at him bravely belonged to that same Thjodhild of many years ago, a sixteen-year-old girl who followed her heart where it led her, perhaps unwisely. Her figure was slim, upright and handsome as ever.

When she was cut off from her family and her home land, he did not think he would ever see her again, and the rumors that reached his ears about the ship from Greenland rendered him highly curious. He approached, taking advantage of his right as an old acquaintance to strike an informal conversation with her.

"Thjodhild," he said, "Is it truly you? I heard of your arrival. You had been through a long journey."

"Longer than you can imagine, Bergsveinn," she agreed.

The sermon had already ended, and they went out of the church together. He matched his stride to hers, unhurried and leisurely.

"I can hardly believe you are here. So much time has gone by. Your father passed away a few years ago, did you know that?" Bergsveinn asked after a few silent minutes.

"Yes," she said, "I got notice of that from my sister Ingvild. Ingvild kept in contact with me throughout all these years. We both learned our letters with the purpose of writing to each other. I look forward to seeing her sometime during our visit."

"How long do you think you will stay?" he asked. She shrugged her shoulders.

"It does not depend on me," she said. "I am only accompanying my son, Leif. You will probably see him soon. He is a brave and clever man, like his father. I do have a lot to be proud of, Bergsveinn."

"I have no doubt of that," he nodded. "The rumors about Leif Erikson have already turned, in part, into splendid tales. No wonder the king himself asked to see him... and we, the commoners, are wild with curiosity."

"I am certain you are not one of the *commoners*, Bergsveinn. You must have your own tales of splendid deeds."

"There isn't much to tell about me," he said humbly. "I lived a regular, reasonably prosperous life, a quiet life. Unlike you, Thjodhild, I did not go into exile; I did not wander through strange lands."

"Is that a hint of compassion I hear in your voice, Bergsveinn? There is no need of that. I chose my path."

"I know. That is precisely the point. Do you have no regrets?"

She hesitated a little. She thought of all the long years of estrangement from her family, about her father, who refused to hear her name mentioned until his last day, about the exile from her home land. She recalled the wanderings, the insecurity, the dangers and poverty and shame and sometimes hunger. She thought of the man for whose sake she made that choice. A slight smile curved her mouth.

"No, Bergsveinn," she said sincerely. "I do not regret. I have had a good life with my Erik."

She remembered how she first met Erik as if it were only yesterday. It was a winter day of rare beauty, on which the sky brightened and the snow shone in the sunlight, so sparkling white it hurt to look at it. Thjodhild, who was terribly bored by being shut up at home during many weeks of harsh Norwegian winter, danced with joy when she saw the bright sun. Her older sisters have already left home to get married, and throughout the long cold weeks there had been no guest, no visitor in their home to dispel the unvarying loneliness of winter. Now she just had to take advantage of so fine a day. Her father warned her, of course, that the pleasant weather might not last long, but Thjodhild still decided to dress in her warmest furs and go out in the big sledge, accompanied by two servants.

Her father's fears proved to be right. Soon, the sky darkened with clouds and snow began to fall thickly. The winds threatened to overturn the sledge, and the reindeer, shaking with cold and fear, were stuck in the snow. They no longer could pull the sledge together with its people against the frozen, harsh wind, and Thjodhild decided to set them free. She hoped that the clever animals will find their own way back to her father's house, and someone will understand that they got into trouble and will send men to look after them. Otherwise, she feared, her father might decide she managed to reach Ingvild's house in time and simply chose to wait there until the end of the storm.

The short winter day was nearing its end and the cold was growing bitter. The two serving men were frightened, and so was Thjodhild, though she attempted to hide it. She tried to look braver than she was, to lift the spirits of the men. Her only hope was that someone would pass by and notice them – someone with enough resources to rescue them or at least to call for help, but the chances of that seemed slim. They offered fearful prayers to their gods.

Suddenly, they heard sounds which were like music to their ears – sounds of men talking, and sledges sliding upon snow – great, strong sledges, pulled by many mighty reindeer that had strength enough to beat the storm. Thjodhild and the two servants began to shout, though their voices were soon muffled in the wind, and waved their hands to ensure these unknown men would not miss them. Of course, the strangers might have been brigands, but in their situation they had no choice but to trust their good fortune – if they continued outside in the storm, it would mean almost certain death and they knew it well.

Their pleas for help were not fruitless. One, two, three, four, five sledges approached, carrying in them almost twenty men, all young, most of them dressed in a modest but respectable way; they could have been warriors or sailors. One of them, who looked not much different from the rest but seemed to be the leader of the party, jumped down from his sledge into the snow.

"I will not ask what a maid like you is doing outside on a day like this," he said easily, "but you are sure lucky to have encountered us."

Their eyes met, hers blue as the sky and his blue as the sea, and the intensity of his gaze threw color into Thjodhild's face. Still, she made herself look at him. His face was broad and pleasing to the eye, despite being thickly covered with freckles. He had a straight nose and a strong jaw. His wavy red hair got out from beneath the fur cap on his head. He was broad-shouldered and well-muscled, but not very tall – not much taller than Thjodhild, who was rather on the short side – and only a couple of years older than her, by the look of him.

Her curiosity was awakened by his looks. He seemed to be someone who had just come back from a long journey, and his companions likewise. But of course, if it weren't for the unusual circumstances, she would not have allowed such a stranger to accompany her. It would not be deemed proper for someone of her birth and station

As it was, though, she had no choice but to climb into the sledge and place herself by his side. The servants were crowded into a corner of another sledge, and together the procession began the slow careful way towards her father's.

At first Thjodhild was determined to say nothing, but soon she found herself stealing shy, curious glances at the young man by her side. And when she looked away she felt his eyes studying her face, which she lowered into the hood of her fur-trimmed cloak against the wind. A rather silly thought occurred to her – that if it weren't for the wind, she could have lowered the hood, and then her dark, shiny hair would be seen in all its glory.

He began to tell her of himself, though she did not recall asking. His name was Erik Thorvaldson, and all called him, as he said, Erik the Red – it was not hard to see why, when she looked at his red hair and the young beard that adorned his chin and jaw. He was not exactly handsome, but something about him drew the eye, so that she found herself looking again and again.

She asked him where he was from, and it turned out he came upon the shores of Norway from Iceland, not too long ago.

"My parents were banished to Iceland," he told her in a tone of most flattering trust, "because of a conflict my father had with someone who invaded his grazing lands. My father was a farmer, a peaceful man really, but in this case he insisted to stand upon his rights in ways that, ah, weren't exactly peaceful. So, that man insisted he was in the right, and there was a fight which my father won – and in which the other man was killed. It was self-defense, of course, but his enemy had been rich and powerful, and his relations appealed to the king, which determined my father's fate. He passed away in Iceland a few years ago and never saw Norway again, but I was allowed to come back. I always thought of Norway as my home, not Iceland, though I was just a boy when we left."

By pure chance, Thjodhild was familiar with the story, and was not at all certain Erik's father was just such an innocent victim of circumstances, but she preferred not to enter an argument. This was the first time she met someone who did not come from the area where she was born and raised, let alone someone who had lived in exile in Iceland. She ventured to mention it.

"The time in which Iceland was the home of exiles and outlaws alone has long passed," Erik told her. "Today it is a prosperous country... though the pick of good farming land is pretty slim, I'll grant that. Anyway, Iceland can expect independence from Norwegian rule one of these days."

"Such talk is treason, is it not?" said Thjodhild with a hesitant half-smile. He shrugged.

"If there is rebellion in Iceland, I will not be the one to lead it," he said. "I never meant to stay there for the rest of my life – nor here, for that matter. No, my eyes look west."

"West?" Thjodhild was surprised. "What do you mean? I heard that beyond Iceland there is nothing but a frozen, empty sea, as far as the edge of the world."

Erik laughed. "The opposite is true, Thjodhild," he said, and so she discovered that she must have told him her name, though she did not remember doing that. "Experienced sailors tell, and I have every reason to believe them, that after many days of journey in the western sea you can reach a land upon which men had never trod. It is said that this land is cursed, that it devours all who step upon it, and woe betide those who reach its shores."

"And is this true?" Thjodhild asked tremulously.

"That is just what I mean to discover," he assured her cheerfully.

"I heard such tales once," she remembered. "That distant shore is called the Black Land."

"But of course. Such tales, meant to frighten children and fools, are told by men who have no hope of reaching Valhalla," Erik said confidently. "It might just be a good, fertile land, with wide rolling meadows for grazing, and who knows what treasures hidden in the earth. But what is most important in my eyes is that this land is uninhabited, and not under the rule of Norway, and in it a free man can live safely, without fear of injustice."

"Live?" repeated Thjodhild. "Do you mean to say you intend to stay there all alone?"

"Not alone, of course," Erik hastened to explain. "I did not mean to say I am planning to raise a tent of sealskins and live in it by the side of a lonely fire on the shore. I will need men to sail with me, brave and loyal men, and I also need money and resources for the journey – enough to start a settlement."

"That is why you came to Norway, then?" asked Thjodhild. "To look for coin and men?"

"Yes," said Erik, "and a wife, too," he added.

These last words surprised even himself, she learned later. The truth was that he had not thought of marrying just then, but as he looked into the pretty face of the girl by his side, colored rosy pink with cold and shyness, he suddenly understood that was indeed his true purpose. In Viking trips, there is no place for women except in the way of loot. He had no desire for such conquests, though. His journey would be of another kind, and yes, he needed a wife who would be ready to share this path with him – a faithful, strong woman, one who would not fear to tie her destiny to the unknown and leave everything behind.

"It must be a fascinating venture, to settle an unknown land," said Thjodhild with a hint of longing. "If you are successful, tales will be written of you, and you shall be remembered even after hundreds and hundreds of years."

The tone of her voice conveyed a simple, serious belief in his success, and he raised his head with boyish pride.

Chapter 5

They approached the place that had been her home ever since she was born, and Thjodhild felt a surprising, faint stab of regret when she recalled that in a few minutes she would say goodbye to this young man who was unlike anyone she had ever met. His conversation was like fresh wind blowing in one's face after a long time of being shut within four walls. And before she was able to stop herself, she invited him to come in together with her – there can be no doubt, so she told Erik, that her father will be grateful and will wish to express his gratitude to him personally.

Erik seemed surprised but gratified, and it took no difficulty to persuade him. After exchanging a few quick words with his companions, he came along with her. Thjodhild, who looked at the other men fleetingly, thought that they seem devoted to him, or perhaps to the promise of new, unknown lands. Some of them would probably abandon him soon after the beginning of his journey; others would follow him through thick and thin.

Her father, as she had predicted, was very grateful and promptly called for food and drink. He was a bountiful host. Bread and meat, beer and hard, smelly cheese, and also dried apples and honey were served. The old man thanked Erik profusely again and again for bringing his daughter home safely, and made his guest promise that if he is ever in need of something, he would not hesitate to ask him for any favor. Nevertheless, the expression of cool suspicion did not leave his eyes. The visit was formal and not too long, and Erik got up from his seat, brushed the crumbs off his clothes, looked at Thjodhild one last time, exchanged a few insignificant courtesies with her father – and was gone.

In the privacy of her chamber, Thjodhild sternly told herself that the sense of loss she felt when the door was closed behind the young man was completely unreasonable. It was a fleeting encounter, she told herself. This lad has a wonderful dream which might or might not come true. But something in her heart told her that she will hear of Erik Thorvaldson again – perhaps in many years, when she will be a wizened wrinkled crone with a dozen children and two dozen grandchildren. Then she will remember that distant winter day, when she was sixteen and met a young sailor who told her something of his heart's desires.

It turned out, though, that things were not meant to happen exactly that way.

Two days after Erik rescued her from the snow storm the day was bright and clear, with no remembrance of the weather's fury. And Thjodhild, whose heart was not at peace ever since she returned home, asked her father's leave to go and visit her sister Ingvild. The permission was granted, and Thjodhild passed her time pleasantly, though she experienced a tiny, irrational stab of regret when she failed to encounter Erik once more on her way home. People like him, she knew, do not tend to frequent the same paths over and over again, yet somehow she had hoped.

When she returned home, she noticed the expression of her father's face was extremely sour. Thjodhild wondered whether it was one of the servants that irked him so. But to her surprise, he sent everyone away, so that they remained alone. She looked at him expectantly.

"I need to speak to you," he said abruptly.

"What is it, father?"

He cleared his throat. "It is about the boy who helped you on your way home two days ago," he said, "that Erik Thorvaldson."

35

"What about him?" said Thjodhild, trying her best to seem indifferent.

"What did you speak of on your way here?" her father demanded.

He told me of his dreams, thought Thjodhild – *and I let him grasp a hint of mine in one unguarded look*. But of course, she didn't intend to say this aloud and made her best effort to look innocent.

"We spoke of nothing significant. Why do you ask?"

"He was here," her father declared, and after a pregnant pause went on, "he asked me for your hand in marriage."

A deep blush flooded Thjodhild's face, and to her good fortune, her expression of astonishment was genuine. Her father noticed that.

"I promise you, Father," began Thjodhild, "that I had never met him before that storm, and there was not the least hint of - "

Her father raised his hand, stopping her, and she fell silent.

"That will do," he said. "Of course, I did not think otherwise. It is obvious that you could not encourage the fellow to form any such ideas. A penniless adventurer, the son of an exiled murderer... I have no idea what he was thinking. Of course, I told him so at once."

"I don't understand what he was thinking either," said Thjodhild serenely, while her heart pounded furiously. "Do I have your leave to go and rest a while, Father? I am rather tired."

She hurried to her room and sat down on her bed. Her head was spinning. What was the meaning of this? Does this mean, then, that their brief meeting was not wholly unimportant in Erik's eyes? But does he really wish to marry her on so short an acquaintance? Why did he not ask to see her? Did he really hope her father would give him a favorable answer? And what does he intend to do now that her father had refused? Will he give up?

All these questions preyed upon her relentlessly, and more than anything she wished to meet Erik again and clarify the matter, but she had no idea where to look for him or how to contact him. The days passed and her life went on as usual. *It was a fleeting fit of madness*, she told herself, resigned. Erik must have understood that only being possessed by some confusing spirit could prompt him to ask for the hand of a maid whose social standing alone would put her quite out of his reach – even if he had met her more than just once. He was refused, as he should have known he would be, and now she will never see him or hear from him again.

A short time after that, there was a market day in the nearby village. Thjodhild went there, and, while she was examining some wool, a tall, lean, flaxen-haired boy two or three years younger than herself approached her.

"Are you Thjodhild, the earl's daughter?" he asked, looking at her with big, frightened eyes.

"Yes," she said, wondering. Almost every face in the village was familiar to her, yet she did not know this boy.

"I have a message for you," said the boy quickly and quietly, "you must have a light in your window tonight at midnight. And I was also asked to tell you that it's tonight or never."

"Who? How?! When?.." The questions crowded on Thjodhild's tongue, but the boy already began walking away, shaking his head.

"I can't tell you nothing else," he said, "this is the message I was asked to pass, an' if I didn't get good pay for it, I wouldn't dare to do even that. It's more than my hide's worth."

And he disappeared among the market crowd.

Thjodhild stood rooted to the spot, and all color drained off her face. Her father and sister tried to talk to her, the salesmen tried to catch her interest, but she could not look at anything and asked her father to allow her to return home, under the pretext of a headache. When her father noticed her paleness he easily believed that she was unwell. And indeed, the blood beat painfully against her temples just as it pumped through her fluttering heart. She could speak to no one, and fled to her bed a short time after returning home.

It was perfectly clear who sent the boy. Erik did not know his letters, probably, so all he could do was pass her a simple message through someone else. She did not know exactly what he was planning, but it was clear to her that whatever it is will be apt to raise her father's fury. The choice was hers. A light in her window will mean "yes" - while a dark window at midnight will speak a firm "no".

It is madness, I don't even know him, I don't understand why I am doing this, Thjodhild thought while she lit the candle and placed it close to her window, which she opened a crack. The flickering candle was a single light in a moonless, starless night.

Thjodhild wore her outer clothes, a warm fur cloak and thick leather boots, but still she shivered uncontrollably. *What will happen? What will come to pass?* She thought constantly.

She heard a brief knock on her window, and when she opened it, she saw a ladder propped against the windowsill. She looked down, to the darkness of the yard below, and as much as she strained her eyes she could see nothing.

And then she stopped thinking and began acting. She placed her foot on the windowsill and started the precarious descent down the ladder. To her surprise, her heart stopped fluttering and she concentrated now on one thing alone – how to place her foot on each step without falling.

It was over, and there she stood, in the empty yard behind her father's house – and there he was, the strange young man from the snow storm, standing before her and smiling; his mouth laughed confidently, but his eyes betrayed his uncertainty. She looked at him in amazement. She still found it hard to believe this isn't a dream.

"I apologize for how it all played out," said Erik. "If I knew my letters, perhaps I could send you a proper message and explain everything, but since I never learned to read and write, my only hope was to meet you face to face. So I had no choice but to send that fool, Bjorn – and he, of course, can hardly string two words together."

"My father told me you came to him and asked for my hand," said Thjodhild. "I found it hard to believe."

"Your father also told you, naturally, what his response was," remarked Erik.

"Why?" asked Thjodhild, studying his face. "We only met once and talked briefly. What would you do if my father had given his consent?"

"That would have allowed me to court you and get to know you better before the marriage taking place," said Erik, and laughter hid in the corners of his wide mouth, "but taking everything into account, it probably won't be possible after all."

"What won't be possible?" Thjodhild was determined to make his meaning clear.

"To get to know you better before we are married. Because that is how things stand, lovely Thjodhild," he added, "either we join our lives tonight, or not at all."

Thjodhild looked at him and a strange peace flooded her soul. After all, deep inside her she had known it would come to this, ever since Bjorn approached her at the market and gave her his jumbled message. Tonight she must decide: will she run away from home with Erik Thorvaldson and tie her destiny to his for as long as they both live - or will she never see him again?

Erik noticed the quick glance she stole in the direction of her window, and said apologetically:

"I am truly sorry it has to be this way. If I could have warned you of the plan ahead of time, I would tell you to take what you might wish to bring with you. Now it is impossible, though. If you go back up to your room, we might not be able to escape. We don't have that much time."

He didn't elaborate, and didn't mention just then which mouths in the house of her father were silent because of a bribe, and which by fear of a sharp blade.

"But wait a moment," said Thjodhild, attempting to squeeze a bit of reason into the entire business, "who says I agree?"

She looked directly into his eyes. She liked the fact that he was not much taller than she was. She will feel comfortable with him, protected but not crushed, not repressed... he will never try to control her in the same way her father always had.

Does this mean she agrees?

"Well," Erik paused, and his voice was softer than usual, "it is time to decide, then."

"You don't know me," said Thjodhild, "I don't know you."

"It is not exactly true," said Erik. "Sometimes, it doesn't take very long to understand the essence of the person standing before you." He did not elaborate, but she knew he is right. At the very moment their eyes first met, her heart sensed unmistakable closeness.

A smile began to spread across her face, and simultaneously across his – a smile of relief. In her case, the relief of having made a decision. In his case, the relief of being accepted, though he had assured himself he didn't doubt very much that he would be.

"Well, if we must escape tonight, it is a good thing I have my thickest boots on," said Thjodhild. "Do we need to walk far?"

"You will not need to walk tonight," said Erik.

He lifted her off the ground in one swift motion of his arms. Her arms wrapped themselves around his neck, and upon her face appeared an expression of giddy happiness that was mirrored on his.

That was how Thjodhild took the first, and most important, independent decision of her life.

Looking back, that night always seemed to her like a dream – the jump into the arms which were good and warm but so foreign, the escape into the snowy, frozen darkness, the humble, secret wedding – when she thought of it, she always told herself that if she had been given enough time to consider her decision, she probably wouldn't agree to such an insane offer – and every time, she told herself how good it was that she wasn't given time to think too much.

If she had known all the difficulties that awaited her and Erik, would she still choose to walk down this long and winding path alongside him? This she could not say. But she was definitely happy that it was her, and not any other woman, whom he had chosen as a companion of his life.

Erik, too, failed to explain how come he did not think that a rich, spoiled sixteen-year-old girl might be a burden to him in his long journey and a life wrought with danger and struggle. But an inexplicable feeling attracted him to this maid in a way that would not allow doubt or mistake – and indeed, it turned out he had gained himself a loyal wife, one who encouraged him even through the hardest times.

Chapter 6

At first Thjodhild still entertained the hope that once she arrives on her father's doorstep, married, and asks his forgiveness for acting against his wishes, her father's heart will be softened and he will take pity on her and receive her and Erik into his household. But this hope was soon gone. Not only did her father refuse to see her, he spoke against Erik to earls who had the utmost influence in the district, and it soon turned out that Erik has no place in Norway, just like his father.

They sailed the Iceland, but there, too, they were unlucky. In a way very similar to what happened with Erik's father, an argument over a piece of land turned into violent conflict, in the course of which one man was killed, and Erik declared as the culprit. It was obvious that there would be no peace for them in Iceland, either.

Where would they go, then? Thjodhild never thought she would be destined to live her entire life in Iceland, a poor outskirt of Norway that siphoned in all the exiles, thieves, murderers, sorcerers, seekers of freedom and betrayers of the throne – she knew her husband's eyes are looking out there, into the unknown, into the land in the west that might exist or might not – and Erik was convinced that it does exist. Now all he had to do was collect about him enough men who would believe him, and prepare to make the journey.

Thjodhild nearly fainted away when he presented before her the men he had recruited. They were daring adventurers, some of them desperate, some but half-sane, and most with very little to lose. All were exiled to Iceland, which meant they all broke some law or other – and though it has been a while since Thjodhild saw every law-breaker as a criminal, her heart skipped a beat when she heard the locals speak of her husband's new companions. She was especially afraid of one man, by the name of Harald Bjornson. He was one-eyed, and scars too numerous to count adorned his face and arms. It was told his wife cheated on him – and he strangled her, and his wife's lover, who was a man of high rank, and all his family. He used no weapon but his own deadly hands to kill all these men and women. He stood a trial and was doomed to execution, but eventually succeeded to soften the punishment by using all his life's savings as bribe.

"I don't care," Erik said stubbornly when his wife told him of her concerns, "even if he is a descendant of Loki the trickster. Bjornson is an excellent navigator and a bold warrior, and this is what will matter on our journey and in the new land. I do not fear betrayal, I do not fear lies, I do not fear murder – my fear is of weakness in the people next to me. That is precisely why I am concerned because some of them insist on taking their wives along."

"But Erik," said Thjodhild, "I thought our goal is to found a settlement in the new land, far from the Norwegian rule, where we can begin our lives afresh as decent men, not despised outlaws."

"That is true," her husband confirmed, "but what if I am mistaken? What if nothing awaits us in the west? What if that land exists – and I am fairly certain it does, I must say – but it isn't fit to be settled? What if it's one enormous glacier throughout most of the year? Such a journey into the unknown is an adventure for men, not women. I would prefer for everyone to leave their wives here, but the women fear that if their husbands are gone for too long, people will take advantage of their helplessness. Actually, my sweet, I would prefer you to remain behind as well."

"No," Thjodhild said firmly. "We already spoke of it. I will go wherever you go."

"Think of little Leif," he begged, "How would such a sea journey affect a child?"

"The journey will do him no harm," declared Thjodhild. "Our son is stronger than any other boy I know, Erik. You will see, a day will come and he will be a great man, surpassing even his father."

They began preparing for the journey, and did their best to get ready in time, so as not to miss the period when the winds and currents are favorable. They stocked up on food, water and various supplies, and every man procured himself warm and sturdy traveling gear and any weapon he could get, in case they were to meet non-compliant local population.

Thjodhild did not like to remember the challenges of that journey, by the end of which she was heartily sorry for leaving Iceland, and feared for her life and for little Leif. But Erik's hopes did not fail, and a land of striking beauty appeared before them, a land of magnificent mountains and fjords and meadows that looked promising enough for grazing and planting, and trees – not too numerous, that was true, but enough to supply the wood they would need to begin a settlement. The expedition, in short, was a success. The people who came with Erik now saw him as a leader, not just a guide who chanced to take them overseas.

The land was wide but, as very few exploring parties sufficed to find out, there was no sense in going much further north, for the northern areas were mostly covered with glaciers. It was decided, then, that the settlement will be founded at the southernmost point of the new land, which Erik had called Greenland. The climate in the area they had chosen was very much like the northern parts of Norway or Iceland.

"Judging from the plants, spring and summer here should be just long enough to make good grazing," Erik said. "We must send a ship back to Iceland to tell people the news, bring more settlers here, and also cows and horses, goats and sheep and pigs. Then we can be truly well-off, and not depend only on fish and game."

Erik feared for his life if he should ever be seen in any area of Norway or Iceland again, so the man chosen to recruit new settlers was Thorbjorn Olafsson, Erik's loyal friend. Thorbjorn was not an outlaw, but decided to go together with Erik into exile, because his noble spirit rebelled against what he called glaring injustice. To the sorrow of his elderly parents, he left the family farm in Norway to his young, reckless brother, who was to have everything in Thorbjorn's absence – although officially, the property would belong to Thorbjorn, and to his children after him, if and when he should return to Norway.

When Throbjorn and his crew left, and only a handful of people remained in the settlement – there was but one longhouse in all of Greenland then – Thjodhild felt terribly lonely. It was as if they had been left alone on the very edge of the world – and actually, it was just so. She pressed her little son to her heart, and he wriggled in her arms. Leif felt he has already outgrown such excessive attention from his mother, and preferred to go on in his play. Thjodhild kissed him and sent him off.

"Erik," she turned to her husband hesitantly, "could it truly be that all this wide land is unsettled?"

A crease appeared between Erik's brows. He feared that just as they had come upon Greenland, someone else might have discovered it before them – and though no sign of human habitat was discovered so far, the land was wide and, despite the parties they sent, mostly unexplored. What if there are local nomadic tribes that might invade their vulnerable settlement, just as they are waiting for the reinforcement that is due to come with Thorbjorn?

But he knew he must not show even a hint of fear. All the courage of his men, who trusted him, depended on his own.

"All the facts point to this land being uninhabited," he told his wife in make-believe confidence. "It is very difficult to reach, and most likely no one had done that before us."

He was wrong, but back then it didn't matter very much yet. Sooner than anyone expected, Thorbjorn returned from his successful journey, and brought with him fourteen ships full of men, farm animals and tools. Thjodhild was relieved when she saw that many women came with their husbands, and even some children appeared, to become Leif's playmates. She knew how dangerous it might be when there are much fewer women than men in a settlement and what strife it may cause. Thorbjorn himself had married during his short stay in Norway and brought with him his new bride, Aslaug, a healthy, hearty, cheerful girl who did not fear the rough life that awaited her, far away from anything she had known before.

The settlement began to grow, and sealskins and pelts of white bears that were exported to Iceland and Norway were the first step towards financial independence. The merchants who traded with them did not care that Erik the Red, the leader of the

Eriksfjord settlement, is an outlaw. They bought the skins and pelts and later sold them at triple price in Norway.

Thjodhild was very proud of her husband, who was now the ruler and the rule, the undisputed leader and head authority of the settlement. What gladdened his heart most of all was exploring new areas in Greenland and the expansion of the settlement he founded. Thjodhild, on her part, was busy running the household and raising the children – Leif, and after him two younger sons, Thorvald and Thorstein, and Freydis, the only daughter.

One day, when Erik, Thorbjorn and a few other men set out to hunt seals, something unexpected occurred.

"Wait, Erik," Thorbjorn touched his shoulder as they were going through the forest towards the shore. By that time, Thorbjorn was a father as well. His son, a big, strong, clever boy, was called Thorvard, and was a good friend of Leif and his brothers.

The group of people who appeared before them unexpectedly was about as numerous as their own party, and its members, too, were armed hunters. Upon the faces of the two leaders appeared a very similar expression – that of suspicion and fear; the balance of strength between the two parties was such that none dared to attack. The locals, who existed after all, were wide-boned, of short stature, with coal-black hair and dark, narrow eyes. They wore furs and skins, and looked hardy, as if they were used to traveling long distances by foot.

At the end of a very pregnant silence, the leader of the locals raised his arm and said a few words in his own tongue. Erik and his men did not understand him, of course, but the tone of his voice was pacifying, and plainly indicated he had no wish to attack. Then he placed upon the ground a sack he carried on his shoulder, and gestured at Erik, who understood the contents of the sack are meant for him.

The group of locals made a few steps back, and Erik opened the sack, which was made of sealskin. It contained long polished walrus tusks.

"Listen, Erik," said Thorbjorn thoughtfully, "we never gave much importance to the walrus, but these tusks can compete with ivory, and that is dearer than gold in Norway!"

Erik, through various gestures, did his best to express his gratitude – and so as not to be outdone, took off his long cloak, which was made of very fine white bear pelt, and this offering was accepted with equal graciousness by the leader of the locals. After that, Erik ordered his men to go back to the settlement. He decided to forgo hunting that day.

"It turns out we are not alone in Greenland after all," he said to Thorbjorn. His friend looked at him, surprised by the heavy foreboding he heard in Erik's voice.

"It doesn't look like those hunters frequent the same paths we do," he said. "They came here by chance, and didn't seem to be interested in confronting us."

"Not today, because they did not outnumber us," said Erik. "How do you know they will not recruit enough men to wipe our entire settlement at once?"

From that day onward, Erik started to post guards each night, but time proved his fears unfounded. The locals did not attack, and even a certain kind of trade with them had developed, though nothing more. They were too different from the new settlers, in both looks and ways. But Erik, who was a shrewd man, made an effort to observe their habits, because he knew that if they wish to fit into the harsh climate and long winters of

Greenland they need to study those who had already done so. He learned from the locals the methods they used to hunt seals and whales, and following them the settlers began to base their food more and more on what came from their surroundings – fish and seal meat.

"There is only so much space we can use for planting and grazing," said Erik, "if we don't want to exhaust the land, we must eat less of what we were used to at home, and consume much more fish. The locals do so, and they enjoy excellent health."

Freydis, when she was grown enough, took this one step further. She managed to learn the local tongue and talked with those who came to the settlement to trade. Some of the things she learned shocked her mother.

"Erik, my love," Thjodhild said to her husband, "I beg you, you must make her stop. I always abhorred rituals of sorcery, and from what people tell about the practices of these local tribes... I do not wish to see such morbid curiosity in Freydis."

"You know why this is happening," said Erik. "Freydis is a quick, clever girl. She grows bored. You encouraged her to learn her letters, something that was completely unnecessary, in my opinion. Now no ordinary pursuit is interesting enough for her... but there is a solution, my dear. Thorvard and Freydis are mad about each other, you know that. Stop saying she is too young, she is almost as old as you were when I met you. Let us get them married, let Thorvard take her to a new home, and all will fall into place, you will see."

All did fall into place, but alas, for too short a time – Thjodhild thought sadly a few years later, at the Norwegian court. Freydis and her doings were, as far as she was concerned, her own most prominent failure as a mother.

Chapter 7

Thorgunna winced when the servant girl pulled the comb too forcefully. Her copper hair tumbled loose down her shoulders and back, shining softly in the light of the oil lamps. A reprimand stood on the tip of her tongue, but she remained silent. After all, she was the one who had asked her maid to hurry.

She was already wearing the green velvet dress she chose for the evening, and the emeralds she had inherited from her mother glittered in her ears and about her neck and wrists. Now only her hair was left, to be brushed and adorned with emerald-studded pins. The slave girl who was responsible for arranging her hair was brought from the shores of Britain; her fingers were especially deft, which was why she was chosen to be Thorgunna's personal maid. The girl appreciated this position, for Princess Thorgunna was gentle and fair. She wasn't apt to lash out at her servants and slaves as many other noblewomen did.

There was still a while until the feast, but Thorgunna was in a hurry because the king had summoned her, and hinted that the matter cannot wait. She was curious. Something made her think that it must be connected with the guests who arrived from faraway Greenland.

After Thorgunna's hair was brushed to a metallic sheen and twisted into two long thick braids that looped around her head as a crown, the slave girl dabbed some perfume on the princess's wrists and on her bosom above the cut of her dress. The dress brought out her slim, willowy figure, and the dark green velvet made the white of her skin seem even fairer. Thorgunna, unlike some of the noblewomen, always had the habit of washing her face and body every day, but today she indulged herself with an especially long spell in her private bathhouse, and spent a while in a large tub full of steamy hot water. She felt, therefore, a pleasant sense of cleanliness all over her, and her movements were more graceful than ever as she stepped through the corridors towards the king's chambers.

She was received almost at once. His Grace, too, was dressed and ready for the feast, in all the glory of his crown, his costly clothes, and his finely made fur cloak and boots. A precious ring of white gold, studded with an enormous black amethyst, graced the index finger of his right hand. The ring had been a gift from his beloved late wife, Geyra. It was told among the smallfolk that Geyra herself had an identical ring that was lost when she died, which had extraordinary magical properties. Of course, King Olaf chose to ignore these rumors. As a devout Christian who took care to demonstrate his faith at every opportunity, he frowned upon anything connected with sorcery.

The king looked benevolently upon his niece as she entered and motioned her to come closer. He took her by the hand and told her to sit by his side, on a bench piled with snow wolf pelts. They reclined on soft pillows, and Thorgunna looked at the king with a curious gaze.

"Well, my dear," he said warmly, "we don't have much time left until the feast. I told the cooks to serve a wide array of dishes tonight, and a skald named Styr Herjolfson will sing for us. Soon we will have the chance to take a closer look at these people who arrived from afar and about whom we have only heard tales until now."

"I look forward to that, my king," said Thorgunna with sincere enthusiasm. "I have heard a lot about Erik the Red and all he had managed to do since he left Norway. I felt sorry that he did not arrive together with his family, but I understand that he was sentenced to exile until his last day, for some terrible crime..."

"Ah, Erik the Red is a brave man," said King Olaf dispassionately. "I think at least half his fault was simply bad luck that made him cross paths with important people. He is not bloodthirsty. All his energy he had put into settling that land he calls Greenland. Anyway, Erik is getting on in years. His son, Leif, will be chieftain of the new settlements. He is the one I summoned here, and he is the one who interests me most right now."

"He is quite an impressive man, is he not?" said Thorgunna, recalling the tall, powerful, red-haired stranger, a glimpse of whom she caught earlier in the day.

"He is," said the king, "and he possesses an influence which has the potential of growing. Despite the harsh conditions which, as far as I know, make life in Greenland difficult, people continue to go overseas and settle there, looking for profit and especially for freedom. This way, they distance themselves from the Norwegian rule. I had the privilege of entering the covenant of our Savior, Lord Jesus, together with all the royal court," the king placed a hand on his chest and fingered the heavy, ornate gold cross, a jewel he started wearing not that long ago. "I sent priests to all the provinces under my rule, to show the light of the Christian faith to my people. But Erik the Red is a stubborn pagan, and so are most of the people who flock to the shores of Greenland and lose the place that is prepared for their souls in paradise, by the throne of Lord Jesus – and simultaneously their place here in this world by the throne of Norway. It pains me to think of all the souls that are destined to burn in hell, without getting even a chance to hear the Gospel."

"I, too, feel sorry for the idol-worshippers," said Thorgunna without a shred of cynicism. The priests at court were selected according to their eloquence, and the princess visited the church frequently and listened to the prayers and sermons. "But what can be done? Greenland is so far."

"There is but one solution," said King Olaf. "To baptize Leif Erikson, make him into a loyal soldier in the army of Jesus, one who will take care of spreading the true Faith among his people. Erikson, his mother, his sister and the people who came with him will spend the winter with us, until the weather improves enough to enable them to sail back to Greenland. By then, Leif Erikson must already be a man of God – and my man, it goes without saying. I intend to offer him a place in my personal guard, at least while he is here – and naturally he will accompany me to church."

"That is a splendid idea, Father," agreed Thorgunna. Since she lived most of her life under the guardianship of her uncle, King Olaf, she got used to calling him Father. "A place in your personal guard! That is an honor many noblemen would gladly fight for. Leif Erikson will, of course, recognize the offer for the compliment that it is, and be grateful. I believe it is much more than an exile like him can expect."

"And still I wonder if that will be enough," said King Olaf, caressing his beard. "I mean, enough to ensure Leif Erikson's loyalty. He is unwed. He will go back to Greenland, and there he will surely marry some pagan woman who will steer his heart away from the righteous path of our Lord Jesus, and by and by will put rebellious ideas into his head. This must not happen."

"It is a reasonable concern," said Thorgunna. "Give him a wife, then," she advised. "Some meek, devout girl. A younger daughter of some not very rich earl will not find it very much beneath her to marry someone like him, especially if he is distinguished by you."

"It might also be that if he is charmed by a woman, Erikson will divulge his plans to her, including what he intends to do in Greenland and where his true loyalty lies... because as of now, I am uncertain about it. I believe that under the influence of a pretty face he may well be much more talkative than if I try to get him to speak using direct means."

"That is true," nodded Thorgunna. "That is why, Father, you should give him a daughter of one of the earls in whose loyalty you can trust. One who would not withhold knowledge that might be important to the throne."

"I cannot think of a maid I would trust with something like that," said the king. "If Leif finds out my intention, he will see it as an act of spying and intrigue, and may become angry - even though it would be nothing but a very reasonable and prudent measure," he hastened to add. He took his niece's hand again. "The only woman who is close enough to me, who is clever enough in addition to her great beauty, and loyal without doubt – is you, my dear Thorgunna."

The princess looked at him, mute with disbelief. She wasn't quite certain of what her ears were hearing.

"Oh, of course I don't mean to *give* you to him," the king assuaged her fears. "I love you as a daughter, and you will marry Sigurd and be the queen of Norway one day. But I do ask you to acquire a... friendship with Leif Erikson – of course, in a way that would not be public, so that no shadow is cast upon your honor. Get to know him. His thoughts, his heart, his plans – and tell me all you find out. Flatter him; let him understand, using subtle hints, that he is a man of such great influence that he may hope to become *much* closer to the king one day. I need Leif Erikson to return to Greenland as a devout Christian, accompanied by a priest – and by an illusion that one day he may win your hand in marriage."

For a moment, Thorgunna was silent. Despite the conviction in the king's words, what he suggested sounded like trickery, and she didn't know whether she will be able to accomplish a mission such as the one he was about to bestow upon her. She was never particularly good at spinning intrigues, nor did she have any great desire to excel in that part. But of course, she didn't dare to refuse the king openly.

"And what will happen when Erikson returns to Norway?" she asked instead. "Because with such encouragement and hopes, of course he will return."

"When he returns, you will be Sigurd's wife," said the king. "But do not worry. By then, Christianity will already be spread in Greenland, and the loyalty to the Norwegian crown together with it. As for Erikson, he will have no cause to complain. He will receive what is due to him as my loyal subject, and I will see to it that he marries well, far better than he can expect now. I will make him an earl and give him a beautiful maid from a noble and rich family. That ought to appease him."

Thorgunna had her doubts. Leif Erikson did not strike her as a man who can be easily manipulated. Questioning the king's decisions, however, was not her province.

"The Greenlanders will spend some months here," the king went on. "I assume Erikson will not refuse my offer to take a place in my personal guard. It means that most of his time will be spent right here, at court. It should give you enough opportunities to extricate all his secrets from him."

On her way to the feasting hall, leaning on the king's arm, Thorgunna made an effort to keep her shoulders and back especially straight, as if trying to shed the heavy weight of the task in which she was now unwillingly involved. The prospect of what she must do cast a cloud over her thoughts. She did not relish the thought of trifling with a man such as Leif Erikson.

Chapter 8

The royal feasts at King Olaf's court were always something exceptionable, and in the eyes of those who came from the modest households of Greenland the feast was full of splendor like none that had ever been seen before. After a plentiful summer's harvest, the barns were full of wheat, barley and oats, salted meat and fresh and dried fruit. The trestle tables in the hall were long, made of polished wood and groaning under the weight of roast pork, mutton cooked in its own blood, rows upon rows of fat salmon and big, fresh loaves of bread that had just been baked and gave off a delicious smell. Servants and slaves walked around the tables and poured beer and mead for all the guests, and close to where the king's family sat – the king himself, the princes, and the princess – they served also excellent wine that was brought from lands far to the south.

Leif was surprised to discover that the king ordered him and his mother and sister to sit so close to the royal end of the table, closer even than some earls who now stared at him with bitter envy. The glance he exchanged with his mother proved to him that she, too, did not expect so great an honor. In their simple garb and few ornaments, Leif and his mother were a striking contrast to most of the Norwegian nobility.

Only Freydis took it all for granted. She took care to bring her finest clothes and costliest jewels, those she got from her father as a gift when she married Thorvard, and now she could be seen in all her glory. The great hall was drafty and rather cold, despite the enormous fire fed by whole tree trunks - and the silk dress Freydis chose for the evening was pretty thin, so she had to cover it with a costly cloak of arctic fox pelts – but be that as it may, she looked impressive. Her lush red hair was pulled away from her face by a ribbon of green silk embroidered in gold, and pearl-studded golden hoops shone in her small delicate ears. Her lips smiled but the cat-like eyes, one blue and one black, were cold and calculated. She looked at every one of the men who sat at the same table with them, and tried to assess the worth of each and surmise how much he might be of help or hindrance to them.

The king's two sons sat on his right side and Thorgunna between them, next to the heir, her intended husband. From beneath her long, downcast lashes the princess examined Leif Erikson, who sat opposite her. Though he wore clean garb in honor of the feast, his clothes were simple and unadorned, like those any of his men might wear. Just a single golden earring graced his left ear, and inside it two tiny precious stones, one of them a ruby and the other a sapphire. Thorgunna wondered whether this earring was given by a woman he had loved, or taken by force from a foe he had slain. On his right cheekbone she noticed an old, long-healed scar, no doubt a souvenir from a fight or a hunting trip.

Compared to the other guests who sat this close to the king Leif looked untamed, although he had had time to trim his hair and beard in the hours before the feast – but the way he held himself and ate was gentler than she had expected to see. His large, work-roughened hands broke the bread in a cautious, unhurried manner, and he bit into his meat and drank from his cup without the obvious greed that some of the guests displayed.

He had a face which would be called distinguished by most men, or handsome by most women, with a straight nose, strong jaw and a red mane of hair. But what attracted the eye most of all was the freedom that was so obvious in his countenance, in the way he looked, in the few words he said. His shoulders were wide, his arms powerful, and even while he sat it was easy to tell he was a man of great height.

The noise in the hall ran high, so Thorgunna did not chance to exchange even a word with Leif or his relations, though she had wanted to very much. For a moment, her eyes met his and he inclined his head politely. A moment later, he called the boy who passed by the table with a tray in his hands and asked him to pour more mead.

At the end of the feast they were served large wedges of goat cheese, apples baked in honey and blackberry-filled tarts. Another kind of costly, sweet wine was brought for the most distinguished guests. While they ate, they were entertained by the performance of the well-known skald Styr, handsome and impressive and dressed in garb of fine, though simply cut wool. His dark cloak was held in place by a polished silver brooch in the shape of a falcon. He entered with quiet steps, and an expression of light melancholy was upon his handsome face. Despite his youth – he could not have been more than twenty – his glory as a singer and poet was already high. He sat in the place that was prepared for him in the middle of the hall, and gave a long, melodic touch to the strings of the harp he held in his hands, leaning against his knees. When he was convinced he caught the attention of every man in the hall, he began his song. And those were its words:

The years might have passed, but you daren't step onto the road,
And try as we might, we could not have held on to the dream.
There is a bed for us among the wild herbs of abroad,

61

But not in the land of harsh snow and locked up, frozen stream.
For us there's a land where the words hold a meaning no more,
Where lilies float upon the surface of moonlight-kissed lakes.
Perhaps we might meet once again, like we have met before,
Or maybe a sweet kiss is no longer ours to take.
Perhaps one day fears will all vanish and haunt us no more,
And we'll strike a path that no man ever traveled before.
Or maybe the dreams will continue to haunt our minds,
And torment the spirits of weak who had been left behind.

Freydis froze in her place, rendered mute by surprised anger. It was a poem she herself had written once upon a time for Thorvard, and he loved it, though the message of the poem was one of glum reproach. He sang it at quite a few gatherings in the house of her father in Brattahlid, in Greenland, and many people had heard it, some of them winter visitors or traders. But who took these words here, to the shores of Norway? And who passed the song to Styr, who sang the foreboding words of Freydis in her own ears, here at court?

Leif and Thjodhild, too, exchanged surprised looks, recognizing the song they had heard a few times at home. It might have seemed that Freydis was supposed to be flattered by the popularity of her poem, but the expression of her face was bitter and defensive, and Leif understood why. She did not wish to recall anything that had to do with Thorvard.

He could understand her. For him, too, it hurt to remember Maura, though unlike his sister, his loss was not his fault. But despite the pain, he liked to feel she is still with him. Often he brought her image before his mind's eye and imagined what she would have said of any new experience that fell to his lot – the journey to Norway, the stay at court and the cordial reception they were honored with, the foreign views, the colorful crowd, the luxurious feast and all the prominent people around them – the proud earls; King Olaf himself, who kept stroking his beard as if pondering something; Prince Sigurd, who was an insignificant, dull-looking type; and his bride-to-be, the princess Thorgunna, who was so beautiful she lit up everything around her as if she were the sun – and like the sun, it was difficult to look at her directly.

The skald Styr began singing another song. To Leif's surprise, the singer looked at him, and inclined his head respectfully, before he touched his harp and began singing the following:

I came from a land that is far out there,
Where the scent of honey fills the air,
Declaring a summer, respite from cold;
I tasted sea waters throughout the world,
I know all the stars in their skyward ways,
And death has been on my heels many days -
Yes, so many times now I know no fear.
I know thrills of journey from there to here,
And sweet is the sound of a shield that falls...

"Isn't this lovely, now?" said Freydis with biting irony, and Leif felt her elbow in his ribs. "You are already quite famous here."

"I would not flatter myself too much," said Leif. "This song was written about Father when I was still in my swaddling clothes." But he still took a few coins from the leather pouch tied to his belt and tossed them to the singer.

Thorgunna was impressed by the song much more. Its bold words and the pleasant voice of the singer made something within her stir. She always possessed high sensibility, and a combination of a keen mind, together with wishes of her heart that were too vague even for her to discern, created a fertile soil for fancy. She knew the song she had just heard was written about Erik the Red, but just as well, she thought, it could have described his son Leif. Was not he as great a traveler and discoverer of new lands as his father, and perhaps even more? His star will rise and shine brighter yet, she suddenly felt sure.

The king is mistaken in trying to manipulate this man, it became clear to her – and he is doubly mistaken in the way he intends to do it. She was young and inexperienced, but not stupid. The tall, impressive stranger sitting before her, with his sharp eyes of a hawk, a laughing mouth and a stubborn chin – he can understand and appreciate honesty. But since when has honesty been a common feature with kings?

... More sweets and wine were served, but Thjodhild felt the onset of a headache and asked her son to escort her to the chambers she shared with Freydis. Leif got up readily, but Freydis expressed the wish to stay longer. She was immersed in conversation with a man sitting next to her, the earl Ingvar Haraldson, a thin man with a thin, shrewd face and auburn hair that had already begun receding, though he could not be more than thirty.

"I had almost forgotten there are courts, with great halls such as this one, and people dressed so finely," Thjodhild told her son with a tired smile as they began making their way back. "After so many years of missing Norway, I did not think I'd so soon miss Greenland. But now all I look forward to here is meeting my sister, Ingvild – and then, I will wish for nothing more than going back to Brattahlid, to your father."

"Father will be glad to hear how eager you were to come back," said Leif. "As for me, I do not expect too much pleasure during our stay here, although some profit might fall to our lot."

And he told his mother of the king's offer to make him one of his personal guards; King Olaf had already broached the subject privately, under cover of the music, during the feast.

"That is quite an impressive gesture of trust, my son," said Thjodhild with satisfaction. "During the months we are going to stay here, you will be close to the king, which is so very advantageous. And there is no knowing – perhaps if the king is very pleased with you, he might consent to remove the taint of exile and outlaw from your father's name, and restore his rights in Norway and Iceland."

"This might be so," said Leif, "though I do not believe Father will be too impressed. He has made his home in Greenland. There, he is the leader, and no one questions that. In Brattahlid, his word is the law – people do not take to heart the laws of Norway, which is many weeks of sailing away – when the season is favorable, that is. I believe that right now, the king might need the Greenlanders more than the other way around. And more than anything, Mother, I believe we are in a pit of vipers, and I have a feeling that we will have to be very careful so as not to step on one. Did you notice the man Freydis talked to so animatedly this evening?"

"Freydis!" his mother repeated, annoyed. "Yes, I did see. A man who wears a cross on display, as if to show he is a devout Christian, but his face is like that of a fox. I sense that in the following months I will have to be as close to Freydis as a hound on a track of deer. I intend to take her on a visit to my sister Ingvild, Leif. There she will not be surrounded by so many people, and she will have less temptation and opportunity to mess up her life and ours. Oh, Leif, where is the source of this cold, calculated ambition of hers, of this readiness to step over those who should have been dearest to her, just so she can have her own way? I grieve for her, and I grieve for Thorvald. If she had truly been my daughter, she would have turned out different."

"Now, it is anger that makes you talk so," said Leif. "Freydis is your daughter, just as the rest of us are your sons. She might not be the child of your body, but you were the one who raised her."

Chapter 9

This was a secret only a few knew.

One summer, after an especially successful hunting trip made by Erik and Thorbjorn, the latter threw a splendid feast in his house for all the hunters. Thjodhild was not of the party, and there was strong ale aplenty – and one woman who threw herself into Erik's arms, filled his cup again and again until he was quite drunk, pulled him by the hand to share her sleeping bench and, as turned out a short time later, became pregnant.

Thjodhild's sorrow and anger were deep. It was true, of course, that mistresses and bastards were not an uncommon thing, but she was always confident that her husband has no need of other women. He always told her so again and again himself, and so he maintained even after it became known that another woman is carrying his child.

"It wasn't me, my love," he said. "It was Thorbjorn's good drink. I can hardly recall her face. I don't mean to see her ever again, although, of course, I will support the child when it is born. I have no woman but you."

Seemingly, Thjodhild was resigned. She wasn't going to leave Erik, of course. But her disappointment was still strong, especially when she discovered, around that time, that she is with child again herself. She wondered whether their marriage will ever become again what it once was.

By a curious play of destiny, it so happened that the two women were brought to the birthing bed on the same night, and almost at the same time, at midnight, two baby girls were brought into the world. But Thjodhild's daughter was born lifeless – while the other woman, the thought of whom brought her so much grief in the past months, died a short time after giving birth, leaving an orphaned child. An hour later, Erik took the tiny, snugly wrapped babe, ran to his home and placed the child in the arms of his tearful wife.

"I knew you were very angry with me, my sweet," he told her, "but this is my daughter, and she is left without anybody in the world – while our daughter was carried off by the gods. Let us adopt this girl and raise her as if she were our own, yours and mine."

Through the tears that blinded her, Thjodhild looked at the babe, who had already begun to look for the warm breasts, full of milk that was meant for another child. The girl's hair was red, like her husband's. Her eyes were closed, so that their color could not be seen, but her features were not unlike those of her son Leif when he was just born. She was tiny and soft, warm and full of life. How much she had longed for a daughter, after giving her husband three sons!

Thjodhild took the child to her breast and adopted her as her own daughter – and their babe, the one whom the gods had taken, Erik laid down next to the woman who died in childbed and the two were buried together. They told no one of the exchange. They raised Freydis as if she was the daughter who had been born to Thjodhild – and so she gained the status of a trueborn daughter, not a bastard; and what is no less important, the girl also had a much better mother than the one who had brought her into the world – a woman of careless behavior and a great fondness for drinking.

Thjodhild, on the other hand, discovered that raising a daughter is not quite what she expected.

She had imagined a little girl to be a gentle, charming creature of naturally pleasant habits. A daughter was supposed to stay close to her mother, observing and learning all the household ways, spinning and weaving, sewing and doing embroidery. But little Freydis knew how to get her own way, and insisted on full independence since about the age of one year, when one of her blue eyes turned blacker than black, to her mother's grief. Soon she learned to insist that her place is together with her brothers, in their play of war, their weapon training and their hunting. While other girls played with rag dolls and took their first lessons with the needle, Freydis would not part from the wooden sword Leif carved for her, and insisted on her hair being cut short.

"Do not let this bother you too much, my dear," Erik advised his wife when she complained to him about Freydis's inappropriate behavior. "All children will have their tricks, and Freydis is a very spirited girl. She has no sister to play with, only brothers, so why should it surprise you she tries her best to become just like them? When she grows a little she will understand what is expected of her."

Erik was right only in part. True, after a few years had elapsed Freydis stopped hacking her hair short and began paying more attention to her dress, but she didn't stop training with Leif, Thorvald and Thorstein, and even joined them at seal-hunting. Moreover, she began learning how to read and write – something that even made Thjodhild happy at first, because it meant Freydis spent more time indoors. She learned not only the Norse runes, but also the Latin writing, which was just beginning to become widespread then. The runes were carved into stone, mostly, and parchment was costly and hard to come by – and so Freydis practiced her letters by writing with a piece of coal over a slate of wood.

During one trip to Iceland on which she accompanied her father – who by then had authority enough to dare being seen in Iceland, if not in Norway – Freydis laid her hands on some scrolls which she read greedily; later, it turned out they contained accounts of witchcraft, something that was highly irritating to her mother, who never supported things like fortune-telling or spells for bringing the wrath of gods upon a neighbor one crossed paths with.

"Nonsene," insisted Erik in the face of his wife's excessive anger. "Many girls of Freydis's age tend to become interested in things that are, shall we say, out of the ordinary. That is the nature of youth."

"You don't understand, Erik," said Thjodhild, shaking her head. "In Freydis's case, it goes much further beyond simple curiousity. Yesterday I caught her looking through one of the scrolls she brought from Iceland. She looked at me in a way that plainly said she did not expect me – a surprised way, my dear, and a guilty one. At that very moment, my ears were filled with a whisper that gradually subsided, as if distancing itself, until it was impossible to distinguish a few moments later. Those were spirits she invited into the house by her sorcery, Erik – spirits that left when I entered. She truly has powers, and I don't like it at all. She is only twelve."

"It will pass, you'll see," promised Erik, but he attempted to convey the confidence he did not truly feel himself.

A short time after that, Freydis angered her father in earnest. She began communicating with the locals and learned their tongue during market days that were held outside Brattahlid.

After that, she began disappearing time and time again, and her father discovered she visits the temporary dwellings of the Skraelings, the tents those nomads made from sealskins.

"I don't like this," he told her openly after catching her red-handed, "I really don't like this, Freydis. The Skraelings are no friends to us. It is true that we trade with them rather than fight them, but does it mean they are glad to see us settling a land that until not long ago was their alone? Of course not."

"They wouldn't hurt me," replied Freydis, proudly raising her red head. "They know who you are, and they know who I am. I am learning a lot from them, Father. You make light of the Skraelings, but they have much knowledge about everything in Greenland, and the seas and lands beyond it, the animals that live here and the resources that are buried deep inside the earth. They also know to tell the fortune, and to find out what lies in the heart of every man," she added off-handedly.

"And I understand these last bits of knowledge interest you the most," remarked Erik.

"Be that as it may," Freydis said elusively, "I believe Leif should consult them before he sets out on his next journey around the coast."

"Be that as it may," Erik cut her off, "I forbid you to fraternize with them."

"Do not underestimate the Skraelings, Father," Freydis said again, in a voice so serious that Erik felt a shiver run down his spine as he heard his daughter's words. "They know of us much more than we know of them. Yesterday, in their camp, I met a man who was born among them, and knew no tongue but theirs, a man about forty years old, and he had narrow eyes with a thick fold of skin, like theirs, and wide cheekbones like theirs – but the color of his eyes was blue, and he was fair of hair. Who is this man? Is it possible that men from our home land have lived here before, and they mixed with the Skraelings and were lost? Who were they, and how did they disappear?"

"This I cannot tell," said Erik, "but I have no doubt we must take care when we deal with them, and you will not go to their camps again."

When Freydis was thirteen she experienced a complete turnaround in her feelings. Actually, perhaps a turnaround is not the correct term. It was a quiet process that had taken some time, but as her transition into womanhood was in full bloom, it bubbled above the surface. It had to do with Thorvard.

Freydis had known Thorvard ever since she was born. He was the son of Thorbjorn, her father's friend, and they played together as children. When the boys had grown somewhat, Leif and Thorvard became especially close, like their fathers have always been. At first glance it was difficult to understand why. Leif was reckless, Thorvard pensive. Leif was sharp-tongued, Thorvard was silent. Leif was a pleasure-seeker and Thorvard shunned pleasure for its own sake; Leif's temper was easy, while Thorvard, even as a boy, was fearsome in his fury.

Even in their looks they were quite the opposite. While Leif was red-haired and blue-eyed, Thorvard had dark eyes, and his raven-black hair was tied back in a long braid. His appearance was striking among the rest of the lads. His face was not as handsome as Leif's, who was remarkably good looking as a young boy, but there was a deep, quiet power in his eyes. Both boys were of a fine build, but Thorvard was a veritable giant, extraordinarily tall, and his shoulders were so wide he found it troublesome to pass through some doors in the settlement.

While Leif had already enjoyed success with some local women, Thorvard was unusually timid on this score and lowered his eyes whenever a woman talked to him, something that was completely at odds with his usual bravery.

But the two friends had something in common deep within their soul, and that caused the great closeness between them. Both had a high sense of inner integrity and courage, both were decisive and clever much beyond their years, and both sincerely cared for the people in their responsibility, be it a few children playing at sticks, some men on a hunting trip near Brattahlid, or the crew of a ship that would sail to unknown lands. These qualities made men eager to follow them and would eventually turn them into well-known leaders.

Freydis and Thorvard failed to understand exactly when, how and where was gone the childhood ease with which they played together ever since Freydis was a babe; when they began blushing as their hands chanced to meet, and when a love bloomed between them, a love so strong that even a short separation became unbearable to two hearts that beat as one. It was a most eligible, desirable union as far as both families were concerned, and all who knew the young people were happy about their attachment. It was clear to everybody that a feeling so powerful cannot be repressed for long, and that the two will marry quite young.

"You will see," Erik told his wife with great satisfaction, "now she will stop her nonsense. Now she will have a proper occupation – taking care of a husband and a household, and of children later on. There isn't and cannot be anyone better than Thorvard for her. Now she will lose her taste for rebellion and sorcery."

But he was wrong.

A day before the wedding Freydis disappeared, and later came home pale and tearful. She refused to eat and acted like someone who had been given terrible news. Thjodhild knew that her daughter visited the Skraeling camp again, despite Erik's prohibition, and saw the old witch she had mentioned several times before. But what was it that she heard? What can bring such misery to a maid so young and beautiful, just a day before being wed to her beloved? Thodjhild prodded and inquired, but Freydis said nothing. She wiped away her tears, put on her wedding clothes and smiled, but the shadow of haunted fear still flickered in her eyes.

Ever since that day her interest in sorcery increased, and she continued to meet and converse with the Skraelings oftener than ever, to Thorvard's great dismay. He did not know how to stop her, and after periods of ignoring what she did there were accusations and outbreaks of anger. So things went on until that accursed journey to Vinland after which the life of Freydis was never the same.

Thjodhild's heart ached for this beautiful young woman whom she considered, after so many years, to be truly her own daughter, as if she were her own flesh and blood just like the rest of her children. If only she knew how to bring peace to her tormented heart! What grieved her most of all, she thought, was that even now she didn't understand why things had to happen this way.

"Leif," she told her son, "you know, I met a friend from old times today and talked to him for a while. His name is Bergsveinn Snorrason, and he told me some things which might be of interest, and among them... Thorvard is here, in Norway."

"Here?" Leif was surprised. "I was certain he must be in Iceland. He sent me a message through one of his men saying that he intends to return to Greenland next year. And who knows what this decision cost him, the poor fellow."

"He is visiting with his father's relations," said Thjodhild, "and, it can be surmised, is recruiting more people who would join him in the Western settlement."

"Are you going to tell Freydis?" asked Leif.

"No, son, I don't think I would dare. Thorvard has been through enough. But you and I, perhaps we can go and see him and Sygni. She had turned three already, you know. I am certain Thorvard will not object to seeing us. Erik and I have always loved him as our own son."

Chapter 10

Just as Leif had expected, his position in the king's personal guard was not very exciting. The most significant part of his work consisted of accompanying the king just about everywhere. He ate with the king and stood guard outside his chamber when he slept, and was by his side while he gave audience to his vassals, important men and distinguished guests. Once in a while Leif picked up a hint or two regarding the political, strategical and financial aspects of running a kingdom. It sounded terribly complicated to him compared to his father's chieftainship in Greenland. There everything was done on a personal basis, as every man was known by reputation if not by sight.

Not too much time had elapsed since the union of Norway, and there were still many earls who, for all intents and purposes, didn't see themselves as subject to the king. They neglected to pay taxes and did whatever they saw fit. Still, it was obvious the kingdom's power lay in union. Separation into small, independent, frequently warring factions would lead to Norway's inability to compete with other, stronger, more united and better organized kingdoms.

King Olaf did all that was necessary to keep about him a group of especially strong, powerful earls which would be loyal to him. Ingvar Haraldson was one of them. He was a clever, ambitious man who acted as an adviser to the king on all matters of profit and loss. Leif didn't like him – the fellow seemed too smooth, too glib-tongued and shrewd to him. He suspected that for this man honesty was a superfluous quality. He didn't like Ingvar's excessively flattering manner to his sister Freydis either. He couldn't suppose Haraldson meant to court her, although he had no wife. *What is it that he wants, then?*

Many times, the king would send away the men of his retinue and go and eat alone in his chambers, while he seemed deep in thought – pondering matters of state, no doubt – or looked through some ancient scroll. The king was a learned man and knew not only the runes, but also Latin and arithmetic. He also possessed vast knowledge about far-away lands and expressed a deep interest in Greenland.

"I have visited England, Ireland and Scotland, and the lands of the Slavs to the east and south," the king told, "and I saw no land as beautiful as Norway. But I should like to see the wild country you grew up in, Leif. If the burden of so many commitments here in Trondheim was not so heavy, I would sail together with you in spring."

"Perhaps a day will come when we are honored with a visit from you, King Olaf," Leif said politely. *Father would love this.*

"According to the maps I saw, Greenland is a vast country," the king remarked, signaling to the serving boy to pour more wine.

"That is so," said Leif. "Greenland looks roughly like a giant triangle, the base of which is in the north and the point in the south, and only close to the point there are some lands fit for growing crops, pasture and, in short, settling, and also some woods here and there, though most of those have been already cut down for building. But this, as I said, is the smallest part of the country. Most of Greenland's territory is covered with enormous glaciers."

"And what is there beneath the glaciers?" asked the king. "Could it be anything worth seeking?"

Leif shrugged. "Most of them are so thick no one would contemplate breaking through them, Your Grace."

"Not even during high summer?" insisted the king.

"It might be possible to break away some parts of the ice," said Leif, "but does His Grace believe we might find something that would justify the great effort involved? Also," Leif went on, "we have more than enough to do without fighting the unconquerable forces of nature. There is all the ordinary farm work, and hunting for our needs and for selling across the sea – sealskins and whale fat, and walrus tusks for ivory."

"Ah," said the king, "with hunting, life is not so very boring. I am fond of it myself and arrange many hunting trips – for entertainment, of course. Do you hawk?"

"I have a few times," said Leif, "but it isn't very common in the place where I grew up, Your Grace."

"Well and good," said King Olaf. "In two days we will go hawking, and then we can all evaluate your abilities."

As it turned out, the promised hunting trip was delayed by a few days of cold rain, sleet and mud – but eventually, a pleasant autumn day came along and the hunters were out on their way early in the morning. They rode underneath a clear blue sky strewn with little puffy clouds. The hooves of their horses broke the thin frost that covered the ground, the yellowish brown dead grass, and the leaves in all shades of earth and fire that fell down from the trees.

Leif was glad for the change. He got tired of standing and sitting, listening and talking. His strong body asked for movement, activity, stretching of limbs and work of muscles, and something that would engage his senses, but not his mind or his heart. Freydis, who was also invited, was all smiles as she rode by the side of Ingvar Haraldson. The king signaled Leif to ride by him at the head of the column, together with the princes, his niece Thorgunna, and the rest of the king's guard.

"You ride well, Leif Erikson," Prince Sigurd spoke to him. "I was certain that you, the Greenland settlers, never sit on horseback and only ride in sledges pulled by dogs or reindeer. Or perhaps by white bears," he added off-hand, to the sniggers of some men about him.

"There is no need to exhibit your ignorance, Sigurd," the king told his son. "Do you truly believe no man of Greenland owns a horse or has had an opportunity to sit in the saddle?"

"I do not pretend to be a rider as skilled as you, Prince Sigurd," Leif replied serenely, "but I daresay I shall live to the end of this day without falling off the back of my horse."

Some smiled, others laughed, and the conversation dispersed. Princess Thorgunna gave him an appreciative stare, but said nothing. She rode very well herself, straight as an arrow, her head held high and proud. The hood of her dark cloak was thrown back, her hair collected in a smooth knot at the base of her neck.

Like countless times in the past five years, Leif's heart was suddenly constricted because Maura wasn't by his side, because she couldn't share with him all that delighted his senses – the colorful shower of falling leaves, the deep green of pines and other evergreens, the fresh, cold, invigorating air, the energetic movement of his body forward on the back of the chestnut horse. So many times he dreamed of sailing here one day together with Maura, of showing her the land of his fathers.

Their time had run out sooner than they expected, though. *No one can tell if there will be time for all we plan.* He shook his head and looked forward. At times he felt her riding just next to him – he could almost see the sun reflecting off her smooth black hair, could hear her soft, pleasant voice talking to him, and on her tongue, as always, were words of wisdom, hope and cheerfulness – all the messages that helped him turn from reckless youth to mature man. Even after she passed away, whenever he was in doubt many times it was enough to think of what she would have said or done to reach the right decision.

All his energy in the last five years was dedicated to fulfilling the promises he made to her: sailing to Vinland, strengthening the ties with Iceland, supporting and advising his younger siblings. Only one request of hers he could not satisfy.

He didn't marry again.

"Leif," he recalled her soft, weak voice on her deathbed, as if the words were whispered in his ear just now. *"Leif, my beloved, thanks to you, and you alone, I was happy as I never thought I could be."*

It seemed as though she had lost almost all her blood, and it was a wonder she was still conscious. Her eyes were enormous and full of ethereal light, her face white as snow. Her cold hands held his, but with every moment their grip weakened, and though he returned the pressure to her fingers, he sensed he could not pass any of the heat of his body to her. She was shaking with cold underneath the blankets and furs.

"You must marry again, my love. I do not want you to be alone for the rest of your life. Be happy. Be happy."

Those were her last words.

... Leif's good fortune did not smile upon him on that hunting trip. While the other hunters had already begun collecting their bounty, his hawk refused to play along.

"You seem deep in thought, Leif Erikson," remarked Princess Thorgunna. "That must be why you have had no success today."

Even in her simple riding garb, she looked radiant. The exercise brought a very becoming flush into her rather pale face. Her hair shone like copper, her eyes were bright, her long dark eyebrows enhanced the clearness of her skin. Her hawk was held upon her arm with the natural grace of a noblewoman who often goes hawk-hunting. Leif smiled despite himself.

"As long as this is not a hunt for profit, I won't be sorry even if I return empty-handed. I am enjoying the ride. Besides, I didn't expect any bounty. Hawk-hunting is a sport for earls, not simple men like me, and I am not used to it."

"Simple men!" cried the princess. "Many years hence, when none of us or our children or grandchildren walk upon this earth, people will forget Thorgunna – but will remember Erik Thorvaldson, the discoverer of new lands, and his son Leif, the expander of horizons."

Without noticing it, they let their horses drop pace and lost their place at the head of the column by the king. Leif was amused by her words.

"Forget Thorgunna, the queen of Norway?" he said. "I find this hard to believe."

"It is not at all certain," Thorgunna said quietly, "that I will be the queen of Norway."

"No?" Leif raised his eyebrows. "But it is well known, and commonly spoken of, that you are promised to the prince Sigurd, Princess."

"Everybody has thought so ever since Sigurd and I were little," said Thorgunna. "But now, when times are turbulent, His Grace believes it might be better for the kingdom to make a different arrangement – get Prince Sigurd to marry so as to secure an advantageous connection, and arrange another lot for me."

A hint of something akin to pity appeared for a moment in Leif's face, and this didn't remain hidden from Thorgunna's eyes. She went on:

"It is so - a maid of my birth and position must be disposed of in a way that will benefit everybody, not merely herself. But I do not fear for my future. I am the king's own blood, and His Grace loves me as a daughter. I have no doubt he will find me a good husband."

She is a clever girl, thought Leif, *but such good reason when it comes to the choice of a husband is unnatural for someone her age.*

The day was so pleasant and the hunt so entertaining that none of the party noticed two couples who were left far behind. The first were Leif and Thorgunna; the second Freydis and Ingvar. The last two were riding very close to one another, as if they were old friends, and seemed to be deep in quiet conversation.

"It is a great pleasure to meet you," said Ingvar, his voice smooth and sweet as honey. "What you are telling is very interesting indeed. I hope I will have the pleasure of conversing with you in a place where no one will interrupt my enjoyment of your company."

Freydis gave him her most charming smile, but her eyes remained cold. She didn't know whether she could trust this man. His birth wasn't very high, but his ambition, his glib tongue and his natural sense for connecting himself with useful people advanced him to the position he now occupied. Freydis had no doubt the man is a double-edged sword. On the other hand, however, it might very well be that he is precisely what she needs.

"I am certain," she said, "that very soon we will have the opportunity for uninterrupted conversation."

Chapter 11

It soon became clear to Leif that there are other, much less pleasant sides, to his position as the king's personal guardsman. He reached this conclusion when King Olaf requested his company at church on Sunday. To Leif's claims of not being a Christian, His Grace replied with great seriousness:

"I cannot and do not intend to force you to accept the light of the Christian faith, Leif, although doubtless my duty as a good Christian is to pray for your soul, so that you might see the true path of Jesus, our Saviour. The least I can do is encourage you to step through the doors of the church, which are open to all, and hope the truth will glimmer in your heart and make you leave the ways of pagan worship, as I have left them myself."

And so it was that Leif found himself among the church pews, listening to a sermon that made various feelings rise inside him, from wonder and doubt to mild curiosity and sometimes outbreaks of mirth he had to conceal as fits of coughing.

The priest, Father Wilhelm, was a small, lean man with long straw-colored hair that looked as if it hadn't been washed in at least a year. But his voice, surprisingly for such a small man, was loud and deep, and his speech energetic and full of impact.

"God made a covenant with the people of Israel," he declared, "but the Israelites have sinned again and again, and worshiped idols, and bowed to statues. And so the Lord dissolved this covenant with His unruly children. He sent into this world of sin his only son, our Lord Jesus, who was crucified and accepted torment and death to pay for all our sins. And here is the wonderful message: he who acknowledges Jesus as his savior is forgiven for all his sins – and it is clear we have all sinned, are sinning, and will continue to sin until our last day. And it is said in the New Testament, in the book of Mark: *He who is baptized shall be saved, but he who is not baptized shall not be saved.* So hurry and accept the path of Jesus, our good Lord, who longs for nothing more than to embrace us all in his boundless mercy and lead us straight to the base of the Heavenly Throne! Hurry and spread the message of Christ to all those near you, all your kin and friends. And since any man who does not accept the faith in our lord Jesus, and pushes away the wonderful gift of atonement for all sin, has but one outcome – an eternity in hell – it is permitted and even encouraged to press and convince him until he accepts the true Christian faith, and even by using power, for it is obviously for his own good."

In his mind, with surprising and unexpected clarity, Leif saw once again the image of Nathan Ben Yosef, the Jew he accidentally met during his travels. Only thanks to this man he vaguely knew who those "Israelites" the priest mentioned were, and the bitter words of the Jew from that one and only meeting echoed in his ears again.

"You will get to know the Christians yet," said Ben Yosef, "and hear what they say. These days it cannot be otherwise. Their gospel sounds convincing. They took our holy writings, made off with them, and twisted and rewrote them so that they will fit their purpose. They talk of peace and justice, but their ways are the same ways of brutal power as of people who do not claim to be so very righteous. They are trying to make us accept their faith and abandon ours, at swordpoint.

I tell you this, Leif Erikson, because you seem like a good man, and a thinking man, unlike many," added Ben Yosef, and then his voice was lowered to a whisper. "There *is* one God, one

Creator of the universe, and he is your father and mine, and the father of all men – and to live by his will you need not join any religious circle, but only believe in Him and live a honest life."

Leif listened more intently. He attempted to understand what the priest was saying, but there was no true sense in his words. It was all one great jumble to him. He has always been a man of sense, and the gods of Asgard amused him in their inclinations and sins, which were so human – material desires, power struggles, betrayals, promiscuity, battles and intrigues. He found no sense in magic rituals, whispers and fortune-telling, either. Sometimes he wondered whether there is any higher power at all – or whether, perhaps, destinies are randomly entwined in a world full of suffering, loss, death and a tapestry of events, some of which are terrible and some glorious. The beautiful and the ugly, the brave, the good and the evil walked hand in hand so often that there could not be, Leif thought, a god so insane as to mix it all together. Such thoughts made him feel very lonely. It was much easier to believe at least in something, no matter if these should be the jealous and manipulative gods of Asgard his fathers worshiped for so long or the innocent, patient Savior Father Wilhelm talked of with so much religious ardor.

His glance fell upon the face of Princess Thorgunna, who sat not far from him, and a sudden pain pierced his heart when he saw the expression she wore – an expression of pure faith, of longing for something that cannot be expressed in words. Her eyes stared at Father Wilhelm, but it was easy to see her soul had taken flight above the polished wooden pews and thick walls of the semi-dark church, and was now wandering far and high above, in worlds quite apart from this one, seeking something pure and beautiful which is alone worth living for. The passionate glow of her soul put a light in her face which was far higher and purer than her natural earthly beauty. Her eyes were moist with emotion and her lips trembled when Father Wilhelm talked of forgiveness, acceptance and boundless love which may be expected by those who walk through the gates of Christ. Unconsciously, her hand rose and rested upon the ornate, gem-studded golden cross that adorned her neck. For her, it was all true, and she saw it all in the eyes of her mind. The priest's words lit within her a fire of ardent faith, a faith that had very little in common with bored righteousness of the king, whose face was expressionless as he listened to the speech made by Father Wilhelm.

Perhaps women simply need this – to believe in something, and it doesn't matter very much what, Leif thought to himself at the end of the sermon, when everybody got up and the crowd of believers began chanting a song in Latin of which he didn't understand even half a word. *Perhaps all they need is innocent faith.* In this world, the men are active. They fight and make decisions, while women are expected to accept the rule of a man, be it their father or husband, during the whole course of their life. They cannot do much by themselves. In such a position, how comforting it must be to believe that the world is run in a good and righteous way, though perhaps we cannot see it!

When the crowd began to disperse, its motion left Leif and Princess Thorgunna close to one another. Her face was now serene, but a special glow was still about it, refusing to disappear.

"Well, Leif Erikson," she said while he walked slowly by her side, behind the king who was deep in conversation with some people of his retinue. "What do you think of the wonderful words Father Wilhelm gifted us with today?"

"They were very interesting," Leif said evasively.

"Interesting?" her eyes were narrowed. "Is that all you have to say?"

"If the princess means to ask," he said, "whether, after I heard Father Wilhelm's sermon, I feel an irresistible urge to run and beg to be baptized, the answer is no."

"In that case, you are an incorrigible pagan!" cried the princess. "I have no other way of explaining your ignorance of the wonderful revelation that floated within the church walls until not long ago. Everyone felt it. I doubt there was a dry eye in the crowd."

"Me, an incorrigible pagan? Not at all," said Leif. "On the contrary, I have always respected the customs of our fathers, but I was never ardent in my worship."

Thorgunna looked pleased enough with his answer.

"You simply have doubts, then," she said. "You must continue visiting the church, and eventually you will see the pure light that is spread by Father Wilhelm's words."

"The princess speaks of feeling and I of reason," said Leif, politely inclining his head. "With all honesty, I don't know whether my desire to analyze everything is a power or a weakness, but always, when it comes to matters of faith, I have endless questions, and more often than not they aren't satisfied. Who is this Jesus Father Wilhelm praises so faithfully?"

"God's own son," Thorgunna supplied willingly, "who was sent into our land of sorrow to bring a message of truth and atone for all our sins. His holy mother, Virgin Mary, was innocent when she conceived Lord Jesus."

Leif suppressed a slight smile, for he felt he might offend the girl's innocent faith, but a stubborn expression appeared upon his face.

"This isn't a new story, princess," he said. "In the legends of almost all people we hear of gods who planted their seed in the wombs of mortal women, and brought giants and heroes into this world. There are tales of the god Odin - "

"Here we do not talk of petty fake gods," said Thorgunna, "but of the one true God, who sacrificed, with endless love, his only son to save our souls from an imminent curse. And it isn't about the lust of a god or a demon for a woman of flesh and blood – but only by God's will, without any physical act, the new life was planted in Mary's womb."

"She was untouched?" Once more, Leif was trying his best not to smile. "Well, that is a better story some maids would come up with."

Thorgunna frowned angrily. "This is sacrilegious talk, Leif."

"To be sacrilegious," he insisted, "I must at least know what I speak against. The words of Father Wilhelm?"

"The words of God," Thorgunna replied quickly, "which can be read, for our comfort, in the holy books - which were written down by the disciples themselves, those who walked by Jesus during his pure and holy life."

"Ah," said Leif. "The holy books. Well, they must be written in Latin. Can you read Latin, Princess?"

"I know a little Latin," Thorgunna said modestly, "enough to understand the Mass, but not enough to read the New Testament in its entirety."

"Well, I cannot read at all," said Leif. "The tradition of our fathers has passed by word of mouth, but here we talk of a

89

mysterious faith written down upon parchment, in a language understood by only a few of our people. And may I ask, Princess, where did this Jesus come from?"

"Our Lord Jesus was born in Bethlehem, in Jerusalem," said Thorgunna, wondering at the question. It was difficult for her tongue to pronounce the foreign names, but Leif recognized them still. "As far as I understand, Jesus was a Jew," said Leif, "not a Roman, and so it is more likely that he recorded his thoughts in the tongue of the Jews, and not in Latin. What of those works that came before the New Testament?"

"The Old Testament was translated by the first people of the church from Hebrew into Greek, and later into Latin," said Thorgunna.

Leif shrugged. "Translations almost always mean mistakes," he said, "and here we talk of writings which had been translated twice, and then explained by Father Wilhelm according to his own understanding. And now tell me, Princess, what is it exactly that I must believe in?"

Thorgunna looked at him with a frown again. "Must I understand from this that you doubt our good Father Wilhelm?"

"All I mean to say," said Leif, "is that the message of Jesus, be it what it may, passed many hands until it reached my ears at church today. Forgive me, Princess, but I cannot ignore a natural sense of suspicion I feel towards a faith which can be truly understood only by a few learned priests, while the rest of us are at the mercy of their interpretation."

"The holy priests are the messengers of God," said Thorgunna, though her voice wasn't very confident. "They are a link between us and our Heavenly Father."

"But even if we ignore my doubts regarding the written sources of this new faith," Leif went on, disregarding her last remark, "there are still many questions. If there is one God who is all truth and justice, why did he need to send his son into this world to save us? And if it is true we were saved by this son, how does that appear to the eye? A thousand years have passed since the birth of Jesus, is it not so? Why is there no less suffering in the world, why does all go on as usual?"

"Only our souls are saved, not our material selves, until Jesus comes back amongst us again," said Thorgunna, but felt her words weren't very convincing.

"Well, I do not feel saved," declared Leif, "and I do not believe my soul will be saved - if it is at all possible in this world - among the church walls."

"You must talk to Father Wilhelm," said Thorgunna, "I am certain he will answer all your questions much better than I can."

"Do I seem like a man who would spend hours conversing with a priest?" replied Leif, no longer denying his being vastly amused.

"The way I see it, there is no man who cannot find his place in the Christian faith," said Thorgunna, "and what comfort this must be to those who inhabit Greenland – a place so remote, so sparsely populated and so cold, with no settlements but those that were founded by your father and his men!"

The thoughts of Leif wandered off to the land where he grew up. He saw in his mind's eye the giant glaciers covering most of the country, and the south shores which enjoyed warm currents in season. He recalled the regal fjords of which made up the shore line, the almost endless fall of mountains, the white bears and northern reindeer walking among the glaciers and in the sparse

91

forests that were still left in the south; the Skraelings, whose mysterious ways were attractive and repulsive at once; and most of all the people, people of brave hearts and free, honest spirit, who were banished from their home and found a new one under the leadership of his father.

"I believe the princess doesn't picture Greenland very accurately," he said eventually. "Greenland is not an empty, silent desert of frost. The climate is harsh, even cruel, of course, but it is a beautiful country. My late wife, who was brought up in a land far warmer than Norway, came to Brattahlid by choice and loved the place very much."

A deep and sincere expression of surprise appeared on Thorgunna's face.

"You had been married? I did not know that."

She didn't know and couldn't know, either, that this was one of the few times in which Leif had mentioned Maura of his own free will since she passed away. Something had dulled in his eyes, as if a candle was blown out, and Thorgunna noticed it, but he made an effort to continue smiling.

"Well," he said, "I am not important enough to have the tale of my marriage reach Norway."

Thorgunna thought that perhaps she should keep a polite silence, but her curiosity overcame her. She furtively examined the handsome, masculine face, the wide shoulders and the well-muscled, rough-looking hands and wondered what kind of woman she must have been, she whom he had chosen as a companion of his life – and how it happened that she left the world of living so soon.

"Your wife – who was she?" asked the princess.

She was a woman unlike any other who had ever lived, thought Leif, *a woman to whom I own all I became, all my achievements, small as they may be.* But he couldn't say the words. The rest of the church-goers had passed along the way already, yet he and the princess remained standing together, and he felt exposed and vulnerable, as he always had whenever the topic came up in conversation. It was cold and very quiet, and rain began to fall, spattering their clothes and reminding them they must walk on. Thorgunna kept looking at him, waiting for his reply with an interest the source of which he could not discern.

"My wife was a simple woman," he finally said, "but brave and loving in a way I would wish upon every one, since this is the essence of true feminine happiness... if I may say so, Princess."

Thorgunna understood that this is not all, of course, but felt it is not the time or place to ask more questions. Leif looked now more reserved than before his wife was mentioned, and some part of her sensed she touched a deep wound, one that had not healed completely despite the time that passed and perhaps never will. She couldn't bear to ask more and cause him further pain, but she felt an inexplicable need to know everything – and privately, she had to confess this no longer has anything to do with what the king asked of her.

Chapter 12

When Leif returned to his quarters he was surprised to find Freydis there. She was sitting on his bed, looking bored. While it was true that his bed was far more comfortable than what he slept on at home – a bench with some blankets piled atop it, because he could not bear to sleep in the bed he had shared with Maura – it still wasn't comfortable enough to spend much time upon in a sitting position, as it seemed Freydis had just done.

"I have waited and waited," she said impatiently, "where have you been?"

"At church," he said shortly.

Freydis made a disdainful noise. "You as well, Leif?"

"As well what?" he asked distractedly, taking off his wet cloak.

"Did you not see Mother there?"

"I did," said Leif, "but had no time to talk to her at the end of the sermon. Why?"

"You might not have noticed," Freydis said sourly, "but any time Mother isn't eating or sleeping, she spends at church. Not only at Mass, but also making all sorts of confessions to this pompous fool, the priest Wilhelm. She consults him about which would be the best way to cast the light of Jesus upon her pagan husband."

Leif chuckled.

"And she wears a cross so heavy it is a wonder it doesn't make her walk with her head downcast," added Freydis.

"Father isn't going to like this," said Leif, still smiling. "It seems the leaders of the new faith are acting wisely, though: they talk to the women, and those in their turn do all they can to convert the men. Just after the sermon I had a fascinating discussion of religious matters with Her Highness, the princess Thorgunna."

He briefly told Freydis of the conversation, and his sister's eyes narrowed in suspicion.

"Leif," she said, "you do know you must be careful, right?"

"What do you mean?"

"First," said Freydis, getting up from the bed and starting to walk back and forth in the cramped space of the room, "have you asked yourself why Princess Thorgunna even talks to you? Not just today - yesterday during the hunt as well, I have noticed."

Leif shrugged. "I suppose she sees me as a curious exhibit," he said. "You know, someone as foreign to her as the Skraelings are to us, only it so happens I can speak her language. Nomads and seafarers always awake the curiosity of those who never stir from home."

"I am not stupid, Leif," remarked his sister. "I saw how you look at her. Do not forget who you are, and who she is."

"I look at the moon rising above the mountains, too," Leif said serenely, "without contemplating the idea of taking it for myself."

"Do not forget that Thorgunna is very close to King Olaf," Freydis went on, "the man who raised himself to be the king of all Norway and united the kingdom – a very impressive achievement. I have no doubt he aspires to get more lands under the Norwegian rule. And you, Leif, must act as if you are loyal to the king, but in truth be loyal to yourself alone."

"It might be news to you, Freydis," said Leif, "but it is in the nature of every man to be loyal to himself alone."

"I mean," said Freydis, "that you must be careful when talking about Vinland to the king – or the princess Thorgunna. If there have already been rumors, you might mention in the most off-handed way some group of rocky islands you have discovered to

95

the southwest from Greenland. For all you hold dear, Leif, do not talk about fields of wild wheat and rivers full of salmon, if you don't want to find yourself carried there, regardless of your wishes, in a ship full of the king's men, and expected to act as their guide. Greenland is cold and hard to settle, and Father had already given all the half-decent lands to people loyal to him – a wise move, I must say. But Vinland is lovely, attractive and virtually uninhabited, and the climate is far better there. I scarcely doubt the king will want to put his greedy hands upon that land."

"There is no need to tell me all this, Freydis," said Leif. "I want to found an independent settlement in Vinland without any strangers breathing down my neck."

"Well, the king won't let you off the hook that easily," snapped Freydis. "He will do what it takes to make you his man."

"I have no objection to becoming his man," said Leif. "On the contrary, it might be profitable for us all, because we are forever running out of resources and people, and loyalty to the king might answer all our needs. But of course I will do nothing that might weaken our position."

"Speaking of needs," Freydis spoke across him, "could you lend me some silver, Leif?"

Leif looked at her suspiciously. "Of course," he said, "but what for, if I may ask?"

"Well," it looked as though Freydis was considering what she should say, "I have thought about it, Leif, and indeed, marrying again is not such a bad idea after all – and I need some new clothes and jewels to look decent. This isn't Brattahlid, you know. What I have brought with me isn't nearly enough."

Leif was unconvinced. He knew his sister well, and realized every sudden change of her ideas or sentiments must be taken with a grain of salt, for usually there was a double if not a triple motive.

"Where does this sudden eagerness for a second marriage come from?" he asked. "If you recall, not long ago you told me you have no wish for it."

"Sometimes," said Freydis, "even very often, a marriage can advance a woman's position more easily than any effort she makes on her own."

"You have not even finalized your divorce yet," Leif reminded her.

"Oh, that is only a matter of time," Freydis replied indifferently, "and it can be easily arranged."

When she walked out, Leif was left with an unpleasant burden upon his heart – and for some reason, the face of Ingvar Haraldson appeared before his eyes again, with his sly smile of a fox and his cold eyes. He didn't like seeing his sister in the company of this man, and he liked even less the idea of Freydis marrying him. But more than that, he was harassed by the thought that their connection was not one of possible courtship, not even an affair – but something entirely different and sinister which he could not quite define.

That night, in his dream, he found himself at church again. He was listening to Father Wilhelm, who talked of a land that grows wheat and barley and sweet grapes. He looked about him, and saw Maura sitting by his side upon the bench, her face smooth and clear and her eyes shining. She held his hand and turned to face him, and smiled radiantly.

"This is what you looked for and what you found, Leif," she told him.

And then the dream was thrown into confusion, and instead of Maura it was Princess Thorgunna sitting by him, in all the glory of her youthful beauty, and her eyes were as green as fresh bright leaves in the bloom of spring. And King Olaf appeared instead of Father Wilhelm, wearing the simple garb of a priest which was surprisingly becoming, and talked of capturing those souls that have not accepted the Gospel yet. Then the walls of the church began to fade away, and Leif found himself sitting in the middle of a sunlit forest clearing on a bright summer's day, and a light wind was in his hair, and all his family was by his side – his father and mother, his brothers Thorvald and Thorstein, and Freydis, and Thorvard – and King Olaf and Princess Thorgunna looked at them all curiously, and the king frowned and the princess smiled.

And this smile was before his eyes when he awoke.

Chapter 13

Freydis tugged on the hood of her cloak so that her face was hidden. Her red hair was pulled into a tight knot today, contrary to her custom, and likewise hidden beneath the hood. The cloak itself was good and warm, trimmed with fox fur, but made in dark, inconspicuous colors. Thus Freydis hoped that even if anyone should see her, she would be difficult to recognize.

She hurried through the narrow streets, lifting up her cloak and skirts so that they wouldn't get wet in the half-frozen slush, outcome of the many cold autumn rains. Trondheim was a town founded not long ago, and most of it was a collection of cramped wooden houses that grew thick around the king's dwelling, and the better-looking houses of some of the earls. Though it was noon, the town was half-dark due to the heavy clouds that hid the sky. People passed by Freydis, hurrying upon their business. Once or twice, an earl rode by on his horse and the commoners were plastered against the walls to make way for him. No one paid any attention to the woman in the dark cloak whose face was covered and whose steps were quick and cautious.

She hastened her stride and hurried over to a large wooden building that had black smoke coming through its smoke-hole. The door was open, inviting the comers and goers to enter the inn, and Freydis crossed the threshold of the large, dark common room, dimly lit by the weak glow of oil lamps that spread a reek of fish.

The landlady, a tall, wide woman whose hair had begun to turn grey, came over to have a look at her, and Freydis threw back the hood of her cloak. The landlady nodded and led her down a stone staircase into the cellar.

The cellar was even darker than the upstairs room and was lit, likewise, by lamps burning with fish oil, but its floor was made of neatly scrubbed wooden planks, and upon the table stood a clay jug of wine and two goblets. Freydis looked around her, her eyes still getting used to the shadows, and for a moment she anxiously thought she must be alone. But then the man who was waiting for her stepped forward, placing himself in the circle of faint, flickering light cast by the lamps. Like her, he was dressed in a long, heavy cloak with a hood thrown over his face – which he now threw back and gave her his mysterious smile that was supposed to express warmth. Freydis smiled back, but as she looked at the long, lean figure of the man, her heart beat with fear and excitement at once.

"Freydis Eriksdottir," said Ingvar Haraldson, "it is a great pleasure to see you. I am glad you could make it."

"Of course," said Freydis, looking about her at the damp-stained walls and the thick, dented wooden table, "though I must say I was surprised by the time and place you suggested."

"I didn't want us to meet anywhere at court, because every wall there has ears," explained Ingvar. "And as for the hour, it is much easier to get away during the day without raising suspicions, while nightly wanderings will undoubtedly look very strange if anyone should take notice. Come over to the table, Freydis, and allow me to pour you some of this wine. The inn is very humble, but that is precisely why I use it for meetings I don't wish to make public. The landlady is a loyal, discreet woman, and for a little extra pay she orders some tolerable wine for me, not the murky water she usually serves."

Freydis took a sip of the wine. It was sweet and strong and burned her throat. Ingvar sat by her side on a rough wooden

100

stool and drank deeply from his goblet, emptied it, and poured himself some more.

"Honesty," said Ingvar, "is a necessary component of successful partnership. Tell me true, then, Freydis – have you mentioned our meeting of today to anyone?"

She shook her head, and her eyes narrowed derisively. "I am not that foolish," she said.

"Of course not," Ingvar replied mildly, "but I thought you might decide to tell your brother."

"Leif tends to be excessively cautious whenever people he doesn't know well are involved in the matter," said Freydis. "Not to mention that he – acting upon the best intentions, no doubt – is insufferably controlling of every step I make."

"That is how elder brothers are, for the most part," said Ingvar, "but I hope this will not bother you too much during your stay at Norway."

"I like it here," said Freydis, "and I like to compare what I see to what my parents had told us. I have got the impression many things changed here in the past decades. King Olaf rules undisputed, towns are built, commercial ties grow stronger – and the Christian priests appear at every turn and corner," she finished contemptuously.

Ingvar nodded understandingly. "The Christian rule of King Olaf is one of the reasons why life in Norway is going to become more and more suffocating. Mark my words, soon a free man will be unable to go about his business if he doesn't frequent the church pews."

"I understand you aren't Christian, then," said Freydis.

"I was baptized," Ingvar shrugged indifferently. "I do not mean to speak openly against what is now the custom at court. But I must say I like the Old Way much more, at least because it isn't full of righteous sermons about sin, atonement, and punishing the flesh to elevate the soul."

"Yes," said Freydis, "this is one of the obvious advantages of our life in Greenland. It's cold and empty there, and sometimes very lonely, but a man may be free."

"Make no illusions," Ingvar warned her, "the arms of the Norwegian throne will reach you too, together with Christianity. Iceland, of course, will accept the New Faith before you. But I fear your father does not have much time left to continue enjoying the freedom that has been his lot all these years. And if it comes to open conflict, he should be wise to submit and swear fealty to the king, for otherwise the consequences can be lethal."

His words hit the spot. He knew it when he looked at Freydis, who paled instantly, even though no muscle moved in her face.

"The king has nothing to seek in Greenland," said Freydis. "We are a distant, poor province – and to think that things might come to an open conflict between my father and the king's men, well, that is preposterous."

But before her eyes appeared once more that terrible vision she beheld in her youth, in the flames of a fire and the clouds of smoke that made her eyes burn and water. Ships, ships and more ships arrive at Greenland's familiar shores, carrying people of fair skin and hair, people of Norway. Her father, Leif, Thorvald and Thorstein, and Thorbjorn and Thorvard and old Harald and the rest gear up for battle. The cries of the warriors make the walls shake and the women weep as they are being carried away as trophies underneath the dark grey sky. Flames lick the abandoned houses and the settlement is burning like one enormous torch of fire and blood. And then the cries cease, and the silence takes over, and she alone, Freydis, walks between the soot-blackened, smoking ruins, and looks at the remnants of those dearest to her through a veil of blinding tears.

She shook her head, forcing herself to come back to the present. Sometimes fortune-telling is only a warning, she told herself. Strong people can take their destiny in their hands and change what is to come. And she, Freydis, the daughter of Erik the Red, will do all that depends on her to ensure that the terrible prophecy will remain but a warning, a horrendous supposition that will never come true.

"King Olaf is an ambitious man," said Ingvar. "He dreams of expanding the influence of Norway, annexing more territories – up to uniting with the Swedes and Danes, and conquering the lands of the Finns to the east. With this purpose in mind, he even offered himself as a bridegroom to the queen of Sweden, and I must say such an act probably demanded the utmost determination of him, for the queen is ugly in a way impossible to describe, and her mustache is far thicker than mine. But she rejected him because she is a devout believer in the Old Way, and cannot abide Christians. I have no doubt the king is concocting a plan to annex Greenland, though it might very well be a plan for the more distant future. I think that at first he will try, probably, to bring about the change from inside, by influencing your brother Leif – but if this doesn't succeed, his resources are plentiful and he will not shun the use of force."

"You paint a rather dark picture," said Freydis nonchalantly, but her heart constricted within her.

"Not at all," replied Ingvar. "I am being realistic. If there is one thing kings find hard to tolerate, it is the independence of those who might have been, in some way, considered their vassals.

Your father was exiled from Norway and from Iceland, and it was expected of him to spend his entire life as a miserable outcast. Instead, he made great success by settling a new land where he is the only authority and dictates the rules, and where people are loyal to him. For this he deserves respect. But the settlements of Greenland are small and sparse. If things come to an armed encounter with Norway... I am sorry to tell you this, Freydis, but your chances to win will be very slim indeed."

"Should I understand we are doomed, then? Should we wait helplessly for the moment when we are made to swear fealty to the king and accept his direct interference in all our affairs – or to confront him and see our home burn?"

"If that had been the case," said Ingvar, "I wouldn't waste my time on this conversation. But you are a clever, strong and brave woman, Freydis – and will, of course, be able to recognize a solution that is right before your eyes."

Freydis said nothing, and only signaled for him to go on. To herself she thought, *if I had known how to make sure the greedy arms of the throne do not reach us, I would have no need of you.*

"Your father, Red Erik Thorvaldson," said Ingvar, "must crown himself. He must be king."

The notion was so ridiculous Freydis laughed openly. "Is that your brilliant idea?" she asked derisively. "The king of what? Of a few scattered settlements along the coast of a frozen land?"

Ingvar sat thoughtfully for a moment or two before going on. He poured what remained in the jug into their goblets and took a sip out of his. Freydis followed his example.

"I know many people," he said eventually, "some of them quite important, so I will refrain from mentioning their names for now

104

– people who are tired of King Olaf's rule and would sail west with all their households, if only they knew they can expect freedom of faith and uncontrolled running of their own matters, and good, spacious territories to settle."

"The areas of Greenland which can be settled are very limited," said Freydis, "and most of them are already taken – as you probably know."

"Of course," he gave her a piercing look, "but I have heard rumors that to the west and south from Greenland, not too far, there are good, empty lands, which are only waiting for people to come and take over them. Of course, this is only a tale. I have no idea if it is true, and where exactly those lands are, if they even exist."

He fell silent, looked at her, and waited.

This is the moment of truth, Freydis knew. Can she trust this man? *Leif would probably say no, but on the other hand, I cannot act alone either.* She did not have the means or the influence, and she needs a partner like this Ingvar Haraldson, a glib, well-connected type, one who knows just what to say to the right people at the right moment. And she decided to make her bet.

"What you heard is true," she said. "My brother Leif sailed to that land, along with me and some others. It is a good, fertile country, with fields full of wild wheat and vines of wild grapes, a green land crossed by rivers in which many fat salmon can be found in season. The climate there is far milder than in Greenland and even than in most of Norway. It is a fine place for a settlement, but," Freydis's eyes suddenly acquired a harsh, metallic shine, "it isn't empty. It is populated by bloodthirsty natives, Skraelings who murdered in cold blood some of the people who came with us. During that journey we were too few to confront them, but we left knowing that if we wish to return, the natives will need to be destroyed."

She decided to omit Leif's words, which were too soft in her opinion, about a possible agreement that could be reached with the local people.

"It need not bother you," Ingvar promised her, waving his hand generously. "What are Skraelings compared to Viking warriors? We will get rid of them so that nothing is left to remind us they once existed."

A strong flush of desire for revenge effused Freydis's face. These were the words she wanted to hear, but she attempted to keep her voice mild when she made her reply to Ingvar:

"Do not make light of them. They are cruel, fearless people, and their elders know a lot of some branches of magic."

"Sorcerers and sorceresses do not frighten me," said Ingvar with a slight smile. "Otherwise I wouldn't be sitting here with you. For, unless I am very much mistaken, you too, lovely Freydis, know quite a bit of magic."

"I have learned a thing or two," confirmed Freydis, and a dangerous smile curved the corners of her mouth.

"So I thought. Well, I will tell you what we must do. We have to gather the people I mentioned, rich and influential people who are sick of the king and of Christianity and will be very glad to hear they will have a possibility to live as they see fit, in a new and promising place, under the official but not intrusive rule of your father, who will be called king, and your brother Leif. We shall take care of the natives, and soon a new kingdom will rise. The news will find their own wings and people will flock west."

The blush in Freydis's face grew deeper. Her father, a true king! They will not depend upon the mercy of Norway, the prophecy will not come true, and she will avenge Helgi, Tur and Gudrid. Still, her next words were cautious.

"King Olaf will go mad with fury when he hears of this."

"He will not hear of this," said Ingvar. "At least not until there is nothing he can do to stop it. The western lands across the sea will slip from his hands. Of course, I assume he will try to do something to prevent our success, perhaps even a military move. But you must remember one more thing, my dear Freydis: the king will not live forever, and Prince Sigurd is a weak, gullible type. Therefore, all we must do is gain time. Trust me, what I offer is a very good, sensible plan, in the course of which we will all profit. We need each other. We shall need guidance to reach the new land and begin settling it, and help from the Greenland settlements during the initial period. Your father, at the same time, needs many brave people close enough to him so that he need not fear an invasion from Norway. He is a brave, ambitious man, according to what I know, and doubtless will agree that such a move will serve the advancement of him and his family. Leif, too, will understand, of course, how important it is to have a well-based settlement in the new regions as well as in Greenland."

"I cannot promise my brother will take a liking to this plan," said Freydis.

"There is no need to mention it to him just now," Ingvar said placidly. "First we shall have to collect the people who will be ready to send all their possessions and households across the sea, and when your brother will see that their number is impressive and their intentions serious, he will be convinced."

Ingvar got up from the table, and Freydis understood their meeting is at an end.

"I will leave Trondheim for a while," said Ingvar. "The king will not be happy, but I will come up with some excuse or other to give a satisfactory explanation of my absence. When we are all ready to meet, I will send you a message so that you might come as well. Prepare yourself."

"Do not take unnecessary risks by sending messages," said Freydis. "I shall know where and when to meet you."

Out of the folds of her clothes she pulled a ring and put it on her finger, to the astonished eyes of Ingvar. It was a ring made of white gold, studded with an enormous black amethyst, expertly worked, and in its deep darkness a blood-red sparkle seemed to appear for a moment.

"Queen Geyra's ring!" Ingvar nearly choked in his astonishment, and Freydis didn't fail to notice the greedy glint in his eyes. "How did it fall into your hands?"

"It is a long and tedious story," said Freydis with affected boredom. "I searched for it for years."

"If I were you, I wouldn't wear it in public," Ingvar advised her.

"Naturally," she replied, and hid the ring in her clothes again.

On her way back to the castle, nagging doubts began to haunt her again. She felt she was far too exposed before a man she did not really know and could never really trust. But what else could she do? *To succeed, one must sometimes take risks.* On the other hand, she was filled with a delightful vision – how wonderful it will be if the plan works! A true kingdom in Vinland and Greenland, not just a few settlements – and her father will be king, and Leif after him... and she, Freydis, will also gain the position and influence she deserves. And the accursed Skraelings will lose their land forever, will flee or die. She need not fear for the future of her home anymore.

Still, her heart was heavy. She never told anybody of the prophecy she saw as a girl. She knew no one would believe her, that she would be laughed at, or warned once more not to contact the Skraelings. *I was there, I and no one else,* Freydis thought savagely. *No one but me saw the terrible prophecy in the fire lit by the old witch.*

Now she pinned her hopes upon Ingvar Haraldson, a man she met but recently, and who – she had to admit– was not trustworthy. She had no love for him, no more than he for her, but they might be useful to one another.

In one thing she knew she had an advantage over him. The secret knowledge she had gained throughout the years was not in vain. It gave her something – sometimes, the hidden became open and clear for her. All she had left to do was hope that this would be one of those times.

Chapter 14

"I know His Grace did wisely by acting upon reason rather than feeling," said Thorgunna, looking alternately at the chess board and at the face of King Olaf.

The king sighed, staring at the board and not seeing it. This was the second game of chess they played that day – and evidently, this was also the second game the king was going to lose.

"I had no choice," said King Olaf. "The situation in the Northern provinces requires a watchful eye, and in such a delicate matter I could think of no one but Sigurd I would be able to trust. Sigurd is inexperienced, that is true, but he is my son and all the might of my men stands behind him. I sent the best warriors along with him."

Prince Sigurd left court at dawn of that same day, accompanied by several hundreds of well-chosen men, and turned north.

"I would have done this myself," King Olaf went on, "but commitments of unbreakable nature require my presence in Trondheim for the next few months - and this mission is something that could not be delayed. The flame of rebellion may spread, and when this fire breaks out in earnest it will be far more difficult to put out."

"You are right, my father, certainly," replied Thorgunna. "I have not the least doubt that your provision for the future will be what saves Norway from danger."

"I cannot comprehend why there are earls who do not see what should be so obvious," said the king. "Only a stable union of Norway will prevent us from being in a vulnerable position. We cannot permit ourselves to break into many separate counties again. But there are, apparently, short-sighted men who are moved by personal ambition alone and deny the fact that Norway needs *one* leader."

"It is said that those who rebel against your authority are men who have not truly accepted the Christian faith, Your Grace," said Thorgunna. "They were baptized, but do not visit the church and continue their pagan ways in secret."

"This does not surprise me at all," said the king, "for it has been a while since I was blessed by the understanding that Lord Jesus is the source of all union, while pagan worship is the cause of rivalry, strife and selfish obstinacy. That is why we need to put every effort into spreading and strengthening Christianity in Norway and outside our borders as well. In the lands of the Slavs, in Iceland, and in Greenland too. And now, my daughter, I shall tell you a satisfying piece of news – the wife of Erik the Red was baptized yesterday. She is a wise, pious woman, and truly devoted to the Faith. I doubt, of course, that she will be able to convert her husband – Erik the Red will agree to be baptized when the glaciers in Greenland melt away. His son Leif is a different matter, though. He can and must be baptized. Have you had the chance to talk to him about saving his soul from eternal damnation?"

"Yes," said Thorgunna, "and I fear that he has some sinful inclinations which make him think too much and ask sacrilegious questions which are preventing him from accepting the light of the true Faith. But I am certain the case is not hopeless."

"Of course not, child, of course not," said the king. "Greenland matters to me. Greenland will develop, even though it is such a distant province. Its importance in the trade of pelts, ivory, and seal and whale blubber is rising with every year. One day, when

111

the chieftainship passes into his hands, Leif Erikson shall be an important man."

..."Don't you think, Leif," said Freydis, arranging her earrings, "that it is a little strange, this invitation to sup in the princess's private chambers? I mean, it is a great honor... *too* great, in fact. What have we done to deserve it?"

"This I cannot say," replied Leif. He was dressed in clean clothes, washed and groomed far more meticulously than usual. He spent a long time in the bathhouse despite it not being Saturday, the day on which he took his customary wash. His mother and Freydis wore their best clothes and waited impatiently for the intended hour. Their curiosity was mixed with excitement and, in the case of his sister, with suspicion as well.

The servants led them to the chambers of the princess, and she got up to receive them with noble cordiality. Her rooms were well-heated so she could wear light garb despite the cold outside. The dress she chose for the occasion was made of expensive Byzantine silk in all the colors of autumn leaves, scarlet and orange and deep dark red, and leaves were embroidered upon it in golden threat. Jewels studded with amber adorned her neck and ears and were entwined into her braids, which looked darker than usual in the light of the scented beeswax candles.

"It is an honor, Princess," said Thjodhild.

"You must have wondered at the invitation," said Thorgunna, looking from Thjodhild to Freydis, but hardly glancing at Leif.

"We have heard much of your famous hospitality, Princess," said Freydis in her pleasantest voice, "and are honored to witness it."

"The truth is," said Thorgunna, "that I have wanted to converse with you ever since your arrival at Trondheim. I have always been highly curious about everything connected with Greenland,

and I have spoken to several men who were fortunate enough to visit that faraway land. And well, you have spent your entire lives there, Freydis and Leif – and you, Thjodhild, your husband was the founder of the settlement. But I haven't had the opportunity to speak with you in a way that would encourage a quiet and pleasant conversation, and I thought... in short, I thought I'd create such an opportunity myself."

She smiled charmingly, and two dimples appeared in her cheeks. She had small, white teeth of an extraordinarily pretty shape. Despite the beauty of her smile, Leif sensed a trace of awkwardness in it. *I can smell the king's guiding hand here.*

The princess called her servants, and the table was covered with delicacies which could only be tasted at festive occasions at the royal hall: wild roosters cooked in a sauce of wine and fragrant herbs, fish in forest mushrooms, fresh wheaten bread, an array of cheese and very choice wine. The wine was truly delicious, and under other circumstances Leif would probably have been tempted to drink more of it, but now something told him he must remain sober.

Princess Thorgunna displayed a true knowledge in everything concerning Greenland, and Freydis was an ample source of tales about life in Brattahlid, and of legends concerning the Skraelings, some of which were told by her in the most amusingly terrifying way. Still, Leif noticed, and honored Freydis for it, that she divulged very little of what could be called useful information – anything that would be useful to someone who'd think of taking over the land.

"I can understand that the place awakens your imagination precisely because it is so far, Princess," Leif said finally. "The truth is that life there isn't too exciting. The settlements are small, the winters fierce, the nature harsh and the work heavy. Most of our lives consist of daily grind. Even exploration trips inside the country or sailing along and beyond the coast, which are supposedly the essence of adventure, include a lot of tedious work such as preparing food, hunting and setting camp, cutting firewood and so on. There is nothing extraordinary in what we do."

"You are being modest, my son," Thjodhild said affectionately.

"I wish I could do something like that sometime," said Princess Thorgunna, "set a camp under the open sky. It sounds so... refreshing."

"What a strange thought, Your Highness!" said Leif and laughed. "Trust me, such things only sound appealing when you have never done them yourself."

"But that is the nature of men," said Thorgunna with a smile, "we find interest in what we have never done... and what we seem unlikely to ever do."

After that, to the vexation of Freydis and Leif, the conversation slipped into the realm of religion, the Church, and the merits of Father Wilhelm, whom Thorgunna and Thjodhild both admired and saw as a spiritual guide. When more and more quotes from the New Testament began to be aired, promising eternal hell to those who do not accept Jesus as their Savior, Freydis started to yawn secretly, and after a few minutes declared that, to her great sorrow, she is plagued by a terrible headache.

"With your permission, Princess," she said, getting up, "I feel I shall moan with pain if I stay any longer. If you give me leave, I shall retire to my chamber and rest."

Thjodhild got up as well.

"With your permission, Your Highness, I will join my daughter," she said with an apologetic smile. "If she is unwell, she might need me."

But the quick look she sent in the direction of her son spelled, *You didn't think, of course, that I would take the chance of leaving her to wander at night alone!*

"And you, Leif?" asked Thorgunna when the servants showed Thjodhild and Freydis the way out, and the door was closed behind them. "Will you stay for a while longer? See, honey cakes are just brought in, and there is also sweet golden wine, even better than what we drank before."

"I am at leisure," said Leif, "I only need to present myself at morning guard. But I beg you, princess, I am not good at talking of religion – and if you forgive me, the name of Father Wilhelm does not excite me. Excuse my honesty, and let us talk of anything that does not have to do with Christianity."

"Well," Thorgunna hesitated and decided to let the matter drop, though his words evidently did not please her. "Tell me of yourself, then."

"There isn't much to tell, Your Highness," Leif said modestly. "I am a simple man, a sailor, a navigator and occasionally a warrior. I have already told you all that is worth hearing of our travels, and of our life in Brattahlid as well."

"Tell me of your youth," asked Thorgunna, "the youth of a man is always interesting."

"I cannot tell of my youth without mentioning my wife, Maura," he said evasively.

"Tell me of her, then," said Thorgunna, and her heart missed a beat as she saw the heavy shadow that passed across his face. "Would that cause you too much pain?" she asked with concern.

"I suppose not," said Leif, though it was easy to tell the words cost him a great effort. "Her death was senseless but probably inevitable, and five years have passed since it. But my wife remains a part of me. When I try to talk of her, I do not know where to begin."

"How did you meet her?" asked Thorgunna.

Chapter 15

Leif was a lad of nineteen years when he met Maura.

He remembered that day as if it were yesterday.

Helgi's ship arrived at Brattahlid – he remembered they had already begun to worry, for Helgi's arrival was delayed longer than they expected. If he had lingered abroad too long, the frozen winds and winter currents could mean death. No one envied an unfortunate sailor who would try crossing the sea between Iceland and Greenland during the winter.

But Helgi returned safely, and with a nice profit from the goods he sold in Iceland and Norway – walrus ivory, white bear pelts and whale blubber. His ship was full of timber, rolls of finely woven wool, dried fruit and spices. And brought something more precious still – a few families of free men, with their wives, children and household folk who came to settle in Greenland. Most of them were Icelandic landowners running away from debts, conflicts with neighbors or with the law, though there were also an adventurer or two who arrived at Greenland because they were seized by the desire for change.

Erik and his family gladly received the new families, but they were highly surprised by a woman who arrived alone – an extraordinary event. She was a young woman, unaccompanied by a father or a brother, and from looking at her it was easy to tell she was not from the north. Her hair was black as coal, her skin the shade of olive, and her eyes intelligent and dark. Her clothes were old and patched, not at all adequate for the cold of Greenland, her hair messy and unkempt, and her expression determined. When she was asked what she seeks all alone, in a foreign, frozen land the tongue of which she hardly speaks, she replied:

"I want to work for a living. I will do all I am told. I can wash clothes and cook, spin, weave and sew, scrub floors and shear sheep – any work that needs doing."

Thjodhild took pity on the lonely woman and took her into the household. Soon it turned out the newcomer is a diligent worker, tidy and precise, and handy in all the womanly crafts. At the end of a day, when her regular work was done, she would sit in a quiet corner, knitting or sewing at her leisure. The rooms were always neatly swept and well-arranged, and the food she cooked – after she learned the local tastes – exceedingly good. She did her work with dedication and goodwill, and Thjodhild was happy for gaining such an efficient worker under her roof.

It was hard to tell what exactly attracted Leif to this young and silent woman. She was far from being a beauty. It was true that her figure was good and her stature upright, and her hair, after it was washed and brushed, turned out to be smooth and shiny, but there was a sort of hardness in the features of her face and in her movements - something which prevented any appearance of feminine tenderness. Thjodhild was generous and supplied the woman with all she might have needed, and her tattered rags were soon replaced by good clothes – but she chose garb of the simplest cut, grey and drab, while all other young women made every effort to look handsome in the eyes of possible suitors. Her hair she gathered in a tight knot, smooth and unblemished but strained and severe, and her overall look was akin to that of a nun. Neither did she like to laugh - and though in a few months she learned the local speech quite well, she remained silent and thoughtful. Even Thjodhild, who was sorry for her loneliness and attempted to make her acquaintance with outstanding kindness and patience, could hardly make her speak. She didn't like to tell about herself, and didn't bother to acquire friendships among the other young women.

Despite all this, Leif soon found out her name – Maura, her age – twenty-two, and her place of origin – one of the coast villages in the land of the Galls, though Helgi's ship collected her from a place along the shores of Britain.

Be that as it may, it wasn't long before Leif found himself thinking constantly of the young, odd woman whom he saw moving quietly about the house and doing the chores efficiently and diligently, though her face looked as if she were somewhere far away.

In Greenland there were always more men than women, and every unmarried woman, even if she wasn't a great beauty, would get her share of attention. The able-handed, hard-working Maura soon received several offers of marriage, all of which she curtly refused. And it wasn't contempt or a feeling of excessive superiority – the thought of marriage just didn't appeal to her, it seemed.

At the same time, nineteen-year-old Leif had already gained quite a few victories in love, with single women and also with married ones, whose furious husbands Erik had to keep quiet by generous compensations. After that, he summoned his firstborn to a conversation during which he warned Leif against the burden of bastard children.

"You don't want to get into trouble, Leif," he said, "nor to acquire enemies. Remember, the settlements of Greenland are small and each man is well known to his neighbors. We are free men, and there is not one ruler who might take the women of his vassals as he wills."

"It isn't about that," said Leif, offended. "What can I do if there are women who won't leave me alone? I just go along," he shrugged innocently, but there was a mischievous gleam in his eye.

His mother was more decisive.

"You need a wife, son," she told him. "Why don't you choose some nice girl and settle down? Thorbjorn would doubtless have offered you Gudrid, if she weren't so young. But there should be no trouble findning you a good, sweet maid for a bride."

"I would marry," said the troublesome Leif, "if I could find a girl with whom I should not be bored after the passage of an hour."

"Marriage is not about excitement," his mother told him. "It is supposed to be a source of tranquility, stability and peace."

"Forgive me, Mother, but this sounds odd from the lips of a woman who had run off with a stranger when she was sixteen," Leif said with a smile. "But anyway, why should I sentence myself to a boring fate when I am so young?"

"Stop this, Leif. It is good to marry young, this way you can adjust to one another easily and live happily later on. Here, look at Thorvard and Freydis – they are already betrothed."

"I had warned Thorvard," sighed Leif, "but what is there to be done if he says he cannot live without her? And here I am, obliged to see how my good friend gets himself into a double snare."

"A double snare?" his mother repeated suspiciously.

"Indeed," said Leif. "One, marriage. The other, Freydis."

"Stop this," Thjodhild said angrily. "Sometimes your jokes are insufferable, Leif."

That had taken a short time before Maura's arrival.

When Leif first noticed her, his attentions were shallow and careless. He was a handsome lad, tall and well-built and in possession of unstudied manly good looks. His blue eyes were startling, and his red hair attracted all eyes to his face like a burning halo. Usually, his road to conquering a woman's heart was short and didn't include much effort beyond a few smiles and compliments. But Maura paid not the least attention to him, and Leif personally experienced the power of the ancient feminine weapon – unaffected indifference.

There had been women who pretended not to care for him, but it was usually a game, and not a very convincing one. Maura, on the other hand, looked at him as if he were a broomstick or a clothes brush.

One of those days he walked into the kitchen. For some reason, lately hunger began reminding him far more often that he needs to seek refreshment – and then, of course, he would step into the kitchen, where Maura could usually be found preparing the food – mixing, kneading, chopping, tasting, salting, cooking and baking.

He didn't know whether he should laugh at, or be vexed with himself because his heart skipped a beat at the sight of a young, stern-looking woman in a simple brown dress, the sleeves of which were rolled up to her elbows, and with hands covered in flour. She was kneading the bread dough upon the large, flour-sprinkled wooden table. Some of the loaves were already in the oven, and on another table Leif saw also some ready ones, warm and delicious-smelling.

"Good morning, Maura," he told her. "You probably had to get up in the middle of the night to have the bread ready by now."

121

She didn't favor him even with a look. "I get up when I must," she said curtly, kneading on.

"The kitchen is dark and cramped," said Leif. "You need to get out of here sometimes, to breathe some fresh air and amuse yourself a little."

"The kitchen is always warm," said Maura. "I don't mind being here even all day long."

As to warmth, he had nothing to say against that. Firewood was costly in Greenland because the forests were so few, and the houses were always cold because they could only be heated for a few hours every day – even though all efforts were made to preserve the warmth within and to seal every crack. The kitchen was one of the places where the baking ovens and the hot cauldrons created a warm, pleasant, dim atmosphere throughout most of the day.

"It must be hard for you to get used to the cold," said Leif. "You came from places far to the south, after all."

Maura left her dough and looked at him grimly. "I assume you didn't come here to ask me when I had to get up or how cold I am," she said.

"Oh no, I simply felt very hungry all of a sudden. Do you have anything for me?"

Maura shook flour off her hands, lifted a large knife and, without a word, cut several thick, even slices of the dark, satisfyingly hot rye bread.

Leif fell silent, sat at the edge of the table and sprinkled salt on his bread, and for quite a while he ate in silence and looked at her without saying a word. Maura continued to work in expert, swift movements, taking the ready loaves out of the oven and putting in new ones to bake, sprinkling flour on the table and kneading dough. Her hands were strong and her fingers deft and Leif couldn't help thinking how these fingers might feel on his skin. At that moment he felt he uncovered one of the secrets of his attraction towards her – her movements were so smooth and full of confidence that they lent her a certain grace, though she was not at all a beauty.

"Maura," he spoke again eventually, "where are you from? And how is it that you came here all alone?"

She threw him a piercing, suspicious stare, and said across her shoulder, "I do not see how this concerns you."

"Is there any butter?" he changed the topic.

"It will be breakfast time soon," said Maura.

"I will not stay to breakfast," said Leif. "Thorvard and I are going out to hunt."

Silently, Maura placed before him a bowl with soft yellow butter. He ate and didn't take his eyes off her. In her eyes there was a certain black chasm of misery and pride blended together, a secret which was beyond this world and which he felt he must discover.

That very same day as he returned from the hunt, he asked Helgi how he had met Maura on the way to Greenland.

"Ah," said Helgi, "that is certainly an interesting story. You might not know this, Leif, but the reason why we stayed away so long this time was because on our way home there was a storm that threw us straight to the shores of Britain."

Leif nodded and signed for him to go on. Helgi had the annoying habit of complaining in a very tiresome way, after every journey, about the hardships he had had to endure.

"Well," Helgi went on, "there was one village we saw from aboard, a pretty large place, and we decided to throw anchor there and to get supplied with more food and fresh water. I gave orders to the boys to raise the oars and we reached the shore – the villagers weren't exactly happy to see us, but after we made it very clear we aren't Vikings and are ready to pay our way, they agreed to let us throw anchor. And well, after one night there, we saw smoke and flames and a great confusion. It turned out a fire broke out, and we knew we had to get out of there as soon as possible. We hurried to go aboard again and were about to raise anchor, when we saw the girl running towards the shore.

And I tell you, Leif, it was a rare sight. Her hair was all a mess, her feet bare, nothing but a thin shift on her back, and in her eyes there was this mad look of a deer preyed upon by wolves.

'Please,' she said, with the last bit of air that remained in her lungs, 'please, take me with you!'

And you might not believe this, but we all just stood there, rolling with laughter. Imagine that, the people living along those shores pray to their god that the Norse ships never reach them – and here, this girl was asking to come with us – we weren't Vikings, true, but she had no way of being sure of that. And this, of course, told me quite plainly she had nothing to lose. At that moment I thought she must be a slave who decided to take advantage of all the mess and confusion of the fire and escape, but I can only guess what might have prompted her to join us – people who could, as far as she knew, rape, torture and kill her without a second thought.

'Woman,' I told her, 'you have no idea what you are talking of. We raise sail and go to a cold, lonely place at the end of the world.'

'I don't care,' she said, 'even if you are sailing to hell. Take me with you!'

'And what do you suggest we do with you?' I said, half-amused.

'I can do anything,' she said decisively, 'all the work of home and field; I can tend to flocks and serve as a midwife and spin wool. In every settlement and every place there is need of working hands. I am a hard and faithful worker. Take me with you, and you will not regret it.'

And when she saw I was hesitating, she added:

'Take me with you, or I shall jump into the flames!'

And I tell you, Leif, my friend, she meant it. She had an utterly mad look in her eyes, one of desperate determination.

'Let's take her,' Bjorn said upon hearing this. 'Let's take her to Red Erik, and he will decide what to do with her.'

We helped her climb on board. She was shivering from cold. The women pitied her and lent her some rags to keep her from freezing to death until we arrived. She hardly said a word throughout the entire sail, and she hardly says a word now. She is very strange. I, too, am curious about the story of her life, but it doesn't seem she's very likely to tell it."

After that Leif decided that other measures are necessary, and for this he came to enlist the help of his brother, Thorvald.

Thorvald couldn't help laughing when heard his brother out. He was then a young lad with fair hair like flax, blue eyes, and the first wisps of a beard. He was no worse-looking than his brother, but his shyness and mildness made him appear younger than he truly was.

"Maura is not like all women," he told his older brother. "I can see it. In my opinion, it will be better if you leave her alone. She is not made for you. And frankly, for some reason I doubt she will want any man in Brattahlid."

125

But Leif insisted and came out victorious – his brother gifted him with the words of a song, which was later recited by Leif to Maura.

I fought for long, but now can fight no more;
The walls are strong, but love shall make them crumble.
Oh, fill for me with mead a heavy horn,
With hands at once magnificent and humble.
How was the red wolf caught in snares of gloom?
You look at him, you see him fret in worry.
You bring me forth my senseless, needless doom
While you can give me life, and hope, and glory
But I shall wait. A week, a month, a year -
I promised to the moon that I shall follow.
The strength of love will set the ice astir
Around the heart of beauty proud and solemn.

He sang her this song in the kitchen while she was busy cleaning fish. She did not look at him until he was done, and even when she finally did, it was as if she did not really see him. Her hands were covered in silvery scales, and no muscle moved in her face. When she spoke, her voice was indifferent.

"Give my compliments to Thorvald," she said, "he has a great talent for composition."

But it wasn't this easy to embarrass Leif.

"I could have been the one to write these verses," he said, "if I had Thorvald's talent. My brother has a wonderful ability to put words together, but he has no beloved to hear his poetry – while I have a sweetheart but cannot rhyme two words to save my life. A pity, isn't it? And here is a solution – Thorvald will make up the poems, and I will give them true feeling when I sing them to you."

"Leif," she said, and he secretly congratulated himself, for this was the first time she said his name. "Maybe I haven't made this quite clear, but I did not come all this way to become the mistress of the landlord's son. I could do *that* anywhere."

"Well, if you are so set against being my mistress, how about becoming my wife?" he asked.

Only after the words left his mouth, he understood what he said, and did not even really know whether he truly meant it or not. He waited for her answer with a powerfully beating heart, but she didn't bestow even a single look on him and went on with her work. Now she gutted the fish, pulled out their entrails and threw them into a clay bowl which stood at the middle of the table.

"Anyway," Leif went on bravely, "I cannot understand why a woman would wish to sentence herself to a miserable existence without a man, no matter whether she is lucky enough to be his wife or has no choice but to settle for the position of a mistress."

Now Maura did look at him, and a glint of anger could be plainly seen in her eyes. Her lips were pursed, as if she was trying hard to keep silent. In her right hand she held the large knife, stained with fish-blood, as if it were a sword.

"My work is enough for me," she said finally, and bent her head to the table again.

Chapter 16

The young woman remained a mystery to Leif. Apparently, he should have given up. Until then he had not been a very fervent pursuer of women, knowing that for each one who did not want him, ten would be delighted to have him, even without the smallest chance of marriage. But in this case the outlook was quite different, and it wasn't only the fact that Maura refused him and thus set him a challenge. He felt there is some hidden secret deep within, away from his eyes. Could it be that she had suffered from unfortunate love and was reluctant to get hurt again? Or perhaps something in his ways clashed too strongly with the customs she had been brought up with? Or maybe it was the fact of him belonging to a different faith? He had never seen Maura pray, but this did not mean she was faithless. He was determined to get closer to her. He had to break the ice encasing her.

And he chose quite a bold way to do that.

When Maura had arrived under their roof, she said she doesn't mind at all where she should sleep, and was ready to settle for a little space on one of the benches in the main hall. But Thjodhild, who was like a protective mother to all the maids in her household, insisted on the unmarried women having their own space, which was separate from the men.

Maura, therefore, shared a room with Ingebjorg, a girl who had big blue eyes, curls the color of wheat, ample curves and very thoughtless ways. Every month she had a different admirer with whom she would disappear for a night or two. About a year after the events mentioned below, Ingebjorg was forced to make certain changes in her behavior. She became pregnant, the man was made to marry, and she became a faithful wife, had five children and grew very stout.

It was the night of the Yule, and the entire settlement was supposed to gather in the traditional celebration – the beginning of the Great Hunt of the gods. Usually, Leif made sure to be in the center of the festivities, but this time he slipped away and made an effort not to be seen.

He knew Maura would remain at home alone, for she never participated in any celebration or dance. Every time there was a gathering, she quietly disappeared to the inner rooms to be alone.

In her zeal for work, she lingered for a few minutes to sweep once more the floor of the big main hall, and Leif quickly and silently darted into the room of the serving girls and hid among the shadows, behind two wooden cases which contained all the clothes and possessions of the women – the bigger one of Ingebjorg, the small one of Maura. He remained motionless and wondered how come she did not hear the beating of his heart when she came into the room.

The little room was cold, and Maura did not hurry to undress. First she released her hair from the tight knot which always kept it from tumbling down, and began combing it. The comb, which was made of deer horn, was one of the few pretty items in her possessions. She passed it in long, slow movements through her raven-black hair, and Leif held his breath.

This was the first time he saw her hair unbound, and it was glorious in its beauty. It fell in soft waves down her shoulders, thick and luxurious, shiny even in the dim light of the single candle.

After she was done combing her hair Maura took off her outer clothes. She wore a simple shift of roughspun wool, and thick warm woolen socks. The Greenland winters were pleasant to none, but she felt the cold especially strongly, being unused to it. She shivered and hastened to get in the bed. Then she blew out the candle.

The room was now utterly dark, and Leif waited until her breathing would steady and she would fall into deep sleep. Then he got up carefully, in dread of making a sound, and began his slow way towards her bed.

When he was close enough to be enveloped by the scent of her hair, he stopped for a moment and inhaled deeply. Her scent filled the cramped space, and she smelled of summer fruit and sea salt and something warm which he could not define in words and which made his head spin. He hesitated for a brief moment, and then put a hand on her waist.

She moved slightly in her sleep, but did not wake. Then Leif gained courage and wrapped his arms around her. She woke with a start, but he put a hand over her mouth and laughed quietly and delightedly, and held her tighter still. He wanted to kiss her, but she kept wriggling, trying to slip away from him, and he could not find her lips in the dark.

A moment later, he felt a sharp pain piercing his arm, and a trickle of something hot which was undoubtedly his blood.

"Oy!" he shouted. "What's the matter with you? It's only me!"

He let go of her, and she lit the candle again. The shadows flickered in the room, mingling with the weak light. Maura's lips were trembling with fury and her eyes burned, and her chest moved up and down to the rhythm of her heavy breaths. In her raised right hand she held the sharp knife she had used to clean the fish. The knife was stained red, and in the light of the candle Leif saw that the sleeve of his shirt was torn and that a lot of blood was trickling from the deep cut in his arm.

"I cannot say I did not expect this," said Maura with terrible calm.

"You are out of your mind, aren't you?" Leif said angrily, trying in vain to stop the flow of blood. "I could have lost an eye!"

She shrugged. "I wouldn't grieve very deeply if it were so," she said coolly. "Your father is a just man, he would have stood by me. When I arrived here I talked to him and told him I am ready to be anything but a man's plaything. He promised me that in Brattahlid, no man would lay a hand upon me against my will. Now get away from here."

The next day, Leif attempted to tell everyone he cut himself on a protruding nail, but the rumor soon traveled about and in no time everyone in Brattahlid were laughing at the expense of the unfortunate suitor.

"Ah, Leif, you are sophisticated, no doubt," chuckled Freydis. "Yes, to be sure, this is the best way to gain the heart of a woman who won't even talk to you – get straight into her bed!"

Leif grimaced and touched the fresh bandage around his arm.

"I must say I did not expect such resistance on Maura's part," his sister went on. "After all, you are not ill-looking, and though I personally find it hard to put up with you sometimes, you know how to flatter girls – and Maura does not look like someone who is used to a trail of admirers. Besides, I'm certain she is no maid."

"How should you know?" Leif asked with great interest.

"Call it a gut feeling," said Freydis with a shrug of her shoulders.

Leif learned his lesson, but by no means gave up. Actually, he was more determined than ever, even though Maura ignored him completely since the nightly incident. If prior to that she was at least ready to exchange a few words with him, now she simply ignored his existence.

"You must apologize to her," his friend Thorvard, who would become his good-brother, advised him. "Tell her you did not mean to offend her - besmirch her honor – well, you just find the right words."

"But it was only a jest," Leif said desperately. "I did not really mean to rape her or anything of the sort! I only attempted to shake off that indifference of hers."

"Well, then, my friend," said Thorvard, "you will probably have to think of another way to do that."

"I suppose so," Leif said distractedly.

A day later, he announced to his family that he is going to hunt seals.

"You are mad," Freydis told him. "The men could hardly dig paths in the snow, which soon pile as high as the windows, and I can bet you that in a couple of hours there will be another storm. How can you think of going hunting?"

"Freydis is right," said Thorvard, "but I will go with you. I cannot allow you to go out on your own in this weather."

"No, Thorvard," cried Freydis, "my brother probably lost his mind, but it's his own business if he wishes to freeze to death or be buried underneath an avalanche of snow. You stay here."

"There is no need to," said Leif, seeing the expression upon Thorvard's face; his friend was obviously torn between worry for him and his inability to refuse Freydis. "I intended to go alone anyway."

But even after Leif had gone, Thorvard could not stop worrying. "It is madness," he said, "he need not have gone."

And as the hours passed, he made up his mind to go and look for his friend.

"I must go," he told Freydis. "I had gone out to hunt with Leif many times. I think I know where he might be. I must look for him."

And indeed, Thorvard returned after a couple of hours, supporting his friend, who was exhausted from walking in the snow. If Thorvard had not set out to look for him, he would doubtless have died.

In the days that followed, Leif was very quiet. He did not go out to hunt or train, but only helped his father run the settlement, and later took advantage of a break between snowstorms and went together with Thorvard to the house of his parents, Thorbjorn and Aslaug, in the Western settlement. There he spent several weeks.

On the day he was back in Brattahlid, he seemed the same as before, and when evening came he appeared in the kitchen again. The pots were already clean, and Maura was sweeping the floor diligently. She made no sign of noticing him, but he sat by the table.

"Forgive me, Maura," he said simply, and she looked at him in a stern, detached way, and said nothing for a long while.

"Of course," she said eventually in a cool voice.

But he understood she did not speak from her heart, and continued sitting alone for a long time after Maura retired to bed. He could not take his eyes off a shawl she forgot, wrapped around one of the stools, a large dark shawl she had knitted herself in her free time. His heart was full of pain to a degree he

133

did not expect, and he felt as if he was knocking on a heavy locked wooden door, set in iron hinges. He put his face on his crossed arms, and sat this way, and did not lift his eyes even when he heard her returning footsteps.

Maura looked almost embarrassed. Her fingers clutched the woolen shawl, which was the reason why she returned to the kitchen. She looked at him as if considering how much she should say, and eventually sat on a stool next to him, and when she spoke, her voice was softer than ever.

"Leif," she said, "do not torment yourself so. I forgive you. I had treated you in the way I did mostly out of stubbornness. I had no idea this would cause you pain."

He lifted his head up and looked at her. He was tired, and understood that what worked faultlessly with other women would never do for her.

"I do not understand you," he said. "I try, but I cannot."

"That is clear," replied Maura. "You do not know me. No one here truly knows me."

"But I do want to know you," Leif said, frustrated, "and I don't understand what harm it will do if you allow me to get near you."

Chapter 17

For a long moment they both looked at the glowing embers of the dying fire. Maura's face was lit by the dance of the red flames, and her eyes were two black wells.

"Helgi told me you had asked how I came on board of his ship all alone," she said.

"Yes," said Leif, "and he told me, but I still don't understand - "

"I was not always on my own," said Maura. "I grew up in a humble little home with my mother, father, brothers and sisters, and I was happy and loved. That was in a small village far from here, many years ago. I was a child, and memories are sometimes shifty, but I do remember clearly that I was happy."

One day, I was playing behind the house, and suddenly I heard loud, urgent voices. At first I thought it is Mother, scolding one of the children – but then I heard screams all around, screams of fear and the hurried receding steps of people running away; and then, though I was little, I understood the worst had happened: the strangers we had always feared reached our shores. We had lived in a perpetual fear of them, and Mother told me many times what to do if the pirate ships reach us – run, run, run to the fields and never look back. But I could not. I was paralyzed with worry for the others, and my legs failed me.

I will not tire you with too long a story, Leif. You are probably guessing what happened next – what usually happens. I was kidnapped and sold into slavery, along with many other unfortunate ones from my village. I never saw my parents or siblings again and I don't know what became of them. Perhaps they managed to escape, perhaps they were taken by a different ship, or maybe they lost their lives in the flames. The last thing I saw before my terrified eyes, from aboard the swift ship, was a great fire where my home had been.

Along with two other people from my village, I was sold to a rich man. The two who came with me were craftspeople – an experienced smith, and a woman who was very talented in making fine lace. They were both appreciated for their skills and treated fairly decently, got a warm place to sleep in and plenty of food. I, on the other hand, was only a child, though I knew all the chores of home and field. I was sent to the rooms and to the kitchen, to do simple work which did not require much skill; and a few years later, when I grew up, I was brought as a plaything into the master's bed. That lasted only a short while, and after he was tired of me he sent me to fill the same place for all the guests and friends who spent a night or two underneath his roof and did not object to a bed-slave. There were times when I attempted to resist and was cruelly beaten. Finally, I gave up resistance because my life, for some reason, was still dear to me."

For a few minutes they both sat in silence, she deep in her thoughts, he staring intently at her. Maura's face looked very hard now, and her eyes burned with a determination he never met in any woman.

"I always believed," said Maura, "that a day will come and I will be free again. And it came indeed. The day on which I was released from slavery was very like the day on which I was taken captive: flames, screams of fear, and a foreign ship carrying me away, far from it all. It probably appears odd to you how I dared ask to go away with the Vikings, when people of their kind ruined my home in the first place."

"Helgi is a sailor and trader, not a Viking," said Leif. "Though I suppose you could not know that. And I... well, I am a lot of things, but this I can tell you with all honesty – I never forced myself upon a woman who did not want me, and never found the idea appealing."

"Living as a slave is torture for one who was born free," said Maura, "but perhaps I could have resigned myself to my fate; I could have said this is the way of the world. For can you not think of people who aren't called slaves, but live as such? But I could not go on living as a source of amusement for an idle hour. Ten years and countless men, Leif. There were times when I attempted to die, but an inexplicable stubbornness didn't allow me to proceed. I owe my life to Helgi, who allowed me to come on board his ship, and to your father, who gave me a place in Brattahlid and a decent life, a life in which I can sustain myself by the work of my hands, be it ever so humble."

Finally, Leif gained the courage to take her hand. She did not pull it away from his, but her fingers were motionless, lifeless and cold.

"You are a brave woman, Maura," he said. "You gained your freedom, and never again you shall be with a man you don't want. But know this, I intend to make you want me. I shall marry you."

She gave a short, mirthless chuckle.

"Did you even listen to a word I said? My spirit is destroyed, my body is broken, I am a miserable shred of a woman. I can never be happy again. I can never give love to any man. I am twenty-two, Leif – older than you by only three years, but you are a boy, while I feel that my life is running out. What would you want with someone like me?"

"Nonsense," Leif said decidedly. "You will see that your life, like mine, is only beginning. I have many dreams I do not intend to give up. I will continue my father's work and strengthen Brattahlid. Thorvard, my brothers and I will take charge of settling other parts of Greenland, and will penetrate the depths of the land – and I shall sail west and south, to lands where no man had ever walked, and raise new settlements there. I will name mountains and valleys, rivers and fjords. And in every dream, you are by my side. I could have chosen any woman, but I need someone clever and brave, someone who will not fear to walk with me into the unknown and stand firm against me when I am wrong, as every man sometimes is. It is you. I need not look any longer, I know it is you."

In the dim light of the candle it seemed to him her eyes are brighter than usual. In her simple roughspun dress, with her dark hair neatly brushed and pulled into a knot, she looked wonderfully beautiful and closer than ever, beloved, belonging to him. And when she spoke, for the first time he heard her voice tremble.

"You are delirious," she said. "It can never happen between us. Not ever."

The young people married not long after that. Their wedding was conducted according to the customs of Leif's forefathers. Rings were slipped onto the fingers of the newlyweds, and a hammer symbolizing Thor's war-hammer, Mjolnir, was placed in the bride's lap. When they shared the traditional wedding chalice, full to the brim with mead, Leif thought the drink was more delicious than anything he had tasted before. And all the guests who drank from the wedding chalice said that there was a miracle and the mead in the chalice was sweeter than the rest served at the wedding feast, though it came from the same barrel – and that was a sure sign foretelling a blessed marriage.

The next five years were happy and busy. If the members of Leif's family were surprised at first because of him choosing a bride of such low birth, their doubts were soon dispelled when they became convinced that no other woman could have been such a good wife and useful helpmate to Leif. She prompted and encouraged him in his journeys and joined him on most of them, fearlessly disregarding the uncomfortable conditions. She was shrewd and clever, and managed his home faithfully, and gave a good example to all the household servants in her diligence and her readiness to take on any work, be it ever so hard or tedious. She never became arrogant because of her uplifted position and never abandoned her quiet, modest ways. She entered her marriage with heavy fears and doubts she could not ignore – but the wounds, as Leif promised her, had healed, and love nourished the hearts of the two just as a clear stream feeds the trees growing on its banks. No one but her husband knew Maura's full story, and he did his best not to remind her of what she had told him on the night when he first became certain they are going to marry.

On account of his marriage, Leif postponed his plans of sailing west. As a wedding-gift he got some good land from his father and built a house. Being a landlord took a considerable amount of his time, though he was happy in all his doings and inspired by the undiluted joy of his wife.

"I came to Greenland thinking I would be a servant," she said, "and here I am, a queen. I have a corner in the world to call my own, something I had not even dared to hope for ever since I was a girl. And I have your love, which is more precious to me than all the world."

"I *had* promised you," said Leif, caressing her hair, "that you will be happy with me."

Leif's relatives soon got over their apprehension of Maura's foreign descent and strange habits. His father respected her sharp mind and her honesty. Freydis found in her a loyal friend, one who is not bogged down by petty littleness and finesse. And Thjodhild, whose tender heart told her of a deep, dim pain hidden behind Maura's dark eyes, adopted the young woman for a daughter and was happy to see how Leif's natural liveliness enlivens her as well, and how Maura's good sense and sound judgment direct and bless every venture of her husband's.

Just one circumstance cast a shadow upon the couple's happiness – a year passed, then another, but a child was tardy in coming. Leif attempted to remain silent, even in the face of his wife's disappointment when her moon's blood returned at regular intervals each month.

"I fear that my body is damaged beyond repair, Leif," she told him one night in tears. "Throughout the years, I had been given a herb tisane to make me infertile, so that I would not have bastard children. Perhaps this is why I cannot conceive now."

"We don't and cannot know that for certain," he said softly. "Do not torment yourself."

"I will not blame you if you take another woman, so that you may beget sons," Maura said quietly, averting her face. "But I will tell you this, Leif – if that is what you decide, we shall part. I cannot and won't tolerate the presence of a mistress."

"I will have no woman but you," Leif said resolutely, "even if it means I will die childless. I will be sorry for it, of course, as you are, my love – but I have two brothers. The family line will go on in one or other of them."

... Leif fell silent. The magic of memories faded away, and Maura, the scent of whose hair and the warmth of whose body he could almost feel a short moment ago, turned once more into a pale shadow smiling at him from a distance, most of the time encouraging and only sometimes melancholy. Once more his senses took in the luxurious chamber, the fire burning merrily in the grate, licking the logs with many red hot tongues. His head swam a little from the wine and the memories, and Princess Thorgunna was sitting in front of him. Her young face put on an expression of sadness, probably because she already guessed the end of the story and didn't dare to ask for its details.

"After four years, Maura was finally with child," Leif said eventually, after a long silence. "You can imagine our happiness. But she died in childbirth, and my son died with her."

"I am sorry," Thorgunna whispered, and he appreciated the honest sympathy he sensed behind the simple words. Still, he averted his eyes, and his face remained expressionless.

"That is the way of the world. There are women who are destined to die in childbirth. Five years passed since that happened." *Five years that sometimes seem like an eternity and sometimes like the blink of an eye.*

Thorgunna got up from her place and approached his seat. Now she was standing above him, and he lifted up his head and looked at her. Her eyes sparkled with tears, and upon her face he saw an expression akin to that which he noticed while they sat at church. She wanted to say something, but only a fleeting tremor passed across her lips. Leif was embarrassed, and something fluttered within him.

"I never meant to distress you, Princess," he said. "I am a simple man, and every man has his story."

She put her hands forward and held his face between her palms, and her touch was like a caress of velvet upon his scruffy cheek. For a moment neither of them moved, and it seemed as though not even a breath of air or the sound of a heartbeat broke the deep silence. It was as if they were both standing on top of a sparkling white iceberg, alone in the middle of the sea, detached from the rest of the world – and in the next instant the decision fell, the iceberg flipped over, the sea waters gushed around them.

She bent and kissed him.

For the first time in her life, a man's lips were touching her own, and the kiss was soft and innocent. But then his eyes found hers, and the passion she saw in his gaze made her head spin, and she fell into Leif's lap, and her arms were wrapped about his neck as if of their own accord. The scent emanating from him was manly and clean and intoxicating. And he kissed her, he kissed her, he kissed her, again and again and again.

Only a few words were exchanged between them, and those that were said in the darkness of the room were forgotten the next moment, and anyway they mattered not. Sapphire and emerald, fire and copper, sea salt and white mountains – got closer, connected and blended together, and finally fulfilled their purpose – to become one.

Chapter 18

When Leif awoke the darkness was complete and his heavy eyelids begged to close again, to pull him once more into the depth of long and peaceful sleep. But as he regained consciousness he felt the softness of the bed and the warmth of the woman next to him. The mist which engulfed him the previous evening had dispersed and his senses were sharp and clear again. He sat up at once.

His movements woke Thorgunna, and without saying a word she reached out and pulled aside the heavy curtain that covered her window. The misty grey of the pre-dawn sky could be seen through the wired glass. The smell of morning wafted in the air, and as she took it all in, her expression became scared but decided.

"You must go now, Leif," she said. "Soon the maids will be here to light my fire and bring in hot water for my bath."

A thousand questions, a thousand words were stuck in his throat, but not one found its way out. She hurried him:

"Go now, quickly. The passages are still empty, but not for long. You must not be seen."

He knew she was right but still lingered for a moment, to kiss her softly on the lips. The extent of the danger was obvious to them now that the night, with its passions and fervors, had passed. When he gave Thorgunna a last fleeting look he knew that she, like him, isn't certain they will meet again.

He bent to pick up his clothes. A few minutes later he was already walking quickly down the path he ought to have made the night before.

It was still almost dark, but he did not lie upon his bed; instead, he walked over to the window and opened it wide. Only the richest could afford the luxury of glass windows, and in his chamber he had simple rectangular frames covered in two layers of thick wooden shutters against the cold and wind. He inhaled the cool, clear air which purified his mind and looked at the sky, which had just a faint pink line on the horizon. Despite the darkness of a late autumn morning, it was obvious that a new day has begun from the sounds and smells of the king's hall – the fresh bread baking in the kitchens, the laughter, chatter and curses of the servants, the clang of weapons belonging to guards and soldiers. He must hurry too, Leif knew. In about an hour he was supposed to arrive outside the king's chambers and replace Snorri Hilmarsson, who had stood guard all night.

He just had time to remember that when someone knocked forcefully on his door. Heart hammering, Leif strode over and opened it. The one who stood in the doorframe was none other than Snorri himself, a stout, strong man with a good face which could sometimes look deceptively soft. Those who had known Snorri for any length of time could tell of his fierceness in battle and his complete mastery of sword, shield, battle-axe and bow.

"Erikson," said Snorri, and it was clear he made all the way from the royal chambers running and panting, "His Grace asks you to present yourself before him immediately."

"But my guard has not begun yet," said Leif. "Wait at least until I change my clothes and wash my face."

Hilmarsson shook his head. "There is no time. I don't know what it is about, but from the tone of the king's voice I got the impression he won't tolerate any delay. I was ordered to bring you to him without wasting a minute. Come along, now."

There was no choice. Leif took his weapons – the hand-axe and the knife – fastened his belt, straightened his clothes and got out of the room together with Snorri, smoothing his unruly hair as he walked. The wheels of his brain were whirring madly. *Can it be that the king already knows?* He knew, of course, that in this place walls have eyes and ears, but still he found it hard to believe the word had spread so quickly – unless one of Thorgunna's servants was paid to spy on her, a possibility that had to be taken into account. *If the king knows, his fury will know no limits.*

When he thought of the night before, he was possessed by a vague feeling of discomfort, even guilt. No, he had no regrets, not even in the face of the possible danger – which could mean losing his life. He could not regret anything when the fresh scent of her skin still clung to his and the warmth of her lips was still impressed upon his mouth, preventing it from setting in a thin, grim line.

He had had dalliances with many women without promising any of them anything, but few of them were as young, beautiful and innocent as Thorgunna, and not one of them had as much to lose. Thorgunna's entire future was now at stake. All she had to do for a glorious destiny was wait and allow the time to do its work for her - lead her safely to a marriage with Prince Sigurd, which would eventually make her queen. She put all that at risk. *Why, then, did she blindly jump into dark waters for the sake of a man she barely knows?*

This question burned in Leif's mind and allowed him no rest. Freydis was right – whatever reason in the world did this beautiful highborn woman have to get as close to him as she had, even before last night? He did not have illusions about his own

145

irresistible charms. It was true that he had observed the princess from afar, admiring her beauty, but who wouldn't? He would never have done more, would never have dared to lift his eyes up to her – and never, not even in his wildest dreams, could he have imagined that what happened between them last night could come to pass.

But now that he looked back upon the weeks prior to that fateful night, he knew there could be no mistake. She had approached him from the start – out of curiosity or out of some other motive he could not recognize. And when she kissed him last night, he could read in her eyes and her lips nothing but sincere feeling. He could not help being concerned about her – but he also knew that if he gets out of the meeting with the king alive and free he will try to see her again, despite the foolish recklessness of it.

... He found King Olaf in a glum and angry mood. The king was pacing back and forth across the handsome, spacious chamber in which he usually received his emissaries, advisers and guests for meetings of a small scale. The fire burning in the grate cast shadows upon his face, upon his knitted brows and uptight jaw, upon the lines which appeared deeper than usual. But when the servants let both men in and he saw Leif, the king's face brightened a little and he sent Snorri away with a gesture of his hand, so that he and Leif remained alone, except for a serving man who poured the drinks and then got out as well.

"You are here, Erikson. Good," said the king.

"I heard that you called for me, Your Grace. I came as soon as I could," Leif said politely. He tried to maintain an expression of dull obedience and told himself over and over, *You do not know what this is about. You will deny every rumor concerning yourself and the princess, be it what it may.*

The king halted his steps and looked directly at Leif. His eyes were small and surrounded by crow's feet, and their color was a very light grey. They were sharp like the eyes of a hawk, and when their stare pierced Leif he felt as if the king can see right through him.

"I have been betrayed," the king said, and the last word remained lingering in the air, and Leif's heart fell within him. *Could it be?* And yet he made himself raise his eyebrows and look back at the king with a stare of polite concern.

"I have discovered, with the help of my loyal informers, a scheme against the throne," the king went on. "A group of narrow-minded earls whose short-sightedness does not allow them to see the importance of uniting Norway under the blessed rule of one God-ordained king presume to doubt my right to the throne, and secretly act against their avowed loyalty to my rule. They are plotting something."

Leif tried his best not to let out too much air when he exhaled and not to allow the expression of relief show too clearly upon his face. His previously constricted heart now beat again and sent blood to his limbs, and his mind functioned once more as it was used to.

"That is very grave, Your Grace," he said, "and I put myself at your service if there is anything I can do."

The king looked pleased. "I am glad of it, Erikson," he said. "As you might imagine, I didn't summon you with such urgency for nothing. My position is not easy. Prince Sigurd, my son and right hand, is not in Trondheim – I sent him to another place where I need a loyal commander. Still, it is obvious this group of traitors must be thwarted at once. And that is where you come into the picture. I have not known you very long, it is true, but you expressed loyalty to the crown – and as a sign of acknowledging this, I give you responsibility over this mission."

"What do I need to do, sire?" asked Leif, expressing readiness in all his gestures, though he could distinctly smell danger.

"I have been informed that the traitors will gather in a certain place in the area of Narvik," said the king. "There are several possibilities regarding where exactly it might be, and all must be checked. I will send you to the area along with a group of well-trained men who can move in secret without raising excessive noise. Your task will be to find the conspirators, catch them red-handed in their plot, arrest them all and bring them to me. I would prefer that you take them alive, but if that does not prove possible, I shall be forgiving."

Leif was not exactly pleased by the prospect. He did not plan on breaking up plots and directing secret missions for the king when he accepted the tiresome but essentially safe position in the personal guard. The way he saw it, his time in Norway was supposed to be dedicated to forging useful ties, promoting the cause of the Greenland settlement, and recruiting brave, strong people who would agree to join him on his journey back west. Still, it was obvious to him he could not refuse the king's command. Should he attempt to evade this mission, his position will receive a desperate blow. All this passed within his mind in a sliver of a moment, while the right words were ready, seemingly without hesitation, on his lips:

"I am at your command, my king, in whatever I might have to do."

"I did not expect any less of you, Leif," said King Olaf. "I understood from the first that you are a man of action, not a useless loudmouth like some of those who presume to advise me. Now listen. There is not much time – the forces that will be sent with you are being gathered at this very moment, including men, maps and equipment. It would be good to take survey, if and as you can, among the loyal landowners in the area and secure their assistance if it is needed. It might be that someone of them had already seen the traitors, or at least anyone suspicions – you will be provided with all details that might help you recognize them."

"Does His Grace believe they are planning to overthrow the throne by force?" asked Leif. The king shook his head.

"No. Not at the moment, anyway. As far as I know, for the time being they intend to keep the plot secret. But this does not mean they don't have a considerable power. You must be careful, for if you fall into their hands your life will be worth less than that of an old lame horse."

At that moment it dawned upon Leif this might be the very reason why he was volunteered so urgently for this mission. He was not close to the king, had not the blood of nobility, he was not even born in Norway – he did not know the land, and in all his movements would have to count on the guidance of locals. But he had at least one obvious quality which recommended him for the task – the king did not value his life very much. If he should be lost while pursuing his duty, the loss shall not be so very great. That was why the king had not given the task to his second son – he would not soon send his own blood to a place of real danger.

"On your way, you might meet Ingvar Haraldson," said the king. "He goes to the same area, but separately – alone, with only a few servants, and his task shall be different. He believes he might penetrate the circle of traitors and discover their exact plans; it is even possible he might find out the names of such supporters of their cause who will not appear at this meeting. If you encounter him, do not act as if you know him, especially if you see him in the company of someone whose loyalty you doubt."

Leif suppressed a smile. If there was someone whose loyalty he doubted - and believed the king should doubt as well - it was Ingvar Haraldson himself. But it was obvious the king put his trust in Haraldson, and so he refrained from speaking.

The king placed a hand on his shoulder, a gesture of cordiality that surprised Leif but gave him no illusions of real warmth.

"Be on your way as soon as you can," said King Olaf. "I shall expect notice of you when you can send it along and will hope for your speedy return. The traitors who are caught will lose all their assets and will be executed or exiled. Be that as it may, they will exist no longer. Their lands will be distributed among my loyal men – and you, of course, will be counted among them if you accomplish your duty. Do not linger, now. There is no time to lose."

Chapter 19

On his way back to his quarters, to gather his few possessions and prepare for the journey, Leif attempted to put some order in his thoughts. It appeared everything is happening very quickly and with very little participation on his side. He was bothered by knowing he will not have the chance to say goodbye to Thorgunna. Due to the great urgency of the mission, he could have no more than a few minutes to exchange a hurried goodbye with his mother and sister. He did not like either this rush or the fact that most of his men will remain in Trondheim, while he will be on his way in the midst of complete strangers.

In his room he was met by another surprise – his mother was there, pacing back and forth and wringing her hands with an expression of extreme concern.

"Leif!" she cried. "Oh, thank God! I was on the point of going to look for you."

"The king summoned me," Leif attempted to explain, but his mother did not let him go on.

"My son, we are in grave trouble. Freydis is gone."

"Gone? What do you mean, *gone*?" Leif asked with mounting irritation. "When did you see her last?"

"Last night we returned to our chamber - Freydis complained of headache and got in the bed. I fell asleep myself, and in the morning I rose early and found her bed empty and cold. She disappeared, together with all our money, her jewels, and her traveling clothes."

"I don't like this," said Leif, walking back and forth as the king had done not long ago. "I don't like this at all. Especially since I know that this rascal, Ingvar Haraldson, isn't at court anymore either."

Thjodhild opened her eyes wide. "Do you think they have – they could have – eloped together?"

"I fear something much worse."

He told his mother about his meeting with the king. When he was done, Thjodhild looked fearful.

"But Leif – you don't think that she – that she might be involved in this plot, do you? Even Freydis is incapable of such folly. We will all be executed."

Leif stared at her gloomily. "I'm afraid no folly is beyond Freydis."

"We must find her," Thjodhild said. "And – oh, I don't want to think of it – if she is involved in this, we must get to her before the king's men do. For her sake as well as ours."

Leif nodded. "Of course, there is still the slight possibility that this disappearance coinciding with Haraldson's journey is pure chance... but I wouldn't pin my hopes on that. If I succeed in catching the conspirators red-handed and Freydis is discovered among them, the king might agree to spare her life as a gesture of benevolence. But I would not count on that either."

"We might claim she had been kidnapped," suggested Thjodhild, "or made to join them by extortion. The most important of all, Leif, is to find her quickly, before she has the chance to do too much damage. Ah, this girl! If only you knew, my son, how sick I am of the trouble she brings upon herself and upon us all!"

"There is at least one bit of luck," said Leif. "The county where I am going happens to adjoin the lands of Thorvard's family, and Thorvard himself is there right now. His relations are loyal to the king. It will only make sense to ask for their help. No one will find that suspicious."

"You do not mean to get Thorvard involved in this, do you, Leif?" Thjodhild asked, and a hint of pity sounded in her voice. "I truly think he - "

"Yes," said Leif, "he had suffered enough, and if I could help it, I would never even mention Freydis's name before him again. I fear we have no choice, though. I must find Freydis, and I must do it as quickly and secretly as possible, preferably without involving the king's men who will go with me. And if I must, I will hold her in a secure place until we return home. I cannot achieve all this without some help."

He was silent, and so was his mother – a silence of fearful acquiescence.

"I will be on my way at once," he went on. "You go too, mother - go to your sister Ingvild while the weather allows. Before you are off, spread the rumor that Freydis traveled ahead of you and has already gone to her aunt's, while you were detained by some reason or other. I trust your ingenuity. Do not worry. I will send you word as soon as I succeed in finding her."

When Leif was on his way, very soon after, he felt a mixture of anxiety and relief as he looked back one last time and then spurred his horse, leaving behind the court and the town – together with the plots, the intrigues, the advisers, the earls, the king, the church... and the princess. He did not know whether he would return victorious or defeated, free or in chains, alive or dead – but he would do everything in his power to ensure survival and liberty for himself and his family. *And to do this, I must find Freydis. I must find her.*

Chapter 20

The fifty men who rode with Leif were supposed to be the most obedient, disciplined, efficient and well-trained of King Olaf's soldiers, but Leif found that hard to believe - though he wisely kept his doubts to himself. It was true that the fellows, all as one, were tall and strong, but the way some of them rode resembled more a drunken farmer on the back of his donkey than a fierce warrior on the back of a battle stallion. There were many who wore their weapons in a sloppy, negligent way, and all along the column hummed with chatter, laughter and jokes. *So much for the hopes of proceeding discreetly.*

Leif would have much preferred his own men to be by his side during this journey instead of those picked by the king, but he had no choice. It was clear that the King Olaf's trust in him was very narrowly conditioned. *Some of the men riding with me are meant to spy on me, no doubt.*

At least he would soon see one true friend, thought Leif - Thorvard, who was like a brother to him. Yet he felt guilty for his intention of getting his friend involved in such a doubtful and perhaps dangerous affair, not to mention that it might bring Thorvard face to face with Freydis, and that would be too cruel. Thorvard had paid his debts and deserved a quiet life.

Freydis. Anger and concern mixed in his heart when he thought of her. In truth, it was not clear why her disappearance should surprise him and his mother so - it was very much in her character to do something stupid and dangerous out of pride and ambition, without using her common sense or considering how her decisions might affect others. If it turns out Freydis is involved in some plot against the king - and of this,

154

unfortunately, he hardly had any doubt left - and it becomes known, they might all lose their lives; himself, Freydis, his mother, even all his men. And even if they manage to save their skins, the king will be in no hurry to forgive them.

"We are getting closer," Bjorn's voice shook him out of his thoughts. Bjorn was one of the few people in the company Leif felt he might trust. He was an experienced warrior, about Leif's age, while many others were green boys. He was shrewd and well-worded, and knew how to make others laugh until tears came into their eyes, though he was stingy with smiles himself - perhaps because about half his teeth were shattered in some fight or other. Bjorn was a great rider, and spent most of his time in the saddle. Those who laughed at him behind his back said that this is how he tries to make up for his insufficient height - he was almost a dwarf - and for his malformed legs. And truly, when he sat in the saddle on the back of his horse, his wide shoulders and long arms gave him the look of a man much taller than he really was. Bjorn was passionate about tending to his horse - he would always brush it, make sure it ate well even when the men themselves hardly had a piece of bread and a bit of salt cod to quench their hunger, and often sat talking to it quietly.

Now he gently spurred his horse onward and left his place in the column so that he could ride by Leif's side.

"The owner of these lands is a good man, and loyal to the king, so I have heard," said Bjorn. "He will probably allow us to set camp in his fields and might even give us some provisions."

"Of course," replied Leif, "Ulf Skullason is a good and generous man, so I've heard from his nephew Thorvard."

Bjorn looked at him, surprised. "You know Skullason's nephew? How come?"

"Thorbjorn, Thorvard's father, joined my father in his first journey to Greenland," Leif said cautiously. He preferred not to reveal his close friendship with Thorvard, nor the family connection between them, out of fear that perhaps in a short while such a connection might not be favorable for his friend. "I've heard Thorvard is spending the winter here. I have no doubt we will be well-received."

He looked on to the bare fields with the neatly marked borders, the black land of which was not covered with snow yet. In a deep valley between two mountains he could see the house of Thorvard's relations. It seemed a pleasant corner, and Leif felt guilty for being obliged to break up its peace.

Ulf, Thorvard's uncle, was a big, fat and strong man, with a long auburn beard that fell to his waist and a thundering voice that could be heard at a great distance. His wife Brunhild, on the other hand, had a lean, handsome figure, though she had borne and brought up eight children, and her ways were quiet and pleasant. Both were exceedingly hospitable and generous. When Ulf heard who Leif was, he refused to allow his men to seek shelter in the fields for the night, and insisted on getting everybody under his roof, though there wasn't much room.

"I will not allow honest men, let alone the king's men, to freeze outside our walls. The boys can find a place in the barns and upon the benches in the main hall. At least this way you'll be dry and warm. And don't be too shy to use the bathhouse. After some days upon the road anyone would need it," Ulf added with a loud chuckle.

156

"I thank you for your hospitality," said Leif, though he realized that some of the men will probably be obliged to sleep *under* the benches. Still, it was far better than the prospect of setting camp in a field.

Soon Leif was in the house and face to face with his friends. Exclamations of surprise and pleasure and bear hugs followed. They exchanged news, and Thorvard inquired after the health of Erik and Thjodhild. Leif also described in broad terms what he was sent for, but was careful not to mention Freydis.

"There are some earls in the area whom I always believed not truly loyal to our king Olaf," said Brunhild. "I will not be surprised to find out they are plotting something."

"Just between us, Leif," said Ulf, lowering his voice, "I don't always agree with every move of the king. Sometimes, I think, King Olaf is too soft, and sometimes he labors under schemes and intrigues where it would be more efficient, in my humble opinion, to show firmness and bravery and to strike with force. Also, I do not at all approve of the massive conversion to Christianity that is encountered at every corner. As you can see, all the members of our household remain loyal to the Old Ways, but it seems that soon we will be unwanted in Norway, despite out loyalty to the king. Still, all this does not change the fact that Norway needs union. If the kingdom falls, our land shall be devoured by our enemies as a deer by a pack of wolves. Far-sighted men must give up selfish ambition for a greater cause, but they do not understand this and will not accept this until they feel the king's might. That is why you can count on us. I, my sons, my nephew Thorvard and all my household men will help you in every way we can."

A young maid of about sixteen or seventeen years, with eyes blue like the summer sky and a long, thick golden braid that fell down her slim back, entered and served them beer, a round of cheese and steaming hot rye bread. Leif did not fail to notice the faint blush that diffused her cheeks when she dared to steal a glance in the direction of Thorvard, who looked as if he didn't notice her and remained indifferent.

"Thank you, Dalla, my daughter," said Ulf. Dalla did not leave, but remained standing in a corner of the room, behind her mother's back, almost as if she were a servant.

When everybody sat down to eat and drink, the door was opened a little, and a small girl ran in on her short chubby legs. This was Leif's niece Sygni, who was now about three years old. Without saying a word, she climbed into her father's lap and held on to him, looking curiously and apprehensively at the strangers. Leif had not seen Sygni since she was a babe. Now he looked at her as curiously as she at him. She had delicate features very reminiscent of Freydis, but her hair and eyes were dark like her father's. *A pretty little one.* He soon captured his niece's heart by playing the fool, and later bounced her up and down on his knee. She gave a long, rolling laugh, jumped down upon the floor, ran around the table and finally got under it.

"I know you are the brother of... Thorvard's *wife*," Brunhild said in his ear quietly, almost apologetically. "But please, do not believe we think any the worse of you for it. Thorvard told us you have always been a true friend and tried to warn him against her."

She spoke in a resonating, dramatic whisper which ensured that her words were heard at every corner of the table. Thorvard pretended to be deaf, but his face was stony.

"Brunhild," Ulf said warningly, and his wife fell silent.

When Leif and his friend remained alone, Thorvard grew somber.

"I expected you to come and visit me, Leif," he said, "but I did not think you would arrive accompanied by fifty men."

"I didn't plan to find myself involved in the king's power games," said Leif, "but I had no choice."

"That is not all, is it?" Thorvard asked shrewdly. "You look troubled. I know you well. Tell me, Leif. What truly happened since you arrived at Norway?"

The beautiful and gentle face of Princess Thorgunna appeared before Leif's eyes, so close to his own in the dim light of her chamber. But his mouth was firmly set and his lips did not mention her name. This secret would remain with him. Instead, he began telling Thorvard of Freydis and the inexplicable relationship that had developed between her and Ingvar Haraldson, and felt deeper and deeper guilt as he spoke and saw how Thorvard's face darkened, how his brows were knitted together and his jaw tightened.

"Do you mean to say," Thorvard said in a voice unsteady with indignation he tried in vain to conceal, "that you are asking me to help you save her?"

"No one knows better than I do that she doesn't deserve any help," Leif said quickly, "but if it becomes known that she is involved in this, we will all be in danger."

Thorvard, despite his gruff appearance, was a kind man, but now his eyes burned with the desire of revenge.

"I cannot refuse you," he said finally. "Only for your sake, and for Thjodhild's - I do not wish you to get a blast of the king's

159

wrath. As for Freydis, forgive me, but she deserves to be caught and put to death. She brought this upon herself."

"Just let me get my hands on her," Leif promised, "and I will lock her up until it is time to sail back to Greenland, and once we're there Father will make sure she never leaves Brattahlid again for all the rest of her life, and never speaks to anyone but the household people."

"Be careful," Thorvard advised him. "Your sister is capable of doing to you what she did to me. She might make your men rebel against you and convince them to sail to Vinland instead of Greenland."

"My men are too experienced to fall into a trap such as this," said Leif. "No, as far as it depends on me, Freydis will never see Vinland again. But you and I, my friend, will sail there yet, and Thorvald and Thorstein with us, and perhaps Father as well."

Thorvard's expression grew distant. "I do not mean to return," he confessed.

"You will stay in Norway?" Leif raised his eyebrows.

"My father had not been exiled. He left of his own free will, and no one will refuse me the right of living here. My days of adventure are over. All I seek now is some peace. I have endured enough storms."

"But Greenland is your home," Leif didn't give up, "and your second home is the sea."

"I shall make a home for myself here," said Thorvard, and though he spoke determinedly, Leif recognized a hint of defeat in his friend's familiar voice. "Uncle Ulf is good and generous to me. I can get some land - a little to the north from here, true, but good fertile land. I have enough silver to set up a farm."

"And Dalla?" Leif threw a cautious guess, after a short silence.

"Dalla is a good girl," said Thorvard.

"And beautiful," added Leif.

Thorvard, in a sharp movement, turned his back on his good-brother and balled his hands into fists.

"You know how hard I had tried, Leif. But Freydis acted behind my back. She shamed me, she betrayed me, she put me and all my people in danger. And she was entirely self-focused. She was interested in nothing but sorcery, ambition, revenge. She cared for nothing else, not even our daughter."

Leif put a hand on his shoulder. "I know," he said quietly. "I did not think to blame you for trying to make a fresh start."

"Dalla will make a good wife," said Thorvard. "I haven't spoken directly to Uncle Ulf yet, but from various hints I picked up it looks like she will consent to accept me."

Humble as always, Thorvard, thought Leif. *The girl cannot take her eyes off you.*

"I am sure she would be very happy to marry you," Leif ventured to say.

"She will be a good wife," repeated Thorvard. "She loves Sygni and will raise her dutifully, and will bear me sons and run my home diligently. If there is anything to make me doubt, it is her age. She is almost a child."

A frightened child, thought Leif. But sometimes there is no harm in a woman having a healthy dose of fear of her husband. Freydis, for instance, could have benefitted from it. However, what he said aloud was:

"No one can hope for a better husband than you, my friend."

"We shall always be brothers," replied Thorvard, and they embraced.

"In the morning we will take two different paths," said Thorvard after a moment's silence. "You and your men will go west, while we turn east. This way, I believe, you have a better chance of finding her - and I do hope I am right, for I have no wish to meet Freydis again. Ever."

The glint of hatred that sparkled in Thorvard's eye made Leif uneasy. He hoped to be the one to find Freydis - for her own good.

Chapter 21

Freydis did not like the way Svein Einarson looked at her. She had always admired powerful men, leaders, but in Einarson there was something almost completely bestial hidden under a very thin layer of human garb and behavior. He was not just a giant of a man – Thorvard, her husband, was as tall and wider in the shoulders. Svein Einarson had the eyes of a wolf, with a vicious, merciless glint.

On the day Freydis arrived, one of the slaves made him angry by not leading the horses to the stables promptly enough. Einarson hit the slave's head with his enormous fist, and the boy never got up again.

"You are unfair to our friend Svein," said Ingvar Haraldson when Freydis privately spoke to him of her repulsion. "It is true that his behavior is not, ah, very refined, but what do we care? Einarson has influence and power, and people fear to cross paths with him. That is just what we need to proceed with our plan. He is not even as stupid as most people would believe. And you cannot deny that he has taken quite a fancy to you. I think you've got yourself an admirer."

That much is true. Freydis shuddered. Yes, she noticed Einarson's admiration, yet it was not the kind to soften a hard man. It was wild lust that might have made him rip her clothes off if he hadn't realized he needs her for other purposes. *For the time being.*

"The man kills his slaves as a means of amusement, Ingvar," persisted Freydis. Haraldson shrugged.

"This is something I fail to understand. Slaves fetch a handsome price these days, and a good serving man is as valuable as undiluted silver. But where does this concern for lowly men come from, Fredyis? You surprise me. You did, after all, attempt to get rid of your own husband."

Freydis scowled. "I did not attempt to get rid of anybody," she said. "I merely convinced the sailors to tie Thorvard up and turn the ship towards the coast of Vinland."

"I'll bet he took that in his stride," nodded Haraldson, a smile of faint amusement on his lips.

Freydis averted her eyes. In her mind she saw Thorvard – a huge man roaring with fury, tearing the ropes off him with a mighty effort of his arms, throwing the rebels into gushing waters... and then turning his burning, fearsome glance upon her. Freydis closed her eyes. She hated that memory, mainly because she could not deny how impressive Thorvard had looked in his fury, compared to her as she cowered in fear before him.

"... Is there any gold or silver in this new land of yours?" inquired Svein Einarson, his small yellow eyes narrowed with greed.

"This I cannot say. I saw no gold or silver on the Skraelings, but this does not mean much," admitted Freydis.

"Perhaps they hide it in a safe place, and guard the mines carefully," Ingvar Haraldson put in. "At any rate, that is what we need to tell people to make them want to follow us. The promise of bounty is so tempting that the glint of a possibility alone will be enough to make people leave everything behind."

Freydis gave him a look of distaste. "Why do we need to lie? There is fertile land for all, plentiful fertile land for farming, and we offer people freedom to worship what god they choose. Men followed my father even to Greenland in their zeal to escape unjust laws. So why would they hesitate now, when we offer something so much more tempting?"

"I'm sorry, Freydis, but *few* people followed your father," Ingvar corrected her. "The Greenland settlements are small, and you never have enough men, you know that. What we are planning is something of quite another scale, if I may remind you. Setting up a new kingdom will require massive immigration. The most important thing is to get as many people as possible to sail to Vinland – and soon. Of course, once the settlement is established and people see how good the land is – if it is as you describe – no one will leave, even if land is all there is."

"And timber," added Freydis, "we could all profit from the timber."

"It is all well, as long as you don't forget Svein Einarson," said their host, and Freydis noticed a subtle threat in his voice. "Svein Einarson, who is gathering the first, strongest group of men for you. Lesser men will follow, but I am helping you start. Remember that."

"And of course, our esteemed friend Svein Einarson," Ingvar added with a slight bow, and though Freydis could detect a hint of irony in it, Einarson seemed appeased. "Without you, the plan could never work. We have a glorious future ahead – all of us. The land is bountiful and all but empty... except for those Skraelings Freydis mentioned, but they will be easily crushed. And we will have freedom – the freedom to live how our fathers lived."

"Brave men will certainly like it more than the weak Christian rule of King Olaf," grunted Einarson. "Half of Norway shall be swayed, too, once we gather our army and send our warships across the sea."

165

Quick as a lightning, Freydis turned her head towards Ingvar Haraldson and shot him a burning, accusing glance. *Why does he not seem surprised?* It appeared that Einarson's words were novelty to no one but her. Suddenly she understood how uncertain her position is among these men, and she felt very vulnerable.

"We talked of settling a new land," she said, "not of conquering an old one."

"Oh, but we are thinking big, Freydis, don't you see?" Ingvar said serenely. "Founding a settlement overseas is a glorious design, but why should we abandon our homeland to a king who can barely hold the reins?"

This was it, realized Freydis. *This was the reason behind all the secrecy.* Her words were stuck in her throat. This was more dangerous by far than she had thought. *They don't just mean to settle overseas, they are planning a rebellion.* And this was concealed from her until such a moment when she would no longer be able to protest or wriggle out of her connection with these men. If they should all be caught now, who will believe she knew nothing? *I wouldn't.*

Leif did not truly do her justice. Freydis was not quite so selfish. When the extent of the danger was revealed to her, she thought not only of herself, but also of what would happen to her mother and brother should she be caught.

But as to Svein Einarson, Freydis had to admit: no matter how much she loathed the man, he was a true leader. People flocked to him and were swayed by his words. Freydis knew how to recognize power; she was the daughter of Erik the Red, after all, and sister to Leif Erikson. She could have been a leader in her own right, she thought bitterly, if only she weren't a woman;

then she wouldn't have had to ally herself with men such as Svein Einarson and Ingvar Haraldson. She could have made it on her own.

When Einarson straightened up and stood tall and fierce in the great hall of his house, a steady silence settled in the place of drunken laughter and bawdy song that reigned a moment earlier. He did not even need to clear his throat or thump on the table to gain everyone's attention. All looked at him, as if mesmerized by the sight of his ugly, scarred, powerful face.

"Men who love freedom!" he began. "Our hopes have been fulfilled. We now know of a place where we can found a new Norway, a kingdom where courage will never lose its luster and no king will ever dare to look upon the Old Ways with contempt."

Ingvar Haraldson leaned back, and a content smile appeared on his thin lips.

"Well, the wheels have begun to turn," he told Freydis quietly. "I am pleased to say my work here is done for now. Tomorrow I shall be on my way back to Trondheim."

His serene, matter-of-fact words hit Freydis like the blow of a hammer. "What?" she said, incredulous. "What about me? I cannot go back to Trondheim. If I meet Leif or my mother now they will never let me out of their sight again. They must be looking for me, and – "

"No, of course you cannot go back with me," Ingvar said calmly, "you must remain here."

"You cannot leave me here alone," Freydis said through gritted teeth.

"You will not be alone," Ingvar contradicted her. He sounded faintly amused and a little bored. "The place is full of excited

167

adventurers and conspirators who will want to hear all about Vinland. And surely you do not doubt Svein Einarson's hospitality. He would be sorry to see you leave so soon."

"In other words," said Freydis in mounting fury, "you got me involved in a dangerous game, and now that things are warming up you slip away to your safe corner and allow others to do all the dirty work."

Haraldson's feathers were not so easily ruffled, though. "Unlike our friend Svein, I do not have the gift of inflaming the crowd, my dear Freydis," he said. "Most of my work is done in secret. I collect information and hoard it or pass it on as needed, I make connections between the right people, I sow ideas. Most of the glory is left to others. I am not an excessively ambitious man, but I am a practical one. I know my limits."

"Coward," Freydis said through gritted teeth.

"Now, do not be so unfair," Haraldson said reasonably. "I take risks too. The king trusts me completely. You can imagine what will happen to me if I am caught. But an overthrow of the existing rule cannot happen without people who are close to the king, people who know all his secrets. Well, I am such a man. I know how to pull the right strings. Svein Einarson, on the other hand, is very poor at diplomacy. That is why he needs me just as I need him. We are two sides of the same coin, together."

There was nothing to be done. Freydis could not stop him from going, nor could she join him herself. She had nowhere to go; she would have to stay put. And, despite everything he said, she would remain alone. The thought gave her a queer chill. Though she never really trusted Haraldson, his presence made her feel secure in a way. He was too clever to remain in a place of real danger. *So what does it mean if he is leaving?*

That night, she pulled the amethyst ring out of the folds of her gown and looked at it long and hard. The red flames flickering in the black depths of the stone were reflected in her wide-open eyes. She saw fire, and the exposed teeth of a snarling wolf in attack. She saw a sword striking, merciless, and a foe falling down. She saw flames taking hold of wooden beams and licking them lustily.

Frightened, she took off the ring, twisting her finger in her haste. This was sickeningly like the black prophecy she had seen in the flames of the Skraeling witch. But no, it cannot be. *All I do, I do to make sure it will never happen.* She wanted to bring strength and safety to Greenland. She cannot be wrong. *I cannot be wrong.*

Moreover, she had no way back. When her father and Leif find out about this plan, they will be doubtful at first, she knew. Perhaps they will even call her reckless for associating with Einarson. But once they see what they all gain they will be forced to change their minds. They will no longer be the edge of the world. They will be part of a new kingdom. *If Leif doesn't find me too soon.*

***

"Well, Svein," Freydis said, looking around her with distaste. "Here I am – gods, what a miserable hovel this is! Why did you bring me here?"

"It isn't the most inconspicuous place, I'll grant you, but it's out of the way. We can have a snug little chat here without anyone sticking their nose in."

"We needn't have gone this far for a chat," Freydis said mutinously, drawing her cloak tighter around her. "We could have remained sitting by the fire in the great hall comfortably enough. It feels like it's going to snow any moment."

169

"Too many people there. Anyway, I have something to say to you, and it won't take long."

"Alright, then," Freydis grudgingly relented. "What is it, Svein?"

"I wanted to speak to you of Vinland once more. The land... it is good land, is it not?"

"Better than most places in Norway, and much less crowded."

"It will soon be even less crowded. I will do away with the Skraelings... that is what you wanted to hear, is it not? I will do that – I want to have the *best* land, though, not merely good land."

Freydis scowled. "I have no way of knowing which land is best, Svein. We hadn't settled in the place long enough to find out."

"No, I suppose not. But then, you also have your... special abilities to rely on."

Freydis experienced a prickling, unpleasant feeling at the nape of her neck. There was something sinister in Einarson's voice. "What does this have to do with anything?"

"Now, Freydis, there's no need to be coy with me. My interests are your interests, after all. Ours is more than a business partnership," his leer was so full of meaning that it was impossible to ignore the latter comment.

"What is that supposed to mean?"

"Do I have to say it? Oh well. I am a single man; you are a beautiful woman. Yes, yes, I know the little snag with your divorce, but matters can be brought forward. I'm sure Thorvard won't mind. And if he does, he can be... persuaded. He is staying with his uncle not too far from here, you know."

Freydis looked at him, startled at this unexpected turn. "Leave Thorvard out of this, will you?"

"What, do you care for him after all?"

"This has nothing to do..." she spluttered. "My daughter is there as well, on Ulf and Brunhild's farm. I don't want you anywhere near there, Svein. Now let me go," she made to sweep past him, but he took hold of her arm.

"Wait, where are you going? We haven't finished our conversation. Come, Freydis. If you hadn't wanted to be near me, you wouldn't have stayed behind when Haraldson went back to Trondheim."

"I didn't – it wasn't – " Freydis was losing track of what she wanted to say, as Einarson stepped menacingly near her. "Let go of me," she demanded, once he put his massive arm around her shoulders. "I will thank you never to touch me again," she added imperiously, but the dangerous flash of his eye showed him to be utterly unimpressed by this command.

"Wrong answer, bitch," he said, his steely fingers digging into her arms. Before Freydis knew it, one hand was clasped over her mouth, while the other tore away her cloak. She struggled and attempted to shout, but she was tossed down to the ground. Einarson pinned her down, crushing her with animal force. He slapped her cheek hard, making her mouth bleed on the inside. "You won't toy with me. It's time someone taught you a lesson."

Chapter 22

Thorvard Thorbjornson chose his warmest and darkest clothes, pulled on his most supple, comfortable boots, ones that made his step as soft as a cat's, and took the sword that passed in the family from father to son. According to legend, it was given to one of his forefathers by the god Thor himself.

His long hair was drawn together in a black braid that fell down his back, so that it wouldn't get in the way. Nothing must get in his way tonight.

Thorvard was a man whose word is written in stone. He remembered his promise to Leif – not to hand Freydis over to the king's men if he does find her. It was disappointing to think he will have to give up the pleasure of witnessing her trial and conviction. Still, he looked forward to seeing her beg –helpless, maybe even asking for mercy – though it was unlikely, given the woman in question.

He did not know exactly what Freydis got involved in this time, but knowing her, he could assume with a fair degree of certainty that it is something reckless and dangerous. He knew of landholders in the area who objected to King Olaf's rule. One of them was Svein Einarson, that great wild boar. *Woe to Freydis if she put her trust in this man.*

A few minutes ago he had stood at the door of the dark quiet room where Sygni slept with the women. The little girl's dark head could barely be seen beneath the pile of blankets and furs. The blurred features of his daughter's face were a dim vision in the faint light of the candle he held in his hand. Her long eyelashes rested on her cheeks, casting deep shadows.

Every time Thorvard looked at her, he felt a mixture of anger and pity. How can it be that even for her - for this sweet innocent creature, the babe she carried in her womb and nursed at her breast - Freydis wasn't ready to stop her antics, to settle down and be a woman like all others? If having a child was not enough to tame her, what would be?

It was a dark night, cloudy but snowless, and he saw it as a good sign. *If I do this, it must be tonight.* Freydis couldn't evade justice forever, and he finally accepted that there might be no one but him to bring it to her.

He brought his hands close to his face and looked at them. Strong, skilled, callused hands. They had been this way since he was a boy, and he always counted on them. Now he could imagine these strong hands of his locking a delicate neck in an unyielding trap. *No, I must control myself. My task is to capture her and hand her over to Leif, and that is all.*

He was ready. Loyal men of his uncle's household were going with him. He opened and closed his fists, flexing his fingers. *Soon, very soon.*

He heard quiet steps behind him. Hesitant steps, as hers always were, as if she always doubted that her presence was welcome. He wished to reassure her, but he was never good with words. There wasn't much need of them, not with Freydis... and Freydis was the only woman he had ever known.

"Dalla," he spoke to his cousin, "we will be gone soon. If we don't come back by sunrise – "

"Sunrise?" she sounded apprehensive. "You are not going so very far, are you?"

"I hope not," he nodded.

"What are you going to do?" Dalla asked timidly after a moment of hesitation.

"Capture them. Get them here. What else?"

"Will it be... dangerous?" The last word could barely be heard. Suddenly, Thorvard realized she must be fearful for her brother, who would be going with him. *He means more to her than I do,* he knew. *I am all but a stranger.*

Dalla's face crimsoned over. This nighttime conversation was most unusual. Most days she hardly dared to raise her eyes in Thorvard's presence, let alone speak to him. "Are you certain they are really acting against the king?"

He gazed at her blankly. Somehow, he didn't even think to question that. "We will have plenty of time to find that out once they are here," he assured her.

...They made their way quickly and quietly, black shadows moving through the dark, cloudy night. Soon enough they reached their destination, which was no more than an old cabin made of roughly hewn logs, with broken shutters and a dilapidated door. It was frosty, and the moon that finally appeared was like an old gold coin shining through the mist in the cold velvet sky.

Thorvard sat quietly, without moving, hidden behind a pile of old dry brushwood. He could hear the ragged breath of Stein, his cousin. The others were waiting in several locations all around, so that the hut could be seen well from every point. Not that there was, for the time being, much to see.

They've continued in complete silence for more than an hour when he moved for the first time. The place was cold and uncomfortable and a smell of rot penetrated his surroundings, but this was not the reason of his disquiet.

"I hear no voices," he said in a hoarse whisper. "No one is coming. We are late."

Stein shook his head. He was a clever boy. "We could not risk running into them on our way. We had to arrive once they are already here."

"But why should they be here? It doesn't make much sense. What if the man who spoke to you was wrong? I cannot imagine Svein Einarson coming to this miserable hovel, certainly not with *her*."

"Perhaps they are on their way."

"Or perhaps they have already left," Thorvard crushed a twig between his fingers. "We must know it so we can keep looking for them. If we intercept them on their way back to Svein Einarson's household, maybe not all is lost."

Saying those last words, he stood up. "What are you doing, Thorvard?" the lad whispered urgently.

"You will remain here, Stein."

"You cannot – this is not what we planned – where are you *going*?"

"To make sure of something," replied Thorvard, staring at the dark hut.

"This is folly. Let me or one of the others go with you. You cannot do this alone."

"No one will move. Is that understood?"

"But – "

"Quiet, Stein." Thorvard's voice allowed no contradiction and Stein was forced to swallow his misgivings.

And so Thorvard began walking, stepping very quietly for a man his size. He approached the old, half-ruined shack and pushed the door. It opened easily, like a wide black mouth. All was quiet and cold and dark.

This was useless, he thought, disappointed. Still, he gripped his hand-axe tightly and stepped in.

The first thing he felt was a strong smell of rot and mold. It was moist and cold, as if he stepped into a burial cave. Another man would have said the darkness was impenetrable, but for his keen eyes it was enough that a few thin strips of moonlight penetrated the cracks in the walls and roof. He made two steps forward – two steady, heavy steps.

Someone was lying down with her face upon the ground, her outstretched arms clinging to the rotten, dirty wooden floor. She did not move and was hardly breathing. She was not, however, dead - though how close to death he could not tell. The fear coming from her was palpable, alive and throbbing.

When she heard him approach, she brought her knees close to her body, drew herself together, and tried with all her might to press into the cold, damp floor.

"Came to finish me off?" he heard her voice, half whisper, half groan. *This can be a trap,* he reminded himself, but something told him she is alone. He could not bring himself to move.

And then slowly, very slowly, she lifted up her head and, with great effort, looked directly at him. He flinched. So many times he had looked at this face, yet now he could barely recognize her. A bloody bruise blossomed across her cheekbone, distorting her features. Her hair was messy and full of dirt and fell into her eyes, one of which was swollen. Her lower lip was broken and bleeding, and what part of her face that wasn't bruised was ghostly pale.

She gasped, recognizing him. *"You?"* she said quietly, incredulously. And then, it appeared that the last remainder of her strength ran out and she bowed her head again, bringing it close to the floor.

Thorvard made himself approach, though he would rather turn around and walk out and forget what he saw.

"Can you get up?" he inquired in a low, rumbling voice.

"Go away," she shook her head without meeting his eye. "Kill me now or go away."

He remained still.

"This was what you wanted, was it not?" she whispered.

He bent and took hold of her shoulders, making her lift the upper part of her body off the floor. He held on not forcefully, but firmly, and she winced with pain. He wished he could avoid looking at her body, but there was no escaping it. It seemed as if she was mauled by a fierce beast. Her clothes were torn and she was covered with blood, bruises and – Thorvard inwardly shuddered – bite marks. He averted his eyes from her breasts, which were exposed. Blood was trickling in thin red lines down her thighs, as if iron-hard nails bit into her flesh when her legs were forcefully spread apart.

"Do not touch me," she begged.

Thorvard made no sign to show that he heard her. He took hold of her chin, lifted it, and carefully studied the disfigured face he had once loved so well. She was now weak and defeated, like a wounded animal that had fallen into a trap and now, trembling, awaits the final blow.

"Where is Svein Einarson?" he asked, not really expecting an answer.

"He... left. Do not... do not make me beg for the stroke of mercy, Thorvard. It must be given willingly to those who seek it. Do it. For the sake of all that had been, do it now."

For a moment, just one short moment, their eyes met.

"He was here before," said Thorvard, surprised by how quiet and hoarse his voice sounded. "And he had his way with you. Did he not? *Did he not?*"

His eyes sought hers, burning, accusing, terrible. Softly, without saying another word, she went limp and, without thinking, Thorvard caught her in his arms to prevent her from sprawling over the floor. Then he heaved her unconscious body across one shoulder and walked out.

His task was accomplished. Freydis was in his hands.

Chapter 23

The walk from the darkness of the hut into the light of the fully risen moon took only a few steps, but to Thorvard it seemed like an eternity. With every step his feet felt heavier, as if they were made out of lead. The woman's body slumped across his shoulder was heavy and almost naked, and he was thankful to know that she had passed out. In a way, he was almost relieved when the others began approaching and he could set down the burdensome weight and straighten up.

"What happened, Thorvard?" Stein cried out. "Just look at her – what – "

"I thought you were going to take her captive," remarked Njall, a vigorous man of about forty years, "not beat her unconscious."

"Don't be a fool, Njall," snapped Stein. "Thorvard would never..." but his voice trailed off as he sneaked a fearful glance at his cousin. "I mean, I'm sure you didn't – "

"Svein Einarson did this," said Thorvard in a hollow voice. "He is gone."

Someone bent over the unconscious Freydis, examining her, gingerly feeling her broken ribs and clucking his tongue. Words, remarks, exclamations, empty guesses blended in the air. Njall looked at the woman's bleeding, bruised thighs, and his eyes met Thorvard's. Though no muscle moved in the latter's face, that one look told Njall more than he wished to know.

"The trail is now cold, I expect," he observed. "We won't get our hands on him tonight." Thorvard only nodded, almost vaguely. "Look, if you intend to keep this woman alive, she needs to be taken care of as soon as possible. Not to mention all the rest, she will freeze to death."

Looking startled, Thorvard nodded again, took off his warm cloak and wrapped it around the woman – around his *wife* - covering her near-nakedness. "We will take her to my uncle's house," he said brusquely. "After me, all of you."

And, having said those words, he lifted her up on his shoulder again and stepped into the night.

The way home seemed longer by far than the route they made earlier that night. Thorvard strode quickly, as quickly as he could, as if anxious to be rid of the weight he was carrying. The others found it hard to keep up with him, although none of them had to bear an unconscious woman.

There was, of course, a commotion once they arrived, and Thorvard took advantage of this to be able to slink into the shadows. He let others do it all – answer questions, speculate about possibilities, and take care of Freydis. Half-conscious by now, she was half carried, half ushered into one of the few separate rooms at the back of the house. A bed was hastily made up and a warm fire lit. He wouldn't have followed the women there, but someone – he didn't actually realize it at the moment, but it was his aunt Brunhild – pulled on his sleeve, and he walked in almost unconsciously after her.

Freydis, who didn't seem to understand where she was or how she got there, was sitting on a bench with furs piled on top of it. It seemed it was all she could do not to slump forwards. A blanket was wrapped around her shoulders, and she was supported from both sides by Finna, the oldest servant in the house, and Dalla, Thorvard's cousin and intended bride. Brunhild stood aside and looked on with a wary expression on her face.

"She should be taken to the bathhouse, I think," she said. "I will tell the servants to heat it. These wounds need to be washed and bandaged... and perhaps some wine will help her regain her senses." She was mistress of the house, but she looked at Thorvard as if asking for his permission.

"Do that," he nodded. "Treat her. Bathe her. Clothe her." And having said that, he turned around and walked out of the room, and no one dared to follow him.

And so it was done. The women gingerly peeled off what remained of her stained and torn clothes, and Finna carried them to the fire and threw them in with a look of mingled pity and disgust. Rather than attempt to move Freydis, Brunhild eventually decided to call for a wooden tub to be brought into the room. It was filled with pails upon pails of steaming hot water, and with the help of Dalla and Finna, Freydis stepped inside. Finna supported her head so that it remained above water, and Dalla mopped her wounds with a soft cloth and washed the mud and blood out of her red hair. Freydis's eyes were open, but she stared vacantly ahead of her, as if looking at something distant and terrible. A goblet of hot spiced wine was forced upon her and she managed a few swallows, but her face remained deathly pale.

Later they helped her out of the tub and toweled her dry. Finna bandaged Freydis's wounds with her wrinkled, deft hands, and Dalla brought her clothes – the thickest, warmest clothes she could find – but still the woman continued to shiver, even though the small space was full of warm steam. During all that time she didn't utter a single word, and when she was led to sit on the bench, her eyes remained closed – as if she were afraid to open them and find herself once more in the abandoned hut.

When the night was almost over and the crisp cold feel of autumn dawn lingered in the air, Brunhild got out to look for her nephew. She found Thorvard just outside the doors, looking at the dark sky, quiet and motionless as a stone statue.

"I always knew Svein Einarson is a beast, Thorvard."

He merely looked at her and said nothing. The expression of his face was unreadable. Brunhild squirmed with discomfort. "Do you believe she knows where he might have gone?" she asked.

"I doubt she knows or cares," Thorvard said. "Right now, she hardly remembers who she is."

"I believe you are exaggerating, but – "

Thorvard turned to face her. "Do you?" he asked sharply. "Freydis is the daughter of Erik the Red," he went on. "If he were here, he would have made certain Svein Einarson is caught – and killed."

"Well, Erik the Red is not here, as it happens," said Brunhild, "he is thousands of leagues away in Greenland. Her brother, though...

She gave her nephew a quick, almost furtive glance. An odd sound came out of his throat. "Yes," he said. "Leif will want vengeance, of course."

"Then let him come and have it," Brunhild said, relieved. "He will be here again soon, will he not?"

Thorvard didn't seem to be really listening. "I gave Freydis all I had, but a day came when she attempted to usurp my place and ruin me in the eyes of my men. I had not seen her for years. She spit in my face and mocked me and rebelled against me..."

"But this isn't the point right now, is it?" Brunhild heard the voice of a short, stout man with a long white beard who approached them without being heard. It was Egil, an old slave

182

who had been with Thorbjorn ever since he was a boy and helped raise Thorvard as if he were his own son. He was treated by Thorvard more as an old and respected relation than a slave.

"What about that plot of theirs?" asked Brunhild. "The conspiracy Leif suspected them of?"

"To know exactly what the plot is, I must get my hands on him," said Thorvard, "and I will do it." He balled his enormous fist, and his jaw was set.

"When such a foul deed is done to a woman, one of the men in her family must make the offender pay," Egil went on impassively.

"She has no family here," said Thorvard, raising his fist ever so slightly. "There is Leif, of course – but a while may pass until he returns - "

"She has you, son," said the old man. "She had rebelled against your authority, of course, but she has no power to call it off."

"My authority and responsibility were never worth much in her eyes."

"The trouble," the old slave went on, "is that you had always been too soft with her."

Brunhild suppressed a mirthless chuckle. *Soft* was not a word man often used to describe Thorvard.

"I could never make her see sense," said Thorvard. "The only one who could ever do something about her folly was Erik... and even his influence came to naught when she was about twelve years old. She has been utterly uncontrollable ever since."

"Why did you take her for your wife, then?"

... Dalla, who stood quietly behind one of the partitions, covered her mouth with her hand. Could the pitiful creature in the back room be the same Freydis, the separated wife of Thorvard, of whom she thought with curiosity, resentment and envy at once?

"This does not matter anymore," said Thorvard, looking above the heads of Egil and Brunhild. "It has been years since we parted. But I will do what must be done."

He got away with quick, hard steps.

"Does not matter anymore..." the old man shook his head, "Whom is he trying to fool?"

"He has a point, Egil," said Brunhild. "In truth, she is no longer his wife."

Dalla continued listening furtively, trying to make a connection in her mind between the miserable woman and Sygni. Many times she thought of how Sygni's mother abandoned her little child – and this made her angry. But now she could feel no anger when she thought of the poor woman she and Finna had bathed and treated earlier, the broken woman with empty, fearful, haunted eyes.

"You treat the annulment of a marriage too lightly, if I may say so, mistress Brunhild," said Egil. "No matter what has come to pass between them, Freydis is still Thorvard's wife. He has a duty to protect her and make the bastard pay with his life. Thorvard must kill Svein Einarson."

Dalla felt goose pimples erupt all over her arms, and the hairs at the back of her neck prickled. She rubbed her arms with her hands against the morning chill.

"Kill him? I thought we were talking of Thorvard capturing him and handing him over to the king's men under accusation of treason..."

"It might be so if, to Einarson's good fortune, Leif is the one to reach him first," said the old man. "But depend upon it, mistress, if Thorvard finds him he will tear him limb from limb."

"Do not misunderstand me," said Brunhild, "Einarson can die as far as I am concerned. He deserves no less. He is a dangerous man in possession of important knowledge. Ulf and I believe he must be captured and interrogated."

"But as soon as the king gets his hands on Einarson," said Egil, "no one will allow Thorvard to have his revenge. Isn't that so?"

"*His* revenge?" Brunhild raised an eyebrow. "I thought he only does what must be done – or what he believes to be his duty... is it not so?"

Chapter 24

Breakfast was a quiet, subdued affair. No one talked much. Freydis remained in her room.

"Had anyone brought her food?" Thorvard surprised Finna with his question. There was no need to ask whom he meant.

"She had eaten," said the old woman. "Not much, though. But if I may say so, master, she should not be given any more wine. She seems to have drunk too much as it is."

"Well," Thorvard nodded, "I will go to her, then."

"Wait, do you mean to question her?" his uncle Ulf interrupted. "I will go with you."

"I will leave the questions for another day," said Thorvard in a low, hoarse voice. "Right now, I have no questions to ask her. I do have a few things to say, though."

She was sitting on the bed and looking at the fire when he entered. She was paler than the night before. Some of her bruises had begun to fade, but the sight of her face was ghastly.

"Came to gloat?" these were her words of welcome.

"You need to stop drinking," he said, hearing the slur of her voice. "You always despised those who do so to dull their pain. Surely you do not want to become one of them?"

An unrecognizable sound, something between a derisive snort and a snarl, was all her answer.

"You brought me here," she said after a few moments of silence, "as a prisoner?"

"Feel free to go, you fool," thundered Thorvard, "but Einarson is still out there, I know not where. Next time he sees you, he will kill you, and you are in no condition to shift for yourself. I do not even know why he left you alive in the first place. Perhaps he thought you will freeze to death anyway."

Or perhaps Einarson knew that what he had done to you is worse than death.

"I would have died," said Freydis, "I did not plan on anything else. He befouled me. I am full of muck and rot. You did me no mercy by bringing me here, Thorvard."

For one pregnant moment, they were both silent.

"Whether you are alive or dead," Thorvard said finally, "*he* must die for what he did to you. Someone must get rid of him. That is the law of honorable men. You know it."

She laughed – a hollow sound, a mere shadow of her former confident, mocking laugh he had heard so long ago.

"The law? I have no law but my own."

"You don't," he said, "but I do. And according to the law you cast off, you are still my responsibility."

Freydis threw him a sharp, calculating glance. "Are you going to kill him?" she finally asked. "Is that what you mean to say?"

He was silent.

"But why?" she didn't relent.

"Because it must be done. I have no choice. It is the law. Right now, it doesn't matter what you had done. It only matters who you are."

To avoid further inquiry, he bent to stoke the fire. Freydis wondered how he guessed she was cold. She did not think it could be perceived, but even in this room, which was quite warm, she was shivering from head to foot. Or maybe it was only because she had just conversed with Thorvard for the first time in years.

It only matters who you are, he said. Well, who is she? She had lost her family, her husband, her daughter, the axis around which her life should have revolved. What did she have left now? Her sorcery and her desire for revenge. And last night, upon the dirty floor of the hut, both were taken away from her.

"The ring," she recalled, "he took my ring."

Thorvard looked at her suspiciously, only half understanding the meaning of her words.

"Would he know to... use that ring the way you do?" he asked.

"Not yet," Freydis replied hesitantly. "But I assume he will soon find out."

Thorvard balled his enormous fist. "I will not give him the time," he said.

Chapter 25

"Forgive me, Father, for I have sinned."

Father Wilhelm wasn't truly surprised. He did, after all, hear these words from Princess Thorgunna at least once a week, whenever she came to confession. Yet there was something different in her voice this time – an anxious, desperate note. He wondered what the matter could possibly be.

"Speak, my daughter," he said. "What is your sin? Remember that God sees everything and knows everything, and confession is only necessary to make your conscience easy. Be sincere, and you shall have peace."

She hesitated, but after another moment spoke again. "I am a fallen woman, Father. I had given my innocence to a man without becoming his lawful wife."

Father Wilhelm cleared his throat. "That is grave, my daughter, no doubt. Very grave. Our Lord hates fornication. But all our sins were forgiven thanks to our Lord Jesus, who took the torture of crucifixion upon himself in order to absolve us."

"I take comfort in that, Father," the princess said in a shaky voice.

"What you must do now is ensure that the man in question, too, understands the gravity of your sin and comes to confess," the priest said.

"I fear that will not be easy. You see, Father, he is not a Christian."

This sounds even more interesting. The number of noblemen who had not yet been baptized was shrinking every day, and this narrowed the possibilities as to the identity of the mysterious seducer.

"You must try and get him to see the light of the true faith," he said. "You will not, of course, wish to think of his poor soul burning in hell for all eternity."

"I am trying, Father," Thorgunna said warmly. "He is an honest man and, I daresay, will not refuse to wed me. But I will never agree to marry someone who is not a Christian."

"The Lord shall bless you for your strong faith," Father Wilehlm encouraged her. "And thanks to your faith and devotion to Jesus, our Savior, you shall be forgiven. I absolve you of all your sins."

"Thank you, Father," her voice was accompanied by the rustle of skirts she got up to her feet. The priest sat still for a while, listening to her receding footsteps.

It is very convenient that Ingvar Haraldson is back in Trondheim, Father Wilhelm thought as he directed his steps to the house of the financial advisor. Ingvar Haraldson did not visit the church more than he had to and never set foot in the confession cell, but this did not alloy his personal friendship with Father Wilhelm. The two were kindred spirits – both blossomed in an atmosphere of secrecy and intrigue, which they knew how to manipulate in their favor, both liked an easy comfortable life, and both had ambitions – although Father Wilhelm would never admit his were dedicated to anything other than the glory of Jesus Christ.

"Father Wilhelm!" Haraldson smiled and spread his arms in a cordial gesture. "You are among the first whom I meet upon my return. What a pleasure. Do sit and make yourself comfortable. I have some good wine – do drink a cup with me."

While they sipped the wine, the narrowed eyes of Ingvar Haraldson studied the priest's face.

"My friend, does something occupy your holy thoughts to such an extent that you are not truly present? You didn't even say a word about the wine."

"I apologize," the priest recollected himself and took another sip. "It is very choice, no doubt. But... I would like to ask you a question."

"I am all ears," Haraldson prompted him.

"What do you think might happen," Father Wilhelm began carefully, "if Princess Thorgunna, for some reason, does not marry Prince Sigurd?"

Ingvar gave him a calculating look. "Do you have reasons to think it might be so?"

Father Wilhelm told him.

"Poor innocent child," said Haraldson, half-smiling. "What a relief she must have felt to have her sins absolved!"

"I told her to pray morning and night to the Holy Virgin, the mother of Jesus," said Father Wilhelm.

"Very true," said Haraldson, "the princess has nothing left to do but pray. You and I, though - our task is to think."

"I wonder if we are both thinking the same thing," said the priest, meeting the eye of his companion.

"For Thorgunna, of course, an end to her betrothal would be a harsh blow," said Ingvar, "although she might not think so now, entangled as she is in her love story with this mysterious man, whoever he is."

"And really," nodded Father Wilhelm, "I wonder who he can be. There are only a very few noblemen who have not yet accepted the light of the True Faith."

"Ah, the identity of this unknown lover is an interesting detail, of course, but not so very important. The private life of Thorgunna does not matter so much, truly. I take far more interest in the future of the kingdom. It is not by chance that the king intended Thorgunna for his daughter-in-law. Just between us, Sigurd is a pretty much insignificant type. The people treat him indifferently, but they love the princess. For her sake the smallfolk would be ready to love Sigurd as well – and this would be a great help to him in establishing his rule. This is the very reason why King Olaf did not seek a foreign bride for his son. He could have made an alliance with the Danes, but he passed on this opportunity . He knows that Thorgunna, so generally beloved, will ensure Sigurd's royal seat better than any other woman – even if the prince himself does not see it as clearly."

"On the other hand, if they do not marry..." Father Wilhelm picked up the thread.

"It might be that when the day comes, Prince Sigurd will fail to hold the throne," Ingvar finished. "Yes. And again, just between us, my friend Father Wilhelm, I am not certain it would be so very bad for Norway. Can you keep a secret?"

"Think that you are at confession," said the priest, and they both laughed. "I hope you do not wish for the separation of the kingdom, though?" he added more seriously. "Surely union is best for Norway."

"Oh no, I do not wish the kingdom to fall apart into many warring earldoms," Ingvar Haraldson assured him. "I do think, however, that many can gain from a change of rule."

"It is rumored there is already a group of influential people who think the same," said Father Wilhelm, probing Ingvar with his cool light blue stare. But the expression of Haraldson's face remained impossible to read. Ingvar was well-trained in such matters - otherwise he would not have survived long in his role as a double agent.

"As much as the king might wish to promote his son's marriage to Thorgunna," he said, ignoring the priest's remark, "I doubt he will consent to ignore the fact that the princess had failed to preserve her chastity – that is, if he finds out, of course."

"You are not thinking of telling the king, are you?" Father Wilhelm asked quickly. "Remember that you were not supposed to know this at all."

"Oh, no, Father Wilhelm," said Haraldson, smiling. "Sometimes it is enough to know human nature and allow it to act on our behalf. I am ready to bet that the princess herself will dissolve the marriage pact."

"But that wouldn't make any sense," protested Father Wilhelm. "To give up on a union with Prince Sigurd and a straight path to the throne? That is madness."

"Believe it or not," said Ingvar Haraldson, "women do not always act rationally. Be patient, my friend. We have seats in the front row of this spectacle, and it promises to be an excellent one."

Chapter 26

Finna entered Freydis's room, bearing in her gnarled hands two wooden bowls upon a tray.

Freydis looked at the tray that was placed before her. One of the bowls was full of berries which were stashed in the frozen store-room and taken out to thaw. The other held thick yellowish cream. Berries and cream have always been the one thing she could keep down when she didn't feel well, and Thorvard knew it. In the years when they were still children and cream was scarce he would sneak into the buttery and bring it to her secretly.

If she was in any doubt before, now she was certain he intends to keep her alive. *But why?*

Freydis knew that deep down, Thorvard had always been a bit of a coward. When they went out to hunt together, often he was the one who could not overcome the frightened, pleading, pain-misted look of the fallen deer, and let others give the final blow.

And last night, thought Freydis, she had been the deer.

She did not like that thought at all.

She picked up the spoon and began to eat.

Later Dalla, the golden-haired girl she remembered from the night before, came in. Freydis looked at her in resentment. She was in no mood to see anyone.

"I came to see how you are doing," said the kind girl. "Are you... are you feeling any better?"

Freydis narrowed her eyes derisively. This was the last thing she needed. "You wouldn't understand," she said curtly.

"I – well, maybe not quite, but I can imagine how terrible – "

Freydis looked up. "There had never been anyone but Thorvard." *Now, why did I say that?* She could have kicked herself. *I'll bet they tell him every word I say.*

"I am sorry," Dalla said quietly.

Freydis lowered her voice to a threatening whisper, and her eyes sparkled with fury. "If you tell anyone what I said just now, I swear I will tear out your tongue even if it's the last thing I do."

"I would never do that," Dalla said urgently, got up, and disappeared with great alacrity.

After the girl left, Freydis sat motionless for a long time, mindlessly staring at the outline of the dark logs the walls were built from. Suddenly, with merciless vividness, she remembered the time when she was just a girl and her love for Thorvard had but begun. She could hardly move or speak in his presence. He was so tall and strong and handsome, and his low, powerful voice made her shiver with excitement. She despaired when she thought he might never feel the same way – until one day, she noticed a furtive look that made her heart flutter with hope.

She remembered the first time she ran her fingers through his mane long, dark, thick hair. "Your hair is longer than mine," she told him then with a mischievous smile. "You need to braid it, so that it will not get in your way when you are out hunting." She braided his hair herself and relished the task, though it took her a while to comb out all the tangles. *I wonder who braids it for him now,* a thought surprised her. *Surely not this girl Dalla?*

There was one summer night when the sky darkened only slightly, and she went to swim in a deep clear stream that was her secret place. There she noticed Thorvard's outline – he was hiding behind the bushes. Her heart hammered violently while she attempted to guess whether he would dare to reveal himself

195

to her, and what on earth she will do if he does. But she took her time and lingered in the water, allowing the cool flow to wash over her. Later she stretched on the grassy bank for a long time before she put her clothes back on. It was sweet torture to know he is looking at her all the while, yet have to feign ignorance. Finally, she donned her clothes and he was gone, and she returned home victorious.

They were married not long after. They were both barely old enough, yet felt they can wait no longer.

"Now you are mine, my love," she whispered in the mist of desire that rendered her nearly mute.

"Now and forever," he said.

The magic of her memories was now forever altered. She gathered her knees close to her body, put her arms around herself and rocked back and forth. Her body was an ugly, tainted vessel, as if poison, not blood, coursed through her veins.

Dalla returned later, leading by the hand a girl of three years old with dark luminous eyes. Freydis felt as if a blow knocked all the air out of her lungs. The last time she had seen her daughter was two years ago.

"Sygni wished to see you," Dalla said.

Freydis looked at the girl, painfully recognizing the mingling of her features and Thorvard's dark colors. Sygni returned her a curious, shy look, and hid behind the skirts of Dalla, whom she knew and trusted.

An unbearable feeling of loss constricted Freydis's throat and prevented her from uttering a word. She was worthless even as a mother.

To her surprise, a minute or two later Sygni left her hiding place, approached her, and touched Freydis's fingers with her chubby warm little hand.

"You see," Dalla said softly, "you do have something to live for."

Even the birth of their daughter did not bridge the gap between Freydis and Thorvard. Not even the sweet bonds of motherhood could pull her heart away from its desires and ambitions. She did not attempt to stop Thorvard from taking Sygni to Norway. She felt sorry for it now. She was a stranger to her own flesh and blood, and it wasn't likely to change – certainly not if it depended on Thorvard.

... "You should never have allowed her to meet Sygni!" Thorvard broke out.

"Sygni is her daughter," Dalla said simply.

"She gave up on her," said Thorvard, his chest heaving with emotion. "She threw away all that was supposed to be dearest to her. I do not understand why she chose this path, but it will be better for Sygni to grow up without such a mother."

"Perhaps she regrets," Dalla made a suggestion that caused Thorvard to snort in derision.

"You do not know Freydis," he said. "She feels no remorse. It is not in her nature."

But little Sygni, when no one noticed her, slipped in to see the foreign odd woman, to whom she felt inexplicably attracted. She pressed her cheek against the woman's limp hand, allowed her to caress her hair in a short, hesitant stroke of fingers, and ran away.

Chapter 27

Not long after, Thorvard's hands were crimsoned with his enemy's blood.

Though Thorvard had always been merciless with his enemies, he never derived pleasure from taking someone else's life – but this time it was different. He stood aside and watched almost gleefully how the blood of his enemy's life trickles down to the ground, and made no motion when the dying man begged for the stroke of mercy. He let Einarson suffer slowly until he very end. He felt as if his heart was made of stone.

When the body was brought before everybody, even experienced warriors looked on fearfully and took a step back. Behind him he heard a retching noise and receding footsteps – that, without a doubt, was Dalla.

Freydis moved forward and looked at the mutilated features of the one who had ruined her. Then her eyes met Thorvard's. His face was inscrutable, and he was covered with blood - his enemy's and, as far as she could judge by the numerous wounds covering his arms and chest, his own as well.

"I killed him," he said, and added nothing, for no explanation was needed.

"I thank you," Freydis said simply. She did not know what she was supposed to feel. The fear that had preyed upon her ever since that terrible night was gone, but in its stead there was an empty space, a gap she did not know how to fill. Her enemy was dead, and she no longer felt anger, desire to fight, lust for revenge – nothing of what had propelled her forward in the past years. It was as if something had crumbled to dust within her, and nothing but an empty shell was left.

All of a sudden, it seemed Thorvard had lost its balance. He leaned hastily against a wall, but people around him already noticed, and concerned whispers broke out all over.

"Thorvard?" Stein said uneasily. "Thorvard, what is it?"

"It... is nothing," Thorvard said with great difficulty. "These wounds are a trifle, I... I just need to rest, and it will pass soon."

But it did not pass. The next moment, Thorvard lost power of speech and collapsed, completely unconscious. His eyes rolled in his head. Brunhild screamed. People ran to him, supported him, lifted him up, talked to him, but all in vain.

With great urgency and greater determination than she would have expected of herself, Freydis pushed everyone aside and looked at his wounds. They did not seem grave enough to justify such a collapse, but they could have allowed for poisoning... Svein Einarson was clever enough in his beastly way, much cleverer than people usually gave him credit for. She looked around her frantically.

"I need someone with knowledge of herb-lore!" she cried desperately.

An old crone, bent and wrinkled but surprisingly agile, stepped forward. "I might be able to help you, child," she said, and her wrinkled brow creased more still when she looked at Thorvard, lying motionless upon the ground and breathing with visible difficulty. "Perhaps we might help him together... because I doubt there is much I can do on my own."

"Show me everything you have," said Freydis. She went with the old woman, and while she walked, she gathered within her the remainder of the powers she had left, and prayed for one thing alone – one last spell that would help her save the father of her daughter.

Later that night, when Freydis approached the still unconscious Thorvard with a smoking goblet in hand, she was shaking from head to foot. If there had been a mistake, she knew it would cost her more dearly than any she had made before.

"One moment," she was stopped by Brunhild's sharp voice just as she bent gingerly above Thorvard, probing the tense muscles of his jaw.

Freydis looked at her with puzzled anger. "There is not a moment to lose," she said.

"If Thorvard comes to harm from this grisly concoction," said Brunhild, "you shall be responsible."

"Comes to harm?" Freydis laughed hollowly. "More than he already had, you mean? I can guess which poison Svein Einarson used. Thorvard will not live to see sunrise. The potion I prepared is his only chance."

"He was not supposed to go and confront Einarson on his own," Ulf joined his wife, and his voice was heavy like a shower of stones. "If he dies because of you, you will die with him."

Freydis straightened and gave them both a contemptuous look. "Let it be so," she said indifferently.

She bent over Thorvard again, lifted his head up a little and pried his mouth open with the help of two fingers. Then she helped him swallow some of the potion. He coughed and moaned. Another swallow, and he opened his eyes. Freydis's hands were shaking so hard that she almost spilled the rest of the liquid in the goblet, but Thorvard was able to take it out of her hands and drink on his own.

"You saved my life," he said in a weak voice once the goblet was empty.

"I did not wish to owe you," replied Freydis with self-control that had cost her a great deal.

Chapter 28

As soon as Leif received Thorvard's message, he returned to the house of Ulf and Brunhild. The message lacked details – all he knew was that Freydis had been found, and this was enough to dispel his worst fears – his sister is alive, she wasn't taken by the king's men, and he and his family are safe from the throne's wrath. But a dull worry still gnawed at his heart, and when he was told of all that had happened, his breath was caught in his throat with fury that was only partially calmed when he heard how Svein Einarson had found his death.

"That bastard!" he cried out in anger. "If only I had known, I would have arrived at once, and we could have gotten rid of him together!"

"I could not wait," said Thorvard. "It was my responsibility, after all. It happened close to my family's lands."

Leif looked at his friend intently. A deep weariness was apparent in Thorvard's face, together with something different, not quite so easy to define.

On the day of Leif's arrival, Ulf and Brunhild received a surprise which was not very gratifying to either Leif or Thorvard. Vidar, a distant cousin of Brunhild's, came for an extended visit together with his two daughters, Aslaug and Ingvild.

"Now of all times?" Thorvard asked his uncle with quiet vexation. "This is your house, Uncle, of course – but was there no way to postpone this visit, at least until the leave-taking of Leif and... his sister?"

"Vidar did not bother to send me notice of his coming, Thorvard," Ulf replief placidly. "But even if he had asked, I could not possibly refuse him. Not after I pressed him so strongly to come a mere few months ago. Just think how awkward that would have been!"

"Why did you press him so?" Leif was curious.

"Vidar's daughters are very good-looking, sensible girls," said Ulf. "His wife had died a few years ago, and now that his daughters have reached the age to marry, the responsibility for finding suitable matches for them lies entirely upon Vidar's shoulders. I believe we have an understanding, which is yet unspoken, that it might be good if his daughters married our Stein and Bjorn, or to begin with, if the young people got to see more of each other. Do not worry. Vidar is our relation, he will not complicate the situation by asking unnecessary questions."

When Leif came to see Freydis, he tried with all his might to harden his heart and drive away pity which, in his opinion, she did not deserve - but it was plain to see how much his sister had suffered. She knew of his arrival and received him without surprise, but pressed his hand more warmly than usual.

"I have been expecting you, Leif."

"You have a comfortable corner here," Leif said, looking at the merrily blazing fire and the bench piled high with sheepskins and furs. "Thorvard is a man of his word – he did as he promised me and kept you safe, which is more than you deserve."

"I assume that was the reason why he did not kill me or just leave me behind to die," remarked Freydis.

"Be that as it may, he brought you here."

"Yes."

"He could have walked out of that hut, said he found no one, and no one would have been any the wiser, is it not so?"

"It is."

"You know," mused Leif, "Thorvard has acted very generously, you can't deny it."

"Yes," she paused, "I hate it."

"If you were in his stead, if you had found him hurt and helpless, you would kick him in the ribs, laugh and go on your own merry way, would you not?"

She rolled her eyes derisively and did not bother to answer. *You know me too well,* that gesture plainly said.

"You have always been an evil, unprincipled creature," observed Leif. "And the years during which there was no one to keep you in check only made you worse."

"I love you too, brother."

"I know," he said.

"You believe I got what I deserved for getting involved with them... with *him*? Right?"

Leif pondered this for a few moments. "I would not go that far, perhaps," he finally said. "Perhaps not quite what you deserved, but – I believe – what you could expect. Those were dangerous men. Ingvar Haraldson is a snake who values your life about as much as the dirt on the soles of his boots, and Svein Einarson was simply evil. Thorvard had avenged you. I hope you understand what you owe him now."

"I owe him nothing!" snarled Freydis. "I saved his life as well, or has no one told you? We are equal now."

But even as she said these words, she knew it was not the same.

"I hope you came to take me away from here," she changed the subject.

"Not quite so soon," Leif shook his head. "We had spread a rumor that you are visiting your aunt and intend to stay with her for a while. If you appear in Trondheim anytime soon, it will raise suspicions."

"I will go by myself, then, if you will not take me," insisted Freydis. "I won't stay here. I do not need your help."

"Truly?" Leif raised his eyebrows. "What, do you have another scheme that will get you into even deeper trouble? Not that I believe you can do worse than you already did. I still find it hard to believe you actually planned to crown Father and push him into direct conflict with Norway!" He laughed mirthlessly.

"It was a reckless plan, not outlined well enough," acknowledged Freydis, "but the general idea was brilliant."

"No," said Leif, "it was pure folly, from start to finish."

"You have no vision, Leif."

"Perhaps not," he agreed, "but unlike you, I have responsibility. Did they let you see Sygni?" he changed the subject

"Yes," said Freydis, "Dalla arranged it so that I can see her sometimes."

Dalla, thought Leif. *She of all people.* "Why are you in such a hurry to get away from your daughter again, then? What else is there for you in Norway before we sail home?"

Freydis said nothing. Actually she knew, they both knew, she no longer has anywhere to go. She dreaded the moment of meeting her mother and had not the slightest inclination to actually see her aunt. In the past, it seemed to her that disconnecting herself from the people she loved was a fit price to pay for being able to make her own way. Now it looked as though the way was lost and she remained alone. Always alone.

Later Leif shared a glass of beer with Ulf while the main hall was being readied for a feast in honor of the guests.

"I thank you," Leif said warmly, "for your hospitality, Ulf. Our lives were all saved thanks to your kindness and help. And Thorvard... I do not know how to even *begin* thanking him. I owe him my life, my honor, my freedom, everything... and so does Freydis. Even she has to admit that."

"We all love Thorvard like another son," replied Ulf. "Did you think we could stand aside when his closest friend was in need of help? No matter what I think of your sister, it was obvious she had to be concealed from the king's men. For your sake and for that of your mother and father, and perhaps for your entire settlement as well."

"Freydis was led into blindness and folly by her own ambition," Leif confessed, taking another draught of beer. "She had far too much influence on Thorvard, and the miserable consequences of that are known to us all. I wish she had not messed up so badly."

The older man sighed. "Would that she had not," he agreed.

"I told her to be ready for the feast soon," added Leif, "I hope I did not presume too much."

A shadow of a doubt passed upon Ulf's face. "I... I suppose it is best. Vidar will stay with us for a while, and we will not be able to conceal your sister's being here anyway. He had better see her at once, ask what he might, as awkward as his questions could be, and have done with it."

At the feast it did not seem as if there was any strain or awkwardness, though. The lads were quite happy to sit next to their fair cousins, but Vidar seemed even more gratified than the young people. He sat on Freydis's right, and made every effort to get her engaged in conversation.

"No, I am not often away from home," he told. "The lands owned by my family are extensive and need much care and supervision.

It is a beautiful area – a pity that you aren't familiar with it. The forests and fjords are so lovely, even in the midst of winter. The land is fertile and there are good places to hunt, and in season the salmon practically leap from the rivers and into our hands."

All Freydis had to do was nod, smile, and say a word now and then. For the first time in a long time, she felt almost at peace. It has been a while since anyone talked to her this way, simply, without an ulterior motive. It was as if she entered, for a little while, into a thin stretch of regular life, something she hasn't had for years.

She didn't notice how Thorvard observed them from the corner of his eye. He did so even when he appeared completely absorbed in the food in front of him. He saw how Vidar's eyes lit up when they first rested upon Freydis, and how they sparkled during their conversation. *My kinsman cannot be blamed,* he thought. Freydis was not a regular beauty, but she was a striking woman – no wonder Vidar couldn't keep her eyes off her.

"So, Vidar," Leif spoke while the two of them happened to sit together on the second night after the arrival of the guests. "Are you passing your time here pleasantly?"

"Yes, very much so," Vidar nodded warmly. He was a handsome, impressive man, almost as tall as Thorvard, though not so wide in the shoulders. "It is always good to strengthen family times, and it appears these ties will even be doubled if my daughters make the right choice... so I hope, anyway. And I wished to ask you..."

"Yes?" prompted Leif.

"Your sister and Thorvard... they had been married, I know. But their separation is final, is it not?"

Leif gave him a long, calculating stare, and recalled that Vidar has been a widower for a while now.

"Everybody knows of their separation," he said cautiously, not missing the satisfied expression upon Vidar's face. *Some very interesting proceedings might develop here.*

..."The moon is very bright tonight," said Vidar, "but not as bright as the beauty of the one beside me."

Freydis smiled, and very becomingly arranged a strand of red hair that got loose. "You do not speak in earnest, Vidar."

They were standing out of doors. The night was cold but no snow was falling at the moment, and they both felt the need for a break from the smoke, noise, laughter and beer fumes of the main hall.

"But I am," insisted Vidar. "I cannot find the words to describe how pleased I am that we met, Freydis. I always say what I think, and I think you are an incredible woman. I have never met anyone like you before."

"You hardly know me," protested Freydis, though not at all in displeasure.

"That is true," he readily admitted. "There is an air of mystery around you, a wall of secrecy I wish to break through. I want to get to know you. I want to know everything about you."

She glanced at him quickly. "Are you certain?" she asked.

"I think I know what you mean," said Vidar. "I am not stupid, you know. I have heard rumors about you, and I know you did not live the quiet life that could be expected of a woman at the furthermost corner of the world. I mean, if it weren't so..." he fell into an awkward silence.

"If it were not so, I would not have separated from my husband," Freydis went on plainly. He nodded, relieved.

"I have no intention to offend you," said Vidar. "All I want is to understand you, even if it takes time."

"What is it that you heard of me?" asked Freydis.

"Many things, only a few of which, I am sure, are true. There are those who describe you as evil itself, and now that I have met you, of course I cannot believe it. You are a woman who has her own opinions, no doubt. Determined, certainly. Ambitious, it can be easily surmised. But from here to blood-chilling descriptions of terrible sorcery..."

"Ah," Freydis cut across him. "Sorcery. I did learn the Hidden Arts, that is not a lie."

"It still doesn't justify all the bitter, unrestrained tongues of people. I want to hear your story from your own lips. Perhaps not today, perhaps not tomorrow. When you are ready."

Was this not what she longed for during all this time – a chance to show the other side of the coin, her own side? But suddenly Freydis felt too weary for speech. She bent her head and said quietly:

"I made many mistakes, Vidar."

"As did we all," he encouraged her with a gentle smile.

"Not every mistake is as irrevocable and has as bitter consequences as mine."

"Do not distress yourself," he said. "The last thing I want is to press you to tell more than you feel like at the moment. I simply wanted to tell you one thing."

"Which thing?"

He hesitated briefly. "It is never too late to start over."

She looked at him, and in her face a painful, silent doubt could be plainly seen.

"Do you truly think so?"

"Yes," he smiled, "of course I do."

Chapter 29

One of Freydis's best comforts was the time snatched away with her daughter, Sygni. *This is a gift I do not deserve,* she had to admit – a gift she received, ironically, thanks to Dalla, that sweet girl who was intended as a new wife for the man Freydis had once loved so much. *She will replace me.* It pained her to see the look in her daughter's eyes, the look of a small girl searching unceasingly for a true mother who would be a loving, stable presence in her life. Well, as far as that is concerned, she had failed miserably. *Dalla is a much better fit for the task.*

Despite everything, I will be forever grateful for the chance to see my daughter. She could stay no longer, though, not even for Sygni.

What would she do next? She had no satisfactory answer. Come spring, she will sail to Brattahlid – there, at least, she can be of help to her father, and spend her days in useful work that might take the edge ever so slightly off the sorrow and regret that will be her constant companions for the rest of her life.

Leif, who was well aware of the awkwardness in his sister's presence under Ulf and Brunhild's roof, settled with her that they would leave together with the guests in the morning after the leave-taking feast and travel together to Trondheim, where she will be reunited with her mother and may begin to prepare for the journey back home. On the day of the feast Leif approached Freydis and pulled her aside, so that no one may overhear them. For some mysterious reason, he looked quite pleased.

"Well, little sister," he declared, "I don't know whether you are aware of this, but I have heard some very interesting rumors."

"I know," she replied, "they are attempting to keep this a secret, but almost everybody already know that a betrothal will be announced tonight. It looks like Stein succeeded, after all, in his conquest of Aslaug's heart."

"Ah, that, of course," Leif brushed her words aside with a negligent wave of the hand. "Well, as you said, it's already known. But that is not all. As far as I know, it may very well be that *another* betrothal is declared tonight."

She looked at him in surprise. "Another betrothal? But Vidar said that his younger daughter..."

"Not the girl, my dear sister," Leif said with a sparkle in his eye. "I know for a fact that tonight, before the visitors say a grateful goodbye to their hosts, Vidar intends to ask you to join him and take his hand in marriage. This is an extraordinary bit of news, is it not?"

Freydis could not reply at once and only looked at him in amazement. Actually, on second thought, she wasn't certain whether she is supposed to be astonished by her brother's words or by the fact that she didn't foresee this herself. After all, it could not be denied that Vidar admired her. They sat together, ate together, walked together, spoke of anything and everything in the world. She enjoyed his company more than she had enjoyed anyone else's company in the past two lonely years.

"Do you have nothing to say?" her brother pressed. "It appears you might have a future after all, Freydis. This would be a great opportunity, wouldn't it? A new beginning for you. A chance to leave behind all the foolish mistakes of the past. Vidar is completely charmed and will do anything to win you. And I appreciate him, you know. He is generous, loyal, well-respected and, above all, not stupid. He is a man you might esteem, otherwise I wouldn't think it is a good idea for you to marry him. You might start a family, be a respectable woman, and this time I hope you will not be foolish enough to lose everything. You can remain in Norway, in a distant province of course, but it's still better than Brattahlid. It might be," the bright expression of his face was dimmed for some reason, "that I will even become your husband's good-brother – Vidar had told me that she has a lovely sister, a young childless widow and not at all portionless, whose husband had drowned during one of his journeys to Iceland. Ever since her family has been looking for someone to marry her and give her children, and I might just be up to the task."

"You, Leif?" she was completely amazed. "Do you mean to say that you are seriously considering marriage - and of all possible matches, with a woman you had never even seen?"

"Why not?" he shrugged. "As you had said many times yourself, it must happen sooner or later. I am tired of fleeting adventures, and Vidar's sister sounds like someone who might be just right for me – good-looking, cheerful and sensible."

Freydis attempted to digest what Leif had told her. *He is right, of course.* This is a fabulous opportunity, the perfect chance to begin anew, probably the only chance she will ever have.

She attempted to imagine Vidar, with his big strong body and handsome face, standing very close to her, taking her in his arms, kissing her... the thought did not exactly repulse her, but the notion was simply so ridiculous that she could not suppress a weary smile.

"What?" Leif looked confused. "What is so amusing? And more to the point, what are you going to tell Vidar?" he waited for her reply with a more serious expression than before.

"I do not know," she said honestly.

For a long moment, Leif looked at her until a hint of understanding appeared in his eyes, along withan expression of both pity and disdain.

"You two," he said, "are the biggest fools I have ever had the misfortune to meet."

"Me and Vidar?"

"You know perfectly well whom I mean," he threw across his shoulder and moved away without another word.

Yes. She knew and he knew she knew, but she would rather cut her tongue out than say the words.

..."Cousin Thorvard," Vidar caught up with him after they both walked out of the bathhouse, where they had scrubbed themselves clean for the feast, "do you have a few moments so that we might talk in private?"

"Of course," said Thorvard, and the two men began to walk slowly down the narrow path leading to the barns which was currently empty but for the two of them.

"You know that my daughter Aslaug has made her choice, and tonight we will have a betrothal," said Vidar once he was certain they could not be overheard by anyone of the household.

"Yes," said Thorvard. "I congratulate you. Stein looks very happy, and it appears to be a good match."

"Thank you. Aslaug comes home with me tomorrow, but tonight we will already announce the betrothal to everyone. The wedding itself will take place soon, so that the young ones can start their life together."

"Well, I suppose you will want to discuss all the details with my uncle Ulf."

"Certainly," Vidar stopped and paused, as if looking for the right words. "Thorvard, I will speak plainly. I believe Aslaug is not the only one to have found her destiny beneath this roof."

Thorvard gave him his full attention and nodded for him to go on.

"You know I had lost my wife a long time ago," Vidar went on, "and it is not always easy to find a suitable bride to begin anew."

Thorvard nodded again. He knew that, perhaps better of all.

"I have been alone for many years, but now I believe I found her."

And yet Thorvard was silent. He already knew what he would hear, but could not think of anything to say to make the situation less awkward.

"I speak of Freydis," Vidar finally said. "Cousin, you do not know how much I wish to find the correct words to say this, without offending you and causing strife between our families. I would never allow myself to try and make away with someone else's wife. But I know that you and Freydis have been long separated. That is why I take the liberty to ask – have you given up on your rights as her husband? Is she free, or is she not?"

Like so often, Thorvard's face was inscrutable, not showing any feeling. For about a minute he stood in silence, immersed in his thoughts. He looked at Vidar, as if trying to figure him out. The expression upon his kinsman's face was of sincere discomfort.

"One word from you," said Vidar, "and I will never speak to her nor look at her again. I would never act so dishonorably towards my own relation."

"Freydis belongs to me no more," Thorvard finally said. "I have long given up on any connection I once had with her. She is free to do as she will and marry whomever she wants. I have no say in the matter."

Vidar studied his cousin's face carefully. This was the answer he had expected, the answer he had hoped for, but the tone of Thorvard's voice made him uncomfortable. The words were said with affected indifference, but one could not ignore the anger and pain underneath.

"And now forgive me, cousin," said Thorvard and began distancing himself from Vidar, "I still have a thing or two to take care of before the feast begins."

He might really have had some things to do, but Thorvard no longer remembered what they were when he moved away to his private place of solitude, behind the water well and the barns. From there he could watch the endless emptiness of the barren winter fields.

He could no longer think of anything but his short conversation with Vidar.

This, then, is how it is going to end. In a way unexpected, yet fortunate for everyone involved. She knew he ought to feel pleased by the knowledge that soon she will be far away. He tried to stem the outburst of irrational pain that caught at his heart and refused to let go. Again and again he told himself that it is ridiculous and humiliating to continue lusting after the one who had lied to him, used and manipulated him, betrayed him, mocked and humiliated him, threw away their love as a worthless old relic, and on top of it all, almost made him pay the price of his life for the mistake he made in trusting her.

Now it will finally be over forever. *And a good thing, too,* he told himself.

Many times he wanted, and intended, to start over with a new wife. Since Freydis had returned to her father's house, new offers began to appear for him, but he felt he could not give his heart to any of them. In fact, he only began to think of a second marriage as a real option when he came here and met Dalla – the pretty, good-hearted, sweet and gentle Dalla, whose mildness of manner reminded him of his own sister, Gudrid. *Yes, here is a woman who will be a good and faithful wife.* And yet he hesitated. Something prevented him from taking the next step – the next obvious, sensible step – and ask his uncle Ulf for his daughter's hand in marriage.

Eventually he came to the painful conclusion that even if he moves forward, no one can ever replace his wife. With her every day was a new world, and without her it seemed as though time had stopped. She was fire and ice, she was a gushing river – compared to her, anyone else was a pool of insipid water.

How can he make her go away, no only from his life but from his very being? She had gotten far deeper than just beneath his skin; she was the blood coursing through his veins, flesh of his flesh, soul of his soul. The bond which brought them together could not be reproduced, nor shared with anyone else.

That night, when he looked out of the corner of his eye at Freydis and Vidar sitting together at the feast, he wondered whether old Egil was right. Had he truly been too soft with her? He was blinded by love, he knew it. In his desperate attempt to keep their marriage from falling apart he forgot his conscience, his principles. He had been a toy in her hands for far too long. He refused to see her doubtful doings, her dangerous alliance with the Skraelings, her deep interest in the darkest sorcery. If he had seen it, and attempted to stop it, would that change anything?

217

Would she have listened to him? Could he have prevented the death of those poor people in Vinland, the destruction of his marriage? Could he have made her see reason before it was too late? Could he have prevented the rape and bloodshed of not long ago?

He didn't know. He could not know, and was not even sure he wanted to.

He only knew it is too late now. He had done his duty by her while she was weak and desperate, and now the obvious path for both of them was healing and a final parting of their ways. What else could he do? Get up from his seat, walk over to them, grab Vidar by the scruff of his neck, throw him aside and beg her to stay? That was impossible. He had taken too much from her already. His former attempts at reconciliation were met by rejection enough times to make him thoroughly absorb the message. She does not want him, and therefore he does not want her either, or at least this is what he must make everyone believe if he wishes to save what is left of his pride.

No one could deny Freydis was especially beautiful that night. It looked as if the nightmare was finally beginning to dissipate for her. Her wounds were healed, a slight smile lifted up the corners of her mouth. She simply looked as if she was having a good time. She was wearing a long blue dress Leif had brought for her, and her red hair was pulled back by a silk band embroidered in golden thread.

"Who is that skald?" Throvard asked Dalla, frowning. "He has the voice of a goat."

"Does he displease you?" Dalla wondered. "He passed through these parts, and my father invited him in tonight. He is well-known for his love songs, and Father thought some of them are fitting for the occasion."

Thorvard looked forward, frowning. He wished for this evening to be over soon.

He could do help observing furtively how Vidar did not take his eyes off Freydis, how he sat by her since the beginning of the feast and poured her cup after cup of sweet mead, how he leaned towards her and whispered something in her ear, how she nodded and got up and how they slipped together from the crowded, noisy hall and left the betrothal celebration behind.

Soon they will be back, Thorvard thought, *and the festivities will double.*

Outside, beneath a winter sky covered with clouds through which the silvery glow of the moon broke out from time to time, Freydis stood in front of Vidar and silently waited for what she knew would come. He had asked her for a private conversation, and now she was looking at his good, handsome face. It has been so long since she saw what lit up in Vidar's eyes as they rested upon her.

"Freydis," he cleared his throat. "I am not very eloquent when it comes to these things... it has been a long time since... but I cannot put this off any longer. Tomorrow we leave. I had not noticed how the time allotted for our visit had passed. It was all like a fleeting moment. I am very happy that we came... very happy for the chance to meet you."

"I, too, was happy to get to know you, Vidar," Freydis said sincerely. "It has been a while since I could talk to anyone as I talked to you. I shall miss that."

"It doesn't have to end tonight," he lowered his voice, took hold of her hand and pressed it warmly, "or at all. Come with me, and we can begin a new life together. Just give me a chance to win your heart, and I swear you shall never regret it."

Freydis was sorry for what must happen, but at the same time, a heavy burden rolled off her heart when she sensed clarity such as she had never felt before. She shook her head, sadly but very resolutely.

"You have been very good to me, Vidar," she said. "Far more than I deserve, and I shall never forget you. But what you suggest is impossible."

"I have thought of everything," he added promptly, "to avoid an awkward situation. I even spoke to Thorvard already, and he said that as far as he is concerned, there can be no objection."

Freydis knew that in the darkness of the night he cannot notice her pallor. Her heart was constricted with pain. *As far as he is concerned, there can be no objection.* Of course. No matter what she does, the divorce will soon be made final, and he will marry Dalla, who will make him a very suitable wife from every point of view.

An unspoken question appeared in Vidar's eyes, but she knew he would not dare to say the words aloud.

"My heart cannot be won," she said, "it can only be given away. I know you had loved your wife, so perhaps you understand what I mean. I could never go with a man who does not have my love already," she paused for a moment, "even if it means I will be left alone for the rest of my life. Can you understand that?"

He nodded, swallowing his bitter disappointment.

"I understand," he said, and pressed her hand again, with warm friendship. "And it makes me appreciate you all the more."

"Farewell, Vidar," said Freydis. "It is almost certain we shall not meet again."

"I will be back soon, for Aslaug's wedding."

"I know," her voice shook slightly, "but I will never return here."

Thorvard felt a hand on his shoulder and lifted his eyes from his cup without saying a thing. He was in no mood for talking. He saw Vidar before him, but to his surprise, the expression upon his cousin's face was far from jubilant.

"My friend," he said, "my daughters and I leave tomorrow soon after daybreak, and I doubt I will have time to take my leave of you in a proper way, so I will do it now. The hospitality of our uncle Ulf, of everyone under this roof, was beyond anything we might have expected. I look forward to seeing you again at the wedding of my daughter Aslaug."

He said nothing else and went back to his seat. Thorvard stared after him, trying to figure this out. He definitely noticed a hint of disappointment in Vidar's voice, and his shoulders were slumped a little when he sat back at the table. It seemed as if he had wanted to add something else but refrained from it at the last moment.

And Freydis did not return to the hall with him.

It could only mean one thing.

Without stopping to consider this, Thorvard got up and walked out of the hall. He didn't notice Dalla, who looked at him with compassionate understanding. She had given up on him, and on her pride, long ago now. She understood that her silent, reserved cousin would not be able to find comfort in her arms.

Thorvard hastened his steps, uncertain of what he intended to do or say, but determined nevertheless.

He found Freydis outside, at the edge of an open field, and her expression hit him hard when he approached. She had an empty, still stare, without either regret or hope. Her head was bent as if in prayer. Her hands clasped a small object, and finally she released it and let it fall upon the snow, where it sparkled in all the glory of black and gold. It was her amethyst ring. Then she got up to go.

"Wait," said Thorvard, his voice low and hoarse. She turned around and seemed to freeze. "Do you leave tomorrow?"

"Yes," she replied in a voice that did not shake, though he could not know what an effort it cost her. "We have lingered here far too long. Tomorrow we leave for Trondheim."

He stopped and took a breath, looking for the right words. He was afraid to speak, but he had to know.

He had to know.

"Vidar is going too, but in the opposite direction," he said. "I thought that perhaps you and Leif might be joining him."

"No," she said simply.

"Why?" The word was almost a whisper.

She looked aside, but he had time to notice her eyes were full of tears. Only a few times before had he seen her cry. Freydis was an excellent manipulator, but she was never good at feigning tears. There was too much steely hardness in her. In both of them, perhaps.

When she finally spoke, her voice could barely be heard. "Did not Leif tell you we are going straight to Trondheim?"

He said nothing in reply, but a question burned in his eyes. He noticed a shadow of despair in her stare, as if her entire life depended on his next words. But he said nothing, and finally she looked aside.

When Thorvard woke the next day, he knew without asking that she was already gone. Leif and Freydis had left at dawn, before most of the household people were up, dispensing with lengthy goodbyes.

Chapter 30

Leif made his way back to court with a heavy heart. It was true that he had completed the king's mission – the rebels were thwarted and hopefully he would be able to conceal Freydis's part in the whole affair, so that he and his family should be safe.

Still, the closer they got to Trondheim, the more confused he felt. He was unsure what to think as far as Thorgunna was concerned, nor how he would speak to her before he left for Greenland - what he might say to her when they meet, so he had imagined, for the last time.

Again and again he attempted to understand her, and could not. Not quite, anyway. He thought that her interest in him was superficial, until that night when he told her the story of his marriage and touched her heart.

King Olaf received him with great cordiality.

"You have served me well, Erikson," he said. "Rest assured, you will be rewarded. I know how to value determination and courage."

Leif inclined his head slightly in thanks. "I had good fortune, Your Grace," he said, "and very timely it was, too - for soon, we must take advantage of the currents that will enable us to return home."

King Olaf looked slightly less pleased. "You are determined to leave soon, then?"

"I fear I have not much choice in the matter, Your Grace. I know my father expects our return. I cannot disappoint him."

"Well, at any rate, this will not be your last visit to Norway," the king said encouragingly. "This thought will cheer you when you return to Greenland."

"Certainly, Your Grace," confirmed Leif, though privately he thought that nothing would cheer him better than the familiar sight of Brattahlid.

His meeting with Thorgunna took place sooner than he could have expected. It was the middle of the night, and the knocks on his door did not wake him until after a while. He was used to noises – the house he grew up in was far more crowded than this place, and there was not a hint of privacy for most of its inhabitants. Once he finally woke, raised his head and blinked, momentarily blinded by the flame of a candle that had not yet gone out, he hurried to the door – and on opening it, saw the figure of a woman in a dress of brown roughspun wool. Her face was covered against the night's chill by a faded dark cloak.

Without saying a word, she stepped forward, closed the door behind her and threw back the hood of her cloak. Leif exhaled in surprise:

"Thorgunna!" He meant to find some polite words, but his tongue failed him, and instead he cried, "This is madness! Someone could have seen you coming here and recognize you, no matter how you are dressed."

"The court sleeps," she said indifferently and looked at him with bold eyes. He made himself refrain from any gesture of intimacy. "I am glad to see you back safe and well, Leif. I was worried, for I knew, of course, where the king had sent you."

The warmth in her voice warmed his heart as well.

"Yes," he said. "I am glad you knew. I had to be gone so soon that there was no time for goodbyes."

"I know you are going home soon," Thorgunna went on. All of a sudden, she drew herself up to her full height and declared firmly, "I am coming with you, Leif."

A wave of gratitude, admiration and surprised happiness washed over him. He had not even dared to hope that she would suggest this, but at the same time his good sense refused to be ignored.

"I don't think that is possible, Thorgunna," he said softly.

Her mouth twitched as if she swallowed something bitter. When she spoke again, she sounded far more reserved than a moment earlier.

"I thought that what had come to pass between us... well, such things always matter more to women than men, I understand that. But I thought you realized, Leif, that I had burned all the bridges. I can no longer follow the path that was intended for me ever since I was born, and I see only one possibility before me."

"There may be several," Leif contradicted her, "but I fear none of them include your sailing to Greenland with me."

In the dim light he could not see the blush of humiliation that sprang into her cheeks, but her voice shook with anger when she spoke:

"You never thought to marry me, then."

"Of course not," he hastened to confirm. "How could I pretend to raise my thoughts to you? When you approached me that night... it was like a gushing river that overflowed, flooding everything around it. I have never planned, nor could I plan anything of the sort. I never thought that someone like you, a princess, could even take any interest in someone like me, let alone..."

"You never meant to say, then, that you do not want me?" she interrupted him, attempting to set things straight, and it seemed the words were painful for her to utter.

"Do not want you?" his voice softened. "What would not I give to change our respective positions, to make mine higher, or your lower, so that I might hope to win your hand! But as things stand now, the king will never allow a marriage between us."

"Of course he will!" exclaimed Thorgunna. "When we tell him what happened no other possibility will occur to the king, I assure you."

"But we will not tell him," Leif was determined. "I cannot allow that. A marriage between someone like you and someone like me is not even a debasement, Thorgunna, it is a fall into a deep abyss – not to mention the very real danger of the king's wrath. We cannot permit this to come out."

"You are giving me up," realized Thorgunna. Furious tears welled up in her eyes and spilled over her cheeks.

Leif didn't know what to say. Guilt caught at his throat with an iron hand. Of course, he was not supposed to allow this to happen! A maid of such beauty and innocence, who had given him her all on a sudden impulse – and how was he supposed to summon the strength to refuse her? *But I must do this – for her own good.*

"If it were in my power..." he began, but Thorgunna made an impatient noise. Her eyes burned.

"Well," she said in an unsteady voice, "I believe nothing but this will make you thoroughly understand the situation. I am with child, Leif."

He felt as if a mighty blow had sent him crashing down and sank onto his sleeping bench. From there he stared at her in amazement.

"How?" a senseless exclamation escaped him. The princess looked all steadiness and determination now.

"And I suppose I do not need to elaborate as to the identity of this child's father," she added.

227

"No, certainly not, but..."

In her face he read the pain of disappointment, and tried with all his might to regain his clarity of mind. *Now what?* He never imagined that such a beautiful, desirable woman will be so fiercely determined to marry him. And a child! After he had already despaired of ever having children of his own! But how can he do this to her? How can he condemn her to such a life?"

"It must be clear to you, then, that there is no choice," Thorgunna went on. "We must go to the king and confess everything. I know my uncle, he will be very angry and disappointed, and justly so, but finally he will reach the conclusion that now he has no choice but to permit us to do what is right and obvious, and get married."

Leif looked at her with amazement and admiration. Her sincerity and honesty, deserved far more respect than his evasiveness and reserve. Still, she was only seventeen, and he was much her superior in both years and experience, and knew the ways of the world.

"If what you wish for comes to pass, Thorgunna," he said softly, "you will lose more than you can imagine right now. Allow me to think of this for a bit."

She looked as if he had slapped her, so deeply insulted she seemed. "Think? What is there to think about? Are you not convinced that there is but one honorable way out of this situation?"

"We shall come to the king in the morning," Leif promised her, "It will not do to wake him in the middle of the night."

...Leif paced back and forth restlessly while his mother and sister sat side by side in shocked silence. Freydis was the first to recover, looking at her brother with an odd mixture of sly irony and appreciation.

"And you have the audacity to claim *I* was the one to put everyone at risk? Leif, what were you thinking? You will get us all killed!"

"That is why you and Mother must leave at once, until the danger has passed. You can go to Aunt Ingvild, she will keep you hidden."

"I see no need of that, Leif," Thjodhild said calmly. "King Olaf is a reasonable, sensible man. He would not unleash his fury upon an entire family simply because a man and a maid committed a reckless deed with predictable consequences."

Leif stopped his pacing. He looked utterly lost. "I do not know what to do," he confessed.

"Well," Freydis said serenely, "if Thorgunna wishes to get rid of it, I can prepare her an herb tisane that always works."

"Freydis!" her mother said angrily. "I do not want to hear a word of this! It is a sin against God, not to mention that you had promised to stop with your whispers and concoctions. Leif, Princess Thorgunna is perfectly right. The straight, honest way is the best. You must go to the king, tell him all, express your deep regret, and ask his leave to marry."

"That would be terrible for Thorgunna," said Leif.

"But she does not think so," insisted Thjodhild. "She chose you, just as I had chosen your father. I married Erik and never regretted it - neither the poverty, nor the loneliness, nor the loss of consequence."

"That is true, but you did not get sent straight from court to a remote corner at the very edge of the world. Thorgunna doesn't realize yet what she is about to lose."

"Something doesn't sound quite right to me in all this affair, you know," Freydis mused. "Yes, Leif, you have your attractions, and yes, many women have fallen for you already, and yes, I understand how your story had touched her heart, but still... something in her behavior... she was much too familiar with you to begin with. All these lengthy conversations, the invitation to her chambers... it was much more than what would have been reasonable. Have you not thought of that?"

"Yes," Leif said slowly, "I'm afraid I have."

"Do you realize what this means? We might all be sitting on a nest of vipers."

"Thank you for pointing this out, Freydis."

"Either way," concluded Thjodhild, "you are going to confront the king, and after he hears you out you will surely get married. I cannot pretend to be pleased by how this was done, but I congratulate you, Leif."

"She was not meant for me," said Leif, turning his back on them. Suspicion was beginning to nag at the back of his mind.

Chapter 31

After her son had gone, Thjodhild left as well – to church, while Freydis stayed in the chamber she shared with her mother. Leif was true to his word and did not allow her to go out unsupervised ever since they got back to Trondheim. His plan was to keep Freydis away from company as much as possible until they sail to Brattahlid, where she was meant to live a quiet and humble life under her father's protection.

Freydis did not object, which could testify to the extent of her alteration. Her great suffering had softened her, burned its terrible imprint into her mind, made her more cautious. She was very quiet now, so much that it made her mother and brother worry.

When Thjodhild got back from church, wshe looked at Freydis with understanding and pity, but also with a sparkle of excitement.

"My dear," she said in a voice that shook slightly with emotion. "I have outstanding news. Thorvard is here."

A moment later she was sorry for giving her daughter this notice without preparing her for it. Freydis paled, shivered and sat abruptly upon the bench near the fireplace.

"Here?" she repeated. "Do you mean to say you've heard he is in here, in Trondheim?"

"Not heard – I saw him and spoke to him, Freydis, and also told him where he might find you. I am certain he will come and seek you soon, as there can be no other reason for him arriving so unexpectedly." She gently smoothed her daughter's hair, "I always thought that your separation from Thorvard was the bitterest mistake that could occur," she said, "but now I believe all will come out right yet."

"Do you believe Thorvard can just pass over all that had been? He does not forget easily."

"Perhaps not forget, but forgive – you never even attempted to ask for his forgiveness! I am certain he was softened after he witnessed all you had gone through, and he probably also knows you refused Vidar, so he will understand..."

"I hope not," Freydis said quietly.

"I am going now," declared Thjodhild. "I want him to find you alone when he comes."

A shadow of hope mingled with terror darted into Freydis's eyes. "You cannot do this to me, Mother! No, you will remain here."

But Thjodhild walked out, and indeed, Thorvard soon walked in, looking awkward and self-conscious. He groped for something to say, and could not, until finally he opened his mouth almost unwillingly.

"Why?" he asked. "I want to know why, Freydis. Why was all I had given you never enough?"

"No one ever understood me," she whispered, lowering her eyes, unable to witness the accusation that burned in his. "You, my parents, Leif... I... I had seen things none of you can even imagine."

"Your sorcery again!" Thorvard exclaimed furiously. "I am so – so tired of it! It was the source of all our troubles!"

"But if you only knew..." Freydis whispered, "if you had known, perhaps you could justify me at least in part."

"If I knew... knew what? You never bothered to tell me."

Freydis swallowed the painful obstruction in her throat and looked in his eyes. "You would never listen," she said, "and even if you did, I doubt you could understand what was revealed to me."

"Try me," Thorvard said curtly through gritted teeth.

Freydis took a deep, steadying breath. She still didn't quite understand the reason of his coming, but suddenly it occurred to her that this might very well be the last time they meet. Unless... unless...

"One night, I was with the Skraelings," Freydis told, "and their old witch warned me of a danger that was looming closer. When I asked to know what she meant, she led me to the fire at the mouth of her tent, and threw in it a pinch of some black powder, and the fire changed its color to blue and purple, and she put her hand in the fire and wasn't burned, and told me to do the same – to put my hand in the flames and look."

Thorvard listened, torn between curiosity and anger, drawn into the tale despite his resentment. But then Freydis fell silent.

"And what happened?" he finally asked, moving his lips with difficulty – a difficulty of speaking on a subject he had tried to suppress for many years.

"And then I saw Brattahlid," Freydis went on, "Brattahlid consumed by flame. I saw our house, besieged by fire. And I heard battle cries, though all was quiet around – I heard them within me. And I saw you, all of you. My father and mother, my brothers... and you, Thorvard – I saw you upon the ground, lifeless, and myself walking among the bodies, the sole survivor of the massacre. And I saw something else – the sails of ships sailing away... ships with the sigil of Norway."

Thorvard was silent for a long time, and finally asked:

"When did that happen?"

"It was just before our wedding. I..."

"I remember," he cut across her, "I remember. I feared that you... that you had changed your mind. And so I feared to speak of it, demand to know what happened. But now I understand."

"From that moment," Freydis went on, "my entire life was governed by that black prophecy. I was certain that Brattahlid is going to be destroyed by the Norwegians, and I was determined to prevent that from happening. I could think of no other way to save our settlement except strengthening it in every possible way – expansion, well-developed trade, recruiting new people and... the powers I had been given - though without the knowledge of how to use them wisely."

"This, then, is the explanation of your foolish conduct in Vinland," growled Throvard. "This is the explanation to your reckless alliance with the Skraelings, which cost three of our people their lives."

"Yes."

"And this is also the reason why you got yourself involved in a hopeless plot against the king, together with that trickster Ingvar Haraldson! Ah, Freydis, Freydis! Could you not see that if there was anything which might have unleashed the king's fury against all of Greenland, it is precisely what you had done? If he had known you were involved, he could certainly decide to destroy your home as a measure of warning!"

"It is clear to me now," said Freydis with eyes full of tears, "but back then it did not occur to me that I am acting precisely in tune with the prophecy, that I am laboring to fulfil it with mine own hands."

"And does it have to come true... that prophecy?" asked Thorvard. Fear seized his heart despite himself, despite his usual lack of faith in such things.

"The old woman I had met while staying in your uncle's house," said Freydis, "you know, the one who helped me get some of the herbs I needed for making a potion that would cure you... she... her powers are great, far greater than mine, but she does not use them the same way. That was her choice."

"The old woman of the woods?" wondered Thorvard. "She is a real witch, then?"

"Yes, and with a talent such as I could never dream of. A greater mind, too. And she told me that, indeed, Brattahlid will be abandoned..."

Thorvard held his breath.

"... But not in my time, nor that of my children, or grandchildren, or great-grandchildren... our settlement will grow strong and prosper for hundreds of years."

"In that case, the prophecy..."

"She opened my eyes, Thorvard. I understood that the Skraelings are no friends to us, I understood that the vision I saw in the flames was not a warning, but a clever trick of that witch, so that we would be certain we are facing death, and thus might decide to leave out of fear."

"I always told you not to trust the Skraelings," said Thorvard. "But you would not listen. You never even told me! If only you had told..."

"Do you truly believe it would have made a difference? Would anyone have given it any consideration? You, my father of Leif? Of course not! I knew from the start that I am alone, that I will have to act by myself, to the best of my ability... and the best of my ability cost too dearly to everyone involved. To Helgi, Tur and Gudrid, to you and me, to Sygni – and if it weren't for your efforts, and my brother's, we might all have been in a lot more trouble now. Only now I feel that the snowball has stopped. I was foolish and full of false pride, Thorvard."

"This," he replied, "goes without saying."

She did not reply, but gave him a look full of hope, stubborn and fearful at once. Thorvard thrust his hand into a leather pouch that hung off his belt, and a moment later, when she saw what he held in his outstretched palm, Freydis made a step back and shook her head.

"I don't want this anymore," she said.

"Can you at least tell me what it is about this ring?" he asked. She hesitated.

"There was a time when I had done much to get my hands on it," she finally said, "but now I believe I shouldn't have. It is a long story."

"Something else I was not supposed to know?" he demanded. "You were always so determined to hide all your doings from me, were you not?"

She stared down at the floor, breathed deeply and linked the fingers of her two hands, so that he would not notice the shiver that suddenly took hold of her. The tension in the air was tangible. Freydis tried to say something, but discovered her voice no longer obeys her.

"You had once called me a sentimental fool," Thorvard said bitterly. "Unpleasant words, but very true. When it came to you I was always a fool. I was a warrior, a hunter, a sailor – people followed and respect me, but with you I acted like a lackwit. I never truly understood who you were. If I had, I would not be so surprised to see all you proved you are capable of."

And still she did not reply, for she knew there was nothing to say. He was angry, she knew, very angry, but she preferred to hear his accusations rather than have him erase her from his life in cold estrangement.

"Damn it," he said quietly, "did it really have to be this way?"

"It can be any way you want," she told him.

"I am tired," said Thorvard with suppressed vehemence. "If only you knew how tired I am of all this."

They were meant to be together, and their unnatural separation cost them dearly – more dearly than those two stubborn ones were ready to admit until that moment.

Propelled by a force that never truly relinquished its hold on him, Thorvard made a few steps forward, towards her. His mind and body were quickly spinning out of control. One moment, and he pressed her against a wall, feeling her quick, startled breaths as her body was crushed against his. Another moment, and he towered over her and split her lips in a kiss that was almost an assault.

For a second he still had presence of mind enough to wonder whether he is doing the right thing, but then he felt her mouth open under his, and she moaned softly and quietly with yearning too long suppressed. Her arms were around his neck, her hands buried in his hair, caressing his face. He longed to say something, anything, but could not draw his lips away from her mouth, her neck, the curve of her shoulder. Nothing but the feel of his body against hers could properly express the passion, frustration, longing, loneliness, fury, pain, love, sorrow and, against all odds, hope.

They were blind and deaf, the world around them ceased to exist. They were clinging to each other as if to stop touching would mean death.

"Don't stop," she begged, "or I will believe you are having second thoughts."

"You are mine, then," he said through gritted teeth, and pulled her even closer. "Mine. Do you understand?"

She pressed against him with a soft moan of longing, of satisfaction, of love and pain.

"I am yours," she whispered, "I could never belong to anyone but you."

A couple of hours later, Thorvard found himself upon the narrow bench, covered with furs, on which Freydis slept. She rested by his side, her head pillowed on his shoulder, and with infinite tenderness she raised her hand and cupped his cheek. It was so good to feel her like this, close to him, that he hardly dared to breathe.

And then, without a warning, she turned her face away and began to weep.

Thorvard raised himself up on his elbow, trying to suppress the gnawing worry. "What is it?" he asked uncertainly.

She gave him a fleeting glance and looked away again, weeping and holding his hand tightly. "I ruined you, my love. I ruined everything."

Thorvard was grateful for the clouds that now obscured the moon, for the possibility to simply hold her and be with her in her grief. He could not find his voice, for it seemed something sharp and painful was obstructing his throat.

"My beloved," he said finally, quietly, "most of all, it is yourself that you ruined."

Her face was now buried in his chest, and tears flowed freely down his cheeks into her hair. He made no effort to stop them. They grieved for all they had lost and all they had gone through, and though he never felt a pain such as this before, he knew it is inevitable if they are to truly go on.

"Have you ever thought," she said, lifting her tear-stricken face up to him, "how it could have been if I had never done what I did – if I hadn't allowed my ambition to rule me – if I had never meddled with sorcery – if I had simply found my satisfaction in our home, in being your wife? We would not have lost our friends. We would not have lost so much time, or lived as if by a dormant volcano. We could have been like everybody else... we could have been happy."

He had often thought of this, and his thoughts were bitter and painful, but now all he wanted was to comfort her. She was consumed with guilt and sorrow.

"It is my fault," she wept, " it was all my fault. I think I – I always knew it, even when I blamed you, when I blamed others. It was easier to accuse someone else. But I was the one who ruined our family. And now there is nothing I can do to change this. Nothing, nothing at all."

She did not say "forgive me". She did not dare. Instead, she knelt by his side, still holding on to his hand with all her might.

"I didn't want them to die," she said, and her voice was so hoarse he could barely make out the words. "Helgi, Tur and Gudrid. It is my fault, but I never meant for them to come to harm. Do you believe me?"

He nodded. "I always knew that," he said softly. "We all did. No one doubted it. At first, you believed you are doing what is right. Later you allowed pride and the desire for revenge to ruin your soul. But Freydis, there is still time to mend everything."

"You must leave," she whispered. "I do not deserve this. I do not deserve to have you stay."

But even as she said this, both her hands caught his and held them as if her life depended on it.

"I forgive you," he said, caressing her hair, and his voice broke. "I forgive you, my love. The debts are paid. You need not punish yourself any longer. You are my wife, and we must be together again."

When she raised her head and looked directly at him, he saw that her face is glazed with tears.

"You are so good, my love," she whispered, "you have always been so good and generous. But I fear nothing can undo the damage I have caused."

Thorvard pulled her close to him. "No one can change the past," he said, "and no one can know what might have been. All I know is that now you are by my side again, and that is what matters, and I will not let anything get in the way of it."

"My beloved," she said softly and kissed him, but in her eyes, in the touch of her lips was such sorrow that he felt as if his heart would break. "If anyone should have told me I must die for this one hour with you, I would do that happily."

"But you will not die," he told her. "I need you. The loneliness had been too great, too long. I need my wife. You are mine again now."

"Now and forever," she whispered, leaning into him.

Slowly, sounds of the world around them began to impose upon their consciousness – the muffled sounds of steps and conversation that could be heard outside the door. They got up from the bench and pulled their clothes on as quickly as possible, expecting Thjodhild to return at any moment. She was not tardy in coming; her face wore an expression that clearly spoke of her being torn between the happiness of seeing Thorvard and the regret of not making her detour longer still.

"Don't mind me, children," she said "I was just going out again."

But Thorvard took her aside and whispered:

"I beg you, do not go. I must go myself soon, and I don't think she should be left alone."

Thjodhild looked at her daughter with concern. "Can you just tell me..." she began.

"I am going back to bring Sygni," Thorvard explained promptly, "and then I will sail with you. I am going back to Greenland."

Thjodhild's face lit up with joy. "Oh, my son, how wonderful! Erik will be delighted to see you back, it will give him such joy!"

"I will be back as soon as possible," promised Thorvard.

"Don't worry, my dear son," Thjodhild whispered, pressing his hand affectionately, "she will be fine. All will be fine now."

Chapter 32

The kind paced back and forth, cloak swirling, his face red with fury. All of a sudden he stopped and spun around forcefully.

"You betrayed me!" he cried with uncharacteristic emotion. "You, Erikson – I had been most generous to you, I raised you up, I gave you an opportunity someone of your descent could hardly have hoped for. I offered you enviable prospects, I put my life in your hands, I promised you my assistance – well, it turns out I made a grave mistake! And you, Thorgunna – you were like a daughter to me, I loved you, I meant for you to be the wife of my heir and the queen of Norway..."

"Thorgunna is almost a child," Leif intervened. "The responsibility is mine, and mine alone. Your Grace, I will not blame you if you strip me of all my possessions, throw me into prison or even execute me, but I ask for just one thing – be fair to my relations. They knew nothing of what had happened; I am the only one to blame."

"*No!*" Thorgunna cried out suddenly. "No, my father, Leif is innocent! I was the one who insisted on remaining alone with him in my private chambers, I was the one who kissed him!"

The king's furious glare burned into the girl's pale face. "You were supposed to make him loyal to the church and to me!" he shouted in an outburst of anger. "You were meant to feed his admiration and hope, not get him into your bed like some cheap harlot!"

Upon hearing these words hurled at the princess, some part of the puzzle fell into place in Leif's mind. He looked at Thorgunna and the king with glum satisfaction.

"Ah," he said, "I knew something here is very odd. This, then, is how I can account for the extraordinary attentions my family and I received from the princess."

"No!" Thorgunna turned to him, desperate, pleading, tearful. "No... I mean, it was so in the beginning, but that soon changed once I got to know you. The greatest part of what happened between us was not planned. You must believe me, Leif."

Well, then, she is not as innocent as I thought. This made things more straightforward and slightly lessened the guilt and compassion he previously thought were her due. He spoke to the king.

"I understand that now His Grace has given up on a marriage between his son and Princess Thorgunna," he said.

"Quite!" the king scoffed. "It will not occur to me to let Sigurd have the leavings of some -"

"There is a solution, though. There must be enough earls in Norway who would be most happy to have Thorgunna for a wife, even knowing of her condition. You might easily find a husband for the princess, one who would take her far from here, and if the notice of the babe's birth is spread with some delay, no one should suspect..."

"In other words," said the king, "you expect someone else to take responsibility for your actions."

"No," said Leif, "I am trying to lessen, however I can, the price Thorgunna will have to pay for our reckless deed. The princess is too young to be condemned to a life of penance for one thoughtless act."

Thorgunna looked at him in pain, biting her white lips, but he avoided her eye. The king frowned, thinking over Leif's words.

"No," he finally said. "I have made my decision. I give you leave to marry, and you *will* marry her." He looked at his niece with a bitter smile. "You get to have your heart's desire, Thorgunna. You will sail to Greenland with your new husband, and as far as I am concerned you may spend the rest of your life there, shivering with cold in front of a pitiful fire and eating seal meat. I wish you good fortune." Then the king turned to Leif.

"Naturally, I cannot permit my niece to marry a pagan. You have the rest of the day to spend in remorse, prayer and preparation for your baptism. I will make sure Father Wilhelm is alerted of tomorrow's wedding, and that will be the last time I see you both. Neither of you will return to Norway for as long as I live. Now get out."

When Leif realized that his fate is sealed, his feelings were mixed. Despite everything, he felt an upsurge of joy for not having to say goodbye. *She will be my wife. She will give me a child.* On the other hand, he had no illusions – this would be a harsh blow for Thorgunna. He was not at all certain that her affection for him, no matter how overpowering it might seem to her right now, is strong enough to pass such a test.

There was also the slight disillusionment of knowing she was involved in a petty scheme against him. All this unexpected attention he so wondered at, the invitation to supper, their lengthy conversations – it was all sanctioned by the king... all except for that fateful moment when she bent over him and pressed her mouth against his.

"I am sorry," she said with a quivering lip. "The king wished me to influence you, to extract knowledge from you... I didn't want to do that, not this way, but I couldn't openly refuse, and – "

She looked so fragile, so wary of his reaction. He felt a hot and powerful surge of pity, compassion and longing all mixed together. "Please," he said, "don't you worry about that. I understand." Gently, he touched her face, brushing a tear away with his thumb. "Fear not," he went on, "the king exaggerates a little. It is true Greenland is a bit meager, but it's not all that bad. We do have good food in season. Only the Skraelings eat nothing but fish and seals."

She took his hand in hers. "I am not worried about that in the least, Leif," she said. "I mean to be very happy in Brattahlid."

Leif shook his head doubtfully, with the forgiving disbelief of a man listening to hopeful but ill-based assumptions of an inexperienced child.

"I do," Thorgunna insisted. "My life will not be what I always thought it would, but it will be beautiful and full of good things – things worth living for, worth remembering."

She spoke openly, bravely, and this put fresh heart in him. *The chance might be slim, but perhaps it will be possible after all.* He looked in her eyes and searched for something that would make him easier, but all he saw was the excitement of a girl going on a fabulous adventure, without the sober attitude necessary for a wife and a mother. *She will learn,* he thought with a stab of regret, *and perhaps sooner rather than later.*

The baptism ceremony was performed just before the wedding, and Leif accepted the entire process with obvious indifference. He hardly heard the pompous voice of Father Wilhelm pronouncing with great importance the words of the prayer; hardly felt the holy water touching his brow.

Right after the baptism, the priest began the wedding ceremony. He ordered Leif to kneel by Thorgunna's side, and made the appropriate vows and blessings. The priest's voice resonated in the nearly empty church; the only ones present besides the couple were Thjodhild, Freydis, and His Grace the king. The bride and groom were dressed in simple, everyday attire, Thorgunna in a dress much humbler than those she used to wear every day while she was a princess, a position she had just lost. *Well, she has no choice but to get used to this,* Leif thought with resignation.

After they exchanged rings, Father Wilhelm pronounced them to be man and wife and wished them a long and happy life together. He sounded perfectly serious, and Leif wondered where he learned such composure.

Thjodhild was the only one among the present whose face expressed undiluted joy, though she attempted to be more reserved in face of the king, who approached the newlyweds with a grave expression.

"You are my niece, Thorgunna, blood of my blood," he said, "and despite the disappointment I rightly feel, I hope you will find reasonable contentment in your lot –I trust you will lead a sensible and humble life, as is appropriate for a woman in your new position."

"Thank you, Your Grace," the princess replied, "I hope a day will come when you are able to forgive my husband and me."

"It is a great comfort to me," the king went on, "to know that even in the remote corner of the world where you are about to travel, the purifying presence and holy counsel of Father Wilhelm will continue to guide you."

"What does His Grace mean?" Thorgunna asked in confusion

"Yes, what?" Father Wilhelm joined the inquiry, paling.

The king looked at him gravely, and continued in a tone of fake heartiness.

"I understand this is quite a surprise for you, o holy Father, but this decision came to me only today, just before dawn, when I was tossing in bed and sleep evaded me. I cannot permit my niece to sail to a place full of idol worship, a place without a priest and a church. There must be a holy man who undertakes to spread the message of our Lord Jesus in Greenland - and who can accomplish this task better than you, Father Wilhelm?"

"I... I... I think..." mumbled the horrified priest, whose fluent, convincing eloquence was suddenly all gone.

"What a good idea, simply wonderful, Your Grace!" Thjodhild exclaimed happily. "I will personally take charge of constructing the church, and I am certain my husband will give his consent as soon as the light of the true faith shines upon him. He cannot remain indifferent after meeting Father Wilhelm."

The king bestowed upon her a nod of consent. Father Wilhelm remained mute with indignation. It was obvious he was shocked and horrified at the notion of sailing to Greenland, but what he said aloud was,

"Of course, Your Grace. Your word is law."

Leif noticed the lack of enthusiasm on the priest's side and pitied him slightly. Father Wilhelm surely wasn't to be envied. The destiny of the priest, however, occupied him for no longer than a moment. He had more important things to consider.

While he stood on board of the ship and watched the coast of Norway fade away, Leif thought it was highly unlikely he would ever return. He didn't regret this all that much as far as he was concerned, but Thorgunna was another matter. He noticed a tear, hastily swept away, rolling down her cheek as she threw a last desperate glance at the homeland that was fading away before her eyes. He came closer to her and put his arm around her, and she leaned into him. *My wife, she is my wife now.* The thought was still disorienting.

He looked at Freydis standing beside Thorvard, close to him, happy, with Sygni held tightly in her arms. Thjodhild was not far off, observing the family scene with great complacency.

The only one who looked displeased was Father Wilhelm. The expression on the priest's face was a mixture of sour, frustrated and cautious. The kind-hearted Thjodhild tried as much as she could to soothe him and quieten his fears at the face of the journey. *Well,* thought Leif, *if Mother decides to stand by his side, perhaps this fool might be able to present himself before Erik the Red without his knees buckling.*

As for himself, he decided, he would try not to miss the moment when his father meets the priest. *This promises to be highly amusing.*

Part 2

Chapter 33

Though the journey to Greenland passed as smoothly as could be hoped for, it was a long, tiresome sail, especially for Princess Thorgunna in her condition. The common morning sickness was given more virulence by the sea voyage, but she gritted her teeth and bore it all without complaining, even when she could barely move or eat. The one who liked to complain and rant was actually Father Wilhelm, who all of a sudden forgot the virtues of patience and forbearance.

By the time the ship approached Greenland's coast Thorgunna felt better and was able to look on with a fluttering heart, surveying the beautiful wild land that was going to be her home from now on. When they reached the fjord of Brattahlid, she found enough strength in herself, and in Leif's arm that supported her, to descend towards the crowd that came to welcome them.

"There is your father!" Thjodhild cried happily, running off like a girl. Indeed, they noticed a stoutly built, wide-shouldered man with greying red hair and a long beard in which the vivid shade was better preserved.

"Erik! Erik!" panted Thjodhild, rushing to her husband with shining eyes and an expression of longing quite unusual for someone who had been married for thirty years. Erik was more reserved, and the warmth of his feelings was expressed only in how long he held his wife's hand as he inquired after her health, and in the fact he had eyes for no one but her at first.

"I am glad you are come back, my wife," he said.

Then he looked upon his eldest son, who hurried meet him, and upon the young woman leaning on his arm – a woman of stunning beauty and of a nobility that shone in her every gesture. Erik had no way, of course, to know who she was, but was nevertheless astonished to hear Leif's next words:

"I hope for your blessing, Father. I am married."

The next thing Erik noticed was the cross that now adorned Leif's neck, as well as that of the girl. A faint shadow of explanation began to take form in his mind. Could it be that his son accepted a baptism to gain this woman? It didn't seem like something Leif would do, but for such a beauty, who knows...

It was then that Erik noticed Thorvard, with Freydis and Sygni by his side. He received his son-in-law with exclamations of pleasure, for Thorvard's return was his dearest wish, and his reconciliation with Freydis a dream he hardly dared to indulge.

"Thorvard, my son! How happy I am to see you! What a pleasant surprise! And if I may ask - "

But his wife already placed a hand on his shoulder, and her lips were very close to his ear when she whispered:

"Erik, please, send the children off to bathe and change their clothes after the journey. There are a few things I must tell you."

..."She is with child, then," nodded Erik. "Well, I do not suppose they would be allowed to marry under other circumstances."

"The king was so furious," Thjodhild told him. "Rightfully so, of course. But what matters is that eventually they were given leave to marry."

"I assume Leif had no choice in the matter," remarked Erik.

"Why do you speak so?" his wife said in reproachful wonder. "You do not mean..."

"The girl is beautiful," said Erik, "and she seems kind. But I am not at all certain she is the kind of woman Leif needs. Life here is very humble compared to what she is used to, and I fear she will grow frustrated. She was brought up to be a queen, not a farmer's wife in a remote land."

"Leif thought so too," said Thjodhild. "But I believe you are both wrong. She loves him, Erik. I have a feeling that this will be a very happy marriage."

"I hope you are right," Erik shrugged in resignation. "What is the point of going over what is already done, after all?"

"I am so happy to be home, Erik. For so many years I have dreamed of Norway, but when I finally came there, I realized that my true home is now in Greenland. And so many times I felt guilty for leaving you here alone..."

"Well, if you had not gone, neither could Freydis," said Erik, "and if she had not gone, Thorvard would not be back now. As Thorvard has returned, this journey was worth everything – my missing you, the complications Leif created for himself, even what Freydis had to go through. If what you had just told me is true, how foolish she must have been to get herself involved in such a scheme! I hope that now, finally, she will settle down."

"Freydis changed," replied Thjodhild. "She suffered much, and Thorvard with her. But they must make it right now. They love each other so much."

"I hope she will be wiser this time," Erik said curtly and pressed his wife's hand. Only now that she was back did he understand how much he had missed her.

"I wanted to thank you, my husband," Thjodhild said, "for your pleasant treatment of Father Wilhelm."

In truth, Erik had ignored the priest completely and very openly, but Thjodhild was content. She had expected worse.

When the holy father's name was mentioned, a shadow passed over Erik's face and he got up, distanced himself from her a little and crossed his arms.

"Let us make this clear once and for all, Thjodhild," he said. "I always gave you free reign – too much so, perhaps, I would say now. You decided to become Christian, and you are within your right. I see you swallow every word that comes out of this priest's mouth. I am surprised, and not favorably so, and I do not like this, but I have no intention of interfering. Just do not get the idea, please, that I'm encouraging any of it."

Thjodhild shifted uncomfortably at the blunt directness of his words.

"I am certain, Erik, that when you get to know Father Wilhelm a little better - "

"I have no such intention," Erik interrupted her. "If you insist on building a church here in Brattahlid, well, you have my permission. But you can be sure *I* will not go near there. And I will tell you something else – this new faith will make all of you soft. I have great fears for the brave spirit of my men."

"What are you talking about, Erik?" protested Thjodhild. "There are some great warriors in Norway, and they are all Christians!"

She was a little disappointed by her husband's reaction, but it had not been unexpected. And he had given her permission to build a church - that is what matters.

But Erik shook his head stubbornly. "Christianity will be the end of the Vikings," he said, "but I do not suppose I can stop this process. There are enough Christians here already, and they, of course, will rejoice in the coming of this priest. He, of course, will have no objection to performing Thorstein's wedding ceremony."

"What?!" exclaimed Thjodhild. "What do you mean?"

Erik looked at her with amusement. It was so like him – to keep astonishing news to himself, and then throw it in her way all at once!

"Thorstein is going to be wed," he announced to her. "Soon, Thjodhild, we will have two married sons."

"But... who is the bride?" Thjodhild inquired, attempting to get over her confusion. "Of course, Erik, this is wonderful, I am very happy, why did you not say - "

"He is to marry Gudrid."

"You cannot mean... Thorbjorn's daughter?" Thjodhild gaped in astonishment.

"The very one."

"But... Erik... how can this be? We were always certain that Gudrid rather prefers Thorvald!"

"It turns out that our two sons have competed for the girl's heart for quite a long time, and eventually Thorstein won, for he is Christian, and so is Gudrid."

"Christian? Are you certain that we are speaking of the same Thorstein, Erik? Our son? When did he become Christian?"

"When he understood that is the way to win Gudrid," replied Erik.

"Well, as far as I am concerned, it does not matter whom of our sons Gudrid chooses, as long as we still have her in the family."

Erik spread a handsome feast in honor of his dear ones' return. *But however generous my father is, this is not the court of Norway* – so Leif thought while observing his wife's face intently, expecting to see the first signs of painful awareness that

253

she had made an irrevocable mistake. Thorgunna looked serene and well-pleased enough, though. The smell of roast meat had hit her nostrils with a force that made her experience another surge of sickness, and she chose the fish.

"This is a very interesting fish," she remarked, looking at the specimen in her plate – a very long fish, silvery and scaly, with wide fins. "I have never seen any like it."

"It is a local fish, daughter," said Erik. "We call it 'the longboat'. I believe it is distantly related to salmon."

Not far from them, Father Wilhelm was playing with his food gloomily.

"Have another drink, holy father," Thjodhild surrounded the priest with excessive hospitality, despite her husband's obvious vexation. "And allow me to put some of this meat on your plate. I hope the ale is to your taste – I'm afraid we have no wine here..."

"What kind of meat is this?" Father Wilhelm asked, chewing a small bite with some apprehension.

"Seal," Leif said lightly. The holy father choked and spat it all out.

"Leif!" his mother exclaimed in anger. "Of course this isn't seal meat, Father Wilhelm. It is salted pork."

But the priest did not touch another bit of meat throughout dinner and claimed to be satisfied, in the good Christian tradition, by bread and fish.

Thorvald sat across from Leif, as far as possible from his brother and rival Thorstein who was sitting on the opposite end of the table. Thorstein was bubbling with unbound joy and telling anyone who was prepared to listen all the details of his upcoming wedding. Thorvald pretended not to hear, and tried to produce as much noise as he could scraping his knife against his plate.

Gudrid, Thorvard's younger sister, was the complete opposite of her brother in her looks. While Thorvard was tall and dark, Gudrid was of a small stature, and had long, thick hair the color of honey, and very clear light grey eyes. She was a graceful, sweet, sensible and good-natured girl. Leif wondered that she should prefer Thorstein to Thorvald. It wasn't that he loved Thorvald better than Thorstein, but the quiet, gentle-spirited, dreamy, soft-hearted Thorvald always needed his protection more than reckless, thoughtless Thorstein – and Leif was sorry that Thorstein, who could have chosen any one out of dozens of girls, should win over Thorvald, who had always loved but one.

Unaware of what either of his brothers was thinking, Thorstein called from his place:

"I suggest raising a toast to my brother Leif and his new bride! People have named you justly - you are Lucky indeed, and those who have doubted it need only look at the lovely woman you brought here."

"Yes, we are quite fortunate in our new arrivals," Erik remarked with quiet vexation, shooting an unpleasant look at Father Wilhelm. No one heard him amidst the appreciate cheering and banging and clanging of cups.

When the feast was over, Leif led Thorgunna to the house he had built so long ago and in which he hadn't lived since Maura's death. The passage of time had dimmed the memories and dulled the pain, but something still lingered in the air when they crossed the threshold. *The first woman I brought here had been a slave, and the second a princess.*

"It is a humble place, I told you," he said modestly, "but there is a nice soft bed, and I took care to have the house thoroughly cleaned and heated so you shouldn't be too uncomfortable."

"It is lovely," Thorgunna said warmly, lifting up the oil lamp in her hands so that she might see better.

"If you have no objection, I still have some directions to give to the household men," said Leif. "It might take a little time. Go to sleep, you need not wait for me."

When he returned to their chamber, Thorgunna was already asleep. Leif observed her peaceful face, illuminated by the weak light of a fluttering candle, and was filled with remorse. The room was so small and poorly furnished compared to what she had been used to, he thought with a pang of sorrow – a simple room with walls of thick wooden logs, without carpets or tapestries. He also noticed that all the blankets and furs in Thorgunna's possession were piled atop her. *She must be cold,* he thoughts regretfully.

Finally, he must have made some very slight noise, for she opened her eyes and looked at him:

"Leif?" she called. "Why don't you come?"

He made a few steps, sat down on the edge of the bed, and took her little hand between both his own.

"Can you forgive me?"

"What for?" she wondered.

"For wavering so much," he replied, "for doubting you."

"You wanted what is best for me," she said after a moment's silence. "I understand."

"Then you have no regrets?"

She gave him a wry smile. "I probably should, as we had sinned," she said, "but otherwise, we would never be allowed to be married."

"You were right," he said. "You were right all along. If I had left without you, I would have regretted it until the end of my days. I just hope that you... should not be sorry," he finished quietly.

Thorgunna smiled and lifted her hand to his face, caressing his scruffy cheek.

"This is the first time we get to be alone since the wedding," she remarked. "I'd say we should take advantage of that. It's a little cold, but you'll keep me warm," she smiled, snuggling close as Leif got in the bed and slipped his arms around her.

Chapter 34

Upon the morrow, quite early, Leif had an unexpected visit from his brother Thorvald. Some of last night's dejection was gone from his face, but he still looked more somber than usual.

"I'm sorry for bothering you so early, Leif," said Thorvald. "I know this is not very gracious when coming to call on newlyweds. But I must speak to you."

"It is no trouble. Thorgunna is still asleep, but I have been up for a while now. Have you broken your fast yet?"

Leif offered his brother milk, hard-boiled eggs, cheese and fresh bread, but Thorvald ate little and spoke even less, slowly and methodically breaking the bread and slicing off bits of cheese with his knife. Finally he looked up at his elder brother.

"I plan to sail to Vinland," Thorvald said.

Leif couldn't say he was truly surprised. "When?"

"As soon as possible. I know we had settled that we'd sail there together," Thorvald hastened to add, "but I suppose you will not want to leave your new wife in her condition."

Leif perked up and raised an eyebrow.

"Freydis told me," explained Thorvald, a little embarrassed.

"Of course," nodded Leif. *How predictable.* Well, it was obvious to him that people would soon guess anyway.

"I understand that you do not intend to stay for the wedding?"

"It would be quite unnecessary," said Thorvald, "and I doubt I will be missed."

Leif pondered this for a few moments.

"If you do not wish to attend the wedding," he finally said, "and believe me, Thorvald, I understand you if that is so, you can always arrange for a journey to Iceland. You don't have to go southwest. Vinland is attractive but dangerous – don't forget, we've already witnessed enough to know the Skraelings are not to be trifled with."

"And yet *you* meant to return there," bristled Thorvald, "or is the danger of the Skraelings so much greater when it is me we are talking of? Do you think me unfit to lead the expedition?"

"Thorvald, do not be offended. You know you have less experience in both navigation and battle, that is all. These is a simple fact."

"But you have a wife now," said Thorvald, "and you are going to have a child. It means you must value your life far higher. I, on the other hand..." he didn't go on, but merely shrugged his shoulders bitterly.

"Listen, Thorvald," Leif began, "for all it's worth, I truly think it would have been much better for Gudrid if she..."

"Please, let us not talk of this," his brother stopped him, wincing. "Gudrid made her choice, and I wish her and my brother every imaginable happiness. Just answer this, Leif – will you help me?"

There is no sense in arguing with him, Leif thought, though a sharp twinge of worry prickled his heart even then.

"You know I would do anything for you," he said. "Just promise me you will take Einar and Stein with you. They have sailed with me before and know all the paces. If I know they are with you, I shall be comfortable."

Thorvald asked to see the maps, and Leif brought them out – the rolls of parchment containing knowledge that was more precious than gold – and unrolled them upon the table.

"See," he said, "always take care to sketch your maps – I hope you bring back some more detailed ones. Here, these should be useful, especially if you have unexpected currents or a storm."

"I should not have any trouble if the west coast is within my sight at all times, should I?" asked Thorvald.

"I believe so, but you never know for sure. Look, you must sail south – past Helluland and Markland. Vinland is to the south – and these are the Skraeling lands across the bay. Stay away from there - those parts are far more densely populated than Vinland, and you won't have enough man with you to feel safe."

"Thank you, Leif. I will take care to have a copy of this map made."

And I will take care to check your gear and supplies at least twice or thrice before you are on your way, Leif thought to himself. He was not at all comfortable with the idea of Thorvald sailing without him, and this wasn't the vexation of an explorer knowing he will miss out on a famous adventure. He was concerned about his brother, and he didn't think this journey was a very good idea. He understood he can do nothing to make Thorvald change his mind, though.

Still, at that point he did not yet completely give up on the idea of preventing the expedition from setting out.

"Thorvald has no knowledge of those parts," Leif told his father, "and let's face it, he's not good at navigation – not good enough, anyway. It would make far more sense if he waits until such a time when I can sail together with him."

Erik frowned. Thorvald, his middle son, quiet, reserved and sensible, always got a lesser portion of the attention which was divided chiefly between Leif – the elder, clever and promising one, and young Thorstein, the reckless braggart and

260

heartbreaker. Thorvald's presence was prominent mostly at such times when he had to take upon himself the task of making peace between his two brothers.

"I agree with you," said Erik, "but I cannot blame Thorvald for wishing to get as far as possible from Thorstein and Gudrid just now."

"He loves her more than Thorstein ever will," Leif claimed with bitter zeal.

"Leif, we all love Thorvald dearly, but Thorstein is a good lad, and will make a good husband to Gudrid, I am certain of that."

Leif even tried speaking to Thorstein, so that his youngest brother might convince Thorvald to stay for the wedding as a gesture of reconciliation – but the rivalry between the brothers, although it never came to a state of an open feud, created an estrangement. Thorstein was indifferent to Thorvald's intended journey.

"It is not my fault," he claimed, "if he cannot stay here and face the fact that he lost and I won. It isn't my fault, either, that Gudrid is too lovely to give up just to spare Thorvald's feelings."

Leif's last hope was to sell Thorvard the idea of joining his brother on the expedition. But here some very material objections arose: Thorvard's father, Thorbjorn, was ill and needed his son at home, and furthermore, Thorvard had no wish of leaving Freydis so soon; he was even less disposed to take her to Vinland with him, out of fear that her resentment towards the Skraelings will drive her out of her senses again.

And so all that was left for Leif to do was make sure that Thorvald is well-supplied and accompanied by the best men upon his journey to Vinland. This didn't make him quite at ease, but he attempted to suppress his concern.

...The wedding ceremony of Thorstein and Gudrid was conducted with great festivity in the new church that was built in Brattahlid within a very short time, under the supervision of Thjodhild, who was Father Wilhelm's boldest champion. The small church did not have space enough to accommodate all the guests, and many crowded outside, waiting for the moment when the newlyweds come out of the dim space into the bright sunlight of the longest day in the year.

Leif and Thorgunna waited outside. Though being among the young couple's nearest relations, due to Thorgunna's condition they preferred not to squeeze in with the crowd. They had already given their good wishes anyway, along with the presents. Thorstein got an expertly made mail shirt from Leif, and Thorgunna gave Gudrid several rolls of beautiful Byzanthine silk.

Finally the bride and groom came out arm in arm, to the cheering voices of their friends – Thorstein, proud and merry as a young cock, and by his side the lovely Gudrid, blushing with excitement. They made their way towards the tables that were spread out beneath the sky which wouldn't grow dark – only soft twilight will mark the middle of the night.

Leif looked at his wife, beautiful despite her swollen belly, dancing with innocent merriment in the women's circle – an array of colorful dresses and waving scarves. The bride and groom, meanwhile, shared a drink from the wedding chalice.

Freydis came and sat down by her brother's side, her face flushed from dancing and her eyes bright. Leif did his best to erase the expression of concern from his face.

"Is anything amiss?" his sister asked.

"I am not sure she should be doing this in her condition," he replied, gesturing in the direction of Thorgunna, who was still dancing.

"Nonsense, Leif."

"She ought to be more careful."

"Thorgunna is a young, healthy girl. A little exercise will surely do her good."

He didn't speak and looked away, to the other side of the table, where Thorvard was bouncing Sygni on his knee.

"I know what you are thinking of," declared Freydis.

"Truly?" he gave her a half-smile.

"Yes. You are remembering Maura, and you are worried. But fear not, Leif. Thorgunna is young and strong, she will give birth easily."

"Maura was young and strong too," he said quietly. "You can never know which woman will encounter difficulties in the birthing bed."

"Look, I just *happen* to know all will be well," Freydis lowered her voice importantly. "Trust me."

He half-smiled and raised his eyebrows. "Truly? I thought you had given up on your attempts of fortune-telling, given the disasters it had brought upon you."

"I did that only for your sake," Freydis said, vexed, "so that you might be at ease, and I expected some little bit of gratitude."

Thorvard should know of this, thought Leif. Sorcery and fortune-telling had remained too strong a temptation for Freydis.

"I hope the last notice of Thorvald subdued your concerns a little," said Freydis.

Indeed, not long ago one of the ships that had sailed with Thorvald's expedition returned home, and its crew brought highly satisfactory news from Vinland – the settlement was being built, there was plenty of timber, more than enough food to put up stores for the winter. And the Skraelings have not shown any sign of life. Thorvald, who knew his letters, sent a short note in which he wrote that he is well, and inquired after the health of all the family. With his letter he sent several updated, more detailed maps of Vinland's coast. The ship that arrived had already sailed back, taking more people and supplies with it.

All this was satisfactory, of course, but still Leif could not help thinking that if things had worked out differently, Thorvald might have sat now in the groom's chair beside Gudrid, the happiest of men, while Thorstein would dance upon the meadow together with the other guests, happy and not at all embittered, as the loss of Gudrid wouldn't have brought his spirits down for a very long time.

Freydis tapped her brother lightly on the shoulder and went to sit with Thorvard again, while Thorgunna left the circle of dancers and came to lean on her husband's arm. She smiled at him with shining and her cheeks were flushed.

"Everything is so lovely, Leif," she said warmly. "If we could have had a wedding feast, I would want it to be just like this one."

All around them the short northern summer was at its peak, rushing to make time for an outburst of abundant life – fields full of golden and white flowers, rich green meadows, blooming woods, the earth humming with the sounds of birds and animals hastening to mate, give birth to their offspring and raise the next generation. Thorgunna's belly, too, was full of life when Leif rested his hand upon it. He felt the kicks of his unborn son and put an arm around his wife, happy in her happiness and ready to do all it takes so that she comes to no harm.

"Do you miss Norway?" he asked her after a brief hesitation.

"I do, naturally. But I am happy here."

"Truly?"

"Truly," she nodded, beautiful as the summer, fresh as the green meadows dotted with endless flowers.

The feast had already reached the happy stage when the bride and groom got up and walked away to their wedding-night, but the celebration refused to stop. Under the light sky there was the sound of merry voices and the tap of dancing feet, and the beer and mead and wine bubbled in an endless flow.

"I feel like this *is* our feast," Thorgunna said.

And Leif felt the same. He reached for his cup and took a deep drink. Suddenly, all his worries seemed insignificant, and he was in the mood to celebrate.

Chapter 35

Leif stopped and wiped his brow. This was the tenth time he went round the house, and no one came forward to meet him, or told him anything, or gave him a soothing message. *How helpless are men in such situations!* He recalled that terrible day, nearly six years ago, when he paced back and forth just like now, waiting for the birth of his son – he was told to keep away so that he would not hear his wife screaming out in pain, but he could not go, he remained close to the house walls, helpless, frightened, horrified, furious at his impotence.

Now he heard nothing. Complete silence, the most terrible silence of not knowing. Screams, groans of pain would at least have told him she is still alive...

His mother came out to him, pale and tired – the labor pains had begun in the morning, and now it would soon be evening. Thjodhild had spent all this time with her good-daughter. Her son's eyes bore into her face in desperate hope, and she placed a hand on his arm in a soothing gesture.

"Please, speak," asked Leif.

"There is not much to tell yet, my son. The labor is progressing slowly, it is common for a first time. With you, my dear, it took me a whole day and night, while my fourth time lasted only an hour."

"So there is no way to know how much longer it will be?"

"I believe, and the midwife agrees with me, that we are nearing the end now. Do not fear, Leif, soon you will be a father."

He nodded, unable to say anything.

"Come inside, my son. I will tell someone to bring you something to eat. You haven't eaten anything all day, you must keep your strength."

"I am fine," said Leif and began pacing again, but the autumn nights were already cold and he came inside the house, where bread, fish and beer were brought in front of him. He poured a cup and drank, but could not bring himself to eat.

He thought of his wife. She gave herself to him in an impulse of a moment which he ought to have stopped. He took her away from her entire world without promising her anything in return, except that he should be as good a husband as he can, and would give her a decent life as much as his resources allow. What could he offer her, after all – a widower, a man much older than herself, of a social position so degrading compared with her own? But to his incredible good fortune she loved him - and how will he feel if this day does not end well?

And then he finally heard something – a flurry of excited voices, and a strangled scream of his wife, and then footsteps, and a small, weak cry of an infant just born. As if in a dream, Leif got up, but could not make even a single step forward and remained frozen in place until his mother came to him, beaming, her eyes shining with happy tears. She reached out to him, put her hands on his arms, and looked into his face.

"You have a son, my dear," she said. "A wonderful, strong, healthy boy. I congratulate you."

A son! His heart leapt, and he pressed his mother's hand with great emotion.

"And Thorgunna?" he asked, holding his breath.

"She is just fine. She is resting now. I am so happy for you! I will go straight away and order the servants to send several jugs of our choicest wine to Father Wilhelm. This morning, when the labor has just begun, I ran over to church and asked him to pray for Thorgunna unceasingly."

The fact that Leif didn't sneer at hearing this could testify to the strength of his feelings. He felt as if an immensely heavy stone had rolled off his heart. He has a son, and both of them – his wife and his child – are alive and well!

"When can I see her?"

"She is waiting for you, my dear."

When he entered he saw Thorgunna upon the bed, reclining on her pillows, and her pale face, which shone with utter joy, was turned towards the small bundle in her arms. When she heard his steps she looked up and smiled. He approached her, feeling awkward due to his great happiness, and kissed her brow softly.

"How do you feel?" he asked, sitting down on the edge of the bed next to her.

"I am fine now, just very tired. I know you were terribly worried, my love."

Leif did not respond – there was no need to. Without saying a word, she held the babe out to him. Gingerly, terrified of breaking this tiny and fragile human creature, Leif extended his arms and accepted his son's gentle weight.

"He is beautiful, is he not?" Thorgunna said proudly.

"He has your hair," observed Leif, noticing the chestnut-colored fuzz on top of his son's head. The little eyes, when they opened, were of a light, indistinct color that could turn into blue like his, or green like hers. The babe, who nursed at his mother's breast not long ago, was resting in his arms in sleepy contentment.

"What shall we name him?" mused Leif. "Which name would you prefer?"

"Erik, like your father?" suggested Thorgunna. "Or Thorvald, like your grandfather? For years I had thought I should name my firstborn Olaf, to honor my uncle, but in our current situation it can only vex him if he hears of it..."

Leif stared for a long moment at the tiny human being cradled in his arms.

"Thorkell," he finally said. "His name shall be Thorkell."

"Thorkell Leifson," Thorgunna nodded in agreement, "that is a good name."

"You must rest," he said, "and eat as much as you can."

"I do not feel as if I can eat yet, but I will be happy to get a cup of warm milk."

"I will make sure it is brought to you. How happy I am that all ended well, my sweet!"

"I had a good feeling throughout the labor, you know, as I knew that a holy man like Father Wilhelm is praying for me."

At another time, Leif would probably take advantage of the opportunity to throw some joke at Father Wilhlem's expense, but right now he couldn't care less. His wife was alive and well, and his son rested in the sweet sleep of a rosy newborn. Even twenty two-faced, hypocritical priests could not have tainted his joy

Chapter 36

The sickness was terrible that year. Actually, the local diseases were always harder on the Greenland settlers than those they had in the Old Country, and they were always hurt first, much worse than the Skraelings. But that year the sickness was especially bad, and deadly to such an extent that no one in Greenland felt safe from it. It reached even the most secure places, which made Leif determined about asking his wife to remain within the four walls of their home, together with little Thorkell, and to avoid receiving any visitor whose health was not thoroughly inspected.

"I know you are going to get very bored during such a long, lonely winter," he told her apologetically, "but I will simply go out of my mind if you or the babe should get sick. I must insist. Forgive me."

Thorgunna's pressed his hand warmly. "You are right, my love. Of course we must all remain at home as much as possible. But what about you?"

"I will try to be as careful as I can, too. But you understand, of course, that I don't always have a choice. Apart from our own affairs, I must help my father run the settlement."

Thorstein, on the other hand, loved to pay visits and didn't see fit to change his habits. Despite getting a good house and a nice slice of land from his father upon his marriage, he preferred to spend his time, together with his new wife, in the houses of his many friends, who threw feast after feast in his honor ever since he was married, and pressed him to stay with them time and time again. And so, in the midst of the sickness and the snow storms, Thorstein found himself cooped up in the house of one such friend. But there was no great festivity in it. Everyone was morose due to the many victims the sickness had claimed, and everyone wanted desperately to know when it will end.

One day during that visit, when Gudrid entered the main hall, she saw with puzzlement that the table and benches were moved aside, and that a little wizened crone is standing in the middle of the room, together with several of the household women. When the crone saw Gudrid, her wrinkled face lit up with pleasure.

"Ah!" she called. "Now we are seven!"

At the same moment Thorstein entered as well, accompanied by some of the men. He was pale and tried in vain to suppress the fit of coughing that raked his throat.

"Are you unwell, Thorstein?" Gudrid asked fearfully.

"I'm fine," he replied bravely, attempting to subdue a fresh fit of coughing. "It is nothing, just a little cold. I should have taken my warmer cloak when I went out last night."

But Gudrid bit her lip with worry. That winter, every cough or cold which in another situation could have seemed as nothing became a source of fear.

"Who is that, Thorstein?" asked Gudrid, gesturing with her head towards the old woman.

The owner of the house, whose name was also Thorstein, looked a little awkward. "We – as a matter of fact... ah... we wanted to ask – we believe she can know what this winter will bring, and when this accursed sickness is supposed to pass away..."

"You mean to say she is a witch!" Gudrid exclaimed angrily.

"Come, child!" the old woman called her, ignoring the exchange.

"It cannot hurt," shrugged Thorstein.

"I am Christian," declared Gudrid. "I do not deal with such things – and neither should you, Thorstein!"

"Please, Gudrid," begged Sigrid, one of the other women in the house, their host's sister. "Without you we can do nothing. We need seven women. All you need to do is stand in this circle."

Besieged by the many requests, the soft-hearted Gudrid could not help but give her consent. The old woman lit three fat, tall candles in the middle of the room. They gave off the smell of a bad egg and a greenish, cold-looking light, spreading no warmth. After that, she ordered the six other women to form a circle around the candles together with her and join hands. One of Gudrid's hands was squeezed in the crone's wrinkled claw, and the other held on to Sigrid's shaking, sweaty palm.

The old woman began a slow, monotonous chant that dulled the senses, and together they all walked round and round the candles, until the flames danced in Gudrid's eyes and her head spun. Sometimes, the crone's chanting was punctuated by strange, high-pitched exclamations such as, "how much longer?" and "let us alone!"

Finally, the chant turned into a whisper, and the going around the candles slowed down, and the flames have steadied, and all stopped. The old woman let go of Gudrid's hand, and she in her turn hastened to pull her fingers away from Sigrid's. Sigrid was breathing heavily with fear.

"The disease will soon leave this house and all of Greenland!" the witch declared with satisfaction. And then she turned to Gudrid, and looked at her, for some reason, with special affection. "And you, my dear, the gods shall reward with a long, happy life, and a rich, kind husband!"

"I am already married," Gudrid replied coolly. What did Thorstein *think* when he brought here this shameless fraud?!

Despite the cheerful predictions of the witch, the condition of the household people did not improve. By the end of that day, Thorstein was no longer strong enough to stand on his feet, and had to go and lie down. He expressed hope for speedy recovery, due to his nature which always inclined to hope for the best, but both he and Gudrid knew deep down that his situation is grave. It was true that the stores of the house had enough food and firewood to hold on for a pretty long time, but the storm cast them apart from the rest of the world, and they had no possibility to call for someone whose knowledge in healing surpassed that of the old bragging witch.

"I shall go and pray for you, Thorstein," said Gudrid and kissed her husband's sweaty brow. "Prayer will surely help more than this crone's ugly spells. Try to sleep. I will be back soon to sit by your side."

"I don't know if you should, Gudrid," Thorstein said suddenly in a weak voice. "It might be contagious."

"Do not talk so," Gudrid said calmly, though fear prickled at her heart as well. "Surely you did not think I would leave you, my love!"

In one of the corners there was a place of prayer for Christians, and a bench next to it. The image of the Crucified Man was upon the wall. Gudrid knelt before it and whispered a warm, fervent prayer for the recovery of her husband Thorstein, and for the sickness to leave Greenland soon, without taking more victims from among the faithful children of Jesus.

After some minutes, Sigrid joined her in the prayer corner, and Gudrid noticed with fear that the young woman doesn't look well either. Her eyes were very bright, her cheeks pale and sunken, her breath heavy and shallow. She looked at Gudrid desperately.

"You know we are lost," she whispered.

"What are you talking about?" Gudrid shivered.

"Me and many others in this house. Your husband Thorstein as well. We are about to die. We will not live to see the end of this sickness."

"Nonsense!" Gudrid said dismissively and got up from her knees in anger.

But when she returned to her place by Thorstein's bed, she saw with a sinking heart that his condition had worsened. He was very weak and pale, had difficulty breathing, and though he attempted to hide this from his wife by coughing into a square of cloth, Gudrid noticed with terror that thick, dark blood was coming up from his throat.

"This is the end, Gudrid," he whispered, and paused a little, "and I fear I did not do right," he added in a voice that could barely be heard.

"What are you talking about, Thorstein?" Gudrid tried to sound confident and soothing, though she understood his meaning very clearly, and felt a twinge of guilt as well.

"If only... if only I had a chance to speak to Thorvald again," said Thorstein.

"You will get well," said Gudrid, attempting to speak in a calm and assured voice, but unsuccessfully. "Thorvald will come back from Vinland, and you will talk and make peace. You must not give up, Thorstein!"

He looked at her with a sudden glint of determination.

"You must save yourself, Gudrid," he said. "This house is tainted by the sickness. Here, now my friend Thorstein has caught it as well. As soon as the storm dies down and you can get out of here, you must do so. I cannot stand the idea that you are in danger because of me."

"How can you talk so, Thorstein?" Gudrid cancelled his words with a desperate hand gesture. "You cannot think I would leave you here and flee!"

But that argument was, as it turned out, pointless. Thorstein passed away even before the storm was over, like a candle snuffed out by a gust of wind, and Gudrid felt his hand sliding from her fingers in his last moments. His breath stopped and his body became cold and stiff. Even before the first tears of grief had dried upon her face, it became known to her that Sigrid died as well.

Gudrid could have returned to her father's house, but she preferred to stay under the roof of her good-parents, Erik and Thjodhild. To that house, which she visited as a young happy bride, she chose to come now as a grief-stricken widow with sad downcast eyes.

"If you consent, I shall try to be a daughter to you, in place of the son you had lost," she said, holding out her hands to Erik and Thjodhild, "so that we may try to comfort one another."

"This house will always be your home, Gudrid," said Erik. "Always, until you marry again."

At one point during that same winter it seemed that the sickness is about to claim Thjodhild as well. The gratitude for his wife's recovery made Erik resign himself, to a certain point, to the death of his youngest son – or at least to contain his grief within reasonable limits.

"I cannot think of taking another husband," whispered Gudrid, and her eyes were hollow.

"Certainly not," nodded Thjodhild, smoothing the girl's hair affectionately. "Not at the moment, at least. For now, we will try simply to... live."

Tears poured from Thjodhild's eyes in an unceasing flow. Her poor Thorstein! To die so young, at the prime of his days, when he was just married! He had no time to beget sons, no time even to live in his nice new home! And poor Gudrid – so young, so pretty, and already a widow! The only thing that could console Thjodhild was the fact that Thorstein died after accepting the Christian faith, and therefore his soul is supposed to dwell in heaven now.

"It isn't right that my son should be buried this way," Erik shook his head when they stood by Thorstein's fresh grave. It was a temporary grave in the snow – they would have to wait until spring and thaw to dig in the ground. "He should not be wrapped in cloth and have a cross at his neck. He should have gone to the next world with his sword and battle-axe, and rise up in flames that would take him to Valhalla."

But he was the only one to think this way. Thjodhild, Gudrid and Freydis simply wept unceasingly for Thorstein, the young man who lived as if he knew he would have such a short time upon this earth, and therefore did his best to enjoy life as much as he possibly could.

That winter, Leif could not quite keep apart from other people, on account of his duties in the settlement. But he deprived himself of the company of his wife and son, unless he knew there is no chance for him to have met someone who would pass the sickness on to them. His efforts were rewarded – Thorgunna did not fall sick, and neither did the babe.

Now he sat in his father's house, facing the young widow of his brother Thorstein.

"I am sorry for your loss, Gudrid," he said.

"And I for yours, Leif," she replied.

"I do not compare the loss of a brother to the loss of a spouse."

He allowed her to interpret his words as she would. He grieved for Thorstein, but that was nothing to what he had gone through when Maura died. Yet Thorstein and Gudrid did not walk the same path as he did with his first wife. For Gudrid, Thorstein was her childhood friend, the love of her youth, someone who would eventually become a tender, sad, but painless memory.

"You know," Gudrid said slowly, "the night after he... passed away... I saw him in a dream."

"Thorstein?"

She nodded. "He smiled at me. He looked so peaceful and content, Leif. His face was illuminated by such light... I had never seen anything like it before."

"You should tell my mother of this dream. It will comfort her."

"He spoke to me, Leif. He told me I will receive a proposal of marriage after not too long a time, and that I must accept it. I shall be happy, so he said, and my husband will be a good man."

"It will very likely be so," Leif replied encouragingly.

"No, you do not understand... he spoke with such confidence, as if he knew something that neither I nor anybody else can. And when I woke, I remembered every detail of the dream with incredible clarity. Even now it stands before my eyes. It was really him, Leif. It was his gift of farewell."

..."I hope you had given Gudrid my condolences," Thorgunna said to him when he came home. "How is she?"

"She grieves very much for Thorstein, but she is young. She will recover and move on, I am sure."

"Maybe," Thorgunna spoke hesitantly, "when Thorvald comes back from Vinland, there might be a chance..."

"No," declared Leif. "I know Thorvald. His pride will never allow him to make a second offer of marriage to a woman who had preferred his brother."

"At least this terrible sickness is over," sighed Thorgunna. "Now we can all try to mend what had been broken, and get back to our lives."

She spoke with hope that was not meant to be fulfilled.

Chapter 37

Thorvald leaned against the hut's wall. His legs were shaking, his body rapidly weakening. He knew that the bar would not stop the Skraelings for long – they could easily set the hut on fire if they wanted to. But this didn't matter, as from any possible view he was already a dead man. The arrow's poison was coursing through his veins and his body was becoming heavy and weak, and the ships of his men have already left the shores in fearful haste, fleeing from the Skraelings who closed all around the camp in an unexpected attack.

Ah, their unforgivable leniency! Some months of peace, and people began to fall asleep on their guard, neglecting the necessary security measures. They thought the Skraelings have been resigned to their presence. Only he, their leader, was always suspicious, always mindful of Leif's last warning.

The enemies attempted to kill him first, to cast fear upon the camp, so that the foreigners might fall easily into their hands with the loss of their leader. But he had time enough to give a last order to Einar – run to the ships as fast as they can, raise sail and turn into the open sea.

The eyes of the good loyal man filled with tears of sorrow, but he knew his chieftain is right. Getting one wounded man on board would take time that might cost everyone else their lives. Their only chance was in abandoning him and fleeing instantly. *The sea is turbulent in early spring, but with the help of the gods, they will conquer it and reach home safely.*

And now Thorvald was about to die alone, in a strange, hostile land, without a familiar face by his side, knowing that his farewells to all his beloved – his father, his mother, Leif and

Freydis – were hasty, awkward and insufficient, knowing he cannot press their warm hands for the last time before passing on to the next world.

But he also knew that before he dies, before his eyes close forever, there is one last thing he must do.

With a shaking hand, he wrote several words upon a scrap of parchment, rolled it tightly and placed it in the secret hiding place Leif had set up when he built the house. What is the chance this letter will ever be received by his brother? Thorvald knew Leif would not rest before his bones are returned to Greenland, and if only the Skraelings don't set fire to the house, the letter might survive intact.

Leif! How much he longed for his elder brother to be here in these last terrible moments, when the mind is already becoming foggy but the body still stubbornly clings on to the last remainders of life. How short, how devoid of meaning his life had been! Gudrid... he hoped she should be happy with Thorstein, at the very least.

At least he managed to save his people. The lousy boats of the Skraelings can never catch up with the Norse ships, and if the bastards try, they will bemoan their sad fate. Thorvald's friends are already in the open sea, on their way home, carrying with them his sad story like homing pigeons bearing a letter.

He could almost see Leif's face contort with sorrow, could almost feel his mother's grief, Gudrid's belated regret. With his last remaining bit of strength he climbed upon his bed, a broad bench covered with furs – and the last thing he heard were the quick, fearless steps of the Skraelings walking through his camp.

~~~

Leif's sharp, well-trained eyes of a seafarer recognized the ships while Freydis, who was standing by his side, had just noticed some movement in the distance.

"These are the ships from Vinland!" he cried, and concern furrowed his brow. "And it appears that all the men are making their way back."

Freydis turned to him sharply, biting her lower lip in fear. "They were not supposed to return so soon!"

Leif didn't need to say more. The arrival of the ships at this time meant that the camp was hastily abandoned, and this could only be because...

...Stein and Einar stood before him, their heads bent, their eyes buried in the ground, knowing full well they had disappointed the trust Leif placed in them.

"Thorvald is not with you," Leif remarked in a calm voice, though pain had already begun gnawing at his heart.

"But we are all back only thanks to him," said Einar in a shaky voice. "Your brother is a true hero, Leif."

Leif could doubt no longer. "How did he die?" He asked.

Einar told, and silent tears rolled down Freydis's cheeks. She could not speak.

"He told me to leave," Einar said with a constricted voice, "and save the men. He was my chieftain, I could not disobey him. I had to leave him behind. And... he was right, Leif. Another few moments of delay, and the bastards would have caught up with us."

"So he was still alive when you saw him last?" asked Freydis, trying to conquer her shaking voice.

"Yes," said Einar, "but he was mortally wounded, and even if his wound left any room for hope, the Skraelings surely would not. Unfortunately, I have no doubt that your brother is dead, but he had died as befits a warrior."

"We should never have allowed him to sail there!" Leif exclaimed with grief, fury, and frustration, turning his back on the men. Freydis placed a hand on his shoulder.

"Do not blame yourself, Leif. You were the one who spoke against this journey more than anybody else. We, on the other hand – Mother, Father and myself – thought it might be for the best if Throvald got away from Thorstein and Gudrid while they..."

"There is one lesson we must all learn from this," Leif went on without listening to her. "We do not have enough human resources to found a settlement in Vinland while keeping the locals under control. They are too numerous. We cannot go back there."

"We must bring Thorvald's bones back," said Freydis stubbornly, wiping her tears away.

"Of course," nodded Leif, "but we must think how to do this so that we don't put more men in danger. Who will sail? Me? Thorvard? And when? Give me time to consider this."

"Our brother must be avenged," Freydis added, and an insane glint appeared in her eyes.

Freydis and vengeance – a lethal combination that must not be allowed, thought Leif.

"I do not intend to get myself into a deadly affair of waging war against the Skraelings of Vinland. They are far more dangerous than those of Greenland."

"I cannot believe this!" Freydis cried disdainfully. "Thorvald was your brother, you knew him. Do you think he would have threatened the Skraelings in any way? If they showed any readiness for parley, be it even in sign language alone, I am certain he would have made every effort..."

"I know," said Leif. "It must have been something they planned all along."

"They must pay for this," Freydis repeated, balling her hands into fists.

"Look, Freydis, for the time being, with Father ill, I cannot even think of leaving Brattahlid. We must wait a while. And... please, come with me to tell Mother. I can't handle this alone."

He made a few steps away from her and stood aside, looking into the distance, at the blue-grey sea, in the direction of the beautiful, tempting and cruel land which took his brother's life. Thorvald, so kind, clever, sensible, reasonable. Thorvald the adviser, the peacemaker, the childhood friend, the keeper of secrets, the assistant of countless plans. Thorvald, who loved and supported and would always listen. *He was better than all of us,* Leif thought with desperate, heart-breaking pride. *Too good for this world* – and he died alone, in a foreign land, away from all who loved him, without a comforting hand to ease his passing! *How odd is destiny,* thought Leif. Here, Thorstein the war-monger, the reckless one, the seeker of fights, had faded away in his bed, plagued by sickness – and Thorvald, who had never raised a hand against any man except to protect himself, had died a hero's death.

When they broke the news to their mother, she turned her back on them and stood this way for a long time – silent, straight as a lance, mute in her pain. When she faced them once more, she was very pale, her eyes wide open, as if attempting to see something that is beyond the vision of mortals.

"Please," she whispered, "tell none of this to your father."

Erik, who had begun to feel a little unwell close to the end of the winter, made Thjodhild fear that she had passed the sickness on to her husband. But the winter was over, and so was the sickness. Erik's condition had improved, and Thjodhild breathed a sigh of relief and thought the threat of sickness is over. With the arrival of the spring, however, Erik's cough had grown worse and he began to lose strength, and in the past few days the old fighter could no longer get up from his bed. Thjodhild was unwilling to admit defeat, she nursed him faithfully and did not leave his side day or night, but understood with painful clarity that she and her children must be prepared for the worst.

Thorgunna gently eased Leif's head into her lap, and her soft fragrant hair caressed his face when she leaned towards him and pressed against him with love and pain.

"My beloved, I am so sorry."

But her gentleness and compassion hurt him, constricted his heart with guilt for all that he had and Thorvald did not, in his life or his death.

"I should have made more effort to convince him to stay."

"I do not see that you could have done more than you did, Leif. Thorvald was a man, a leader – nobody could keep him home against his will."

"That expedition wasn't meant for him. It was to be my task. I know Vinland, I could have foretold the ways of the Skraelings better than he had..."

"Do not torment yourself, my love. You did all that was required of you, and much beyond that."

284

A knock on the door interrupted their conversation. Leif raised his head in frustration. "Who in hell..?"

But his wife's face lit up. "It must be Father Wilhelm."

Leif suppressed an impatient groan. *Not this accursed priest now!* But enter Father Wilhelm did. An unconvincing expression of shared sorrow was pasted onto his placid face. If someone had profitable handsomely from the terrible sickness that passed through Greenland, it was Father Wilhelm. Scared, desperate people came in droves to be baptized and receive abolition for their sins, instructions of prayer, hope for the future, and consolation for their lost loved ones who had gone from this world.

"Leif," the priest said in a deep, impressive voice. "Allow me to express my sincere condolences for the death of your brother at the hands of those bloodthirsty savages. I am very sorry I had not time enough to walk Thorvald through the gates of the true Faith..."

Leif could contain himself no longer. He stood up on his feet and looked disdainfully in Father Wilhelm's face.

"Well, *I* am not sorry for it," he said, stressing every word. "If Thorvald had been Christian, we could not burn his bones so that he might rise with the smoke straight to Valhalla."

And having said these words, Leif turned around and stormed out. Father Wilhelm looked after him, astonished and furious.

"Your husband cannot mean that, Princess!"

"I am no longer a princess, Father Wilhelm," Thorgunna said calmly.

"To burn a body! It is a grievous sin, the way of pagans..."

"You must forgive my husband, holy father," Thorgunna said with gentle determination. "It is the pain speaking through him now."

Once he had escaped, Leif closed his eyes and allowed the cool spring air to refresh his face. He turned around to the sound of hasty footsteps and saw Stein, looking pale and straight.

"Leif, you must go to your father now."

No, thought Leif. *Please, not yet, not now.*

He didn't say a word, but broke into a run. Freydis was already there when he arrived, and his tearful mother led him to his father's bed. Erik had melted like a wax candle in the course of a few weeks. His stout body had drained of flesh, and a grey beard covered a thin, sunken chest.

"Leif is here, Erik," said Thjodhild.

Erik turned to look at his son, and it was plain that this slight movement cost him a great effort.

"Come here, Leif," he said. Leif approached the sickbed with slow, measured steps.

"My son," said Erik, "my hour has come. From now on, you shall be the leader in Greenland."

"I do not believe I am ready, Father," whispered Leif.

"Of course you are not. But you will step up to the task, and I know you shall do well. Keep the people safe. Take care to protect and strengthen the settlement."

"I will, Father."

Erik coughed weakly. "I am sorry you have not stuck to the Old Way, but I suppose you had no choice. Still, try to keep Greenland as independent as possible. Make it so that we need not bow to anyone's will."

"I will do all I can to that end."

286

"And take care of your mother. Now that we had lost Thorstein, and Thorvald is far away, you are the only one left in Brattahlid to watch over her. I understand it will limit you in the journeys you wanted to make... will tie you to this place... but I fear there is no choice."

"That is of no account, Father."

"I have already told Freydis not to commit any more follies, but I tell you to keep an eye on her as well... and so I would have told Thorvard if he had been here. She needs protection, although she doesn't always know it."

Freydis, in her corner, made a strangled noise, something between a moan and a laugh.

"I will do my best to uphold the family's good name, Father," promised Leif. He searched for more words, but none came. His father gave a slow, satisfied nod.

"That is all, son. May the blessing of gods go with you, and with your son Thorkell, and with all your descendants until Ragnarok."

Leif reverently kissed his father's hand upon hearing this blessing, which would have made any good Christian revolt.

"Thjodhild," Erik called in a weak voice. She hastened to his bed and knelt by his side, pressing his hand to her heart in a desperate plea.

"I am here, my husband."

"You were a good wife to me, Thjodhild, although our life wasn't always easy. I hope you did not come to regret the day when you decided to run away with me and leave your father's home."

Thjodhild's eyes filled with tears, and her voice shook when she answered:

"Never, my love. Even after both of us are gone from this world, people will still remember how much Thjodhild, the daughter of Jorundar, had loved you."

Footsteps were heard outside the chamber, followed by a cautious knock upon the door.

"It is Father Wilhelm, my dear," Thjodhild said hesitantly.

Leif felt a rising wave of fury within him. *Is there no place in Brattahlid where one might go without the threat of meeting this damnable priest?*

"What does this fool want here?" asked Erik with a frown, and Leif felt a rush of affection and pride towards his father.

Thjodhild pressed Erik's hand and spoke fervently:

"I have one last request to make of you, my love... one single thing... please, accept the faith in the one true God, and his son Jesus, our Savior. Do this, Erik, so that your soul might be saved from hell and we can meet in the world to come."

Father Wilhelm came in, but at least had the decency to remain in a distant corner of the room.

"This priest had better take his sorry hide out of here," said Erik with his last remaining strength. "I will stick to the ways of the Fathers until my last breath. May the gods grant me entrance into Valhalla."

He closed his eyes and spoke no more. Within minutes Erik the Red, the admired leader and stubborn pagan, had passed away.

People came in and out, talking, shouting and crying, but Thjodhild did not move or speak. She simply remained there, kneeling, as if made of stone, holding with a desperate force onto her husband's hand, which grew steadily colder. Finally, with a supreme effort, she got up and turned to face her son. Her lips were trembling.

"Thorstein, Thorvald, and now my Erik as well," she said, "Now you are the only son who remains to me, Leif."

She lost the last shreds of resilience, now that it was no longer needed for Erik's sake, and collapsed into her son's arms, weeping. With wonder and pity Leif noticed how fragile her body feels, how thin and weak her arms are. Could it be the same strong, confident, comforting mother who gathered him in her arms when he was a child, making him feel safe and secure? He caressed her hair and noticed that the grey struck through it with powerful presence, overlapping the dark color of her youth. How her back had bent, how much older she had grown in so short a time!

Leif got out of the grief-stricken house and looked again at the sea, at the infinite, comforting, rolling vastness which might soothe any pain. His father died as an old man and his brothers had been taken young, Thorvald by an enemy's arrow and Thorstein by sickness – but the death is the same, black, silent, eternal, inconceivable - and it makes all equal.

Thorgunna approached him from behind and placed a soft hand on his shoulder.

"I can never go to Vinland again," Leif said with mournful resignation. "Not even to look for Thorvald's body."

"I wish I could contradict this, my beloved," said Thorgunna, "but you are needed here."

He knew it was so. He was the last heir, the last son left to his father, and he must step up to his task now, hoping that Red Erik's shoes will not prove to be too big.

"Well," he straightened his shoulders. "The first thing we must take care of is the funeral pyre."

"Do you truly mean..." Thorgunna began hesitantly.

"Yes. This was what he wanted, and this is what I mean to do."

They placed Red Erik's body in a boat. He was clad in his best battle gear, in a mail shirt and helm, and by his side was all that he would need for his journey into the next world: his sword, battle-axe and shield, a jug of mead and sacks of food, and a pouch of coins in case he needs to pay for his passage. Apart from that, gifts from all the men of Brattahlid were placed in the boat; even the most devout Christians came out to pay their last respects to the leader.

When the pyre was ready and Leif stood before it with gritted teeth and a torch in hand, Thjodhild turned away. Her face was glazed with tears.

"I am sorry, my son," she said. "I cannot bear to look."

She stood at some distance and turned her back on the great fire which began to consume the boat. It grieved her that her husband would not have a place of burial, but she knew he would always be with her, until her last day. And she knew that their faithful companionship will not be forgotten even in Valhalla, or wherever his poor soul, which did not acknowledge the presence of Christ, might go on from here.

Father Wilhelm observed the scene from a distance, with a distinct expression of mutiny upon his face. It vexed him exceedingly that Leif Erikson insisted on performing this pagan ritual in public. *To burn his father's body, shame on him! And this is the man who will be remembered as the chieftain who brought Christianity to Greenland!* The pious soul of Father Wilhelm found it hard to accept such glaring injustice.

Leif stood as close to the fire as its great heat would allow. The smell of burning wood engulfed him, and beads of sweat covered his face. He did not bend his head, but continued looking forward and upward, with courage which, he knew, his father would have expected of him.

When all was over, he came to his mother, wrapped his arm around her shoulders, and so they stood together for a long while.

"Now you stand in your father's stead, Leif," said Thjodhild. "Brattahlid is yours."

"Yes," said Leif, "although I fear I will never be more than Father's pale shadow."

Thjodhild smiled with sad forgiveness of his humility.

"You will be greater still," she said. "Your father was very proud of you. He passed away knowing he leaves a worthy heir after him. The day that comes will be yours, and yours alone, Leif."

Chapter 38

"I believe we should go and live with your mother," Thorgunna said a few days after Red Erik's body was consumed by flames.

Leif, to whom the idea had occurred as well, felt a rush of gratitude towards his wife for bringing it up herself. Within a very short time, it was settled and done.

With the constant company of her son, her two good-daughters and her little grandson, and with frequent visits from Freydis, Thorvard and Sygni, Thjodhild began gradually recovering from the blow she had suffered in losing two of her sons and her husband, to whom she had been married since she was a girl of sixteen. But still they all passed a glum, joyless summer, a summer of incessant rain and loneliness within the four walls of the house.

It was obvious to all that at some point another expedition must be sent to Vinland to look after Thorvald's body, but nobody was going to do that anytime soon. Leif himself was still adjusting to the many tasks and responsibilities of a chieftain such as Erik the Red had been, and didn't expect he would be able to lead the expedition himself. Neither could he think, as much as he tried, of anyone who could go in his stead, except Thorvard – but it so happened that his friend was in a situation very much like his own. His father had passed away too, and Thorvard had inherited old Thorbjorn's estate with all its business and responsibility.

And so summer passed by in Brattahlid, until at the beginning of autumn the uneventful solitude of its inhabitants was somewhat relieved by the arrival of an unexpected guest.

That day, one of the servants ran to tell Leif there is a merchant ship in the harbor, recently arrived from Norway and probably intending to spend the winter in Greenland.

"It must be Thorfinn Thordarson," Leif told his mother. "I remember Father saying we may expect his arrival next autumn."

"True," nodded Thjodhild. "I recall that now as well, although, naturally, I completely forgot all about it earlier. Your father would have been glad to see Thorfinn. He was always a good friend."

Thorfinn Thordarson, more commonly known as Karlsefni, was a rich Norwegian merchant who had been to Greenland many times. In his age he was closer to Leif, but most of his business was always done with Erik. Though most of his time had been invested in trade, Thorfinn was a brave man who also knew how to hold a battle-axe and sword, and pretty well-learned for someone of his descent – he could read and write well, and was a man of vast knowledge, a keen mind, and well-developed sense for profitable ventures.

..."It is a great pleasure to see you, Thorfinn," said Leif, leading his guest into the house. "And yet I fear that this winter in Brattahlid will not be very merry."

"I am grieved indeed, Leif," Thorfinn shook his head sorrowfully. "Last time I saw your father, he was stout and healthy and looked as if he would live for another fifty years at least... and your brothers - this damn sickness..."

"And the Skraelings," a bitter grimace twisted Leif's lips.

"How is your mother coping?"

"She is a strong woman," replied Leif. "Gudrid, please tell the servants to prepare the bathhouse for our guest, and meanwhile to bring us something to eat."

Gudrid set her sewing aside, gave Thorfinn a fleeting, curious glance, nodded and left.

"Who is she?" asked Thorfinn, looking after her.

"Gudrid, my good-sister."

"What do you... oh, but of course, she must be Thorstein's widow."

"You probably remember Thorbjorn, her father. Another valued and deeply respected man whom we lost to the accursed sickness. He had been a faithful friend to my father for many years."

"Yes," said Thorfinn. "That is great ill luck. Yes, I remember Thorbjorn, of course. He probably left no considerable portion to his daughter?"

"Not anything significant, but that shouldn't concern Gudrid. She will always have a home either here or with her brother Thorvard."

"Yes, but still... the poor girl was widowed so soon..."

"You, on the other hand, look as if you have had good luck lately," remarked Leif.

"Business isn't going too badly," Thorfinn said modestly. "You know, I now trade in southern spices as well – quite a profitable line."

Thorfinn is being his usual humble self, thought Leif. The man had never been a braggart. Even now, his clothes were obviously new and costly, but not flashy. Thorfinn could not be called handsome, but there was something pleasing in his face. He looked like a decent, sensible man, one to be trusted.

"I congratulate you on your success, Thorfinn."

"God has been good to me," he replied piously.

Of course, thought Leif, looking at the silver cross hanging from a chain around his guest's neck.

"If so, the help of one god served you more than that of many," he said slyly.

Karlsefni looked at him with surprise. "You are Christian as well, Leif, are you not?"

"Mostly for my wife's sake," confessed Leif. An expression of great curiosity spread upon Thorfinn's face when the subject was brought up.

"With all these mournful news, I have not had the chance to give you my good wishes, Leif, upon your marriage and the birth of your son. Do you even know your story rolled like thunder all over Norway and Iceland? It is told in many different variations, starting from one in which Virgin Mary revealed herself to the king in a dream and ordered him to give you Princess Thorgunna for a bride, and ending with one saying that the princess was put under a spell, or the king was, or you, or all of you at once. The only thing all the story-tellers agree on is that you and Thorgunna sailed to Greenland quite unexpectedly."

Leif laughed, and it felt good. In the past months he had almost forgotten how to do that.

"I will not presume to ask you for details, of course," stressed Thorfinn, although it was clear he burned with curiosity.

"She forced me to marry her," said Leif.

Now it was Thorfinn's turn to laugh. "What? You cannot be serious..."

"No," said Leif. "Indeed, I won't be serious as long as I can laugh."

Their conversation was interrupted by the entrance of Thjodhild and a servant who carried a platter of bread, cheese and ale, and announced that the bathhouse will be ready in a short while.

"Thorfinn," Thjodhild's face lit up at the sight of him, despite the perennial sadness that now always subdued her features. "Be welcome under our roof. You will always be an honored guest here, just as you were when Erik had been alive."

"I am very sorry for your husband, Thjodhild," said Thorfinn. "He was a great man. And I am grieved beyond words for what happened to your sons. I heard on my way here that Thorvald's body was not returned to you, is that so?" he asked Leif.

"It is."

"But if I understood correctly, he was still alive when he ordered his people to flee Vinland?"

"True. He was wounded, and they would never have had time to escape the Skraelings if they had stopped to take him. Thorvald understood that, and would have no delay. He ordered them to leave him there."

"And you don't think he might have..."

"Survived? Desperately wounded, alone, in the hands of those bastards? No, Thorfinn. We must not lead ourselves into false hopes. The most I can hope for is that Thorvald died of his wounds quickly, so that the Skraelings wouldn't have had the chance to torture and humiliate him."

When he saw the pained expression upon his mother's face, Leif hastily fell silent and took a drink of ale.

"If there is anything I might be able to do for you, Leif," said Thorfinn, "do not hesitate to ask. I owe your father many favors."

"I thank you, but it doesn't seem as if there is anything you can do, unless you intend to sail to Vinland and search for my brother's body..."

"That is an idea," Karlsefni said suddenly.

"I beg your pardon?"

"I said it is an idea, and not a bad one. Ever since I heard of Vinland, I have been curious to see the place."

Thjodhild and Leif looked at him in wonder. "You cannot mean that," said Leif. "You are a trader, Thorfinn, not a warrior. You are a brave man, of course, no one doubts that... but you don't want to confront those Skraelings."

"Not confront them," Thorfinn corrected him, "trade with them."

"My son attempted to do that too," said Thjodhild. "Thorvald believed it can be possible to reach an agreement with them and live peacefully by their side."

"Well," said Thorfinn, "I don't know all the details of what Thorvald attempted to do, but I hope Leif will have the chance to tell me all about it during the winter. And now," he drained the last of his ale, "I hope the bathhouse is ready. It was a long journey and I'm very much in need of a good wash."

... "I hope your stay here will be pleasant enough, Thorfinn," Leif said later, while they all sat around the table, "though I do not pretend to be more than a very mediocre substitute of my father."

"You are too humble, Leif," said Thorfinn. "Although, of course, I miss Erik, and will probably feel it every time I arrive at Brattahlid."

"Erik will be missed for many years by all the people of Brattahlid," said Gudrid, "by all of Greenland."

"Yes, with the possible exception, of one two-faced, narrow-minded priest," Leif said tartly.

"How can you speak of Father Wilhelm in such a manner, my son?" Thjodhild scolded him. "A holy man such as him, spending all his time in prayer, attempting to absolve the people of their sins..."

Attempting to make the best possible use of the secrets that are revealed to him at confession, thought Leif.

"You know he and Father couldn't stand each other's sight," he said. "Surely you do not pretend to say Father Wilhelm is sorry for Red Erik's death."

"Yes, your father never accepted the True Faith - it wasn't anything personal against the holy priest, and yes, Father Wilhelm was very sorry for how Erik passed away, without having had the chance to accept Jesus Christ as his Savior and thus gain an eternity in paradise for his soul."

Leif preferred to stop the argument, and concentrated on his food and drink instead. Close to the end of the meal, a skald appeared before them and sang them a lovely solemn song that was composed in Greenland in honor of Thorvald Erikson:

It isn't in vain that the sunrise falters,
It isn't in vain that the crow is calling.
The pine trees are covered in mist of sadness,
And snow underfoot doesn't crunch – it's moaning.
It isn't in vain there's no dance or laughter,
And songs of the battle had fallen silent.
It isn't in vain that your sail won't billow,
Your proud ship won't slip above salty waters.
It isn't in vain that the wolves grow bolder,

In woods evergreen and in sunny clearings,
It isn't in vain that our foes come fearless
To lands we once won, to the house of Erik.
It isn't in vain that the spring is dawdling,
And powerful sea had come down in sorrow,
Its waves do not fall upon rocks with power;
For you shall never be back, o Thorvald.

"It is a good song," said Gudrid, "but I am not certain it does Thorvald justice. I believe it should have told of how he gave up on his chance of survival to make sure all his men may get away unscathed. He saved them... he..." she trailed off, and a mist came into her eyes.

"Yes," said Thjodhild, wiping away a tear. "That was my son. He always thought only of others, never of himself."

Gudrid lowered her eyes. Ever since the deaths of her husband and his brother, so far apart in distance but so close in time to each other, she felt a kind of inexplicable guilt towards both men. Irrationally, she couldn't help thinking that perhaps, if she hadn't married Thorstein, Thorvald wouldn't sail to Vinland so hastily and wouldn't have been killed there – and Thorstein, maybe, wouldn't have visited so many houses during the dangerous time of the sickness, and perhaps he wouldn't have fallen sick then. Of course, she never expressed such thoughts in words, and knew that Thjodhild, who loved her as a daughter, would never blame her, but the vague idea took hold in her mind and wouldn't let go.

After everyone had eaten, the Norwegian guest came over to the widow and said:

"Gudrid, allow me to express my sorrow for your husband and your father. These are painful times for you, I know."

"I thank you," said Gudrid, inclining her head slightly.

"I do not suppose you remember me. I had known your father, Thorbjorn, but last time I saw you, you still played with your dolls."

Gudrid looked at him, and a dim childhood memory was awakened in her – the memory of a dark-bearded, quiet fur trader who came to her father to talk of business, and drew the attention of her brother Thorvard by tales of distant lands which he visited. She felt herself warming to this man, whose participation in the family grief looked as something more than common politeness.

"I have heard of Thorstein's marriage, and brought him a wedding gift. In no black prospect could I expect, of course, that I might arrive too late to give it to him. But I hope you will consent to accept this from me as a gesture of sympathy, and as a symbol of hope for a brighter future."

He ordered his men to bring a wooden chest, and inside it, carefully wrapped in cloth, were a dozen goblets of colorful Byzanthine glass, expertly made. It was a very generous gift.

"I thank you for your kindness and generosity," said Gudrid. "Since I now live with my good-mother, Thjodhild, these goblets will be my contribution to her household."

"Certainly not, my dear," objected Thjodhild. "They will remain yours, and you will take them to your new home when you are married again."

"I cannot think of that yet," Gudrid said quietly.

"There is no need to think," Thjodhild replied gently. "It will simply happen in the natural course of things. No one expects a young, pretty woman like you to waste your life accompanying an old crone like me."

"... Your brother Thorvald made several mistakes from which I intend to learn," Thorfinn said to Leif one day, when they were both hunched over a map. "First of all, I will not sail there with thirty men. I will take three large ships with me, and at least a hundred and fifty men... well-armed men. Certainly, I intend to avoid confrontation, but these Skraelings have to get the message that it's in their interest to stay away from us. And... you told me that your sister Freydis knows their language?"

"A little, but not as well as she knows that of the local natives. The Skraelings of Greenland speak a tongue which is, apparently, vastly different."

"Well, the lack of common language never prevented me from successful trading. And in Vinland, judging from what Thorvald's men brought with them, we may find many goods – furs, timber, walrus ivory... and if we are able to set up a mine of silver ore, like Thorvald hoped to do but never had the chance..."

"It sounds promising, Thorfinn, but under no account I would want you to risk your life. Be careful. You intend to sail in the spring, isn't that so?"

Thorfinn lifted his eyes from the map, and Leif could read hesitation in his face.

"I want you to understand me correctly, Leif," he said. "I am not changing my mind, but... but I am not certain I will be able to sail to Vinland so soon. You see, I... I intend to get married."

"Married?" Leif was pleasantly surprised. "Well, I wish you joy. How come did you not mention this before?"

To his wonder, this respectable, serious, sensible man suddenly blushed like a young lad.

"I... she... I mean, I haven't had the chance, exactly... she doesn't know that..."

"You mean to make an offer of marriage," Leif interrupted him, "but the maid doesn't know of it yet?"

"Yes. I mean, no. She is not a maid, I mean."

"You are confusing me," remarked Leif.

"It is Gudrid," explained Thorfinn. "If she consents, of course."

Leif wasn't very surprised. An unwed man and a beautiful woman thrown together under the same roof for many weeks – why should he wonder?

"I wanted to ask your permission first."

"My permission?" Leif repeated in confusion.

"Why, yes - Gudrid entered your father's household when she was widowed, and with Erik's death, she is now under your protection. So, Leif, I ask you for her hand."

"Gudrid can marry whomever she likes, whenever she chooses to be wed again," replied Leif. "And I believe she is very fortunate to have gained the attachment of a man such as yourself."

"You think she will agree, then?" Thorfinn asked hesitantly.

"Why would you doubt that, my friend?"

"I am much older than her."

"Not too much," said Leif. "You are only a year or two older than me, and Gudrid is just ten years younger than I am, or thereabouts."

If Thorfinn had come to Brattahlid a year ago, his chances would have been slim indeed. As a young girl, Gudrid clearly showed her preference of a gay spirit and impressive gestures over a sensible mind and mild manners. But widowhood, grief and regret made her far steadier and more mature, and this would naturally count in Thorfinn's favor.

"She hardly knows me," Thorfinn continued to doubt his prospects.

"It doesn't matter very much," Leif said with a smile, "and it can always be remedied."

... Thorgunna heard all the details of this conversation from her husband, and therefore wasn't very surprised when, a few days later, Gudrid approached her with downcast eyes and flushed cheeks, and asked to consult with her. Thorgunna encouraged her with a nod, already guessing what this is about.

"Thorfinn asked me to marry him," announced Gudrid.

"How wonderful!" said Thorgunna. "I congratulate you, Gudrid. He is a good man."

"You do not sound surprised. I understand that Leif already told you that Thorfinn spoke to him."

"He did," confirmed Thorgunna. Leif's relations soon they grew to see Thorgunna as part of the family, despite the wonder she evoked in them at first, with her stunning beauty, noble gestures and the impressive clothes and jewels she brought from Norway and wore on special occasions.

"And what does Leif think I should do?" asked Gudrid.

"Leif told Thorfinn that in his opinion, the two of you will somehow settle this between you," Thorgunna said lightly. "What interests me more is what *you* told Thorfinn."

"I asked him for time to consider this."

"To consider? What makes you hesitate, Gudrid?"

"I... I don't know," the young woman said quietly. "I... I have no doubt he is a good, kind man, but..."

"If you don't feel for him the same kind of passion as when you married Thorstein, it is understandable and natural."

"I don't know. Don't know how to explain this. Back then, all felt so clear and simple, yet now... Thorfinn is a respectable man, and he is so good to me..."

"Thorfinn is well-informed, generous, pleasant and wealthy. And he had never even been married, so you wouldn't have to accept stepchildren into your home. He does have a few bastards, as I have heard, but what else can be expected of a thirty-year-old man who never married? That shouldn't bother you. I think, Gudrid, that if you consent to marry him, you shall have a good life, and shall never want for anything."

"He *is* a very wealthy man," mused Gudrid, "perhaps *too* wealthy."

"This is the first time I hear a woman speak of her prospective husband's multiple assets as if they were a drawback," Thorgunna remarked with a faint smile.

"You know I don't have much, I cannot bring anything of significance as a dowry..."

"I am certain Thorfinn knows that and doesn't mind."

"That might be so, but what of his family? What if they think he had married someone far beneath him?"

"Well," said Thorgunna, "I find it hard to even estimate how many marriages wouldn't take place if every couple thought first of what the family is going to say. Sometimes, you just need to think of yourself."

Gudrid squeezed her hand with relief and gratitude. It appeared that her resolution had begun to take form.

...Thorfinn and Gudrid were married at Yule, and the wedding celebrations lasted deep into the winter. During all those months of sleepy cold, the atmosphere at Brattahlid was festive. Thjodhild was happy to arrange something as full of life and hope as a wedding, feast after feast was being held, and Father Wilhelm did his best to ally himself with the wealthy Thorfinn, who also happened to be a devout Christian. In the priest's eyes, Thorfinn's appearance was an auspicious sign for the strengthening of Christianity in Greenland, and for disperding the last strongholds of pagan worship, which was rapidly falling into disfavor ever since Erik's death.

Gudrid encouraged her husband to go on with his plans of sailing to Vinland as soon as the weather conditions would permit it, and even announced to him that she intends to go with him.

"But, my dear," protested Thorfinn, "You don't know what you are about. Think of how crowded it's going to be on board and how uncomfortable you will be... and then, in Vinland – it is known to be a dangerous place, and though I do not intend to pick fights with the Skraelings, one may never know what the future holds."

But Gudrid remained firm. She didn't want Thorfinn to put off the journey, and she didn't mean to let him sail without her.

"We have but just wed," she said. "I don't want to be separated from my husband so soon, but neither do I want to delay the search for poor Thorvald's body."

When Thorfinn spoke to Leif of his doubts regarding the upcoming journey, Leif privately thought that Gudrid's determination to go probably stems, at least in part, from the guilt she was still feeling about Thorvald's death. But he didn't say this aloud and instead replied:

"I understand why you hesitate, my friend. It is difficult to sail with women on board."

305

"Three of my men have wed here this winter, too. If I take Gudrid with me, they will want to fetch their wives along as well, and if I don't let them, they will grumble. Also, I will need some woman or other to wait on Gudrid."

"It will make things more complicated, but perhaps, of all choices, it is still the best. Because in truth, you don't *want* to leave Gudrid behind so soon after your marriage, do you?"

Eventually Gudrid won and, together with a few other women, joined the crew of the ships, which was just beginning to take final form.

"Gudrid is right, Leif," said Thorgunna, when she saw the three ships that Thorfinn was taking – three ships which were large and well-equipped but, naturally, would still be crowded and afford no luxuries during the journey. "I would have done the same thing if I were her."

"To your good fortune, my dear," Leif said with a slightly mournful smile, "you needn't expect to have to make any such decision. I do not see how I can ever leave Brattahlid for any length of time."

His wife's eyes stared at him appreciatively. "You always do what must be done," she said.

"I have no one I might leave in my stead, and the tasks that need to be taken care of are too numerous to mention. I remember how I tried to talk Father into joining me on my journeys, how Thorvald begged him to come along when he sailed up the coast. We never had the wit to understand how many demands there are upon a leader such as my father had been. Ever since he began the settlement, he did not belong to himself alone."

"I wish I had had time to get to know him better," said Thorgunna.

But I could have gotten to know him better, Leif thought regretfully. At any rate, he could have spent more time with his father, could have learned more from his experience – the experience he now so strongly felt he wanted. And his brother Thorvald – there, too, he suddenly saw a gap which he can never bridge over now. The closeness ought to have been deeper, steadier, more constant. *We must never live thinking we have time,* he thought. And now he cannot even go to search for Thorvald's bones. Another man, a man who isn't even directly connected to the family, is going to step up to this task.

He caressed his wife's hand, and in his other arm he held the little child that was playing with his beard. For this, for his marriage he was more and more thankful with every day that went by. He no longer saw Thorgunna as an inexperienced girl caught up in an undesirable situation. She has become his source of comfort throughout all this terrible time since Thorstein's death. *Whether there is one god or many, I thank them for giving me this woman.*

Chapter 39

"I'm afraid I cannot allow this."

"Why not, Thorvard?"

"Because... because women are nothing but a hindrance on an expedition such as this." *And because I promised I will never allow you to go back to Vinland, where you have already caused enough trouble.*

"Well, I already went there once, did I not? And this time, unlike before, more women are going, even Gudrid – your sister Gudrid, that little hen who spent her whole life at home!" Her voice softened. "You don't really want to leave me behind, do you, Thorvard?"

"Separations are a necessary part of life," Thorvard said bravely, though his heart was constricted.

"We have already spent too much time apart, my love. Now all I ask is that you allow me to be by your side."

"You are right. I do not wish to go so far away for so long, and I don't really have a trustworthy man to leave in my stead. I believe I will give up on the journey. Thorfinn will do fine without me."

"Give up? Oh no, Thorvard! Just think what a fabulous opportunity this is for us, what venues of profit, what a fascinating journey! No one can arrange it all as carefully and with as much attention to detail as Thorfinn."

"Well, then, and what do you believe we should do about Sygni? We cannot take her to Vinland with us."

"We will leave her under my mother's care, of course. Sygni loves her very much, and Leif and Thorgunna will be here as well. She will be just fine."

Thorvard suppressed a sigh. A mother who can leave her little child behind so easily... well, he was under no illusion – he didn't think his life with Freydis would suddenly become all peaceful and devoid of conflict. He knew she hadn't truly changed; she was only more careful. But he had expected a little more... perhaps... submission? *Yes, you truly are an incorrigible fool.*

..."I cannot approve of this either," announced Leif.

"I knew you would say this," said Thorvard.

"Of course you knew. You know me, and I thought you know your wife as well by now, but this decision of yours... it is, shall we say..."

"I know, I know. But Freydis swore she had abandoned all her plans of seeking revenge. She promised to make no contact with the Skraelings, to remain inside the camp with the other women for as long as we stay in Vinland..."

"Thorvard, my friend, such reasoning could be somehow justified if you had known Freydis no longer than a month or two, or at least if you weren't married yet. But after all you had gone through with her..."

"I believe she has a firmer understanding of reality now, Leif. She knows the situation."

"Oh, yes. Of course. But I don't think you will be astonished if I say Freydis will always be Freydis – ambitious, unprincipled, reckless, and absolutely uncontrolled."

"These aren't very kind words."

"I love Freydis – her courage, her wit, her readiness to disdain danger. But you, Thorvard, must be warned. You are my oldest friend, and you are dear to me."

"You are right," Thorvard replied, defeated. "I know you are. I know how ridiculous it is that I can never refuse her, but..."

"But you cannot," Leif finished in resignation. "Listen, Thorvard. You must watch my sister very, very carefully. And there is something else, something I intend to tell you alone – not to Thorfinn, though he will be the leader of this expedition, and not to Freydis, though she is my sister."

"Speak, Leif," said Thorvard. "Your secret will be safe with me."

"It isn't exactly a secret – actually, I am not certain. Listen. When I built my cabin in Vinland, together with my men, I made a hiding place in it and told of it to no one but my brother Thorvald, just before he set out on his last journey."

Leif explained the exact location of the hiding place, and Thorvard nodded.

"Do you believe Thorvald left something for you there?"

"I do not know. Perhaps... I don't know how much time he had before he died. Perhaps he hid a letter, a newer map, or perhaps an object of value he did not have a chance to hand over to his men. In the last message I got from Thorvald, he tells that some of the Skraelings have more gold and silver than we had imagined before, but he had no intention of letting this be known among his men. He wanted to avoid sowing seeds of greed and reckless actions driven by lust for gold."

"That fits him so well," said Thorvard.

"It does. Search that hiding place for me, Thorvard. Thorvald and Thorstein are gone, but you are my brother as much as either of them had been, and perhaps more. I trust you as I would trust myself."

The day of departure had come. The men, who made up most of the crew, occupied themselves with last inspections of the equipment, the ships, the oars and the sails. The women were mostly busy expressing their fears to one another – except

Freydis, who was looking forward with sparkling eyes and pacing back and forth, impatient to be off.

Thorfinn came over to Leif and pressed his hand warmly.

"Thank you for everything," he said. "The winter I spent here in Brattahlid was the happiest of my life. I owe you a great deal, Leif."

Leif noticed the affectionate glance Thorfinn sent in Gudrid's direction, and laughed. "I wouldn't put it quite that way," he said.

After the ships had taken sail, he looked after them for a long while. The vision was good and clear, and for a long time he was able to see Thorfinn's wide shoulders and dark beard, Gudrid's golden braids, the red waves of Freydis's hair and Thorvard's tall, upright figure. He was looking back and waving at those who came to say goodbye. Finally, it became impossible to distinguish the people, and the ships turned into tiny black spots on the horizon. It was then that Leif looked at his mother and wife, who stood by his side, and allowed them to lean into him, one on each arm. Little Sygni concealed her tearful face in Thjodhild's skirts.

"Will they be back?" asked the girl in a small voice, and Thjodhild replied simply:

"We shall pray for that every day, my dear."

She was careful not to make promises, and Leif well understood why. Such a long journey always meant a great risk, and Vinland had already taken the lives of some of their men. The sail there won't be a trifle either. At some point during the journey, they will need to go ashore and renew their supply of fresh water. And wherever they stop, they might run into Skraelings, and one cannot foretell what such encounters may bring – trade or battle. And there are women with them, which makes the expedition more vulnerable. Gudrid and her servants... *and Freydis*. He had to confess, though, that Freydis is likely to be a greater threat upon Thorvard's peace of mind than the actual safety of the expedition.

I wish I could have gone with them, he thought with unrestrained longing. He could almost feel the ship shifting underneath his feet, almost strained his well-muscled arms lifting an oar for the first time in a long time.

"My love," Thorgunna told him when they were left alone, "I know how frustrating it must be for you, having to remain behind, yet I... I cannot help but rejoice."

"You are entirely within your right to be happy that your husband remains in Brattahlid," he smiled, making an effort so that his smile wouldn't seem sad.

"I mean, precisely at this time that... I am with child again, Leif," she said with shining eyes.

"Are you certain?" he asked with joyful surprise.

"Yes," she nodded. "I recognized the signs earlier this time. Are you happy, my love?"

"That our Thorkell should have a brother? Of course I am. I wish he is to Thorkell what Thorvald had been to me."

Chapter 40

"There is no doubt it is him, then?" Thorfinn's voice was grave.

"It is him," replied Freydis, looking away from the sad remnants of her brother. "These are his clothes, his weapons. It is Thorvald."

"We must prepare a coffin for him," said Thorvard. "He may rest in it until we return to Greenland."

Gudrid hurried outside for a draught of fresh air, fighting an urge to vomit, and left Thorfinn, Thorvard and Freydis with the bones of the one who had once loved her so much, and who arrived here because of her. She didn't remain alone for long, though. Thorfinn came out to her.

"Are you unwell, my love?" he asked, offering her his arm. She leaned on him gratefully.

"I am fine, Thorfinn," she said, forcing her voice to sound steady.

"Do you regret coming here now?" her husband inquired with concern.

"No, of course not! I... I simply need to rest, and soon I will feel better."

Thorfinn gave her a worried look. It was true, though, that Gudrid seemed weak, pale and tired, but not ill. Nothing a good long rest, a decent meal and a refreshing wash cannot improve, he told himself.

"We won't have to live in this cabin, will we, Thorfinn?" Gudrid asked with a shudder.

"Of course not," he reassured her. "There are more cabins here, though they are smaller, and we will begin building a spacious longhouse directly. There is plenty of timber for the taking."

Thorfinn's men began working in the camp without delay. There were a lot more people in their expedition than with Leif back on his first journey or with Thorvald later on, and they would need far more living and storage space. Thorfinn also ordered that a tall strong fence should be erected all around the camp, and that guards should stand at the gates at all times.

"It will have to be so during the entire time of our stay," he made clear to his people. "Even if the Skraelings come to trade and look friendly. We must not forget what happened to Thorvald – not because we seek revenge, but because we wish to learn valuable lessons for the future."

Thorvard noticed the burning fire which leapt into his wife's eyes as she heard these words, but Freydis decided to hold her tongue for a change.

As Thorfinn had predicted, the Skraelings weren't tardy in coming. They allowed the Greenlanders to see them from a distance, waved green branches, and expressed a desire for peaceful interaction in all their gestures. The Greenlanders came out to them well-armed, but their hands didn't reach for the handles of their battle-axes, and a market was soon spread near the camp.

The Skraelings were short people, black-haired, with a wide build, and their skin was slightly darker than that of the Greenland natives. Their attire was made of fur and leather. They expressed great interest in the Norse weapons and, communicating by sign language, expressed their readiness to purchase several weapons for a very generous quantity of luxurious furs – but Thorfinn had predicted this and forbade selling any weapons to the locals. "That was one of Thorvald's mistakes," he said. "Their weapons aren't very effective,

314

compared to ours, and we want things to stay this way. It is unwise to help a foreign, hostile people gear up with good steel."

Instead, Thorfinn offered the Skraelings cloth, glass beads, copper dishes and other goods which were, as he guessed, very special in their eyes. In return, he got from them pelts of bears and wolves of varieties he had never seen before in any country he had formerly visited, ornaments made of deer horn, and expertly made clay dishes. The Skraelings also expressed great curiosity when they saw milk, cheese and butter, which formed an important part of the Greenlanders' ration. Thorfinn, who was a man of far sight, took care to bring along cows, goats, geese and chickens. The animals which had grown weak during the journey served to enrich the men's rations with fresh meat, and the rest were brought to the camp in Vinland – Thorfinn planned not only to keep them for the production of milk and eggs, but also to breed them as part of the permanent settlement.

When the Skraelings saw the fair-skinned strangers consuming the unfamiliar white beverage, their curiosity knew no limit – and their interest grew more powerful still when Thorfinn's people explained to them, in gestures and grunts, that the milk is the source of their great height and strength. The Skraelings exchanged rapid comments in excited voices. They traded for some in exchange for furs, and drank it not far from the camp. Shortly after that, they began to bend and writhe in very odd ways, and hold on to their stomachs with a grimace of great discomfort upon their faces. Later they hastened to disappear into the bushes, to gales of laughter from the new settlers.

"I suppose their stomach just isn't fit for drinking milk," said Thorfinn, after he was done laughing.

315

"What do they eat, then?" asked Gudrid.

"Mostly fish, I suppose, and deer, and the wild wheat and berries we have found in the woods," her husband said. "And perhaps some of those sour little grapes Leif made such a fuss about."

"These Skraelings are very interesting, aren't they, Thorfinn?" remarked Gudrid. "I believe we must learn all we can from them, as they no doubt are learning from us. Every time they get near the camp, I see how they look at us, examine the houses, stare at our ships. It is as if they are trying to record every detail, and I cannot help but wonder for what reason."

"You need not fear them, my sweet," said Thorfinn, caressing her golden hair. "It is obvious they fear us. But you are right, we must learn all we can about them."

Indeed, he and his partner Bjarni Grimolfson were carefully watching the ways of the Skraelings, and discovered that these were nomadic people, who had no permanent homes and dwelt in tents made of skins in their seasonal camps, not unlike the tribes of Finnmark and Lapland.

"They also have boats," remarked Bjarni, "but they aren't as fast as ours, they have no sails and can only move up and down rivers inland. In such boats they can never venture out into the open sea."

This knowledge gave Thorfinn a certain measure of security, but he ordered his people to watch the ships more carefully. The vast numbers of the Skraelings worried him, and he surmised that there were far more of them on the other side of the bay, where the lands were even more fertile and tempting, and the hunting better. In the meantime, the Skraelings showed no intent of attacking, but so it was at the beginning of Thorvald's stay, was it not? Thorfinn shuddered just thinking that the Skraelings might get the idea of burning the ships and attacking the camp at the same time.

Further negotiation with the locals could not take place yet, due to the language barrier. Meanwhile, they settled for relations of trade and cool distance.

Freydis, on the other hand, was quite at ease. While Gudrid mostly remained within four walls from nightfall till dawn, Freydis had no fear of going out at night. One night, when she went outside to make water, she was surprised to see her frightened good-sister standing at the door of the house and looking about her. She held a broomstick as if preparing to hit someone with it.

"What is going on?" asked Freydis.

"I heard a suspicious noise," Gudrid replied in a trembling voice.

"One of the men probably went out for a leak," Freydis suggested.

"I... I am not sure. I heard a slight noise, the sound of a branch breaking... if these are steps, they are very quiet, and... why would anyone from our camp take such care to be quiet?"

"So as not to wake the others?" shrugged Freydis. "But if you are so concerned, let us make a round and check."

"What, alone?" Gudrid opened her eyes wide in fear. "Do you not think it would be better to wake Thorfinn and Thorvard?"

"If we wake the men because of every slight noise we hear at night, they will soon be asleep at their day's work. Wait here," Freydis ordered Gudrid, entered the house again with light, quick steps, and came outside within a moment, holding in her hand the axe Thorvard used to cut lumber with.

"Where did the noise come from?" she asked. Gudrid glanced fearfully at the heavy axe and pointed to the space behind the cabins.

"Take off your shoes," commanded Freydis.

"But..."

"Take off your shoes, I tell you. If there is anyone who isn't supposed to be here, you will thank me."

Gudrid obeyed. Barefoot, the two women stepped noiselessly in the direction of the animal pens. Freydis had a firm grip on her axe. A few moments later, a long, furry tail sped past them in the silvery light of the moon, and Freydis lowered the axe and smiled disdainfully.

"Just a fox, Gudrid. We should have a better fence made around the chicken coop."

Gudrid exhaled with relief.

Chapter 41

"You should have told me," Thorvard was furious.

"I don't understand why you should be so angry," Freydis played it innocent, attempting to subdue her sly smile. "Have you not told me you would like to have more children, my love?"

"Do not act as if you don't understand! You knew you were pregnant before we left home, and you knew very well that if you tell me, you will have to stay behind!"

"But I did *not* know, Thorvard," insisted Freydis. "Here, look, your sister is also with child, probably from the time before we took sail, and she only discovered it now, too."

"This is Gudrid's first time, and so it is natural she might have assumed it was only seasickness. But you must have known! I am certain you did."

"What does it matter, anyway, where I should be while I am pregnant, and where I give birth – here or at home?" said Freydis. "It will happen just the same way. And the climate here is more comfortable."

"We don't even have an experienced woman who might help you when your time comes," Thorvard said darkly.

"There is no need, Thorvard. I am perfectly capable of doing it on my own."

Gudrid, who was carrying her first child, was not quite so sanguine, and attempted to obtain from Freydis every bit of knowledge her good-sister could recall from her first time.

"It is just lovely that we are going to have children so close together, Freydis," Gudrid said. "If we stay here for a while, the little ones will each have a companion of their own age."

Thorfinn was torn between excitement about going to become a father (lawfully, at any rate) for the first time, and anxiety for the well-being of his dear Gudrid. Her three servants were young girls, and he regretted he didn't take in the stead of one of them someone older, with experience as a midwife. As things appeared now, Freydis would probably have to assist Gudrid during birth – if they don't both go into labor at the same time, that is. If it were possible, Thorfinn would send his wife back to Greenland or to any settled place, but this wasn't a feasible option – and even if it were, another such journey in her condition could do more harm than unassisted birth.

During all this time, Thorvard didn't stop thinking about Leif's request, but he could not obtain a quiet hour during which he might search undisturbed the hiding place his friend had described to him. Finally, he rose one night when the entire camp was already asleep, and only the guards prowled around its fence. He took an oil lamp, which he lit carefully so as not to wake Freydis, and got out of the cabin. He hoped that even if someone should notice him, it will simply be assumed he got out to make water.

He slowly edged towards the cabin which used to belong to Leif, and to Thorvald after him, and now stood abandoned because none of the men agreed to live in it, out of fear of ill luck. He opened the door carefully, and waited a few moments to make sure no one heard the slight creaking sound.

The cabin was empty. Thorvald's body was already resting in a coffin made of pine-wood, which was to be taken to Greenland when the currents and winds allowed it. Apart from the place where the arrow struck, no other wounds were found on his body. It appeared that the Skraelings had simply allowed the poison to do its work.

Thorvard began knocking around the walls, as Leif had explained to him. He moved patiently and slowly from one end of the cabin to the other, until he found a section of wall that made a hollow noise in response to his knocking. Using his axe-handle as a lever – according to Thorfinn's instructions, all men were required to keep an axe, a sword or a knife close to them, even at night – he carefully broke and pulled it apart, and placed the oil lamp upon the bench, so that it will light the depression that was revealed to his eyes.

He saw a sheath of oiled leather, picked it up and extracted a roll of parchment out of it. After much prodding from his wife, Thorvard finally learned his letters, for which he was now grateful. Leif instructed him that if he should find a letter, he must read it without delay.

"You can never know what might happen," his friend had said. "It might be that you return but are unable to preserve the letter. In such a case it is better that you should at least know what was written in it."

And so Thorvard spread the roll of parchment and began reading what Thorvald Erikson had written with a trembling hand in his last hour.

"My dear brother Leif,

I do not have much time, my wound leaves no hope, but I trust I will be able to complete this letter - and maybe once, someone or other of our men will return here. Perhaps you will even come yourself, and think to check the hiding place you told me of.

Do not blame yourself for my death. You did all you could to prevent what happened. Know that I leave this world without any regrets.

Before my time finally runs out (Thorvard noticed how the writer's hand became unsteady and the lines began to lose their shape) *I will say a few words about the objects you will find here, together with this letter. I obtained them from a greed-induced Skraeling whom I was able to tempt by our best weapons..."*

Thorvard shook his head mournfully. This mistake might have been what cost Thorvald his life! It was very possible that the Skraelings attacked the camp out of desire to get their hands on more weapons which were better than any they ever had before.

"...But the price was well worth it. As soon as I saw these treasures, I understood they are ancient artifacts of great worth, and certainly weren't made by the locals, although I do not yet know where they came from, nor how they were brought here.

One of them, the one you are holding in your hands now, I placed here immediately upon receiving it..." Thorvard strained his eyes. With every word, it was becoming harder and harder to decipher Thorvald Erikson's writing. The letters were becoming less and less clear. *"... while the other..."*

The letter ended here abruptly. This, no doubt, was the moment when Thorvald, with his remaining strength – which, as he understood, was rapidly running out – pushed the letter into the leather sheath and concealed it together with the treasure.

Thorvard picked up the wooden chest which had been resting next to the letter. He opened it and froze in astonishment.

He took the object in his hands, with gentleness and awe, not as a Viking who finds loot but as an explorer wondering at the power flowing into his fingertips as he touched the beautiful and mysterious thing.

Not even for a moment could he suppose that this precious treasure was made by the Skraelings. And it wasn't just because it was obviously made of pure gold. If he was any judge, its worth far exceeded the weight of gold it was wrought from – and the Skraelings, of course, had not the craftsmanship necessary for making something like this. *Leif must see this, but Freydis mustn't know it exists.*

Thorvard carefully hid the precious object underneath his clothes, intending to conceal it among his personal possessions until his return home. Apart from it, there were some small gold coins in the wooden chest, and a few rather tasteless silver jewels. These he placed in the leather pouch that hung from his belt. They can be safely shown, so he decided, to the others in the camp.

When Freydis saw the coins and the jewels, the glint in her eye convinced Thorvard even further that he was right not to show her the most important treasure of all.

"Where do you think these gold coins came from?" she asked, holding one coin between her thumb and forefinger, staring as if mesmerized at the sunlight reflected off the beaten gold. "I personally have never seen any gold upon the Skraelings – and as far as I know, they use no metal at all. Have you seen the letters on these coins, Thorfinn?"

"Yes," replied Thorfinn Thordarson. "Without boasting, I have been to many lands and traded among many peoples – but these letters, I cannot say to which land they belong. Still, they look familiar, as if I have already seen them once. It isn't Greek, nor is it Arabic... but I scarcely doubt these coins have traveled for a long time and reached this place in some obscure, mysterious way. Maybe when we come home we can find someone who recognizes their source."

"Perhaps the Skraelings might be able to tell us more, if we could speak their language better," said Freydis ponderously. "Perhaps I might try to converse with them and compare their language to that of the Greenland natives..."

"No," Thorvard said with determination. "I forbid this, Freydis. Make no contact with them. Events of the past have already taught us that these people cannot be trusted. They will stab us in the back as soon as they see we are letting down our guard ever so slightly."

Thorvard's warning, it turned out, had not been in vain.

It was night, and Gudrid, always slightly anxious, was the first to hear suspicious noises. She raised herself on her elbow.

"What is it, my love? Are you feeling ill?" Thorfinn asked in a sleepy voice.

"Thorfinn..."

"Yes? Did anything happen?" he rubbed his eyes, attempting to ward off the persistent sleep.

"Not really," said Gudrid, "but I thought I heard something odd."

Thorfinn strained his ears. After some moments, he understood what his wife means.

"It could simply be a few deer wandering near the camp," he said soothingly, though it was obvious to him this didn't sound very convincing. "I will go and make a check right away, at any rate."

He hastened to pull his clothes on. "Wait, Thorfinn!" Gudrid called out in fear. "What shall I do?"

"You stay here, Gudrid," he ordered. "We are in the middle of the camp, it is safest here." His voice was strained, his movements hasty, and only a slight, confident nod gave some comfort to his frightened wife.

Outside, the noise was more obvious, and the smell of burning torches carried in the air. Bjarni ran to Thorfinn, and there was anxiety in his face.

"Thorfinn!" he breathed out. "The Skraelings... they killed one of the guards outside, they are surrounding the camp!"

One look around told Thorfinn that the situation was grave. The camp was surrounded by a burning wall of torches which could easily set all the buildings on fire. The nightly attack and the fact that the Skraelings could get so close to the camp without raising alarm were due to their knowledge of the territory, with which they were familiar, of course, much better than the Greenlanders. Thorfinn had never seen so many of them at once – *it might be that several tribes united for this attack*, he thought with horror.

All this passed in his head within a fraction of a moment. It was clear this was not the time to stand around and think – if they want to survive, they must act, and quickly. The Skraelings began attacking from a distance – they used strange-looking catapults that hurled rocks right into the middle of the camp and sowed destruction and panic among the people. All the men were already out of the cabins, and people were running around, waving battle-axes and swords, shouting to each other, confused, devoid of sense.

"We must get organized, now, or these bastards will do away with us all. Bjarni, collect the people and lead them to protect the camp. Snorri, to the ships, now – prepare to take sail, and no matter what, don't let the whoresons get near you. Thorvard..."

"I cannot believe this, Thorfinn," He heard Freydis's mocking voice. "You think we should run?"

Thorfinn looked at her in astonishment. "What do *you* think we should do, Freydis?" he asked with impatient anger. "They are about to break into the camp!"

Thorvard came back running, his face grave. "It won't do, Thorfinn! They blocked the passage to the bay! Freydis, what are you doing here? Get inside the house right now! A woman in your condition..."

"Even a woman in my condition isn't supposed to fear these pitiful Skraelings!" called Freydis with furious pride. "Not to speak of you, men!"

"We are surrounded!"

"Do Vikings tremble with fear when they are surrounded by a flock of sheep? Are you warriors or not? Are you even men? Give me a sword, and I shall fight no worse than any of you!"

But of course, no one thought to give her a sword. Thorfinn, Bjarni, Snorri and Thorvard lunged forward, to meet the Skraelings face to face, for it became clear there is no other choice – and Freydis, heavy with child, lagged behind.

And yet she had no intention of yielding. Far from it. The battle was now all around her, everywhere. Arrows whistled and battle-axes landed deadly blows, people swung swords, pushing aside the clumsy flint spears of the Skraelings. There was a stampede around buildings which were already set on fire by the enemy. The scared noises the animals made mingled with the cries of the people.

The Skraelings weren't very skilled warriors, nor were they very well-equipped, but their sheer numbers were terrifying. Some of the Greenlanders have already paid with their lives, such as Thorbrand, Snorri's son, whose skull was crushed by a stone. His sword was lying next to him, having fallen out of his slackened grip, and Freydis bent and picked it up, and went ahead after her husband as quickly as she could.

When she reached the very heart of the battle, where each of their men was fighting no less than five Skraelings at once, Freydis climbed a tall rock, waved Thorbrand's sword and yelled:

"You will not win over us, filthy dogs! We will kill you one by one, even if there is a hundred of you for every one of us! Come here and feel Thor's wrath!"

Most of the people in their group were Christians, but even they felt a renewed outburst of determined hope when they heard these words, which were shouted above their heads in the torchlight-dotted darkness. "Thor, Thor! Thor's Hammer!" people picked up the battle cry.

The Skraelings, of course, didn't understand a word of what Freydis said, but her image, that of a raging pregnant woman with her hair loose, her clothes torn and a sword in her hand, shining in the torchlight – it was terrifying, and their rows trembled. This slight hesitation was enough to spur the Northmen on, and they pounced upon the natives with bloodlust, encouraged by the battle cries of Freydis, who presided over them like a red-haired Valkyrie.

When the sun rose, the meadow next to the camp was strewn with the bodies of the Skraelings. The number of the natives who were killed was tenfold to the number of the Greenlanders in the camp. The rest of the Skraelings vanished without a trace. Their defeat was complete.

"You were wonderful, Freydis," said Thorvard as they made their slow way back to the camp, leaning on each other. He looked at her with obvious admiration and his face lit up with joy, and it seemed he completely forgot about his injured arm. Blood from his wound seeped through the bandage his wife hastily made for him out of the hem of her own dress.

"I suppose now you no longer regret taking me with you, right?" Freydis replied with a winning smile.

"I just hope all this effort caused no harm, my love," he said with concern, "to you or the babe."

"Stop this, Thorvard," she said, vexed. She took his hand and placed it upon her belly. He felt the powerful kicks of his child, as if his unborn son was just as agitated as they were. "See? I am just fine. My condition is far better than yours. As soon as we get to the cabin I will take off this dirty bandage and treat your wound as it should be treated so that it isn't infected."

"Freydis," he lowered his voice. "I hate to be a spoilsport, but we must be prepared for the possibility they will be back."

"Nonsense," Freydis replied off-handedly. "They already got a taste of our wrath. We needn't fear such pitiful creatures."

"Not them, Freydis – but their number, which is many times our own."

"They will not be back," his wife said confidently. "They would not dare."

"Perhaps not for a while," agreed Thorvard. "But if we are out of luck, they will return just when you are at your confinement, and what will happen to us all then?"

...Gudrid was the first to go into labor, while Freydis was in the last month of her own pregnancy. Like for many women with their first child, Gudrid's labor pains lasted a long time, and close to the end she was already completely exhausted.

"I cannot do this," she breathed between contractions. "I cannot, Freydis!"

"You *are* already doing this, you silly!" her good-sister replied firmly. "Whether you want to or not, so go on! Another short push and he will be out, I can feel it!"

"I am about to die," whispered the exhausted Gudrid. "I will die, and Thorfinn will never forgive himself..."

"Don't be stupid," said Freydis, and wiped Gudrid's face and cracked lips with a damp cloth. "Here is another one. Concentrate!"

Indeed, Gudrid's fears, it turned out, were baseless. Very soon she gave birth to a strong, healthy son, whose powerful cry made the people all over the camp cheer.

"Snorri Thorfinnson," said Thorfinn with pride and joy, holding his son in his arms. "The first child of our people to be born in Vinland."

"So how does it feel to be a father, Thorfinn?" asked Freydis with an evil smile. She, too, have heard rumors of Thorfinn's bastards. But he made no reply to the hidden sting of her words, and perhaps never even noticed it. He looked at her with profound gratitude.

"She could not have done this without you, Freydis. I owe you my wife's life, and my son's as well."

"Don't be a fool," said Freydis. "Any healthy woman can do it on her own. Someone just needs to be there to take hold of the babe when he slides out."

When Freydis's own time came, which happened a week later, she refused the presence of any of the women, and brought her son forward all alone. When her groans and the babe's first cries have subsided, the women came in and helped Freydis to get to bed, and to wipe and wrap the newborn babe.

"His name shall be Erik," said Freydis, lovingly looking at the boy whose red hair was just like his mother's and grandfather's. "You have no objection, do you, Thorvard?"

"Of course not," replied her husband, who was dazed with joy and relief of having the birth pass so smoothly, and of holding a healthy, rosy babe in his arms.

The Skraelings never dared to show up anywhere near the camp again, but this didn't put Thorfinn at ease, and when Gudrid and Freydis began to recover from their births, he began to speak of returning home.

"What?" Freydis was stunned. "But we need not all go back, Thorfinn. Thorvard can take one of the ships, sail to Greenland and bring more people and supplies back here."

Thorfinn shook his head, and his expression was morose. "I don't think you understand our situation, Freydis," he said. "The Skraelings will not allow us to settle here."

"But we won the battle! We flattened them!"

"We won, and it was a brilliant victory which we owe mostly to you, but I do not dare to hope that the conflict ends here. Another such attack, if it happens now, can cost us all our lives. We lost ten men..."

"And killed hundreds!" Freydis called out with pride. "And the others ran off like dogs with their tail between their legs!"

"The men who were killed left families back home," said Thorfinn. "When we set out, I promised them a safe return."

"I have never heard of such a foolish promise," Freydis said disdainfully. "It is known that journeys such as this one take their toll, especially when we talk of lands which are yet almost unexplored. And ten people for such a brilliant victory, as was ours against the Skraelings, is not too high a price to pay."

"Perhaps you would think differently if Thorvard was one of those ten," Thorfinn remarked furiously.

"My brother was killed here," Freydis reminded him, "and I still don't think we should leave."

"Well," said Thorfinn, "to the good fortune of our people, this expedition is not under your authority."

She turned his back on him and began to walk away. While she did, she turned her head and threw at him across her shoulder:

"I knew I shouldn't expect much from you, Thorfinn, but I did not imagine you are *such* a coward."

Thorfinn didn't bother to reply. He already had the chance to learn that arguing with Freydis is about as efficient as drawing water with a bottomless bucket. For every argument of his she could offer ten of her own, and while she spoke they even sounded convincing. All he could do was trust his own good sense and do what had to be done.

Chapter 42

There was much noise in Brattahlid upon the arrival of the ships from Vinland. Thjodhild hurried down to the harbor, laughing and crying alternately with happy relief, when she saw her dear ones descending upon safe land – Freydis, Thorvard, Gudrid, all alive and well, thank God! And Gudrid and Freydis with babes in their arms, what a joy! She led little Sygni towards the parents who have almost become a dim and distant memory to the girl. Sygni averted her face shyly when her father bent over her, attempted to gather her in his arms, spoke to her and showed her the little brother that was born in a distant land.

Thjodhild looked around her. Wherever she looked, families were reunited, speaking excitedly to each other, embracing – and she recalled all the times when Erik had come back from a journey and gathered her in his arms, and she felt the familiar male odor of his body and hair, of sweat and damp wool and salt and leather.

Her eyes sparkled with tears when she heard how Freydis had named her son.

"May this boy grow up to be like his grandfather," she smiled at the babe she held, and gently placed the small, sleeping child back in the arms of her adopted daughter.

"We all miss him, Mother," Freydis suddenly said with uncharacteristic softness.

Yes, Thjodhild thought sadly. *But I alone will continue to miss him until the day I die, be it near or distant.*

"Tell me," she hesitated, "Thorvald..."

"We brought him home," Freydis said quietly.

"Thank God," Thjodhild said bravely, suppressing a sob. "I could not have borne the thought that he... is there..."

Distancing himself from the group comprised by Thjodhild, Freydis, Thorvard and Gudrid, Thorfinn came near Leif to speak to him. The two men shook hands warmly.

"Welcome back, Thorfinn," said Leif. "I haven't had the chance to see you and give you my congratulations yet. You and Gudrid were blessed with a fine, healthy boy."

"And you, so I heard, now have a daughter. Accept my good wishes as well."

"Thank you. We named her Hallfryd."

"It is a fine name."

"Tell me a little more about your journey," asked Leif.

"I assume you have already heard from Thorvard about our battle with the Skraelings."

"Yes," replied Leif, and glanced quickly in his good-brother's direction. "Who would believe I might be obliged to eat my words, and be happy that he had taken Freydis with him."

"Freydis is a remarkable woman. Her courage blew the spirit of battle into us all, and thanks to her we were saved, I am certain of that, but... Leif, that attack left me greatly disturbed. We had lost people and couldn't afford to lose more. The Skraelings are too numerous. I... I do not believe we will be able to settle Vinland, at least not anytime in the near future. To do that, we would need far more people than we could ever hope to recruit. Otherwise, we would never feel safe there."

Leif struggled to find an answer.

"Freydis claims otherwise, of course," Thorfinn went on apologetically. "But I believe it would be unwise to - "

"Ah, I can well imagine what Freydis claims," Leif gave his friend a tired, slightly disappointed smile. "Thank you for your sincere opinion, Thorfinn. Of course, I do not feel within my right to put more people at needless risk, while I must remain behind myself because of my duties in Brattahlid. Thank you for everything, especially for the effort you made in returning Thorvald's bones here."

Thorfinn placed a hand on his shoulder for a second, nodded, and walked away.

Vinland! The green meadows, the wide open lands, the rivers teeming with salmon, the wild vines and thick forests – all this came before Leif's eyes with amazing clarity, and the disappointment constricted his throat. The country overseas is so fertile – while here in Greenland they only have a strip of cold, hard land with scant vegetation, which can scarcely support the settlers. And it is so cold here, always so cold. How he had hoped to found a permanent settlement in Vinland! But it wasn't in his nature to sink into melancholy, not even when forced to bury a dream of many years. He squared his shoulders, determined to move forward.

"Prepare the pyre for my brother Thorvald," he ordered his men, "with weapons and gifts, and all the tokens due to a warrior fallen in honorable battle."

"Leif," said his tearful mother, "I know that Thorvald had not a chance to receive the Gospel, but I thought that... perhaps it will still be more appropriate, you know... to bury him underneath a cross. I am certain that if only he had had a little more time, he would have..."

"No," Leif replied resolutely, "Erik the Red must meet at least one of his sons in Valhalla."

When the flames began to lick the wood and a thick column of smoke rose into the air, Leif stood and looked on for a long time, unblinking and silent. Once nothing but a few last red embers remained in the pile of ash, Thorvard came over to Leif and placed a hand on his friend's shoulder.

"Can we speak... alone?"

Leif nodded, and the two friends came inside, into the house, into one of the inner rooms. When they were quite alone, Thorvard rummaged in the pouch hanging upon his belt and took out what he had brought for Leif – Thorvald's letter and the object he had concealed with such care during the entire long journey home.

"You were right," he said. "Thorvald had hoped you would come to look for him, and left this for you."

The eyes of Leif, who learned his letters only recently and wasn't a very expert reader yet, passed slowly over the lines of this last, unfinished message from his brother. Then he raised his eyes with a mute question.

"Open it," Thorvard nodded towards the wrapped-up object.

Leif did so, and just like Thorvard, fell back in awe, amazement, and an inexplicable longing that was entirely unconnected to the rich shine of gold.

"It is... a goblet," said Leif. Yet these words were hollow, and he knew it. It was much more than any goblet he had ever seen.

"I didn't show it to anyone," said Thorvard.

"Not even Freydis?"

"Especially not her. I know my wife, Leif. I am no longer under any illusions regarding her. Freydis... her heart is in the right place, but she is ambitious and reckless, and seeing something like this would make her come up with insane plans I don't even want to contemplate. You know, Leif, how dissatisfied she is with our situation..."

"Your situation is just fine," said Leif in an attempt to dispel his friend's embarrassment. "And if it doesn't fit Freydis's expectations, it is her problem." He stopped a little, and then asked, "You do know what this means, don't you, Thorvard? Someone was there before us. Some foreigners have reached Vinland before we did. Where do you think the Skraelings got this from?"

"I do not know," Thorvard shook his head. "But perhaps this might shed some light over the matter?"

Out of his pocket he drew one of the gold coins with the mysterious letters. "Do you know such writing?"

"No," said Leif. "It isn't Latin, nor any other writing I have ever seen. But perhaps one of the men here might know these letters. Let us consult our most experienced sailors."

To their vast surprise, the man who offered a key to this mystery was none other than Father Wilhelm.

"Unless I am much mistaken, these letters are like of the most ancient holy texts," he said, "of the Old Testament. These are Hebrew letters."

Well, thought Leif, *even this ridiculous fool was bound to turn out good for something sometime.* "Thank you, holy father," he said.

Thorfinn and Gudrid didn't linger in Brattahlid too long. Thorfinn had received notice from his old, ailing father in Iceland. Old Thordar begged for his son to come and help him run his farm and business ventures. Thorfinn accepted the offer – which threw Gudrid, who never stopped feeling slightly inferior for being almost entirely portionless when Thorfinn took her to wife, into a whirlwind of anxiety.

"I will miss you all so, so terribly," she told Thjodhild tearfully while they were packing. "I will miss Greenland. It has been my only home."

"We will feel your absence too, my dear," Thjodhild replied affectionately, pressing her good-daughter's arm. "But I know you will have a wonderful future in Iceland. I have heard that the lands and farms in possession of Thorfinn's family are fabulous. And Thorfinn will still come here to trade, so I hope we will see each other again yet."

"I do hope so," said Gudrid. "I cannot bear the thought I am leaving forever, and might never see you all again. And meeting Thorfinn's family, too! I have heard that his mother, in particular, is a very proud woman, and casts fear over her entire household. I also know she had hoped Thorfinn would marry a rich girl from his country, someone with a large dowry that would increase his wealth. What will she say when she discovers her son married a woman who has nothing?"

"Do not let this bother you, Gudrid," said Thorfinn when she voiced her concerns before him. "I am wealthy enough so as not to be swayed by the bride's dowry."

"Still," persisted Gudrid. "You could have married a rich maid, and instead you took a widow who, in addition, brought you next to nothing."

"I married the woman I wanted," he said warmly, caressing her hand. "What is all my money good for, if I cannot do that? I am certain that when my relations meet you, Gudrid, they will love you, and will not be able to think of any other woman who might have fit me better than you."

Once Thorfinn and Gudrid have left, it seemed as if a large part of the cheerful, vibrant life of the place had left with them. For many long hours, Leif used to sit alone, reserved and distant, staring at the mysterious goblet Thorvard had brought back from Vinland. He ran his callused hands over the smooth golden surface, and an inexplicable melancholy took over his heart.

One night, as he was thus sitting by himself, his wife disrupted his loneliness.

"Thorkell and Hallfryd are already in bed," she said. "And I came to see whether you need anything, my love."

Leif looked at her with gratitude and reached out to her with his hand. She came and placed her small hand in his large, tough-skinned palm. He wrapped his arm around her waist, which was still as slim as when she was a girl. She leaned forward, and her soft auburn hair tickled his face.

"I cannot stop thinking about this goblet," he said. "Here, come over and rest your hand upon it."

Thorgunna did that, but soon recoiled. "This will sound strange, Leif," she said in a strained voice. "But... but I feel as if I am not supposed to be doing this."

"I know," he replied. "I feel the same way."

And for another moment they were silent. "I know you will not rest until you solve this mystery," Thorgunna finally said. "But I simply do not know how you might do this without sending another expedition to Vinland, to search for the other object Thorvald hid before he died, God only knows where..."

Leif shook his head gloomily. "I cannot do that," he said. "Vinland has become too dangerous a trap. People already know that, and I... my personal interest does not justify such a risk. But as to this," he gestured towards the goblet, "I cannot help

338

but think that maybe... years ago, my love, I had met a man who, I believe, might shed light this mystery."

"Truly? Who is he?" Thorgunna inquired curiously.

"To reach him, one would have to sail a long way. Not at so much peril as a journey to Vinland would entail, but still..."

"And do you intend to do that?"

"I do not know," mused Leif. "Perhaps... not just now, though. Mother needs us now, and... if I go, I would like you to come with me, if possible. Together with Thorkell and Hallfryd."

"Of course, my love," replied Thorgunna. "Wherever you go."

"We will journey with the greatest comfort possible for you and the children. I believe you will find the journey pleasant enough – it is far to the south, where summer is so warm, and the trees grow fruit as sweet as honey... but of course, if you think it might be too difficult for you..."

"If there is any possibility of doing this without being apart," said Thorgunna, "I will prefer it."

..."And why should you hesitate, my son?" wondered Thjodhild. "Do not think of me. If you wish to journey, do so. Do not be concerned, your old mother is yet able to look after herself for the time being. Besides, Freydis and Thorvard will remain with me."

When the ship sailed out into the Northern sea and the shores of Greenland have almost faded away, it seemed to Leif that the dead who were dear to his heart walk beside him still. Before his eyes he saw Maura, shaking flour off her hands – Thorstein, cheerful and reckless, on their hunting trips and in fistfights away from which his elder brothers pulled him by force – Thorvald, his confidante, dreamy and fair-haired, reciting his poems to people who have gathered around the fire on winter nights – and his good, brave father, Erik the Red.

The ghosts walked alongside him, smiling at him lovingly, and in his heart each one of them was as tangibly real as those of his loved ones who were, to his good fortune, by his side still. The dead ones will be waiting for him. They will be there, always.

The years did not make him forget the way he had traveled so long ago to the home of the Jew Nathan Ben Yossef, but when he came to search for the man, it turned out he lives there no longer. He had grown very wealthy, so Leif was told, and traveled to a nearby town, where he became a respected member of his people's community.

Leif wasn't too sorry for the unexpected delay, for his wife was enjoying every moment of the journey, enchanted by the fertile green landscape of the southern land. They made their leisurely way to the foreign town, and found the house of Ben Yossef.

Leif did not expect the Jew would remember him, but to his vast surprise, right upon his entrance the man got up from his seat, and an expression of astonishment spread upon his face.

"You!" he cried. "Leif, son of Erik!"

"You did not forget me, then."

"You can be certain of that. I heard about you in past years. But I did not expect..."

Leif stared at the man, wondering where he should begin.

"Neither did I forget you," he said. "Years have passed, but some of your words still echo within my mind."

"Why are you here?" asked Nathan Ben Yossef.

Leif hesitated for a moment. "I suppose there is but one single reason for this," he finally said with surprising confidence.

"Because in this world, there is a power higher than myself or anything I can possibly imagine."

From his pouch bag he brought out the precious object, the one that caused him so many sleepless nights, and instantly understood he was not misled. The look upon the face of Nathan Ben Yossef expressed boundless astonishment – his eyes widened in awe, and he made one step back and covered his mouth with his hand in reverence. His power of speech had left him for a few moments.

"How did you come to possess this?" were his first words when he spoke again.

Leif explained where and how the goblet was found, and the expression of awe upon the Jew's face grew even deeper.

"But how? I do not understand. As far as I know, none of my people had ever reached those shores!"

Leif shrugged. "We probably cannot obtain enough knowledge to solve this mystery. But," he paused, "can you at least tell me what this is?"

"It is a holy artifact," the Jew told him. "It was used for service in the Temple we once had, and which is no more. I have never indulged a hope to see anything like it. I will give you all I own in return for it, if only you consent to sell!" he added with zealous fervor.

Leif shook his head. "I do not need your gold," he said, ruled by a sudden impulse, and looked directly at the man. "I will give this to you. I have a feeling this is what I must do."

But the Jew refused to accept such an arrangement. "Allow me to pay you," he said, "so that no one can doubt the transition of ownership was done in an honest manner." With deep reverence, he placed both hands upon the treasure. "Did you not say that, according to your brother's message, it may be understood there is another such object, or something similar to it, close to where your camp was?" he asked.

"Yes," nodded Leif, "but my poor brother did not have time to complete his letter before he died, and so I have no idea where exactly it might be."

"I will pay you any sum I am able to collect, if you consent to go back to that place and search for this artifact for me," the Jew said earnestly, but Leif shook his head in refusal.

"I cannot do that," he said. "I am a man of family, a landowner and a chieftain. I must go home, I cannot allow myself to risk my own life and the lives of my men for such a purpose."

"Then perhaps somebody else might do that?" inquired Ben Yossef. "I promise you, the prize will be such that even a man who has nothing will become as rich as a king, if only he succeeds in finding the holy object and bringing it here to me."

"I wouldn't indulge too many hopes regarding this, if I were you," said Leif. "I will try asking among the men of my country to see if anyone is interested, but if you want to know what I think, the chances of another expedition setting forth are very slim. The journeys there have grown more and more perilous. No one will agree to take such a risk, if he has anything at all to lose."

Chapter 43

"And now?" asked Thorgunna. "It has been a pleasant journey, but now I am beginning to feel anxious to be home."

"You speak the truth, my love. Would you like us to stop in Norway before going back west?"

Thorgunna hesitated for a moment, and then shook her head nay. "It is true that we could go back there now that my uncle, King Olaf, is dead – but for what? There is nothing for me in Norway."

"In that case, our final stop before the last part of our journey will be in Iceland. I trust you will not object to meeting Thorfinn and Gudrid again."

"That is a wonderful idea, Leif," his wife's face lit up. "Yes, I would dearly love to meet them."

Their visit with Thorfinn and Gudrid, though short, left them with a feeling of deep satisfaction. Thorfinn's family owned lands which were probably the finest in Iceland, good fertile lands which provided amply for their great stock of sheep, goats and cows. The herds were of excellent quality and supplied great bounty. The farmhouse itself was excellently built, comfortable and spacious. Thorfinn's father, Thordar, had passed away shortly before their coming, but his mother was still in good health, and it appeared that the company of her son, good-daughter and grandson does her all the good in the world. Just as Thorfinn had expected, the relationship between his mother and his wife became affectionate and warm, and his mother didn't stop praising Gudrid. The rich girl from the nearby county had been long forgotten, and Gudrid was the mistress of the house, fulfilling her role with gracious modesty, and loved by everyone.

"If only you had let me know of your coming beforehand, Leif, the food wouldn't be so scant," Thorfinn said time and time again during a feast which reminded Leif of the Yule celebration during the best days of Erik the Red. "But this is all we can currently offer you, so it will have to do. Bring us more drink, girl!" he told the servant.

"I see things are going well for you," Leif remarked with a smile.

"Cannot complain," replied Thorfinn. "The lands here are very good, the herds are thriving, and there is even a hot underground spring nearby, so that this area is less cold, compared to others next to it. I did not give up trade, but now I run most of my business from here, through young, vigorous, strong people who sail my boats. Of course, this means I lose some deals which require personal involvement, but I can afford to pay this price in order to spend most of my time hereA, together with my family. I am fortunate to have a wife who prefers less profit made in a year, and a husband at home, rather than the opposite. I have had enough journeys, Leif."

"I can understand that," said Leif. "I am no longer sorry for not being able to settle Vinland. Now all I wish is to return home, to Brattahlid, and grow old in peace."

"All is well, is it not?" Thorgunna asked Gudrid at the same time, on the other side of the hall.

"All is just fine," replied Gudrid warmly. "Of course, everything seems twice as good now that you are here! But my life grows better by the day. Everyone is so good to me, and Thorfinn spoils me so! I have everything I could ever want, except for... for you. You cannot imagine how much I miss you all – every single day I think of yourself and of Leif, of Thjodhild, of my dear brother Thorvard and of Freydis. We are supposed to spend the next winter in Greenland," she went on. "So Thorfinn settled with Leif in his last message already, before you came here."

"I know that," Thorgunna nodded.

"Of course. Well, I am so looking forward to that, I can hardly wait! Snorri, to be sure, will come with us, as I cannot bear to be away from him for too long."

"Only a very affectionate heart," Thorgunna said with a smile, looking around, "can make anyone want to leave such a place in favor of a winter in Brattahlid."

"You, Thorgunna, left a place far more luxurious than this one, to spend in Brattahlid all the winters of your life," Gudrid reminded her.

"It is true," said Thorgunna, "and I think I have been looking for Brattahlid all my life, without even knowing it."

Leif used part of the money he got from the Jew to buy goods which were much needed in Greenland, among them a hefty portion of timber for building – something that was always in short supply. His profit was high enough so that no one would raise an eyebrow in face of his long absence. No one knew the true purpose of his journey, except for his own wife and Thorvard.

Leif might have said that he is ready to settle down and get old, but he felt like a giddy young boy when he descended from the ship in Brattahlid and saw his mother hurrying towards him with a wide smile, her arms open. When she held him at arm's length to look at him, Leif observed her too. He was relieved to find his mother in good health – but even more than that, her eyes sparkled again and she looked more energetic than she did when they left. *Time does its work,* thought Leif, *it dulls the pain bit by bit.*

"Is everything well at home?" he asked. "How is everyone?"

"You have no reason to worry, son," Thjodhild reassured him. "All is fine. As a matter of fact, everything has gone smoothly during the entire time of your absence, except for that unfortunate business of Thorvard's broken leg..."

"What?!" Leif cried out. He only felt at ease during his journey because he was able to put his trust in the stable, constant presence of Thorvard in the settlement. Now this security was instantly dissolved.

"Not to worry, Leif, Thorvard is almost completely recovered now. It is true that we were quite at a loss when this sad accident happened, but to our good fortune, Freydis took the matters into her own hands."

Thjodhild noticed her son's wary expression and hastened to reassure him:

"I know what you must be thinking, but she did quite well, she truly did. See for yourself – the herds are thriving, the hay was collected in time, everybody did their work as they should. I did my part by watching over Sygni and Erik most of the time. Freydis sent them to me, and spent most of *her* time going about the settlement. She personally supervised everything, not even a single little detail was left unattended. We did so well all this time mostly thanks to her."

"I want to see Thorvard," said Leif.

"Go on, son. He is here now, in Brattahlid. Freydis has gone to the Western settlement, but we expect her back today."

Thjodhild then devoted her attention to Thorgunna, Thorkell and Hallfryd, and Leif was left alone to look for his friend, whom

346

he found limping slowly around the yard, leaning on a heavy walking stick. At the sight of Leif, Thorvard's face lit up.

"Leif! I cannot believe this, I missed the ship's arrival... but perhaps it is for the best that you didn't see me in this sorry state without being forewarned."

"Let us sit. I want to know how this happened," said Leif.

"No, we should remain standing – or better yet, let's walk slowly. The healer just took off the bandages that held my leg in place, and it appears that the bones have been nicely put back together, but to recover my strength I need to work my muscles as much as I can. How did this happen, you ask? I had an argument with old Svein about which would be the best way to patch up a hole in the roof of the big barn, and I suggested that we should both climb up ladders and have a closer look at the state of the roof. And well, Svein is supposed to check the condition of the ladders once in a while, you know? But I guess he didn't have the chance to do it in the past ten years, and the wood had rotted, or perhaps the ladder was simply fit to hold Svein's weight, but not mine..."

"Why are you laughing?" Leif was puzzled.

"Freydis," grinned Thorvard. "You should have seen how she had given poor old Svein a taste of her wrath. She swatted him on the head with a big wooden spoon until he went running with his tail between his legs. I was lying right here, on this bench, with my leg up, groaning from pain and laughter. I didn't know how we would go on until your return, but Freydis sent me to bed, sent the children to your mother, and took everything under her control."

"That is precisely the part that concerns me," remarked Leif.

"It wasn't the solution I would choose, either, but don't forget that Freydis grew up here in Brattahlid with three brothers. She sailed to Vinland twice, to Norway once, and learned a thing or two in between. So, perhaps she didn't have much experience in running a settlement, and she made a few mistakes, but about one thing there is no doubt, Leif – no one dares to mess around with her. Not if he wants to avoid being smacked on the head with a wooden spoon," Thorvard laughed again. "She just went ahead and took the reins into her hands."

"A pity I wasn't here to see it," grinned Leif.

"I will tell you more than this, Leif. She has been so busy while I laid here with a broken leg that she was forced to set aside all sorts of odd plans and impossible schemes, and now there is a lot more peace around here. I finally understood one thing: Freydis is not the kind of woman that can be locked within four walls and expected to find her happiness in spinning wool and wiping children's snot. She has far too much vigor for that."

"Well, that much is true," agreed Leif. "So what now? Do you intend to go on resting on this bench and pass the Western settlement under the permanent leadership of my sister?"

"Of course not, but I certainly intend to ask her to be more involved from now on, and I think it will be best for us both."

"What will be best for us both?" asked Freydis, who had just entered, and was still wearing her traveling cloak. Her face was pink from the wind.

"If you climb ladders instead of Thorvard," explained Leif.

"Naturally," said Freydis, "as I weigh about three times less."

She walked over to her husband and. "How are you feeling now, Thorvard? Are you doing better? Come, lean on me, put this stick aside, and let us go check on the children."

That night, the main hall was full of conversation and laughter, almost like in the good old days of Erik. The return of Leif and Thorgunna, and the notice of the anticipated visit of Thorfinn and Gudrid, lifted everyone's spirits. Leif enjoyed the presence of all his near relations so close to him – his wife and children, his mother, Thorvard and Freydis with their children – until he suddenly felt he must be alone, and retired to his own room. The muffled sounds of jokes and easy conversation he heard through the wall filled him with deep satisfaction, as if a last, and highly important, missing piece of a mosaic had been found and fitted just into its right place.

Then he realized he doesn't truly wish to be alone. He longed for his wife, and she wasn't tardy in joining him. The understanding between them no longer depended on words, and she smiled without saying a thing as she put on her long, warm woolen shift, and got into bed by his side.

"You know," he told her when his arms were wrapped around her and they both looked at the flickering light of the candle, "there is something final in this return home. I have sailed away and back again many times, but now I have a feeling I will never leave Brattahlid again."

"I feel the same way," agreed his wife.

"And this doesn't bother you?" asked Leif with a sudden shadow of insecurity.

"I didn't expect to leave Greenland even once after marrying you, my love. Now that I have gone away and come back, I understand I want for nothing."

"Neither do I. Does that mean I have grown old?"

"It means you have grown," whispered Thorgunna, caressing his stubble-covered cheek. "You have grown into a great man, Leif, and I am so proud of you."

He stroked her hair until she closed her eyes, and looked at the flame. It fluttered, about to go out.

"We had better try to get some sleep, isn't that so?" he said. "Tomorrow will be a long day."

He closed his eyes as well. Winter is looming closer, and there are still crops to gather. Some more decisions about the livestock must be made – which animals will be left for next spring and which will be butchered, for there isn't enough fodder to feed them all. Some minor alterations must be made around the house, too, and... his thoughts began to wander, and he had almost fallen asleep already, but then something suddenly woke him and he just remained lying there in the darkness, wide awake, for some time, and a strange feeling swelled up in his chest, a feeling he could not quite define. Not joy – satisfaction? Resignation? No, more than that – it was the knowledge that he is just where he is supposed to be, and he has accepted it and doesn't wish for a better fate. He will get up tomorrow morning, prepared to begin a new part of his life, a part which perhaps won't be full of exciting adventures like the first – but its meaning won't be any less, and the happiness to be found within it perhaps even more.

Knowing this warmed his heart, and upon the morrow he woke full of strength and vigor, just as the rooster began to crow. His wife was still asleep, it was still dark outside, but he no longer felt sleepy and got up from the bed. It is the beginning of a good long day, he knew. A good day in his home, in Brattahlid.

Part 3

Chapter 44

"What is your name, boy?"

"What is it to you?" the youth scowled. "I assure you, you have never heard it, nor are you likely to ever hear it in the course of your life." He took a sip of his wine. It was lousy, weak and sour. Nothing to the good rich ale back home.

"I cannot recruit you without having a name to call you by," the fat man presented a reasonable objection.

The youth hesitated. "You can call me Falcon, then."

The the boy's vast annoyance, the fat man laughed.

"I'm not sure what you young ones are playing it," he said, "but I always seem to have at least one Fox, one Hound, one Wolf and one Bull. It appears to be a sort of fashion among you Norse boys, to move south, hire out your services as sellswords, and adopt new fancy-sounding names... but none of you seem to be layabouts, this can be fairly said. Well, barbaric raids are becoming less frequent – praise the Lord! - ever since you Northerners accepted the true Faith of the Saviour, and you do have plenty of good swords – makes sense for them to be occupied in righteous ventures. Your people are mighty warriors."

"I am not so sure what you mean by *my people*," said the boy, still scowling, "but I am almost certain you are off the mark."

"Why," mused the fat man, "judging from the way you speak, you come from somewhere at the very edge of the world – Denmark or Norway or..."

"Believe me," the youth let out a hollow laugh, "to you, Norway may seem like a dreary province, but where I come from, it's like the center of the world."

The man decided to let this matter go for now.

"How old are you?" he asked instead.

"What does it matter?" the boy said evasively. "Can you not tell whether I will serve your purpose without knowing my age? I am more than up to any task that involves wearing a sword and standing vigils, and it seems to me this is just what you are looking for."

The man's eyes scanned him. True, the boy was tall, broad-shouldered and, despite his beardless face, had the look of a warrior.

"Are you a Christian?" the fat man continued his interrogation.

The boy looked more and more displeased with every moment.

"Now, what does *this* have to do with anything?"

"Everything!" countered the man. "We are talking about an important mission on behalf of the church, and I would not trust an unbeliever with a task of such delicacy. I am a man of discretion, Falcon, or whatever it is you prefer to call yourself."

"Surely, if it's such an important task, the church can provide its own men to set forth with it?"

"Well," the man hesitated, obviously in doubt regarding how much he should say, "the matter was presented to me with an air of... urgency. I was instructed to assemble a trustworthy guard as soon as possible, and in this small town I can, perhaps, have my pick of drunken fishermen who cannot tell one end of a sword from another. So I counted upon my discernment, experience and knowledge of mankind, to turn instead to those who seem honest, deserving of trust, skilled with a sword, and above all, those who know when to keep silent."

"Well, you weren't mistaken about me," said the boy. "I am all those things."

The fat man gave a short, booming laugh. "You are surely not in any danger of doing yourself injustice by excessive humility!"

"I wasn't brought up to undervalue myself by false humility," remarked the Falcon.

"So I see. Which brings me back to my original question – are you a Christian, Falcon?"

Grudgingly, the youth pulled from under his clothes a silver cross on a long, finely wrought chain.

"I was baptized. This is a gift from my mother."

The fat man sighed. He supposed this would have to do. "Well, in that case I will tell you more about the task... not all, mind – none of us, I believe, will know all. But enough to make you understand what it is that you ought to do."

"I am all ears," interjected the youth. The fat man ignored his remark.

"Some years ago," he began, "an object of sacred value fell into the holy hands of the church. It has been kept here since, in this inconspicuous but reliable place. In Rome, you see, they take the wise policy of never putting all the eggs in one basket."

"Right," the boy nodded, fiddling with his belt buckle and not looking as if his curiosity was aroused by this beginning in any way.

"Well, then," the man went on, "you know, of course, that we are now fast approaching the ten century mark from the day when our Lord Jesus was sacrificed on the cross, atoning with his blood for all our sins."

"I know that."

"Pardon me, but I would rather not be interrupted. Now, as you might have heard – since this is proclaimed by the simple men and the learned, the lowborn and the noble, the secular and holy alike – it is generally believed that, come year 1033, or at most the dawn of 1034, a mighty battle will ensue at the place of our Lord's suffering, in Jerusalem, the heart of the Holy Land. This battle, according to the prophecies, shall take place between Christians, who are heirs to the spirit of Israel, and the anti-Christ, an entity the nature of which we aren't entirely certain of, which will seek to bring the true believers down. Two outcomes are possible to this crucial battle. Redemption for all – or hell."

"Sounds impressive," remarked the boy, "but as far as I know, there are no Christians in the Holy Land."

"True," said the man, "the holy places our Lord spent his earthly life in are now in the hands of the Saracens, which is precisely why the church is planning on a continent-encompassing military campaign to liberate the Holy Land and establish a Christian kingdom there."

"When do you think that will happen?" asked the boy with a first trace of real enthusiasm.

"I know what you are thinking," the fat man winked at him. "What honor it will bring to the holy church! What glory to the righteous warriors of the Lord! But not quite so soon, I fear. The church does everything slowly and thoroughly, and it is possible that decades will pass before knights and soldiers are actually recruited for this mission."

"Oh," the Falcon said with slight disappointment. "Why did you bring this up, then?"

"Ah, but I am getting there. Once Jerusalem is in the hands of the righteous – and there is no doubt it will happen sooner or later – the church plans to restore the ancient Temple of Solomon in all its former glory, and to witness that we indeed are the rightful heirs of Israel, the holy fathers will present objects that have been used for worship in the Temple in the distant past, as described in the sacred texts."

Seeing that the boy's attention is captured, the man went on:

"Throughout the centuries, the church has been on the lookout for such lost objects, which were scattered all over the world since the Temple was destroyed. Some of them did, after much effort and search, end up in Rome and in other places monitored by the holy church. One such item, as I already told you, has been kept here until now, but recently orders were given to move it to Rome, to keep it there in higher security, in preparation for the journey it will eventually make to Jerusalem."

The boy nodded. His interest awakened, but he knew the fat man won't tell him what the object actually is, and he wasn't going to give him the pleasure of denial.

"So, all this brings us to a task which is really very straightforward," said the man. "The item we discussed must be safely conveyed from here to Rome, where it will be deposited in the most secure vaults of the church. We will set out in a group of five – you, myself, and three other men, on middling horses and in simple, inconspicuous garb. All valuables must be taken off and carefully hidden," he looked pointedly at the silver amethyst-studded brooch that held the boy's cloak in place.

With a sour expression, the Falcon removed it, pinning his cloak with a simple whale-bone carved hook instead.

"If this thing we are supposed to be guarding is so important," he said, "doesn't it merit better protection than five men can give?"

"A question I had asked myself repeatedly," the fat man readily replied. "However, a large group will move more slowly and attract more attention, and furthermore, I was told the transfer must be accomplished as soon as possible, which didn't leave me much time to assemble a large guard of reliable men. So the five of us will have to do," he concluded. "We will put on an act of ordinary travelers headed for Rome – no galloping, no riding during the night. We will travel by day, possibly stop at roadside inns for the night. You look like a clever boy, so there will be no need, of course, to tell you we must look as uninteresting as possible, and in no way arouse anyone's suspicion that we might be carrying something valuable with us. I don't expect ordinary robbers would understand the sacred meaning of the object we are to deliver to Rome, but it is of high value even if only its material worth is taken into account. High enough for an unscrupulous man to slit all our throats without a second thought."

Unconcerned, the Falcon asked:

"And the reward?"

"You and the other young one I hired here will receive your payment upon our arrival in Rome. You have no need to worry on that account. The church is generous with those who help her."

"So I have heard. Can I consider myself hired, then?"

"You can," said the fat man with a wry smile, "so why don't you tell me your real name, Falcon?"

"Harald," replied the youth after a heartbeat's hesitation. The man didn't seem convinced in the slightest.

"Well," he said slowly, surveying the boy's handsome face, his mop of thick chestnut hair and his sparkling blue eyes, "I suppose it really doesn't tell me much anyway."

"I don't know *your* name yet, either," the boy suddenly said.

"I will readily tell it to you," said the fat man, smiling again. "I am brother Gregorius."

"Brother?" the Falcon looked over the man's leather jerkin, his iron-studded belt with a sword dangling from it, his muscular hands and close-cropped neat beard. "You don't look like a monk."

"The church makes its uses of people whose piety is not immediately perceivable," said brother Gregorius, now grinning openly, "such as you and me. We will be setting out right after dawn," he added, "Meet me outside the town gates. Do not be late."

Chapter 45

When the Falcon rode out of the town gates at dawn, the other four were already waiting for him. Brother Gregorius acknowledged his presence with naught but a curt nod. As for his other companions, two of the men were so inconspicuous it was hard to define a feature in their overall appearance that would distinguish them; they were neither short nor tall, neither dark nor fair, and one tended to forget to forget their faces the second one took his eyes off them. Judging from certain unmistakable signs, the Falcon concluded they were familiar with Brother Gregorius from before, possibly being monks in disguise just like him.

The last member of the company was a sandy-haired youth about the same age as the Falcon, and one look at his face, his garb and his weapons instantly convinced the Falcon that here is another Northman, though in all likelihood not from his homeland. The other young man clearly made the same observation right away, naturally, and made a move to approach and strike a conversation, but the Falcon edged away from him almost imperceptibly.

Without saying much, they set off in the misty drizzle of a bleak morning. The Falcon noted no sign of the valuable object they were supposed to be guarding. It must be small, then, he presumed – small enough to fit under the cloak of Brother Gregorius.

They slowly and steadily rode up a narrow road, with the drizzle subsiding by mid-afternoon. The boy's cloak, boots and hair were damp, but the Falcon didn't mind – he had had many far worse salty sprays on his voyage across the sea from his homeland.

Come evenfall, Brother Gregorius called a halt and they busied themselves by setting camp in the midst of a shallow clearing a little way off the road. One of the two unremarkable silent men took upon himself the task of starting a fire, the other went to collect water from a nearby stream, while Brother Gregorius began to take provisions out of a large bag that was attached to the saddle of his horse.

The Falcon could no longer ignore the fair-haired young man who approached him with a grin and spoke in his own language: "Fancy finding myself in the company of a fellow Northman here."

"Hello," said the Falcon, without displaying excessive enthusiasm. His comrade, however, seemed to take no notice of that. He settled down on a fallen log and fixed him with a friendly, curious stare.

"I'm Bjarni Olafson, of Thordarsfjord to the west coast of Iceland," he said.

"Harald," said the Falcon, shaking hands. "Sigurdson," he added after a heartbeat.

"Where are you from?" asked Bjarni.

The Falcon frowned. "Greenland," he said after a moment, with some reluctance. He knew he could not avoid this question for long, and he hadn't really been anywhere else in his life until now, so he would have a hard time making up convincing details about life in other places.

Bjarni eyed him with the liveliest interest. "Are you, now!" he sounded impressed. "I have met some people from there, and brave, good people they were, too. Does your whole family live there?"

At that moment, their conversation was interrupted by Brother Gregorius, who called out:

"Fox and Falcon, or whatever it is that you prefer to call yourselves, come here and help keep the fire going!"

While the Falcon was stoking the fire, and one of the silent brothers filled a blackened iron pot with fresh water, Brother Gregorius began to add the contents of various packages to the pot: lentils and peas, some dried meat, a couple of onions he skillfully peeled himself... it was an odd kind of stew for a Northman's taste, but it smelled good and it was hot, and after asking for some additional salt, both youths managed a second helping of it.

After supper, Brother Gregorius took the first watch, while the other men were told to go and rest.

"I know I'm going to wake up with my neck all stiff," grumbled Bjarni, wrapping himself more snugly in his cloak.

"Tomorrow, if we are lucky, we'll reach a good inn before sunset!" called Brother Gregorius, obviously overhearing this complaint. Bjarni swore under his breath.

"It's bloody cold for autumn, and that's saying something if you consider where we come from," he said, propping himself up on his elbow and fixing the Falcon with a curious stare. "So, Harald... if you are from Greenland, do you know the local chieftain, Leif Erikson?"

"A bit," admitted the Falcon after a brief pause.

"There are many tales about that man," Bjarni went on, "they say he was a great warrior in his years, and an excellent navigator, but now he must be getting on in years... isn't he?"

"Yes," the Falcon nodded reluctantly, and it was obvious he takes no pleasure in this conversation. "I suppose so."

"But he has a son, doesn't he? About our age, so I have heard – do you know him?"

"We've met," the Falcon replied evasively.

"What is he like?" asked Bjarni. "Do you think he will be as great a chieftain as his father?"

A wry smile appeared on the Falcon's face. "People say Leif Erikson's son is a good-for-nothing scoundrel," he told Bjarni. "A pampered boy with a taste for fine wines and other men's wives. They also say his sister, Hallfryd, or his cousin, Erik, should do better to govern over Greenland once Leif passes away."

"Well," Bjarni shrugged, curling up to sleep, "someone always picks up the reins, one way or another, right?"

"I guess so," replied the Falcon, and he thought this was the end of it, but after a few minutes of silence he heard Bjarni's sleepy voice:

"And we are actually going to Rome, eh? If someone told me a year ago I would get to see the place in a twelvemonth, I would laugh in his face. I'll bet you didn't think you'd go to Rome either, did you, Harald?"

But the question hung in the air as if no answer was really expected. The Falcon kept silent, and in a few more minutes, he heard Bjarni's snores.

As Brother Gregorius promised, the next day's end found them on the front step of an inn, which was most welcome, for the day was much colder than the previous one, with a thin brittle layer of frost that broke under the hooves of their horses as they set out in the morning. The night promised to be colder still, and though the stuffy, smoky air in the inn's common room made the travelers' eyes sting, at least it was warm. They didn't fancy spending the night under the open skies.

The inn was full of travelers seeking refuge from the cold, and the air was thick with bawdy jokes, off-tune singing, and raucous laughter. Someone was strumming a lute in the corner, the same few ill-tuned notes over and over again. The oil lamps gave just enough light to notice that the floor and trestle tables alike were thickly covered in grime.

It took the innkeeper some time to shuffle forward to greet them and ask if they will be ordering supper.

"The rooms are full to bursting," he warned, "but I can let you make beds for yourselves in the barn for half the charge."

"What?!" Brother Gregorius exclaimed in outrage. "You sneaky thief, you'll be charging us for sleeping in the barn?"

The innkeeper shrugged indifferently. He was a heavily built, slow man with an impassive face.

"Word goes around I'm not chargin' for sleeping in the barn, and next thing I know, my barn's full of vagabonds and beggars," he said. "Can't blame me for doing all I can to keep my business safe. How about that supper, then?"

"What do you have?" asked Brother Gregorius.

"A fine joint of pork, roast with onions, carrots and turnips," said the innkeeper.

"Fine then, boys," said Brother Gregorius, turning towards his companions. "Since you endured my cooking without any complaint yesterday, I think you deserve a decent meal tonight. Supper for all, and a flagon of beer," he told the innkeeper.

The man nodded and shuffled away. Some minutes later, a girl approached their group. She had the same heavy-set jaw and lank hair as the innkeeper, and her face was pockmarked on top of all, but she was curvy and buxom, and the sway of her hips pointed out an unwavering confidence in her own charms. Her playful smile revealed good teeth, too, even and white. Falcon thought she looked no older than sixteen, but in the scant shifting light of the lamps it was hard to tell for sure.

"Your supper will be brought to you soon," she said. "Anything to drink, good men?"

"We ordered beer," replied Brother Gregorius, "but our drink seems tardy in coming."

"How about something stronger, on a chilly night like this?" suggested the girl. "We have good wine we made ourselves last summer. I could mull some for you with raisins, if you like."

"I'll have some wine if you take a cup with me," said Bjarni, jingling silver coins in his pocket.

The girl gave him an appraising look and another flash of her white teeth.

"Alright, then," she nodded, walking away.

Soon, their supper arrived, and the companions concentrated on satisfying their hunger and quenching their thirst. For a while, no sound was heard but chewing, the scraping of knives on plates, and a soft thud whenever a tankard was replaced upon the table.

The Falcon enjoyed his food thoroughly – it was possibly the first really good meal he had since leaving home. The pork was brown, sizzling and dripping with fat, and the beer was light, strong enough, not too sour. Brother Gregorius took the role of host upon himself, making sure everybody has enough to eat and drink.

As the inn slowly emptied and the other guests either wandered out of the door in a drunken sway or staggered off to bed, Bjarni occupied a corner further from his comrades, and sat there with the innkeeper's daughter, pouring wine for them both from the jug he had paid for. The level of noise was still too high to make out what he was saying, but the girl's laughter grew louder with each minute, proportionally to the content of wine that was poured out. The innkeeper observed this scene with a silent scowl, and when he couldn't take it any longer, his sharp voice could be heard across the hall:

"Bella! Come into the kitchen and help your mother clean up!"

The girl got up obediently, but with a gesture in Bjarni's direction that plainly hinted she is quite willing to continue their conversation later.

Soon after that, the companions headed off to the barn for the night, to make themselves as comfortable as they could in the heaps of straw. Mysteriously, Bjarni was nowhere to be seen, but Brother Gregorius made no comment on his absence. The boy who called himself Harald was pretty sure he recognized Bjarni's footsteps outside the barn, coupled with a girl's giggle.

Come morning, Bjarni was still missing, and Bella, who served them breakfast in the common hall, looked distinctly puffy-eyed and tousle-haired. She put a loaf of hot freshly baked bread on the table, along with a slab of cheese and a crock of butter, then walked off without saying a word. They could see the innkeeper shuffling his feet in the distance and looking very grumpy.

"Do you have an idea where your friend could have gone to?" Brother Gregorius asked the Falcon, frowning. "I had not counted on losing one of our number so soon in the journey."

"He is not my friend," the Falcon replied with a shrug, but there was no chance to elaborate, because at that precise moment Bjarni walked in from the yard, lacing up his breeches as he strolled up to their table as if he had no care in the world, slumped down on the bench, grabbed a thick slice of bread and a chunk of cheese and began to eat.

"What?" he said defensively, noticing the reproachful glance of Brother Gregorius. "Can't a man go outside for a leak?"

Brother Gregorius teetered on the verge of speech, it seemed, but then decided to let it slide. He took the jug of milk – it was fresh and frothy, with cream on top – and poured some into his cup.

"Eat quickly, boys," he prompted his companions. "Make sure you have your fill, but do not linger. We ought to have been on the road already."

Over on the other end of the hall, the innkeeper sharply said something to his daughter, who scowled and disappeared from view. He then resumed his business, glaring malevolently at the guests from time to time.

"Our landlord looks none too pleased," remarked the Falcon in Norse, under his breath.

"Yes, well," grinned Bjarni, "I can understand him, but I hope he doesn't think I was the first one to gain the favor of his daughter. No, that flower had been plucked already, and a good long time ago, as far as I could tell."

Brother Gregorius, who couldn't understand a word of what they were saying, cut Bjarni off:

"Quite enough chat over there, boys! The sun is high in the sky, let's get on our way!"

The first part of the day's journey passed uneventfully, and when they stopped for a midday break and Brother Gregorius opened his saddle bag to take out some bread, cheese and olives he had bought at the inn, Bjarni stretched out on the grass and yawned.

"Feeling tired?" asked the Falcon, smirking. "That poxy wench gave you no rest last night, did she?"

"Come off it, she wasn't that bad-looking," Bjarni gave him a disarming smile, "certainly not after a few cups of that strong wine she brought me, and in the dark you can hardly tell one girl from another anyway. Besides, it has always been a slim pick for me," he added, "and I assume it must be even worse in Greenland. I've heard all the women there are big and bulky, like the seals you eat every day."

"We don't eat seals every day," the Falcon corrected him. "Only when beef and pork are scarce. And it is true a woman needs to be strong, rather than a pretty dainty thing, to be considered a worthy bride in most households. There's just too much hard work always to be done for it to be otherwise. But there are some beautiful women in our land, too – my sisters among them. I have three sisters," he added. "The eldest is only fifteen, but can mount and ride a wild stallion grown men have despaired of taming, and is so beautiful that a dozen suitors were already vying for her hand when I left."

As he said that, words which his mother told his father about Hallfryd rang in his ears:

"She seems to have taken much more after her aunt Freydis than after me. She even *looks* more like her."

"She looks more like *me*," his father replied with a smile, "but I agree with you, Hallfryd reminds me of Freydis, when she was her age. Let us just hope our daughter acts more wisely."

"Wisdom at fifteen! Nay, we ought to find her a proper husband, Leif. That will tame her."

"My parents had tried that approach with Freydis. It did not work."

...Bjarni's voice cut through his musings. "Do you have brothers as well as sisters?"

"No," a cloud passed over the Falcon's face. He had often thought how much simpler things could have been for him, had Hallfryd been born a boy. *There would have been another son to make up for my father's disappointment.*

"What, are you an only son?" Bjarni looked surprised – and impressed. "Why did you leave home, then? Or were your parents so badly off that they couldn't offer you much?" he added sympathetically.

The Falcon searched for a noncommittal reply, but was saved from the necessity of answering – just then, the sound of hooves could be heard, and seven riders appeared at their roadside clearing by a merrily bubbling stream; seven warriors on swift, tall horses, with the visors of their helms pulled down. As the men pulled the reins and the horses came to a halt, neighing, the man in front of the group took off his helm. He had a pale face framed by black hair and a black, neatly trimmed beard, a hawk-like nose, and lively brown eyes.

"A pleasant day to you, good men!" he said. "Do you mind if we join you here and offer you to share our humble meal?"

"We were just about to leave," said Brother Gregorius, getting up and motioning to the others to start gathering their belongings. "But by all means, take advantage of this spot to rest. It is dry and sheltered from wind, and the water in this stream is uncommonly sweet and clear."

The black-bearded man gestured to the others to dismount, just as the five companions mounted their horses.

"Where are you headed?" asked the stranger off-handedly.

"To Rome," Brother Gregorius replied in a polite manner that did not, however, encourage further questions. "I have a brother there who trades in saffron and cloves. I am recruiting some men for him," he gestured towards his comrades, "who will be ready to receive cargo and sail to Sicily in a fortnight."

He nodded curtly to the stranger, and hurried to depart.

"I didn't like it one bit," Brother Gregorius later said under his breath to Falcon, who rode by his side at the head of the column.

"Those men?" replied the boy. "If they had wanted to do us ill, they could have. They looked like skilled warriors, and we were outnumbered."

"That is true," agreed Brother Gregorius, "but I still cannot rule out the possibility that we are being followed. In our situation, better be safe than sorry. When we stop for the night, we will go further off the road, and we will keep a low fire for just enough time to cook supper and warm up for a bit. And, although I know your friend Bjarni will be greatly disappointed, there will be no more stops at inns for us until we reach Rome."

"He is not my friend," the Falcon said again, "just because we speak the same language..."

"In a foreign country," said Brother Gregorius, "it is often enough to make friends out of people."

"So... these men," the boy changed the subject. "Do you think they have an idea of what you are carrying?"

"I do not know," Brother Gregorius frowned. "I had tried to conduct this affair with the utmost secrecy, but it is impossible to know for sure when there is more than one man in the secret.

Especially," he pierced Falcon with a stern glare, "as I have two men whom I hardly know riding by my side."

"I did *not* mention anything to anyone!" the boy said defensively.

"So you say, and something tells me I can trust you... Harald. But how, I ask you, would I know for sure? And what about your not-friend Bjarni? However I look at it, you two are the weaker links in this chain."

When time came to set camp for the night, the two silent monks did all the chores of collecting the wood and water, tethering the horses and starting a fire, as effectively and swiftly as usual. The Falcon was assigned as cook's helper, and Bjarni was sent to scan the surroundings of the camp.

"All quiet," he announced upon his return. He sat down next to the fire and accepted a wooden spoon from Brother Gregorius. He dipped the spoon into the heavy iron pot, out of which the others were already eating a hearty stew of lentils, onions and cured bacon.

Tonight, they were in luck. They came across a hastily built and abandoned hunter's hut. It was cramped and drafty, but at least they had a roof over their heads. Bjarni, of course, took care to make a sleeping place for himself next to the Falcon, and when everybody settled down, said in a whisper:

"So, Harald, you didn't tell me yet why you left home."

"Neither did you," the Falcon reminded him evasively.

"Well, with me it's all pretty much straightforward," Bjarni said dispassionately. "There are five brothers in our family, and when my old man passed away, the land left over after him just wasn't enough for us all. So, my oldest brother took over the old place, the second built himself a new house at some distance, and the other two decided they will go into trade. For some reason they didn't want me to go with them, probably because they knew I'm lousy with numbers, letters, and rubbing the right people the right way.

Now, farming was never my most precious dream, if you understand what I mean to say, but I always assumed that's what I'm going to end up doing. But staying at the farm that now belonged to my brother, without a hope of ever getting a place of my own, seemed like a ratty deal. So what was left for me to do? I *am* good with a sword, sort of, but it seems the good old days when just about anyone could go Viking are over. So, I've heard people saying that down south, on the Continent, they value Northmen as good swords for hire. Why not try my luck, I thought? If I do well, I can come back home with enough money to buy me some land and slaves, build a house, get married, and... start farming. Which, again, isn't what I dreamed of," even in the darkness, the Falcon could tell Bjarni is grinning. "But for the life of me, I can't imagine how else I would live steadily and decently. Traveling from place to place as a hired sword does get old after a while."

"Have you been doing it for a long time, then?" asked the Falcon.

"I've been wandering around Europe this past year," said Bjarni. "Worked as a bodyguard for some rich man, got paid well, saved some money, not as much as I hoped. Saw some amazing places, now heading to Rome here together with you. As I said, all is pretty much straightforward with me. Many a young man from our parts is now doing the same. So what about you, Harald? Were you driven away from Greenland by hope of gain?"

"No," said the Falcon, finally resolving to loosen his tongue, if only a bit. "It was a woman."

"Oh?" The smirk in Bjarni's voice was clearly audible. "Pangs of disappointed love?"

"Had it been disappointed, I wouldn't have to leave," said the Falcon. "She was another man's wife."

"I knew you are not as quiet as you look," remarked Bjarni appreciatively. "And so the affair came out and you were forced to leave, eh? Was she worth it, now?"

"Women are never worth as much as it seems to us when we desire them," the Falcon said sagely.

Bjarni laughed, then stifled his laughter quickly, remembering there are other people sleeping – or rather, trying to sleep – right next to them. "You are too young to think that way!" he protested.

But the younger boy already rolled on his side, his back to his companion. "Night, Bjarni," his muffled voice was heard from underneath his cloak.

Chapter 46

"Tell me about her," asked Bjarni the next day, as the travelers were idling away a morning of incessant rain. Brother Gregorius was sitting in a corner, merrily humming to himself while he whittled a flute out of a piece of wood he had procured from his bag. The two silent warrior monks were immersed each in their own employment, one polishing his sword, another reciting prayers from a holy book.

"Who?" asked the Falcon, playing for time. Bjarni nudged him in the ribs.

"Don't kid me, Harald. That woman who was the reason you left home! Who was she?"

The Falcon sighed. It seemed he had no choice. The rain showed no intention of relenting anytime soon, and bored Bjarni had sniffed out an interesting story and was now following it like a determined hound would a track of deer.

"She was married to a friend of my father's," the Falcon told him, "her name was Ingeborg."

"Was she pretty?" asked Bjarni.

"Yes," the Falcon said reservedly.

... Yes, she was lovely indeed. She had a tall, strikingly beautiful figure, a long plait of shining copper-colored hair, fine, delicate skin, and eyes the color of spring grass. The look of them was bold, impertinent even, and when her long thick lashes quivered, it changed into proper seduction. In his mind's eye, he saw once more the day when he approached her house stealthily, under a hooded cloak, and quickly, furtively knocked on the door.

His knock was promptly answered by her, and she drew him inside, wrapping her arms around his neck and bolting the door shut. She had clearly washed her hair not long ago, as it was still damp, and her clean, fresh smell was accentuated by a musky foreign fragrance she had sometimes used.

She kissed him long and deep, and it took all his willpower to pull back for a moment and ask:

"Are we alone?"

"Yes," she smiled wickedly, revealing pointed little white teeth. "Gunnar told me he will be absent all week, he had gone to old Thorketil's farm to discourse on buying some cattle or a flock of sheep or some other boring thing. He is forever going away on business, you know."

"And the servants?"

"I sent them all out on some errand or other. Even the women are out, doing the washing, it will take them all day. There is nobody to stand in the way of me and my handsome, my sweet, my strong young Falcon," she purred, unlacing his breeches in swift, deft movements of her dainty fingers.

"Wait," said her lover, catching her wrists. "Wait just one moment."

"What?" she stopped, looking both surprised and vexed.

"Gunnar. I heard rumors that he is suspecting something."

She gave a derisive laugh. "What, that old goat with his big ale-filled belly? Let him suspect for as long as he likes, he will never dare to mention it unless he sees it with his very eyes, and I am a great deal too clever to ever let him catch us."

"Still," he insisted, "We have got to make sure..."

"*You* have got to make sure you please me," she whispered, pulling off his tunic and kissing his chest. Her mouth was hot and moist, her hands nimble, and as always, she was enough to make all rational thought fade away. He easily lifted her and carried her in the familiar direction of the vast bed with its down mattress, losing himself in the softness of her skin, the feel of her body against his, the scent of her hair...

Afterwards, they laid side by side, exhausted, but already Ingeborg propped herself up on her elbow and began to make those playful and cajoling moves that plainly hinted she was expecting him to be up for action again before long. This always made him feel both flattered and a little harassed. Even he, with all the ardor of a boy towards his first woman, was hard-pressed to satisfy her appetites. Ingeborg was a couple of years older than him, and by the well-trained way of her pillow play, it seemed highly unlikely to him that she had come a maiden to Gunnar, whom she had married only last year.

Suddenly, unexpectedly, a sharp rap on the door could be heard in the languid silence. Startled, Ingeborg bolted up, yanking the bedcovers so that they covered her breasts, and leaving her lover stark naked. Without further prompting, the boy made a scramble for his clothes, pulling his tunic back on and lacing up his breeches faster than ever before. He buckled his belt with trembling hands, careful for a clink of metal not to be heard.

"Ingeborg?" The unmistakable deep voice of Gunnar sounded on the other side of the door. "Are you in there? The servants told me you locked yourself inside and sent everyone away, are you unwell?"

"Quick," Ingeborg muttered under her breath. "What are you doing with these boots? Take them off, your steps will be heard. Come on, I will let you out of the back entrance. Then I'll open the door and pretend I've been down with a headache. *Hurry!*" She hissed, pushing him forcefully towards the back door, which led to the barns.

And so the young Falcon, the bold lover, made an unseemly escape from his paramour's house through the shit-laden mud of a cattle yard, his bare feet squelching through puddles of stinking goo, his boots held in his hands.

..."That was ill done, Thorkell," his father frowned, "very ill done indeed."

An irritable expression passed over the boy's face. He was in no mood to hear remonstrations.

"Gunnar was always a friend to me," his father went on, ignoring his dismay. "He has known you since you were at your mother's breast, had often held you on his knee, looked at you as if you were one of his nephews. Imagine what state he was in when he came to me..."

"What will happen to Ingeborg?" asked Thorkell. His father shrugged indifferently.

"Since Gunnar will not divorce her, which I suggested he should do, by the way, I expect she will continue whoring once he permits her to get out of the house once more. But not with you," Leif raised a threatening finger.

Thorkell chose to let this remark pass.

"It is hardly possible to marry a young beauty like Ingeborg to a fat old man like Gunnar, and expect her to be content," he said, "however rich he might be."

"Gunnar is not old," countered his father. "Oh sure, he *might* be considered as such by a green boy of seventeen, but he is only thirty-five, and strong as an ox. Personally, I worry more about what will happen to *you* than to the unfaithful wife who is now undoubtedly softening Gunnar's heart with fake remorse and a great deal of tears."

"I had not really planned this, you know," said Thorkell with a jolt of regret. "I just... the first time it happened, I simply found myself alone with her, and then... she... came at me. She was always touching me before that," he went on, "smoothing out my tunic, ruffling my hair, pressing to me as if accidentally when Gunnar invited us to feast with him last harvest-time... she chose me," he finished, his face burning with humiliation for the lameness of his own excuses. "Can you understand this?"

"I can," said Leif, and Thorkell thought he could see his father's beard twitch with a suppressed smile, which he considered a good sign. "But still, this doesn't change Gunnar's feelings one bit. He wants justice... and I must say, Thorkell, he is entirely within his rights."

"You mean to say, he might try to kill me?" Thorkell frowned. His father sighed.

"Had the matter been known only to him, you and myself, he might have been willing to smooth things over – provided a hefty sum is offered to him as compensation, of course. But such things get out and about, Thorkell. By now, half the settlement knows Gunnar was cuckolded by his young wife and the chieftain's son, and all who know Gunnar as a self-respecting man expect him not to take this in his stride."

"So what am I to do?" asked the boy.

A shadow passed over his father's face as he replied:

"Leave, and promptly."

Thorkell's heart jumped into his throat, beating violently. This was a door which he had very nearly despaired of opening - yet here was an opportunity, ready to fall into his lap.

"But where would you have me go?" asked the youth, holding his breath. On this account, he knew, he was not to expect treats. His father fixed him with a stern gaze.

"I have been asking myself the very same thing," he admitted, the lines on his face more prominent than ever.

His son did not wish to betray his tension by further inquiry. He waited.

"I have made many mistakes with you, Thorkell," said his father. "I have been too indulgent with you, too complacent, I demanded very little of you, and here is the result. By your age, you are almost a man – yet you are immature, irresponsible, idle, flippant and vain."

Thorkell continued in silence, but his face showed every sign of defiance. Leif Erikson went on:

"When your renowned grandfather – my own good father, Erik the Red - was your age, he was already a leader, with people rallying around him. When I..."

Here Leif stopped; an honest recollection he couldn't ignore reminded him that at the age of seventeen, he was perhaps more like his son than he cared to admit. He also recollected that he owed his reformation of character largely to his first marriage, a prospect which didn't seem likely for his son anytime soon.

"No, I don't have much to boast of, I fear," he concluded, "but when you have children of your own one day, you will understand how natural it is for us, as parents, to want our offspring to be better than ourselves. Hallfryd, Gudrun and Sif were brought up by your mother, and they are all, it appears, turning out remarkably well. Your upbringing, in contrast, was my responsibility, and there I abysmally failed. Yet I know nature has endowed you well, son – you have a bold heart, an eager mind, a proud spirit, and a pure soul. Your being thoughtless and spoiled are the failings of youth which, I hope, can and will be corrected in time."

"Thank you for this allowance, Father," Thorkell remarked tartly.

"There is no need to be cheeky. As I said, my primary concern for the time being is to get you well away from Brattahlid – nay, away from Greenland, for as long as you are in the same country as Gunnar, I will not be at peace. But where should I send you? This is something over which I lost my sleep all last night."

"I am not a cargo of seal-skins to be *sent* anywhere!" said Thorkell, firing up. "Do you mean to tell me I have no say in the matter?"

"Be quiet and listen. Is there a mission, I asked myself, an expedition, any business worthy of your situation and fitting for your abilities? But I fear there is none. There are not many ships at this time of year. Yet go you must; and so, I concluded, Thorhall is leaving for Iceland in three days, and you will go with him. From there, you can find passage to the continent, where they value a good sword. This is not what I would wish for my son, but hopefully, a year as a hired sword will be enough for you to gain some experience and see some of the world and, more importantly, to have the gossip die down."

"So my exile is to last only a year?" Thorkell asked ironically.

"I am hopeful that a year abroad should suffice," said Leif. "In the meantime, I shall do my best to try and appease Gunnar, perhaps find him another, better piece of land in another part of the country, and persuade him to sell his farm to me. I will be loath to part with Gunnar," he added, "He is a loyal, trustworthy, sensible man. But I fear that in the current state of affairs, I have no choice."

Thorkell's fate, therefore, was decided and sealed. He felt relief and even a certain sort of nervous anticipation; he knew he was irrevocably separated from Ingeborg, too, and his own resignation in the face of this fact surprised him slightly. He was not desperate to see her again – he hardly wished for it, even though their meetings were so ardently desired by him before! Nothing seemed to attach him to home now... nothing but one person he yet dreaded to meet.

When he came to see his mother, her face was composed and she even met him with a smile, but the distinct redness and puffiness of the delicate skin around her eyes betrayed that she had been crying.

"Come and eat, son," she said, gesturing towards a plate of cheese and dried apples.

At thirty-five, Thorgunna was still a beautiful woman, of noble manners and a queenly stature, but right now she looked helpless and lost.

"Mother, I..." he began, hardly knowing what it was that he wanted to say, but she rendered him silent with a gesture of her hand.

"There is no need to justify yourself, Thorkell. I know your blunder stemmed more from weakness than wickedness, and besides, many a lad your age is gone from home to see the world. It is only a mother's heart that brings tears to my eyes upon so sudden a parting. In a year, I hope, we shall see you again, and I expect that, when you return, you will take a larger share in your father's concerns about the settlement."

But here Thorkell became defensive. "I doubt I am made for this," he said.

"What do you mean by *this*?" his mother didn't understand.

"This," he gestured around the room, "all of this. Worrying about shortages of timber, settling disputes, traveling to celebrate the harvest with farmers all over the country, buying and selling of cattle, strengthening our defenses and cheering people up through endless winters. My grandfather was good at this, so is my father, but not I. I am unequal to carrying such a burden."

"You are like your father," said Thorgunna, nodding. "When your grandfather died, Leif, too, felt that he is stepping into shoes that are much too big for him. Yet he succeeded; he is as good a chieftain as Erik the Red was, and no less admirable a man."

"My father knew his duty. By the time Red Erik died, Father was his only son."

"As are you," his mother reminded him.

"There is Hallfryd."

"Hallfryd is valiant, open-hearted and clever, but she is a girl. She will marry, and even if she settles close to us, she will no longer be part of this household."

"You are forgetting Erik," argued Thorkell. "He is responsible, sensible, reliable... everything I am not, according to Father," he bitterly concluded.

"We all love Erik dearly," said Thorgunna, "yet the fact remains that he is your father's nephew, not his son."

"More's the pity," shrugged Thorkell, "because Erik seems a lot better suited to the position I must have but don't want."

"What would you do instead, then?" asked his mother.

"I can hardly tell you," Thorkell shook his head, "but I do know I would like to have a choice, something that no one is very keen to give me, somehow. Perhaps I would like to sail unknown seas and explore new lands, like my father did in his youth. Or make myself into a successful trader, or travel far to the East and engage myself in the mysterious sciences that are only learned there. I could even pledge myself to the church..."

He had achieved his purpose. His mother could not suppress a smile.

"That," she said, "is unlikely."

"You are right. But the occupation I feel suited for least of all is being the leader of a far-flung colony, which is exactly what you all are expecting me to do. Now, perhaps I will not return in a year. Perhaps I will stay in Europe a while longer..."

"Thorkell," said his mother, "I didn't wish to say this, but it seems that I must."

Her eyes filled with tears again. His attention was captured, and something sank deep in his stomach.

"What is the matter?" he asked anxiously.

"Your father."

"What is wrong with Father?" asked the boy with a feeling of foreboding.

"He is nearing fifty, and although I had always been sure he would live many years longer," his mother's voice broke, "now I am not so certain we can count upon that. He hides it, he does his best to go on as always so as not to worry anyone, but I know he hasn't been the same since his bout of illness last winter. He needs more rest, he needs someone to care for him..."

"You can care for him, Mother," Thorkell said quickly. "You and my sisters."

"I do all I can to make Leif more comfortable, but he needs more than a wife who runs his house and makes sure he has a good meal. He needs someone who could share his burden."

"He has Uncle Thorvard and Aunt Freydis," said Thorkell, "and..."

"... and above all," his mother cut across him, "he needs to know that, on the day when he is finally forced to let go, his son will be there to take over his duties."

Again, Thorkell made to speak, but she silenced him with a mute plea.

"As Leif's wife," she said, tears now streaming freely down her cheeks, "I don't know what I should do without him. But as Thorgunna, the mistress of Brattahlid, I know well what arrangements I need to make to get the settlement running smoothly for a while longer. All this, however, won't be worth much without you. If Leif dies without a son who is ready to take his place, Greenland will be plunged into strife and conflict."

"What you say makes me leave with a heavier heart than I otherwise would have," said Thorkell, "yet I find it hard to believe my father's life is in any immediate danger."

"It was not my intention to make you believe that," said Thorgunna, "but merely to stress it to you, my son, how crucial it is for us all to have you back home safe and whole – and soon."

She pressed his hand, not requiring a reply, for which he was grateful.

"Swanhild will be very disappointed to hear that you are leaving," she sighed wistfully, as if voicing an afterthought.

Swanhild was a gentle and pretty girl, about Hallfryd's age, and her bosom friend since childhood. She had taken a fancy to Thorkell a long time ago, but was always so shy in his presence that he didn't know what to make of her. Neither was she the type to attract attention to herself by breathtaking beauty. While her figure was good, she was of small stature; and although her features were regular, and her dark hair and big deep grey eyes with their long dark eyelashes were even uncommonly fine, there was nothing striking in her face, none of Ingeborg's seductive charm.

"Mother, I do not wish you to be deceived on this account," said Thorkell. "Swanhild is a very good sort of girl, but there isn't, and never was, an understanding between us."

"I know," his mother nodded sadly, "for had there been an understanding, all this unfortunate business might not have happened, and you would not be going away.

Hallfryd, his sister, was less inclined to take things in stride.

"This is *so* like you!" she exclaimed angrily, pushing him squarely in the chest.

"What is?" inquired Thorkell, rubbing the spot where she shoved him.

"All this!" she snapped. "Giving mortal offence to a good man. Getting Father into so much trouble as he is trying to smooth it all over. Going away just when you are needed..."

"Father is *sending* me away," he pointed out.

"Don't pretend this is not what you always wanted!" Hallfryd pushed an accusing finger into his chest. "To get away from Greenland, see the great wide world with all its wonders..."

"And what is wrong with that?" he challenged her. "Our father did his fair share of traveling when he was young - "

"Not when *his* father was ill," Hallfryd's eyes were slits.

"Father is not ill, it's just that he – you know – he is getting on in years, and everybody who knew him when he was young is having trouble to... to adjust the way they see him."

"Fine," said his sister. "If you wish to deceive yourself... but I'm still telling you this cow Ingeborg gave you far more trouble than she was worth."

"You cannot understand," Thorkell said with an air of superiority, "you are not a man..."

"I am glad I'm not a man, then," huffed Hallfryd.

"To tell you the truth, I am surprised you even know about this," remarked Thorkell. "I thought you weren't home."

"I went out as soon as I heard," explained Hallfryd. "I thought I ought to tell Swanhild before someone else does," she shot him a dirty look.

"I don't know where you and Mother get such ideas," he said, "but..."

"Don't be surprised if you find her married when you return," interjected Hallfryd, waggling her finger at him.

"What about you?" he teased, eager for a change of subject. "Have you and Erik settled it all between you yet?"

"Very amusing, you are," was all her grudging reply.

"I thought you were fond of Erik."

"Of course I am," she nodded, "just as I am fond of *you*, even though your stupidity exasperates me sometimes. I could never think of marrying Erik, though. He and I are too much like brother and sister. I will miss you, Thorkell," she added, her gaze suddenly steadfast and serious. "Oh, how I shall miss you, you stupid, ignorant..."

"I will miss you too," he admitted, clumsily patting her sister's arm, "more than anything in Brattahlid."

When the small crowd came to bid farewell to Thorkell, a contrast could be strongly seen between the stooped shoulders of Leif and Thorvard's tall figure, still bold and upright. Freydis, less than a decade Leif's junior, looked many years younger than her brother.

Gudrun and Sif hung about their brother until the very last, together with their mother; but Hallfryd merely stood to the side, her arms folded, a frown upon her face. Erik, her cousin, hovered close to her.

"They will make a nice couple, those two," Freydis whispered to Leif, fondly staring at her son, who was now nearly as tall and broad-shouldered as his father. "And a good thing, too, because things have been a little dull at our place ever since Sygni left home."

"Do not make any illusions," countered her brother. "Hallfryd plainly told Erik it can never be. No betrothal will take place."

"Oh, and you still take seriously what young girls *plainly say*, do you?" smirked Freydis. "You are hopeless, Leif. Mark my words, though they are very young, they will in all probability be wed next year, or at most the year after."

"She told Erik that, as far as she is concerned, they are like brother and sister."

"Well, so were Thorvard and I," grinned Freydis, "until one day, we weren't."

Thorkell took leave of everyone, embracing his mother and sisters, shaking hands with his father, uncle and cousin. He made a tentative move in Hallfryd's direction, but she turned her back on him. He shrugged helplessly and climbed on board, ushered by Thorhall. Only when the ship took off and began to gain speed did Hallfryd finally consent to turn in his direction.

And a gust of western wind brought to Thorkell his sister's parting words:

"Thorkell Leifson, you are a complete *arse!*"

Chapter 47

"Pay attention now, boys," said Brother Gregorius, "we are going to pass through Genua. Not what I would wish," he scowled, "but if we try to bypass the city, it will take too much time. So we go through as quietly as possible. No delays, no dawdling, is that understood?"

"We won't stop even for a night?" Bjarni asked glumly.

"I fear not," Gregorius said briskly. "Just ride through, is that clear? The serving girls in the port taverns won't know what they are missing," he added with a smirk. "Now, of course we are going to stop at the market, as our food supplies are beginning to dwindle, but other than that, no delays."

"He is a killjoy, the fat one," Bjarni said quietly in Norse. "I can't wait to be shot of him. When we get this bloody who-knows-what to Rome, we'll visit every tavern on our way, eh, Harald?"

But Thorkell didn't partake in these sentiments. "There will not be much silver left for you to take home, at this rate," he pointed out.

"Well, yes," Bjarni admitted sheepishly, "but what's this to you? You are not in want of coin, judging from how you told me your father gave a heap of silver to that offended husband, to prevent him from getting an axe through your head..."

Thorkell felt a vague pang of regret for telling him the details of the episode in which he escaped barefoot from Gunnar's house. Bjarni made for a good listener, though. He relished the story.

"So," he said shrewdly, "was she worth all the hassle, then, this Ingeborg?"

Thorkell shrugged. "To tell the truth, I can scarcely remember her face," he admitted.

"Aye, one is hard pressed to remember faces after a while," Bjarni nodded understandingly. "It is the tits that stay in your memory longer, so I've noticed. One always remembers the tits of his first woman," he added with the air of fond reminiscence. "Did she have a nice pair?"

But in Thorkell's mind, the whole of his paramour's image was beginning to seem fuzzy, indistinct, as though covered by the fog of many years. All he could remember was the sultry look, the vapid smile, and the forcefulness of the seduction.

"... I don't understand why raisins should be so costly," complained Brother Gregorius as they replenished their stock of supplies at the local market. It was teeming with people. The air was filled with the calls of merchants, the smell of fish, and the haggling of countless customers.

"You need not buy any if they are too costly," advised Thorkell indifferently. He was observing a distinctly unfamiliar kind of fish in the seafood row.

"I would not, but it's still a long ride to Rome, and in the years I have been traveling on horseback, I never found something that gives strength to a tired rider as quickly and easily, and in as wholesome a way, as a handful of almonds and raisins."

And, sighing resentfully, he bought some raisins and tied them securely in a rough clean cloth.

As they passed by the port, Thorkell felt a tug of longing at his heart, induced by the sound of waves, the salty spray and the sight of many ships, some of them large and magnificent, others old and shabby. This lively, colorful southern place was as different as possible from the silent fjords of Greenland, where the sight of a single longboat was a cause for exhilaration. Yet essentially, all ports are the same – places where one can get on a ship and travel on to the next destination, and he found himself thinking of the dear ones he left home, all those weeks ago. It was the first time he left home for long, and he wondered whether he will find them all much altered upon his return – whether his father will be well, Hallfryd married, and Gudrun and Sif much grown, when he is back.

"Are you listening, Harald?" sounded the voice of Brother Gregorius. "I was saying we turn around now - the sun will set soon and I don't fancy finding myself in the port area after dark. Come, we are moving into a quieter part of the city to try and get out of the gates as soon as possible."

The sun had already set while they were riding through a quiet street on their way to the gates. As darkness fell, the streets emptied rapidly. There were no lanterns, no torches in this part of town, and the riders retained tolerable visibility only thanks to the light of a bright half-moon. The hooves of their horses squelched loudly through the accumulated mud of lengthy rains.

It was then that they suddenly heard the ominous beat of more hooves, both in front and behind them, and seven men appeared – four at their front, three at their back. One of the men in front rode a little forward. Even in the faint light, there was no mistaking his dark hair and beard, the pale skin, and the distinct features. He was the stranger they met by the roadside stream.

"I know you have it," his quiet voice, directed at Brother Gregorius, could be heard clearly in the silence. "Hand it over."

Brother Gregorius didn't say a word. Neither did he move. His eyes darted around, confirming that there was, indeed, no way of escape. This knowledge was reflected in the pallor and the grim expression of his face.

"Hand it over," repeated the stranger, holding out an outstretched hand, "and no one need get hurt."

Thorkell, however, knew better than to believe this. The way he saw it, they'd have to either fight their way through, or die at sword point. In a fraction of a moment, he analyzed it all and saw their situation with cold clarity. Almost without thinking, he drew out his sword with a clang – and in the moment that followed, the narrow street rang with the song of steel.

He was not bad with a sword, but this was his first real fight, and shamefully, just as his sword collided with the back of someone's helm and sent it flying away, the weapon was knocked out of his hand. This proved to be a blessing in disguise, though, because it made him resort to his battle-axe, which was less pretentious but speedier and more familiar in his hand. He swung it forward, and it sank into something soft, and then there was the crunch of splitting bone, and he felt sickeningly exhilarated; but just then, he heard Bjarni's urgent exclamation behind him, and his horse reared, and he was thrown off and plunged into total darkness.

Next thing Thorkell knew, he was resting on something very soft and comfortable, with warm coverlets heaped up on top of him. He felt no pain, actually, just extreme weakness, to the point of being unable to lift a finger. In his consciousness, he felt as though mere seconds have passed since he fell, yet that couldn't be right – someone had lifted him up, after all, carried him away from the fight, brought him here, into this unfamiliar room, undressed him, placed him in this bed and skillfully, tightly bandaged his left leg from the thigh down.

Two voices were conversing near him, in a tongue he couldn't recognize; one was low and guttural, the other sounded like the song of a bird in a high summer sky. A voice that would certainly have made him think he has stepped out of the world of living, mused Thorkell, if it weren't for the increasing clarity coming back to his mind, and the growing discomfort in his body.

Footsteps approached, and a third, anxious voice he recognized as belonging to Brother Gregorius spoke in Latin:

"How is he?"

"His fever has subsided," the low voice said, "his delirium is over. Hopefully, sleep will now serve to heal him."

But with the return of consciousness pain began to creep over him, and Thorkell let out a low moan, upon hearing which the two men were rendered silent and hastened towards his bed. He heard light, retreating footsteps as well, and opened his eyes just in time to see a slender figure disappear in the door frame.

Upon perceiving that his eyes are open, Brother Gregorius came closer.

"Harald?" he sounded deeply concerned. "How do you feel?"

His tongue felt like parchment, and his voice came out extremely hoarse as he replied:

"I've been better."

"I shall tell one of the servants to bring him something to drink, and perhaps he can eat a little as well," the other man said quietly to Brother Gregorius in Latin, and went out as well.

"We feared for your life, my dear boy," said Brother Gregorius anxiously, once they were left alone, "but now it appears that, with the help of God and the Holy Virgin, you will make a full recovery in time."

"How long have I been like this?" asked Thorkell. He was beginning to feel each of his wounds separately now, a burning scorch at his left thigh, a throbbing pain in his right arm and shoulder and a dull, pressing headache. Even breathing brought pain with every expansion of his chest.

"Two full days, and all this time you had been hovering between life and death," Gregorius told him. "It was a nasty blow you received to your head, but if Bjarni hadn't pulled you off your horse, your skull would have been hacked in two. A deep long cut to your thigh, right through muscle and flesh, but all has been done to prevent inflammation. A cracked rib, we suspect – not much one can do on this account but rest – and a horse kicked you in the shoulder and arm as you tumbled down – a miracle you weren't trampled."

"What about the others?" asked Thorkell, feeling a sharp stab of dread.

A shadow passed over the plump, usually cheerful face of Brother Gregorius.

"Brother Michael is dead," he said, "and Bjarni is wounded, but his injuries were by no means as serious as yours. He has been up and about for a day already, and is very anxious about you. Brother Lazarus and myself escaped unscathed."

"I regret to hear this, about Brother Michael," offered Thorkell. "Have you known him long?"

"These twenty years," replied Brother Gregorius, thus confirming Thorkell's earlier suspicions. He sounded very somber. "A good, loyal man he was, may God rest his soul. But you, Harald – you were brilliant. They were surprised when you charged right at them so fearlessly, and this gave us a split second's advantage, which decided the entire outcome of that encounter. Had it been otherwise, we wouldn't live to tell the tale. You brought one of them down with you, and Bjarni killed

392

two. The rest scattered. It was a lucky day for the church when I made the decision to contract you and your countryman."

Bjarni was no countryman to him, of course, but Thorkell had no energy to point that out. "Those were the same men we met back then," he remarked instead.

"I told you even then that I didn't like their look, did I not?"

"And you still have no idea who they might have been?"

"No, I fear not. But as I said, even excluding our own group from suspicion, there are too many people in on this secret to vouch for perfect discretion, in my humble opinion."

"The thing we are supposed to be guarding... is it still safe, then?" asked Thorkell.

"Yes," nodded Brother Gregorius, "as safe as ever. All thanks to you two brave young men. Have no doubt, you will be amply rewarded when we reach Rome."

A question sprang up to Thorkell's mind, and he was surprised it took him so long to think of it. "Where are we?"

"Ah, now, I am glad you asked," replied Brother Gregorius in a satisfied tone. "You see, the racket we made on that street when those bastards caught up with us could be clearly heard at a distance, but most home-owners bolted their doors and windows shut, the cowards. Well, I can scarcely blame them," he added as an afterthought, "if I had a family to protect, I might just have done the same. But the owner of this house," he gestured around the comfortable spacious room, "opened his doors for us as soon as our foes were driven away, and has been a most gracious host to us ever since. He has done everything in his power to get the best treatment and every possible relief for your wounds, so that you probably owe him your life. Still, I would tread carefully around him," Gregorius went on warningly, "he is not a man of the True Faith, you see. He is a Jew. Under regular circumstances, in the course of a delicate mission such as ours, I would not be staying under a Jew's roof, for it is known these people cannot be fully trusted. But due to your condition, we will have to trespass upon his generous hospitality a little longer, as unwilling as I am to delay our journey."

"You could leave me here," suggested Thorkell, "and tell me where I should seek you in Rome, so that I can collect my payment later. I trust you shall not deceive me on this account."

Brother Gregorius looked genuinely offended. "Certainly not, but did you think we would go on and leave such a valiant comrade behind, in the hands of people who aren't even Christians? I would consider this the height of dishonor. No, we will wait for your recovery, Harald."

Soon after that, a servant came with a cup of warm honeyed milk. Throkell's stomach reeled at first, but he was able to keep it down, and after drinking, he felt better.

"Excellent," Brother Gregorius nodded approvingly. "You are still very weak, of course, after two days of fever and no nourishment. I will leave you to rest now, and after you sleep some more, I shall tell Bjarni he can come and see you. He has been very worried."

There must have been something more than milk in the cup that was brought to Thorkell, because as soon as he finished drinking and set the empty cup aside, his head fell upon the pillows and he sank into peaceful, painless, dreamless sleep.

When he awoke, the sunset was already glowing ruby red outside the windows, and he felt vastly better. Just as he was debating within himself whether he might attempt to prop himself up to a sitting position, the door was slowly, quietly pushed open.

Thorkell forgot that he wanted to move; that he needed to exhale. It was as though an invisible hand seized his lungs, only allowing him to draw quick, shallow breaths.

A maiden walked into the room – presumably the one he had earlier vaguely, fleetingly glimpsed walking out, but then he had no chance to observe just how lovely she was. Her figure was tall and so slender that it would have appeared fragile, if it weren't for the unmistakable confidence of her movements, the easy grace that defined her air. Her hair, tumbling loose down her shoulders, was as black as the wide velvet ribbon that held it off her forehead, but it shone like silk. The black locks framed a face of exquisite whiteness, yet with a visible rosy bloom of health underneath its delicate pallor. The line of her jaw, the curve of her eyebrows, the contrast between the whiteness of her forehead and the dark of her hair – it was all perfection, but most mesmerizing were her eyes, the color of dark aged honey. They were heavily shadowed by long, thick, black eyelashes, with an expression unusually steadfast and serious for a maid of around sixteen.

If Thorkell had been a religious Christian, he could have sworn he just saw an angel descended straight from heaven. If he had upheld the ancient beliefs of his forefathers, he could have thought she was a vision the gods sent to taunt him.

He didn't even dare to blink, for fear that she will be gone within the second. But the girl showed no intention of going; on the contrary, she looked purposeful and busy. In her arms, she carried a basin of water and some fresh clean cloths. In an unhurried, efficient way she put those down and came near him. When she saw that he was awake, an expression of satisfaction appeared upon her face.

"I was told you have awoken. Are you feeling better?"

Instantly, he realized it was her voice that he heard when consciousness first returned to him. He, however, seemed to have lost the power of speech. He made to try and rouse himself, but the maid restrained him with an alarmed gesture.

"What are you doing? Do not exert yourself. You have been very ill."

Obediently, he sank back into his pillows. He realized that, because of his silence, it might occur to her that he does not speak Latin, so he cleared his throat and, with effort, rasped something that could pass for "alright".

"I will need you to roll over to the side, though, if you can," added the girl. Her Latin, he noticed, had an accent not typical of the locals. "I want to check whether your bandages need changing."

"Was it you who treated my wounds, then?" Thorkell asked in amazement.

"Certainly," she said. "An uncle of mine is a great physician, and he taught me quite a bit about nursing ever since I was little. Can you roll over, then?"

Thorkell did so, feeling dizzy – from the change of position, or from the fact that her hands were touching him, he did not know. Her fingers were very nimble, her movements purposeful, and he didn't wince at all as she changed the bandaging of his thigh.

"Did you change my clothes, too?" he asked with a sudden upsurge of horror. For the first time, a slight smile lifted up the corners of her lips.

"Of course not," she assuaged his fears, "we have enough men-servants in the house."

Now that he looked at her without the immediate fear of being blinded as though by the sun, he noticed that she was wearing an obviously costly, richly embroidered dress, though of a queer fashion. Earrings of gold and amber were dangling from her ears, and reddish gold bracelets gleamed at her wrists.

"Are you the daughter of our host?" asked Thorkell.

"Yes," she said. "My father's name is Maimon Sofer. I am Tzipporah. Now rest," she told him firmly. "I will give orders that something nourishing should be brought to you."

And without looking at him again, she picked up the basin of water with the used bandages, and walked out.

When the last trace of light disappeared below the treetops, and after a servant passed through the room to light an oil lamp, Bjarni stepped in. His left hand was bandaged, and so was his brow, but otherwise he looked unscathed.

"Harald, you are awake, that's good – how are you?"

"Never been better," Thorkell replied distractedly, dazedly, still seeing the ethereal beautiful face before his eyes, still hearing the melodic voice with an exotic lilt.

"What?" Bjarni squinted suspiciously. "They nearly hacked you to pieces, my friend. I thought we were both goners."

"You saved my life," said Thorkell.

"And you saved us all by hauling yourself straight at them," countered Bjarni. "A reckless move, but brave – one which would have earned you a place in Valhalla, when the old gods were still in power," he grinned. "Anyway, it was not what they expected. So," he said, after a brief pause, "what say you to being here? Looks like this house belongs to a mighty rich man, does it not? I have never seen so many embroidered tapestries and so many servants in one place. I suppose we should consider ourselves lucky that he took us in. And a great good care he is taking of us, too. This Jew's daughter is quite a skillful nurse. Not to mention a fair maid," he grinned. "But have you not seen her?"

"I did," confessed Thorkell.

"Beautiful girl, is she not?"

Thorkell remained mute. He felt it was almost sacrilegious to try and describe her in simple, mundane words. Instead, he changed the subject.

"Brother Gregorius says he has no idea who the men that attacked us were," he said, "but I don't believe him. I think he has his own guesses, but prefers not to share them with us."

"Well, he is within his right to do so – we are only hired swords, after all," Bjarni said reasonably. "What would induce him to trust us?"

"Nothing, apart from the fact that we saved his life," Thorkell said tartly.

"We were saving ours at the same time."

"Bjarni," Thorkell said, struck by a sudden idea, "you didn't mention the task you were hired to do to anyone, did you?"

Bjarni was silent for a moment, considering this. "Now," he frowned, "the night before we set off, I spent some time in a tavern, and I've had a few drinks. What exactly I said, I don't remember, because it all became a bit mixed in my head after some tankards of ale. But even if I said something I shouldn't have, I doubt common brigands would have followed us all this way. There are more than enough unwary travelers carrying valuable goods, after all."

"But what we are guarding isn't just an object of value," said Thorkell. "It is supposed to be a unique treasure."

"Supposed to be," nodded Bjarni, "but we don't even know what it actually is, do we?"

"No," conceded Throkell. "We do not."

Just as Bjarni was walking out, he passed a servant that came into Thorkell's room, carrying a tray laden with a bowl of lamb broth and a small loaf of bread. Thorkell managed a few chunks of the bread, which he had softened by dipping it in the broth, but he didn't have much of an appetite – and soon, instead of eating, he found himself staring at the bowl. It was made of clay, beautifully glazed and covered with an intricate design. Even the simple wooden spoon that was brought along with it was fastidiously sanded and polished until it was smooth as silk. Everything in this house implied wealth, prosperity, good taste and attention to detail.

Unexpectedly for himself, Thorkell reflected once more on the events that have led him to leave home. Ingeborg's image looked more indistinct than ever, but all of a sudden, Gunnar's face appeared clearly before his eyes – a broad, good-natured freckled face with a bulbous nose and heavy eyebrows. He remembered how Gunnar had played with him as a child, let him ride on his mighty shoulders and gave him treats such as baked apples and roast nuts, and felt a stab of burning shame. His glorious journey suddenly appeared to him no more than a cowardly escape, and he resolved within himself that if he chances to come home in one piece, he will not avoid Gunnar. He will take care to meet him and try to make what amends he can.

Chapter 48

The days passed by, and Thorkell gradually recovered his strength. Brother Gregorius often came to see him and expressed deep satisfaction about his speedy recuperation. Bjarni visited even more often, and soon, leaning on his comrade's arm, Thorkell was able to descend from the bed and stroll around the quiet, well-kept, fragrant garden behind the house. That place touched his senses in a way none other ever did. Until now, Thorkell had never known anyone who put work – and hard work it was, too, that was plain to see – in a plot of land solely for the sake of beauty. Back home, people grew turnips, carrots and radishes, and though often he felt something expand in his chest when he looked at a meadow full of flowers in the height of summer, more often than not he would remark to himself, "this is going to make good hay".

Tzipporah, the unattainable maiden of unearthly beauty that became known to him by such a sudden chance, came too – to check on the healing process of his wounds or to suggest fortifying foods. She was always purposeful and practical, and seldom allowed a word that was not strictly necessary to escape her lips, but those she did utter were cherished by him as treasure. He hoarded every look, every word, every mild gesture that might have indicated she is not completely indifferent to him – although at the same time he cursed himself for an insolent fool.

He soon learned that the elderly Jew under whose roof they were staying, Maimon Sofer, was a widower. He had four other children beside Tzipporah – two sons older than her and two daughters younger, but his middle child was without a doubt his favorite, the one on whose judgment he most readily relied and the one whom he cherished most. This was easily understandable - for, besides possessing exquisite beauty, Tzipporah had a clever mind that would have done honor to any learned man. Also, her temper was sweet, but there was something unyielding in her, something mysterious and attractive unlike anything he had known before.

When Thorkell got well enough to have his bandages removed, Tzipporah stopped coming into his room, for it became obvious her help is no longer needed, and this he sorely regretted. But sometimes he caught glimpses of her around the house. It appeared to him that she was always employed; she was amazingly well-learned, knew several tongues, and when she wasn't busy transcribing some orders for her father, she could be seen teaching her younger sisters, reading to them out of beautiful leather-bound volumes, or doing needlework with them. She seldom left the confines of the house and gardens, and when she did, she covered her face with a thick veil. Thorkell well understood why that might be – beauty such as hers was bound to promote greed. Jews were respected at Genua at that time, in particular rich, well-connected men like Maimon Sofer, but their position, as always, as anywhere, was precarious. Thorkell shuddered with the thought that lustful hands might stretch out to Tzipporah, and that he will be able to do nothing if that happens.

As he got steadily better, Brother Gregorius began to talk of their imminent departure. Such notions threw Thorkell into an agony of despair. He didn't know what he would do when inevitably, soon, he would have to quit this house without a valid excuse to return. Yet return he must, under whatever pretext, in whatever position – a sellsword, a servant, a suitor – to be close to the maiden who with so little effort took such thorough possession of his heart.

If his thoughts could be at all diverted from the prospect of parting from Tzipporah, he would have observed that it was, perhaps, more than a little odd that up until now, he had seen nothing of their gracious, generous and most benevolent host, the rich merchant Maimon Sofer. Finally, one day when he was almost completely recovered, he was stricken with the thought that he is probably going to leave without glimpsing even once the face of the man who owned this luxurious mansion.

The meeting between them, however, took place the very same night.

After knocking on the door and receiving permission to enter, a man came into Thorkell's room; a plump, short, hook-nosed, dark-haired middle-aged man dressed in the fine garb of someone who had never wielded a sword. He smelled of rosewater. He could only be the master of this house, and when he spoke, Thorkell recognized his low guttural voice as the one which spoke next to his bed when he first woke and found himself here.

"We have not met before," said the man. "My name is Maimon Sofer, and it is I who had the pleasure of receiving you and your comrades here."

"I know," said Thorkell, not knowing why his heart began to beat in alarm.

"You are a brave boy. I am glad you made a full recovery."

Thorkell gave him a silent, expectant nod of thanks.

"We are due to part tomorrow," Maimon Sofer went on. "Brother Gregorius decided it must be so, despite my entreaties that you all stay longer."

"You are very kind," said Thorkell, "but we have been delayed as it is."

"That is so. At any rate, I did not wish to miss the opportunity of speaking to you."

"To me?" Thorkell was puzzled. "Why me?"

"Because," Maimon lowered his voice conspirationally, "you seem to be the one, of all your companions, with whom I can most easily reach... an understanding."

"Explain yourself, if you please," Thorkell frowned, "because right now, I don't understand you at all."

"I know what you are up to," Maimon said sharply.

Careful, thought Thorkell, and his heart beat ever faster. *This could be a trick.*

"What do you mean?" he said, playing for time.

"I mean to say," Maimon went on, "that I know what you are to convey, and where, and why. But maybe," he paused, "maybe *you* know nothing of the matter. Maybe you were merely hired as a sellsword, and no one thought to give you further information."

"No," Thorkell said defensively, then caught himself just in time. "That is to say, I... I was sworn to secrecy," he finished lamely.

"But secrecy cannot exist between two people who are both informed of the same thing," Maimon pointed out.

Thorkell surveyed him warily. The man seemed reserved, cautious, not someone he would trust.

"Perhaps you know," he said, carefully choosing his words, "even more than I do. But the question is, how?"

"We have our ways," Maimon said mysteriously. Thorkell was reminded of the warning of Brother Gregorius regarding Jews.

"What do you want of me?" Thorkell asked him directly.

"The... the thing your commander is so zealously guarding," said Maimon. "Do you know to whom it belongs?"

"The church..." Thorkel began slowly, wondering whether he isn't saying too much, but Maimon broke him off:

"The church is a lying whore. It is a sacred object, an ancient treasure that belongs to my people. It was lost for many centuries, returned to us some years ago, and stolen by the conniving bishops of Rome through a combination of trickery and force."

Thorkell merely stared at him, too astonished to speak. There was sudden power which was bared in this man, until now so soft-spoken and well-mannered. He now appeared downright dangerous. His eyes sparkled with fury. *A trick,* Thorkell repeated to himself.

"Why should I believe you?" he inquired. "And why would the church do that? Why would it be on a hunt for an artifact that belongs, as you say, to the Jews? Even if it is exceedingly valuable... why go to all the trouble of procuring it?"

"The Christians mean to defile the holiest of the holy places in Jerusalem," said Maimon, "the place where our great Temple had once stood. They believe this plan of theirs isn't known to us, but it is. They mean, in mockery of our faith, to construct a Christian church that would look like the Temple and use the remaining Temple artifacts, which they are now assembling in zealous fervor. Thus they mean to show how they have displaced us as the Chosen People of God. But they will not succeed. They will not," he repeated forcefully.

404

Thorkell frowned. "Give me one good reason why I should trust you," he said. "I swore to help protect this treasure, whatever it is, and help convey it safely to Rome - "

"Has Brother Gregorius ever shown it to you?" asked Maimon. "Has he ever displayed even as much confidence in you?" he carefully looked into Thorkell's face, and upon seeing the answer he expected, he continued: "No. Of course not. You do not, then, know exactly what it is."

"No," confessed Thorkell.

"The recovery of this treasure," said Maimon, "has been unexpected. Shall I tell you of it?" He paused, and though Thorkell remained silent, nodded decidedly. "Yes, I must – otherwise, how will you understand? Some years ago, at a great distance from here, a traveler from a far-away land arrived at the home of the leader of the local Jewish community. He brought this artifact with him, vaguely guessing that it originally belonged to the Hebrews, and that it might still be of importance to our people. He willingly passed the treasure into our hands – and of course, the grateful Jewish leaders rewarded him handsomely for it. Now, as a sign of me trusting you more than Brother Gregorius does, I will tell you what it is. It is a chalice, not large in size but beautiful to behold, made of pure gold, with twelve different precious stones surrounding its edge..."

"... and letters engraved around its base, spelling out the holy names of the Lord," Thorkell heard his own astonished voice, which completed the old Jew's phrase of its own accord.

Maimon Sofer looked extremely bewildered. "But – but you said you haven't seen..." spluttered the Jew, not understanding.

"I have not," confirmed Thorkell, "but I have heard tales of this treasure all my life. It was my father, you see, who sailed from Greenland and returned it to your people."

For a few moments, Maimon stared at him, too amazed for speech. "And what," he finally said after a long silence, "is the son of Leif Erikson doing here as a sellsword?"

A slight shadow passed over the boy's face. "Do you know my father?" he inquired instead of answering, eager to change the subject.

"I have never seen your father, but his name is known to me. As foreign as the ways of your people are to ours, I heard of Leif Erikson, and know him to be a good, just man."

"He is," said Thorkell.

"I am glad to hear he is still alive, then," said Maimon. "It is most extraordinary that of all people, it was you who ended up here. It must be the hand of the Lord that guided you; we need your help," he concluded passionately.

"Help you?" Thorkell looked puzzled. "But what is it that you would have of me?"

"You must help us recover that which is rightfully ours," said Maimon, heavily stressing every word.

Thorkell's eyes darkened; he quickly grasped it all, and his very being revolted in protest. "Would you have me rob the man I had sworn to protect?"

"You will, of course, receive ample compensation..."

But here the Jew had miscalculated. "You show me great disrespect if you think gold can buy my way out of my sworn word," said Thorkell.

"I do not apply to your greed, oh no," the Jew hastened to correct himself, "but to your sense of justice. That chalice is ours, we were robbed of it – the church took it for its own, just as it had annexed and distorted our holy texts. Or do you think, like many Christians, that all who wear the robes of a priest are saints?"

No, Thorkell did not think so. He grew up with a father who, much to the grief of his own innocently devout wife, had questioned every religious assumption and every dogma of the church, and laughed out loud about the supposed holiness of any human creature... even, to Thorgunna's horror, the Lord Jesus himself.

"Well," Thorkell said, struck by a sudden idea, "I do not understand why you are applying to me at all. We are under your roof, surrounded by your people, at your mercy. If you want this thing so badly, why don't you seize it at once?"

"I cannot do that," replied Maimon. "My people are suspected and persecuted by the church as it is. If we are charged with stealing a valuable object from a man of the church... no, someone else must do it, and at such a distance from my home that renders us beyond suspicion."

"The men who attacked us," Thorkell looked at him intently, overwhelmed by suspicion that darted into his head. "Did you send them?" He did not expect a honest answer, but he stared intently at the Jew's face, ready to detect any symptom of guilt.

"No," Maimon Sofer met his stare unflinching. "This object Gregorius is guarding is of great importance to me, but I would not take a man's life to obtain it."

"Neither would I," said Thorkell, "certainly not for gold. What you want me to do is called betrayal. Yes, betrayal," he interrupted the Jew's protest. "I would never do harm to Brother Gregorius. He has behaved kindly and decently to me all along."

"You do not owe him anything," Maimon argued. "He only hired you – but there will be no need to do him harm. All I am asking is that you return the chalice to us, and you shall name your own reward."

An idea struck him, too beautiful and terrible to contemplate for long. He attempted to push it away, but instantly it took root in his mind. He might return here! And it might be possible after all – what he hardly dared to dream of! The image of Tzipporah, graceful and lovely, her face full of spiritual power and hidden knowledge, her healing hands quick and skillful, came before him with almost unnatural clarity. It would be terrible audacity, he knew, but... but he sensed she has no aversion to him, as much as he could tell from the behavior of so modest and discreet a maiden. And might it not be what this Jew has in mind even at this moment? *You shall name your own reward...*

"I can ask for anything I want – anything?" Thorkell made sure.

"Yes – and if it is not in my power to give it to you, I will ask my kinsmen and friends to assist me. What say you, Thorkell son of Leif? Will you help me?"

And slowly, almost imperceptibly ,Thorkell gave the tiniest of nods.

Chapter 49

They were supposed to leave early the next morning, and Thorkell was up at cock's crow. He had no wish to linger now; on the contrary, he was impatient to leave, eager for what he meant to do to be over.

To his vast surprise, it was Tzipporah herself who brought him his breakfast, the last meal they were to have in this house. There was a tray in her hands, with a fresh crusty small loaf of bread, a jug of milk, a crock of butter, a pot of honey and some prunes.

He expected her to leave the tray and remove herself from his sight, as has become her custom, without speaking. Instead, she lingered by his side, evidently hesitating. A faint nervous crease appeared between her arched dark eyebrows, barely visible against the smooth pallor of her skin.

"You are going further on your journey today," she finally said. "Be safe."

Does she know? Has her father divulged his secret plan to her? Did her voice shake ever so slightly, or did it only seem so? No matter; if it was but an illusion, it was a cherished one, not to be easily relinquished.

Slowly, her hesitation now clearly perceived, she removed a delicate chain of spun silver from her neck. A tightly sealed silver locket was hanging from the chain. She made one step towards him, holding the locket in her outstretched hand. Thorkell took it, looking into her eyes and forcing his fingers not to tremble.

"What is it?" he asked.

"A roll of parchment is sealed within," she said, "with sacred words engraved upon it. It is meant for one's protection."

"What words are these?"

Her eyes were dark, so dark, and yet full of secret, hidden light. "I cannot express myself well enough to translate them," she told him, "and you don't know the holy tongue," she added.

Latin? Thought the bewildered Thorkell who, though not pious enough to read the holy texts for his pleasure, was quite good in grasping languages. But then he understood – Hebrew, of course. No, he didn't know a word nor letter in that ancient tongue.

"You don't need to know the words to benefit from their protection," said Tzipporah. "It is enough that you keep them close to your heart."

Thorkell's eyes never left hers as he slipped the chain about his neck and let the locket rest right above his heart, next to the cross he had received from his mother on the eve of his journey.

I will return, and I will name my own reward, he swore to himself. *I will name it.*

"There was good food and soft beds in that Jew's home," said Bjarni cheerfully sometime around mid-morning, when they were already at some distance from Genua, "better than anything we're like to have in a while. But it sure feels good to be on the road again! I was starting to feel a bit restless, being cooped up there in that great house where everybody stepped so soft and spoke so quiet... what about you, Harald?"

Thorkell did not reply. He still felt dazed, possessed by a single thought, at once attracted and repulsed by the idea of what he meant to do. For the first time in his life, he was deliberately going to make a turncloak of himself, and he hated himself for it, but felt as though he had no choice. He was not fully convinced of Maimon's truthfulness – though his arguments, he conceded,

410

did make sense – but nevertheless, he felt as though his life depended on the outcome of the mission he took upon himself.

The rest of their journey, up until they reached Rome, was uneventful. They had left Maimon Sofer's house well supplied with provisions, and although they had to set camp all the way, and didn't have a roof over their heads but once, and the frost was getting bitter in the mornings, they were comforted by the closeness of their destination.

Upon their arrival in Rome, which occurred close to sunset, they were promptly lodged in a house with the owner of which Brother Gregorius appeared to be long acquainted. The house, though without the opulence they had enjoyed at the manse of the Jewish merchant, was spacious and comfortable. Thorkell and Bjarni got a room to themselves, which was sheer luxury to anyone who had been used to endless winters spent shut up in the crowded stuffiness of a Norse longhouse, with not even the illusion of privacy.

Bjarni, refreshed by a much needed bath and a good supper, fell asleep very soon – not before cheerfully expressing his hope of him and Thorkell having a good time of fun and drinking once they receive their appointed reward for completing their task successfully. When Thorkell heard this, he felt a stab of regret for what was to follow.

"If you ever return to Iceland," he said after a moment's pause, "and want to find me, I might be at the estate of Thorfinn Thordarson, also known as Karlsefni. Do you know the man?"

"By name," said Bjarni. "There are few men in Iceland better known than old Thorfinn Karlsefni. Is he a relation of yours?" asked Bjarni.

"After a fashion. But most importantly, he has been a friend to my family for many years now. Business had brought him to Greenland many a time. Now, he has the property of several farms, very profitable ones, too, and he resides at..."

"Well, you will have plenty of time to tell me the particulars, won't you?" said Bjarni. "We aren't saying goodbye yet, are we, Harald?"

Thorkell remained silent, deciding it is safest to pretend he has fallen asleep; and soon, the snores of his unsuspecting companion filled the room. He didn't feel remotely sleepy himself, however. If he truly intended to carry out what he had intended to do, now was his last chance. He had already placed himself in danger by allowing himself and the chalice to be brought under the roof of a man who belonged to the church in spirit if not in name. He got up, quietly so as not to wake Bjarni – a completely unnecessary precaution, as his companion was deeply asleep. Thorkell put on his gear and his cloak and soundlessly walked out of the room.

He was vexed and relieved at the same time to find Brother Gregorius still awake in the sleepy silence that filled the house. The traveling monk apparently had no intention of going to sleep; he was deeply immersed in writing a letter by the guttering light of a single candle. He was hunched close to this single source of light, scribbling hastily with a battered quill, which produced an untidy scrawl. This could make matters more difficult, Thorkell knew, but at the same time he felt it would be somehow more honorable to declare himself before doing what he decided he must.

Brother Gregorius did not appear in the least perturbed by the sight of him at so late an hour. He merely gave Thorkell a benign look and said:

"Not asleep, Harald? I find that sleep eludes me tonight, too. The excitement is too great – tomorrow morning, we shall appear before the holy bishops of Rome, and I will present them with the holy artifact that we have so carefully guarded to deliver here safely."

"No," Thorkell said blankly.

Gregorius put his letter aside and finally gave him his full attention. A frown appeared on his face. "What do you mean, *no*?" His eyes were intently fixed on Thorkell, yet still he didn't suspect.

"It is not yours to give away to anyone," Thorkell said, gaining confidence with every word. "It was taken from its rightful owners in a dishonest way, and it shall be returned where it belongs."

And, to give his words more convincing air, he drew his sword out of its scabbard. In the honor of Brother Gregorius it must be said he didn't appear remotely frightened, even though he was unarmed himself, and his weapons were far beyond his reach.

"That Jew," he said calmly after a lightning-speed process of conjecture. "That treacherous snake poisoned your mind, I can see it plainly. I knew he was not to be trusted."

Thorkell said nothing.

"Listen, my dear boy," Brother Gregorius spoke softly and kindly, as if he didn't have a bare sword hanging over his head. "You come from a place which this tribe has not yet reached, but I have had a vast number of dealings with Jews, in the days when I was not yet confirmed in the decision of dedicating my life to the church. I have had ample opportunity to study their nature, and can rightly testify to their being deceitful, greedy, ambitious people with no shred of honor, as befits a nation that betrayed our Lord Jesus to torture, suffering, humiliation and death. You should remember that before you act upon any agreement with them, Harald."

"That is not my name," said Thorkell, deciding time has come to reveal this truth. "I am Thorkell, the son of Leif Erikson, chieftain of Greenland. You've probably never heard of my father anyway, though."

The eyes of Brother Gregorius widened, and his surprise was by no means unpleasant. "But I *have* heard of your father," he said. "I have traveled and heard much, and met many people, remember? Leif Erikson is a Christian, and your mother is well-known as a devout woman. Surely you will not disgrace them by setting yourself against the holy Church of Rome!"

"That would be nothing, compared to the disgrace I have already brought upon them," said Thorkell impassively.

Brother Gregorius looked at him in a shrewd, calculating way. "I do not know what that sly Jew promised you," he finally said, "but the church is benevolent and powerful, and whatever it is that you are supposed to get from him, we can offer you more; moreover, we can give you honor and consequence, and make you a distinguished, respected man forever. Perhaps you think," the monk went on, "that after this display of weakness, I will never be able to trust you again. Yet I assure you, my friend, it is not so. We all have been tempted at one time or another, and heroes are those who were able to resist. Do not commit this folly, my good companion. Do not betray your brothers in Christ for a deceitful promise."

A shadow of agony passed across Thorkell's face, and he swallowed painfully. "I..." he shook his head. "No. No," he spoke louder, firmer, "you will not dissuade me. I must do this. I must."

"That Jew," Brother Gregorius now looked very somber. He sighed. "He did very well for himself, very clever. He chose to turn to the youngest of us, the most susceptible, with the most ardent mind. Well, he succeeded in swaying you; you are determined to do his bidding. Very well, then; I am at your mercy. Are you going to kill me?"

"Never," Thorkell replied at once, "I am not yet sunk that low."

"In that case," said Brother Gregorius, "I am giving you an honest warning, Thorkell. The church will send men all over the country to look for you – starting from the house of that wretched Jew."

"I don't doubt it," replied Thorkell.

"You are making a grave mistake, my dear boy, by choosing the wrong side... the losing side, I would say, if it hadn't already lost," Brother Gregorius concluded in a placid, disappointed tone, as if he were a teacher and Thorkell a pupil that was failing to grasp an obvious fact.

Thorkell was far from doubting him, though. He almost knew, even then, that he is making a mistake. *But if it is a mistake*, he thought savagely, *it is one I cannot help making.*

He only stopped when he was well out of the city gates, and then only for a short time. He didn't sleep a wink that night, keen to put as much distance as possible between himself and Rome. The light weight he was carrying seemed to be weighing him down, burdening him far more than what he would have esteemed reasonable. *Or is it the burden of guilt?*

It was only on the second day that he dared to remove the simple roughspun cloth that covered the chalice, and take a good, thorough look at it.

His breath was taken away. He was looking at a work of art – no, more than that, at a work of perfection, something that seemed to be out of this world, not made by human hand - so flawless were the curves, so smooth and polished the gold, so radiant the gemstones. For an instant, he forgot where he was coming from and where he was headed, the danger he was in, and the dearest hope he scarcely dared to put into words. He forgot who he was, and what he was. He simply sat there and stared, filled with inexplicable despair and hopeless longing.

Chapter 50

When Thorkell presented the treasure before the eyes of the old Jew, he beadily watched for the man's reaction. There was no trace of avarice or greed on his heavily lined face; just awe, wonder and trepidation. Finally, Maimon Sofer looked straight at him. His eyes were glittering.

"You did it," said the Jew. Well, that was kind of stating the obvious.

"Yes, and I think no one followed me on the way here, but you will still have to flee," said Thorkell. "The church will know where to send its people to look for it. I wish I could have done it more stealthily, but..."

"No matter," said Maimon Sofer. "I can move to Antwerp, leave a nephew of mine in charge of the business here. You have rendered us a great service. May I?.."

Thorkell nodded, and Maimon reverently took the cup in his hands. He gently ran his finger over the silky smooth edges, the carved letters. Thorkell, as if mesmerized, watched how the precious chalice caught the candlelight.

"There is one thing," Thorkell ventured to say after a moment's silence, "which neither my father nor I were ever able to understand while talking about it. Considering where Vinland is," he briefly explained its estimated location, relative to both Greenland and Europe, "how on earth could these objects, which belong to your people, end up there? And I don't only mean this chalice, but also coins, tools – I saw them, all with letters in your language."

"Well, there can only be one possible explanation, isn't that so?" said Maimon. "Some Jews must have crossed that vast ocean before your people did – though how, and when, and who exactly they might have been, I cannot even begin to guess. One thing I feel I can conjecture with relative safety, though – to have these valuables fall into their hands, these people must have been important. They must have had a glorious heritage. And I cannot conceive that any circumstance might have induced them to willingly part with these sacred treasures."

"You believe they were robbed, then?"

"Who knows?" Maimon heaved a sigh. "Assaulted, robbed, possibly murdered and disposed of without a trace... we can only guess. We do not know how many of them were there, or how long ago, exactly, since the treasures of the Temple have been missing since ancient times. We are left to wonder over this. It is a miracle we have this object returned to us, as is; and though I know it is supposed to have a twin..."

"There is one," said Thorkell. "It is my uncle Thorvald who first found them both, and he was killed in Vinland. Just as he was about to die, he managed to write a letter, which he concealed in a secret place. In the letter he wrote that he hid the other object someplace else, but he didn't have enough time to finish the letter, and so when my other uncle, Thorvard, came there and read it he was left with no instructions on where to look for it – nor did he have any leisure for treasure-hunting, either. They were all too busy trying to survive while dealing with the local tribes, you see. That was years ago, and none of us ever returned there.

The Jew gave him a long, appraising, calculating look.

"You might, though," he said. "You are young, brave and clever. You could do it."

"Yes," Thorkell nodded impassively, "I might."

"Which brings us to a very important question," Maimon went on. "You returned this treasure to us, Thorkell son of Leif. It is priceless, yet still some price must be set on it, so that you can be properly rewarded. Tell me, what do you want in return?"

The moment he both dreaded and longed for had come. Thorkell hesitated for the briefest moment, and then took a deep breath and said:

"Your daughter."

The Jew blinked. Either he had not expected this, or he could put on a very good act. Astonishment, disbelief and indignation all passed upon his features within mere moments.

"I don't know what you can possibly mean," he said finally.

"I am sure you understood me perfectly well," Thorkell replied, trying to keep his face impassive and his voice from shaking with suppressed anger.

"Well, then, I am sure you, in your turn, understand that this is unthinkable." The Jew's voice was very clear-cut, aloof and cold, yet Thorkell wouldn't be put off so easily.

"Anything I want, you said," he insisted. "I will name my own reward, you said. These were your words."

"True," confirmed Maimon with a twinge of impatience. "But not this. Not what you ask. It is impossible."

Thorkell raised his head. His eyes were like chips of blue steel. He saw the mounting panic in the Jew's face, and observed it with cold fury.

"You *said* I will name my own reward," he repeated, "and I have. I want nothing else."

"I cannot give my daughter away as if she were a trophy," Maimon said very slowly and clearly, as if explaining an obvious concept to a dim-witted child. This enraged Thorkell beyond words. "Certainly not to an outsider - "

"Perhaps I didn't make myself quite clear," said Thorkell. "I will never be as rich as you are, but I am sure to do well, and Tzipporah will be cherished far above how your people treasure this chalice. I do not want her for a slave or a plaything. I want her for my wife."

"I am sure your intentions are... most honorable," said the Jew, "and your motives pure. But this... this has nothing to do with any personal fault of yours, understand that. Quite simply, we only marry among ourselves."

"What about your daughter?" insisted Thorkell. "She is as clever as she is beautiful. She must have guessed. She could not be mistaken about my intentions. Does she have no say in the matter?"

"My daughter," the Jew said slowly, calculatingly, "knows her duty."

"I want to see her," Thorkell rose from his seat.

"No," the Jew said firmly.

"Well, then," Thorkell brushed the Jew's possessive hand away from the chalice, "I fear our agreement is cancelled."

There was such cold despair and unbending confidence in his voice that Maimon Sofer forgot that the young Northman was all alone, in a household full of Jews who were quite capable of overpowering him if need be. His expression faltered as he said:

"Very well, then. I will permit you to talk to Tzipporah, and you will see for yourself."

Was it only imagination, or did she grow thinner, paler during the time he had been absent? She was as beautiful as ever, but there was a tinge of anxiety spread over her features. Or was it just the dark blue dress she wore that brought out the delicate pallor of her face? There was a silver sash around her waist, a silver-embroidered ribbon in her hair, and silver bracelets and earrings studded with moonstones about her arms and in her ears, but she looked dejected, a sad beauty that tugged on his heart and made him, like that thrice damned chalice, forget where and why he was; he merely stood there and looked at her, as though he could never look enough. It took him a minute or two to regain his senses and his purpose.

"You know I did it for you," he said, "it was all for you. You never doubted it, did you?"

Her lips moved as though she meant to speak, but no sound escaped from them. Her eyes filled with tears, and the sight of them was ample reward for all he had done. Whatever she was, whatever he was, she was not indifferent.

"I said as much to your father," Thorkell went on, emboldened. "I asked him for your hand, openly and honorably. But he turned me down, and wouldn't have let me see you if I hadn't insisted."

"Why did you insist?" Tzipporah's voice was barely more than a whisper. "Why?"

He caught her gaze and held it, steadily and relentlessly, until she looked away.

"I do not mean to say that bringing some ancient relic to your father turns me into someone who deserves you," he said. "I probably do not deserve you. Perhaps I never shall. But if you do me the great honor of accepting me, I..." he paused, searching for words. "I know it will be the making of me," he finally said, "and I will do everything in my power to make sure you never regret it."

She swayed slightly, almost imperceptibly on the spot, as if she lost her balance.

"It can never be," she whispered, "and you know it."

"No," Thorkell stubbornly resisted, even while he felt the ground being swept from underneath his feet. "I don't."

"I cannot marry someone who is not of my people," she said.

He felt an upsurge of hope which, however faint, went straight to his head like wine. "I will become one of your people, then," he said hotly. "I will go wherever you go, believe in whatever you believe, and be loyal to your kin for as long as I live. If you just tell me to, I will forget I had ever been anything else. All you have to do is to say the word. Say it, Tzipporah," he repeated, shivering as he called her by the name for the first time.

Her eyes, her beautiful penetrating eyes were full of mercy and sorrow and all that made Thorkell feel next to naught when he was in her presence. Slowly but firmly, she shook her head.

"You are not at liberty to dispose of your life as you see fit," she said, "no more than I am. You are to be a leader of your people, is that not so? They depend on you. They are waiting for you."

He felt everything was beginning to swim before his eyes. He could dispute, he could present more arguments, but he knew in his heart it was no good. His fate was decided even before he set off on this pointless hunt, but he didn't know it. It was all in vain, then. All of it. The risk he ran, the breach of honor, the loss of his companions' good opinion. He never stood a chance.

He bent his head and removed the amulet she had given him before their parting.

"This has served its purpose," he said in a horrible, hollow voice, holding it out to her. But Tzipporah shook her head again, and didn't take it.

"Keep it," she said, her voice barely audible, "and let it keep you."

She turned on her heel and stormed out, and Thorkell though he might have heard a stifled sob from behind the door that was slammed shut. It was so faint, though, that he could not be sure.

Chapter 51

The approaching frosts could already be felt in the air when he reached Iceland.

He had never been to these parts before, and was impressed despite his recent lack of enthusiasm about anything whatsoever. The property looked wealthy and well-established; good land, good stock, solid buildings. An old man was walking across the field, carrying a basket of turnips in his arms. When he saw the stranger, he stopped in his tracks and stared suspiciously, saying nothing.

"Is this the farm of Thorfinn Thordarson?" asked Thorkell.

"One of them," the old man replied grudgingly.

"But he lives here, does he not?"

The man nodded. "And who would you be?" he inquired, eyeing Thorkell up and down. That was understandable, Thorkell thought. *I must look rather like a foreigner, after all this time down south.*

"Thorfinn is my uncle," said Thorkell, wishing to keep things simple. It was true in a way, after all – Thorfinn was married to Gudrid, who was sister to Thorvard, who was the husband of Thorkell's aunt Freydis. "Do you happen to know where I might find him?"

"'Course I do," the old man said contemptuously. "Inside, where it's warm."

Three years have passed since Thorfinn last visited Brattahlid, and Thorkell had turned from boy to man since their previous meeting, but still Thorfinn recognized him right away, and wrung his hand with surprised delight, while Gudrid, whom Thorkell hadn't seen for an even longer time, was fussing about him and ordering a meal and drinks, and inquiring after everyone in Greenland whom there was the faintest chance Thorkell would know – everyone but his nearest relations. This left him wondering. *How much do they know?*

"We got a letter from your mother not long past, you see," Thorfinn explained, and a crease suddenly appeared on his brow. "So it's not *quite* a surprise for us to see you here, Thorkell. Leif and Thorgunna did think you might be stopping here for the winter."

"Would it be fine by you if I stay, then?" asked Thorkell.

Thorfinn and Gudrid exchanged glances. For some reason, they didn't look quite comfortable.

"Nothing would delight us more than to have your company for the winter," Thorkell said finally, "but there might yet be a way to send you home before the frost fully sets in."

"I am not in any particular hurry to get home," said Thorkell.

"I gathered as much from Thorgunna's letter," nodded Thorfinn, "but given your father's condition, she is anxious to see you back in Brattahlid."

The words pierced Thorkell like a hot knife. *Your father's condition...* "What is wrong with my father?" he demanded urgently, feeling as though a horrible dead weight is sinking into his stomach, bearing him down.

"Do not distress yourself," Thorfinn told him reassuringly. "There is nothing critical yet, but unfortunately, it appears that Leif's strength is waning, and he needs your presence more than ever."

Thorkell nodded grimly. *You are not at liberty to dispose of your life as you see fit*, Tzipporah's voice rang in his ears again. "What do you suggest I should do?"

"Now," said Thorfinn, "we can discuss your options. You see, Thorhall the Bear is setting forth to Greenland with a cargo of lumber in a week - "

"Thorhall always cuts it very thin before winter," interjected Gudrid. "Too thin, if you ask me. Personally, Thorfinn, I'd rather see Thorkell through the winter here. As much as Thorgunna wants him home, I am certain she wouldn't want him to take any risks."

"Well, Thorhall had gone there and back every year for the past two decades, and nothing ever happens to him... though there *were* some close cuts, I have to admit," conceded Thorfinn. "We will see how the weather plays out. If the sea is too threatening, I will send a message with Thorhall saying that Thorkell is staying with us, which should set Leif and Thorgunna at ease – provided Thorhall doesn't get blown off course and ends up in Ireland instead of Greenland, as it once occurred." Thorfinn gave a short, booming laugh and clapped Thorkell on the back. "Come, lad. Let's get you warm and fed."

Every comfort of his was apprehended with the utmost care. He was led into a clean, steaming bath-house, provided with plenty of hot water and fresh garb, and after he was clean, warm and dry, he was led back to the spacious main hall, full of the smell of roast meat and the crackling of a handsome fire piled up high with wood that would have cost a small fortune in Greenland.

It was very merry there; there was singing and laughing, and someone was playing a flute in one of the corners. Snorri, the eldest son of Thorfinn and Gudrid, was roasting chestnuts over the fire, while his two younger brothers sat not far from him, hunched over a complicated-looking game board dotted with polished stones. Following Thorfinn's call, the boys rose to greet their relation, looking up to him quite as if he was a man fully grown.

His flagon of mead was frequently replenished by the solicitous Gudrid. She was a kind, good-natured, motherly sort of woman, and Thorfinn was a most liberal man. Their household showed every sign of established prosperity, the food was abundant, the drink even more so, and yet Thorkell was unable to feel at ease. It was more than the concern about his father and the regret of being far away from his family at this time. It was as though a thorn was embedded in his heart, too deep to remove, too painful to ignore.

At some point during supper, the conversation was steered into the direction of Vinland and Thorfinn's journey there all those years ago.

"As fine a country as I ever saw," said Thorfinn, tearing a loaf of bread. "Good pasture, plenty of fish and game, timber for building... it has everything a man needs to make a decent living. Pity those bloody Skraelings were there to mess things up for us. The way it is, it would be damn hard to gather people and resources to settle there, because only a settlement of proper size could withstand those bastards. No wonder no one attempted it after we left."

"Things could have changed there, though," said Thorkell. "Those people are nomads, you said so yourself, didn't you, uncle? They might have migrated."

"I wouldn't count on that," said Thorfinn. "Even if the area is temporarily vacated, one would need many men to feel reasonably safe there... more men than are ever likely to come."

"I would like to go there," Snorri piped up. "I was born there, after all, wasn't I?"

"Yes, both you and your cousin Erik," said Gudrid, "and although you don't remember it, you two had quite a time there, too."

"Perhaps I will go there," Thorkell said unexpectedly. "Maybe not to settle, just explore and cut some timber to bring back home."

"If you make up your mind to go, could you send a message here so that I can come to Greenland and join you?" Snorri asked enthusiastically, sounding rather like an eager puppy wagging its tail. The lad was thin and stringy, and looked no more than thirteen, but his appearance was deceiving. There was strength in his thin, sinewy arms.

"You don't have to go as far as Vinland to cut lumber," Thorfinn pointed out reasonably, taking a sip of mead. "You would find it difficult to make the round trip in one season, especially as the boat will be weighed down with timber, and there's wood aplenty on Markland, which is much closer to Greenland... I am sure you know it, too, for your father's men go there sometimes."

Thorkell knew all that, and he wasn't about to enter into an argument. He had already made up his mind.

On the third day of his stay with his relatives, Thorkell was woken up rather rudely by an unceremonious prod in the ribs.

"Get up, you lazy slug," said a familiar voice. "It's morning."

"Bugger off," Thorkell muttered sleepily, too drowsy to figure out whom the voice belonged to, although it definitely wasn't Thorfinn or Snorri or another of his cousins.

"Not a very nice way to talk to someone who had just gone off across the country to look for you," persisted the voice, and the grin in it was clearly audible.

This time, something registered in his slowly awakening mind. He opened his eyes and saw Bjarni standing above his sleeping bench.

"Hey, there is no need to look so thunderstruck," said Bjarni, noticing Thorkell's bewildered expression. "You were the one who told me where to find you, after all."

"Right," nodded Thorkell, sitting up and pulling on his boots. "I didn't reckon you'd come to Iceland so soon, though."

"I figured I might as well come home after we received our payment," shrugged Bjarni. "Especially as I noticed how the coin was trickling through my fingers down south... drinking, women, gambling... I was just wasting my time, not really making anything of myself."

"Right," repeated Thorkell, not sure what else he might venture to say.

"And also," Bjarni went on after a moment's pause, "I thought that if I find you here, I can put my mind at ease and know those bastard bishops didn't lop your head off."

Thorkell looked mildly curious. "They went looking after me, then?"

"Oh yes, they bloody well did. The very night you made off, Gregorius dispatched someone to go after you, and it didn't take a genius to figure out exactly where they went. I sure wasn't blind, I knew you were not the type to run such a risk simply out of greed – and when I found out who you truly are, I thought it even less likely... and I noticed how you had been looking at that old Jew's daughter all the time we were in his house, though of course back then I said nothing because it wasn't my damn business; and I didn't miss its that you were shut up with him for a good long while the night before we were due to leave, either.

So, I put all this together, and I pretty much figured out the whole story by myself. I also knew there was no chance in hell that sneak of a Jew would ever let you have her," Bjarni added sheepishly.

"It is a pity," Thorkell said tartly, "that you didn't enlighten me on this score earlier. It could have saved me a lot of danger and ridicule. Not that I'm blaming you," he hastened to amend. "I would hardly have listened anyway."

For some moments, silence hung thick between them.

"Anyhow," Bjarni went on, "your uncle and aunt are good people. When I said I was a friend of yours, they were happier to see me than the brothers I had gone home to for a few days before coming here. Thorfinn said I'm welcome to stay as long as I like – and a mighty good place they have here, too. Must be the best pasture in the country, and pretty sheltered from the bitterest winds. Are you planning on staying the winter?"

"In all likelihood, no," said Thorkell. "Unless the weather takes a sharp turn for the worse, I will be sailing to Greenland in a few days. I'll spend the winter at Brattahlid, and come spring, I hope to be off."

"Off?" Bjarni sounded puzzled. "Off where?"

"To Vinland," Thorkell said curtly.

"And where on earth is that?" Bjarni asked, bewildered.

Thorkell explained. "It sounds like a really wonderful place," he said.

"Your uncle was killed by the locals there," Bjarni pointed out warily. "And more locals tried to do away with Thorfinn and his people, isn't that what you said?"

"I should like to settle there," Thorkell pressed on. "All my life, I have been under my father's shadow in Brattahlid. It is time I made something worthwhile on my own."

"You know what," Bjarni said slowly, "I will come with you. If you will have me, of course," he amended.

"Would you do that?" Thorkell didn't hide his surprise, but found himself rather warming up to the idea. Bjarni was an easygoing type, and handy with all sorts of things. He wouldn't be the least useful man to have aboard a ship.

"Sure," said Bjarni. "My homecoming showed very plainly that my brothers don't really want me here. Or rather, it doesn't make much difference to them either way. Here in Iceland, I will never mean much. The welcome I got at home would make even a winter in Greenland seem warm. So," he stopped and studied Thorkell's face, "do we have an agreement?"

Chapter 52

The weather was not very daunting, the sea seemed as safe as it could be at this time of year, and Thorfinn and Gudrid deemed it safe to allow Thorkell to take the ship to Greenland. On the appointed day, Thorkell and Bjarni set out with Thorhall and reached Brattahlid at a good time, wet and cold but unharmed.

The setting sun shone straight into Thorkell's eyes as they arrived, which was the reason why he couldn't quite make out the silhouettes of the people hurrying towards him, calling out his name.

"There's a fair maid come to greet you," Bjarni pointed out with sudden interest, squinting so that the corners of his eyes crinkled. "Who is she?"

Thorkell could only shrug. *Not Swanhild,* he thought he could decide with fair certainty. As the ship came to halt, Thorkell saw her more clearly- a tall, stately girl with a beautiful figure and a long thick plait the color of ripe wheat. He squinted like Bjarni did, but couldn't tell who she was - until the very moment when they came ashore and she rushed forward, straight into his arms, and he recognized his sister Gudrun.

As it often happens with maids her age, a few months have changed the promising innocent beauty of her childhood into a full blossom of young womanhood. She beamed at him, and the dimples in her cheeks grew more visible.

"Thorkell! You are back!" she cried. "Oh, we hoped, but we didn't dare to expect you here so soon! Mother said - "

She stopped, apprehensively eyeing the strange young man who had come with her brother.

"Gudrun," said Thorkell, "this is my friend Bjarni."

Bjarni mumbled something indistinguishable, gave Thorkell's sister one quick look and cast his eyes aside. Thorkell looked at him with surprise. He was not used to seeing Bjarni act so bashfully.

"Oh, let us go home," said Gudrun, tugging on her brother's arm. "Mother will be so happy to see you safely back!"

"Where is Hallfryd?" asked Thorkell. "How come she isn't here, bouncing up and down, waving her kerchief with tears of joy in her eyes upon her big brother's return?"

"Hallfryd? Well, I expect she will be wherever Erik is," said Gudrun, smirking.

"Erik?" repeated Thorkell, pleasantly surprised. "Did they finally settle it between them, then?"

"Ah, that is a really good story," told Gudrun, as the three of them started walking in the direction of Brattahlid. "Perhaps even too good to be told in a hurry. You see, there was a merchant here during the summer, a man called Gunnbjorn Greybeard..."

"The fur-trader from Norway?" interjected Thorkell. "Sure, I know him. Go on."

"Well, and this time he brought his daughter along with him. We all wondered why, until it became clear that she is a... *natural* daughter," Gudrun paused with embarrassment, and tucked a strand of hair behind her ear. "And apparently, although she was only fifteen and a real beauty, and Gunnbjorn was ready to give a very handsome dowry with her, in Norway no man of any consequence wanted to marry a bastard, so he hoped that perhaps in Iceland and Greenland he will find someone not quite so – so - "

"Finicky," supplied Thorkell, glancing side-ways at Bjarni, who was still unusually silent.

"Right," nodded Gudrun. "So, this girl, Ulla, took a great liking to Erik straight away – Erik was staying with us at the time – and sat many an evening talking to him, all smiles – and well, you know Hallfryd. She wasn't going to put up with this."

"I imagine not," grinned Thorkell. "I always thought there is nothing like a good healthy dose of jealousy to set her mind to rights. I expect it won't be a year now before Erik marries her, poor fellow."

His mother, when they met her, burst into tears of joy and embraced him as though he had been absent no less than ten years.

"Oh, Thorkell," she sobbed, "what a swift, what a merciful answer to all my prayers – you are here, alive and well, and arrived in time before the frost, too! I was afraid you would venture something too risky - "

"Mother, don't," Thorkell attempted to gently disentangle himself, well aware of the eyes of Bjarni, Gudrun and Sif, his youngest sister, but to no avail. His mother held on to him tighter until, having spent her excess of emotion, she stepped away from him, still squeezing his hand, her eyes brimming with tears of gratitude.

"Is all well?" he asked her quietly, subtly drawing her away from the others. "I stopped at Thorfinn's farm on my way home, you know, and your letter reached me there. My father... what should I prepare myself for?"

Her loving, gentle smile faltered. "You will understand when you see him," she said.

Thorkell felt at once that perhaps he would rather not see his father so soon, but to say so would have been a display of cowardice. "Where is Father?" he asked with a feeling of foreboding creeping over him.

"In the church."

"In the..." he stopped, not quite believing his ears. *The church?*

"Oh, not from any sudden outburst of piety," Thorgunna laughed shakily despite herself, seeing his incredulity. "Quite simply, when he wishes to be alone during the day, the church is the likeliest place to be quiet and empty."

Thorkell, therefore, walked with quickened pace in the direction of the little church that was built under the devout instruction of his grandmother Thjodhild.

Sure enough, his father was there, and although Leif's whole countenance lit up with surprise and joy once he saw his son, Thorkell couldn't suppress a jolt of worry. The few months that had made such a startling difference in the appearance of Gudrun had quite the opposite effect on his father. Leif Erikson had grown visibly thinner and weaker, and his hand, when he touched Thorkell's, felt bony. Still, Thorkell attempted to hide his concern by greeting his father with a smile and warmly embracing him.

"My son," said Leif, holding him at arm's length, "let me look at you. You are all of a man now."

But just at that moment, Thorkell didn't feel like a man. On the contrary, all the old feelings from that conversation with his father when he was told he must leave surfaced once more, and he was again a foolish boy caught red-handed in a dishonorable act.

"I came back earlier than was expected," said Thorkell, "I hope it won't cause any trouble."

"None at all. If you refer to Gunnar, he has gone into trading, and the farm is now taken care of by some cousin of his. He moved Ingeborg to the Western Settlement. She is now with child, and there is even a fair chance Gunnar might be the father. I know I would be insulting you, Thorkell, by warning you against going to see her."

Thorkell nodded vaguely. "You haven't had too many concerns, then, since I've been gone?" asked Thorkell.

"Not really, unless you count your mother worrying herself constantly, as we had not the remotest idea of where you might be. Wherever that was, though, and whatever you did, it seems to have done you good. You look steadier now, Thorkell, more serious, more mature. That much is obvious at first sight."

Thorkell then proceeded to telling his father all about his adventures, omitting the mention of Tzipporah altogether. He knew his story had sounded awkward because of it, with frequent pauses and uncomfortable silences, but Leif was too wise to pry further, although he listened with baited breath, unwilling to miss a word.

"It seems like the hand of destiny," he said finally, thoughtfully, "that you should come across the very object Thorvald died for and Thorvard brought back from Vinland."

"You know," said Thorkell, "these Jews are the queerest people I have ever met. It is as if they are... not quite of this world. They have their own laws," he finished, guarding his voice against sounding bitter, "some of which I could not understand, much as I tried."

436

"Yes," Leif said distractedly, "but Thorkell, I don't think you will be able to go to Vinland to look for the rest of the treasure. I am terribly sorry to disappoint you, son," he went on, "but you are much too needed here."

He didn't go on, since the expression of his son's face told him plainly he need not have said even that much. Thorkell seemed instantly resigned.

"Well," he said, "it is all for the best, of course. When I think of it thoroughly, a man would have to be mad to join an expedition to Vinland under my leadership, and I do not want to assemble a crew of madmen."

"Perhaps in the future..." began Leif.

"I will stay home," Thorkell interrupted him, "and try to make myself useful. This would be more than I have done so far, so it will be a point of satisfaction."

For a moment, Leif closed his eyes.

"I now have nothing more to wish for but time enough to properly introduce you to the affairs of the settlement," he said, "and nothing to regret but the imminent sorrow of your mother." And the shadow of death hovered about them, but Thorkell could not face it, not yet. He turned away in mounting fear. "Father, please..." he hardly knew what he wanted to say. Leif raised a hand, silencing him.

"From your mother and the girls I can hardly expect this," he said, "but you, my boy, must be prepared. Whether in a month, in six, or in twelve, death is coming for me. I can feel it in my bones, and all that is left for me now is to make what arrangements I can to make sure it doesn't catch me unprepared."

Thorkell looked at his father, rendered mute by distress. He couldn't imagine Brattahlid without his father's presence; his constant, reassuring, unchanging presence. Even less could he imagine himself stepping into his father's shoes.

"Come, now," Leif said with a twinkle in his tired eyes, "no need to look at me so mournfully. I am not dead yet, after all, and tonight we are going to celebrate your return. Let us go and give orders for a feast as good as we have on the night of Yule."

Thorkell thought he would see a twinge of disappointment on Bjarni's face once he realizes he is going to spend the winter in a place vastly inferior to Thorfinn's house, but his friend looked quite content, ready to be pleased with everything, and after supper he settled quietly to play chess with Gudrun. Bjarni was usually pretty good at chess, but this time, for some reason, he kept losing.

Hallfryd, who had done her best to appear haughty and reserved, now appeared at his side, and Thorkell noticed she was trying her best to keep her face impassive. He grinned at her, and she gave him a rather hard poke in the ribs.

"Back with your tail between your legs, brother?" she teased.

"That's no way to talk to a warrior who had fought heroic battles," he said seriously.

"Heroic? Ah, but you are probably referring to your battle against the sea sickness. Tell me, Thorkell, how did you do it? How come your unfortunate companions weren't all covered in puke?"

"Where is Swanhild?" Thorkell asked, ignoring her remark. "Weren't she and her father invited? I haven't seen her since my arrival."

"Oh, and are you wondering she didn't run out and throw herself at you?" Hallfryd asked tartly.

"Does she know I am home?"

A curious expression, something between satisfaction and wariness, appeared on his sister's face. "I told you not to be surprised if you find her married when you return," she said.

"Is she?" Thorkell inquired. "Married, I mean?"

"No," Hallfryd admitted rather grudgingly, "but everything is pretty much settled between her and Ottar Bardasson."

"Ottar – not Ottar Pimple?!" exclaimed Thorkell in a voice of mixed incredulity and disgust.

"A few pimples can be overlooked, you know, considering how well Ottar did for himself on his two last trading trips to Norway," said Hallfryd. "There are many girls who quite envy Swanhild her good fortune."

"I still can't believe she would have him," Thorkell shook his head.

"And I can't believe you would miss out on the chance to have *her*," retorted Hallfryd. She then went off to the side and helped Sif to collect the plates from the table, and they didn't return to the subject that night, but next morning, soon after breakfast, Hallfryd cornered her brother with her hands on her hips, looking menacing.

"*Well?*" she demanded. "And what exactly are you waiting for?"

Thorkell didn't bother to pretend he didn't understand her meaning. "I thought you said it was too late."

"It certainly will be, if you keep on hanging around," she said, taking him by the arm and steering him out of the door into the crisp cold morning. She then continued to stand in the frame, blocking the entrance as if unwilling to offer him a route of retreat.

Swanhild's father owned a farm within walking distance from Brattahlid. The news of Thorkell's return have already spread there, and he was warmly greeted by everyone, including the farmer Hallvard Bjornson, a portly middle-aged man who wrung his hand enthusiastically. All his warm effusions, however, weren't enough to prompt Thorkell into talkativeness. Today, he had a purpose.

He found Swanhild inside, busy spinning wool and chatting to one of her younger sisters, who was gathering the yarn into a ball. When she saw Thorkell, she got up and welcomed him cordially, but without excess of emotion. *Am I too late?* He asked herself. He could not stand and wonder, though. He had to try.

"Do you think you could give me a little time... alone?" he asked, casting a sweeping glance around the longhall, which was full of women – Swanhild's mother, sisters and the household servants - going busily about their work. Swanhild's younger sister kept glancing at them furtively, though she pretended to be immersed in her yarn balls. "I think this is one of the last fine days before the frost," said Thorkell. "We could go outside," he suggested.

"That would be fine," she nodded, putting her work aside. Together, they went out of the house and into the poultry yard, and stood leaning against the wall of one of the barns.

"I have something for you," he said, and in his outstretched hand he held a silver brooch shaped like a swan. She hesitated for a split second, but took it with a shy smile.

"This is pretty," she said, turning it in her fingers.

"I bought it from a merchant in Iceland who had a hoard of nice things for women," said Thorkell. "Brooches and hair pins and

440

walrus ivory combs with silver inlay... I thought of my mother and sisters when I saw these – and of you."

Swanhild's eyes were suddenly wet. He wondered whether he had said the wrong thing, and tried to make amends by reaching for her hand.

"Swanhild," he said in a low voice, "I wish I could say I was sorry for leaving, but I can't. If I had not gone, I wouldn't know that my place is right here after all."

"You have no reason to feel guilty," said Swanhild. She didn't pull her hand back, but neither did she return the pressure of his fingers. "You betrayed no duty. You broke no vows."

"No," he conceded, "but nor did I make any. I kept running from duties and vows... until now," he added, and tentatively, he raised his hand and brushed it gently against the soft outline of her cheek. The slight smile that appeared on her lips, hopeful like a dawn after a long winter night, was all the answer he needed.

"I guess I won't be going to Vinland after all," he announced to Bjarni not long after.

"Figures," Bjarni nodded understandingly, "what with you getting married, and being an only son, and your father – great man, he is, I like him a lot, but he isn't young anymore and not in the best of health... of course you need to stay here."

"You must be disappointed," said Thorkell, "it will be a long dull winter in Brattahlid for you, and without the diversion of planning an exciting journey come spring to make the cold season pass more quickly."

"Disappointed? No, not really," said Bjarni. "Back home, all we have to eat during winter is salted cod, some cured bacon and stale oat cakes as hard as rocks. And my eldest brother's wife is always in a fuss about the fire wood, going on about how costly it is and how it's not going to last until the thaw, so we're always skimping on wood and freezing our backsides off. So really, as far as I'm concerned, winter here is an improvement."

"So where are you planning to go, once the thaw comes?" asked Thorkell. To his vast surprise, Bjarni looked awkward, almost as if he was caught at some mischief.

"Well," he said, hesitating, "I – it so happens that I asked your father whether he'd be interested in another pair of working hands around the farm, mentioned I'm pretty good at hunting and trapping, too – if I do say so myself. He very kindly said he would be happy to have me stay."

"You are planning to stay long-term?" Thorkell frowned in disbelief. "As a farm-hand? *Here?*"

"There are certain... attractions that I wouldn't find anywhere else," said Bjarni, clearing his throat and blushing crimson up to the tips of his slightly protruding ears.

Thorkell looked aside, following his friend's involuntary stare, and saw Gudrun with her head bent over her sewing. She looked busy at work – far too busy, actually, it seemed to him. He had never seen Gudrun so deeply immersed in her needlework before. It looked almost as though she was trying to show she isn't listening.

"I understand Gudrun is too young now," said Bjarni was an apologetic half-smile, "and that I might not stand a chance either way. But I will wait. A year, two years, three. However long it takes. She is worth it."

Thorkell couldn't suppress a wide grin and clapped him on the shoulder. "With two brothers-in-law such as you and Erik," he said, "life in Greenland is bound to have its compensations."

442

Epilogue

Eighteen months later, all the people of Brattahlid stood together by the freshly dug grave, heads bent, and many eyes brimmed with tears.

"Go, son," urged Thorgunna, relinquishing her hold on Thorkell's supportive arm. "Go, I will follow you and the others later."

"I don't want to leave you alone, Mother," he said.

She lifted up her head and gave him a brave, though tremulous smile.

"Leif lived a long and worthy life," she said, though her voice trembled as she spoke. "He was happy to see you and Swanhild, Hallfryd and Erik, Gudrun and Bjarni married and settled. Ever since you returned from your journey, he knew he has a son who will replace him with honor and dignity when the time comes. And he lived to see this spring," she added, and her voice quivered even more, "spring had always been his favorite season."

Still, Thorkell hesitated, unwilling to leave her side.

"I will be well," Thorgunna whispered. "I just... I just need a little while longer alone with him, and then I will go home."

Thorkell squeezed her hand, nodded, turned around and walked away, to where his wife and his sisters with their husbands stood. Swanhild looped her arm through his and glanced worriedly at Thorgunna. "Will your mother not come?" she asked in a low voice. "It is getting chilly."

"Soon," he said quietly, drawing her away, and the others followed. "It is better to let her be for now. Give her time."

When she was left alone, Thorgunna knelt by the grave and ran her hands several times over the mound of soft, cool earth that now concealed what was left of the only man she ever loved.

Part of her wanted to be laid to rest right then and there, together with him. Their life together, outwardly so humble and simple, was effused with beautiful meaning, with secret understanding, like a fairy story, like a beautiful song. She was not forty and might yet have many years of life ahead of her, but without Leif it all seemed empty, pointless. Ever since she was a young girl, she had surrendered her life to being his wife. She had no identity of her own anymore. How was she to go on?

Yet she knew he is there, there still, she knew he couldn't have truly left her. She almost felt his hand on her shoulder, firm and reassuring, almost heard his voice, steady and warm, pointing out those duties and comforts that will enable her not to snap under the burden of grief. Her home, her children and her young grandson, Thorkell's son; all the people who looked up to her. They need her. She cannot fail them.

Thorgunna gently smoothed out the mound of earth and got up from her knees. For a while still, she stood and looked down, then turned and began walking home, and with each step she felt more and more as if Leif walked behind her. She didn't look back, unwilling to part with this reassuring illusion.

She looked at her son and daughters with newfound, aching love, struggling to see Leif in them. With bittersweet emotion, she observed how the features of them both blended in the faces of those who were their flesh and blood.

Thorkell noticed that she was back, approached her and embraced her. She leaned into her son's arms. He was as tall and strong now as his father had been when she met him. Being

444

enveloped by his arms like this brought acceptance, peace, and the startling realization that she had given him her all, all she had, and from now on, there is nothing more left to do for her son. It is his turn now, his hour, his responsibility – and what is more important, he had fully come to terms with that.

She closed her eyes and saw Leif again. Leif with salty spray in his tangled hair, Leif in the great hall of the longhouse, settling disputes and making announcements. Leif in moments of carefree joy, humming a song and bouncing the children on his knee. She had seen him and comforted him in mourning his father, both his brothers, and his mother. She had often wondered about this source of inner strength that seemed to feed him and made him go on so steadily. She understood now that it must have been the sense of doing his duty, doing what is both expected and right. That was how they began their life together, and it was the same thing that would give her sustenance now.

There was one memory of him that particularly stood out in her mind. They were newly married and she was pregnant with Thorkell, and it was a summer of busy, never-ending work. All the men had been called off their regular chores so that the hay would be cut in time, and Leif joined everybody else.

As the day was drawing to a close, she stood at the door of their home and saw him coming towards her, tall and strong, breathing with health and life, his hair matted and sweaty and his shirt sticking to his back. He approached her slowly, and in his eyes she read both longing and apprehension. Perhaps he thought she would be taken aback by seeing him after a day's work in the fields, like any common farm hand. She had smiled sweetly then, and pressed herself close to him, and guided one of his hands to rest on the swell of her belly.

Those were her memories. They belonged to her. It was a life they had built, a life they had shared, a life that still went on seamlessly, flowing like a river, and no one could take that away. The blue eyes she had loved so much shone in her memory even now, bright with a combination of manly strength and the tenderest devotion. Those eyes, she knew, are watching her from above still, and it is their appraising gaze that will determine each step she takes from now on, until the end of her life. From now on and until the very end, she will be guided by what he would have thought, said, or done.

And the image of Leif with blades of grass in his hair, a pitchfork in his hand and a wide smile upon his face will stand before her, up until the end of it all, until the day when the borders of space and time are crossed and they finally meet again.

66999093R00247

Made in the USA
Middletown, DE
16 March 2018